Cradle of the Scots

AN ARGYLL ANTHOLOGY

Edited by

BRIAN D. OSBORNE
RONALD ARMSTRONG
RONALD RENTON

Birlinn

First published in 2000 by
Birlinn Limited
8 Canongate Venture
5 New Street
Edinburgh
EH8 8BH

ISBN 1 84158 041 4

British Library Cataloguing in Publication Data
A catalogue record of this book is available
from the British Library.

Typesetting by Textype Typesetters, Cambridge
Printed and bound in Finland by WS Bookwell

Contents

NOTE: Titles given in quotation marks do not appear in the original and
have been provided by the editors.

1
FOREWORD

'Lord of the Isles, whose lofty name
A thousand bards have given to fame'

So the Borderer Walter Scott describes the hero of his long narrative poem, about one of the hereditary chieftains who held sway over that large proportion of the western islands of Scotland and of the adjacent territories generally called Argyll.

Argyll or *Earra-ghaidheal* means the Coastland or Boundary of the Gael. The current local government unit of Argyll (and Bute), based on the douce town of Lochgilphead, seems a modest though charming bearer of a title once associated with fierce warriors like Somerled and Red Hector of the Battles. The history of Argyll is a staggering litany of great names and deeds and institutions, of places such as Dunadd and Iona and Islay, which played a key role in the political and religious development of the nation. Moreover, Argyll or Dalriada was the impetus for a spiritual, cultural and civilising influence spreading from the very edge of Europe to lands far from Scotland. This anthology includes extracts in prose (both fiction and non-fiction) and poetry reflecting this importance. Argyll's part in the linguistic history of Scotland is a crucial one, and we have tried to reflect the important Gaelic heritage by including a wide range of familiar and less familiar material from both the oral and written traditions. The texts provided have been faithful to the punctuation and spelling of the editions from which they have been taken. Full translations have been provided for all the Gaelic material.

Much of the influence and the fame of Argyll down the years has been derived from the jewel of Scottish islands, St Columba's Iona:

> That man is little to be envied, whose patriotism would not gain force upon the plain of Marathon, or whose piety would not grow warmer among the ruins of Iona.

So Dr Johnson wrote on his visit in 1773. The linking of Iona, 'the luminary of the Caledonian regions', with Marathon in Greece was fitting because of the common quality which these historic sites inspire, of what Kenneth Clark called 'a sense of peace and inner freedom'. Moreover, the rest of Argyll with its severely indented coastline and garland of islands might fancifully be compared with Attica and the archipelagos of the Aegean. Legends and tales of Viking and Scots sea-raiders also awake echoes of Homeric deeds and of course the bardic tradition flourished in sea-girt Argyll as it did in Ancient Greece.

In the literature of previous centuries, which makes up the bulk of our selections in this anthology, it is this same epic scale that is encountered most often. This may be because all knew Argyll as an important place where stirring deeds were done. The battle at the Pass of Brander, during the Wars of Independence, when Bruce won a famous victory against the MacDougalls of Lorne, was just one instance celebrated by writers then and since. Or, to take another example, when in 1411 the 'Islesmen' of Argyll crossed the mountain barrier and came down into mainland Scotland to 'The Red Harlaw' near Aberdeen, it was clear that these followers of the Lord of the Isles were major players on the national stage. Material such as the epics composed by the bards of the chiefs, descriptions and first-hand accounts given by travellers to Argyll, and differing versions of history are all included in this book. Some trace the rise to dominance of Clan Campbell and, later, their ignominy in the Wars of Montrose. From then can be seen the beginning of a decline, of a gradual reduction of the importance of Argyll – the place if not the ducal house – on the national political stage. Macaulay's masterly (if biased) version of the Glencoe massacre can be seen as a fitting postscript.

The many travellers, from Pennant to Mendelssohn, who visited these parts in quieter days were drawn to imbibe the beauty of the scenery as well as the historical and literary associations. In particular they came in large numbers to see Iona, because of its historical and sacred past, to the other little island of Staffa, because of its unique geology and associations with the legendary Fingal, and to the town of Inveraray, with its cultural links and the amenities offered to the traveller from its two fine inns.

Today, although the beauty and charm remain, the modern Argyll is a sleepier place, with less of the bustle, even, of the nineteenth century. We have selected pieces from various modern visitors to the area as well as those who know it better but love it no less. The last hundred years or so has seen the writing scene in Argyll dominated by novelists and short story writers like Neil Munro, although George Campbell Hay and Argyll's adopted son Iain Crichton Smith have produced first-rate verse, bilingual in Gaelic and English.

In order to create a structure for the wealth of material written about

Argyll and by Argyll folk, we have arranged our selections of writings in four topographical-based chapters. Throughout it has been our object to choose items that are substantial and satisfying in length as well as being rich in interest, and to provide introductory notes and analysis which assist the reader to appreciate the background of the item and understand the context in which it appeared. In addition to the commentary on the individual passages, each of our chapters has an introduction outlining the main features and characteristics of the area and providing further illustrative material.

Drawing boundaries in a country so indented with sea-lochs and strewn with islands ('on a coast intersected with many arms of the sea, and in islands divided from one another by wide and dangerous firths': James Macpherson) is far from easy. A benefit derived from this topography, however, from this interpenetration of land and water, is that the people 'acquired a considerable knowledge in navigation'. This added to the importance and power of Argyll in past centuries. At a time when travel and transport on land was slow and difficult and in a country where the great mountain spine of Drumalbyn stands between Argyll and the rest of Scotland, sea-borne traffic was extremely efficient. Not surprisingly therefore, several of our extracts describe the influence of the sea. The sea brought invaders but it also was the basis for mini-empires like Somerled's or the MacDonald Lords of the Isles with their galleys and birlinns. Later still came the fishing fleets, the puffers and the steamers of MacBrayne.

In this collection we have adopted fairly modern descriptions of the different areas of Argyll but in a sense we have chosen to describe an Argyll that no longer exists, perhaps appropriately for a land that has so much of Celtic mystery about it. Consequently this book refers to places like Morvern and Ardnamurchan which are not part of the modern local government unit, but on the other hand *our* Argyll does not include Bute nor indeed the *arriviste* Helensburgh.

For each of the four chapters we have identified a site or sites with exceptional interest or powerful associations act as a stimulus for literature. In the chapter which deals with Cowal and Mid-Argyll the principal site without question is Dunadd. This is because of its undoubted status as the heartland of ancient Argyll and arguably of Scotland when it was an 'emergent nation'. Within the same area, however, is a later focus of power in the Inveraray seat of the Dukes of Argyll, which features in several of the historical novels of Neil Munro.

The area of Mull and North Argyll has of course Iona, much praised by travellers and inhabitants alike, the greatest centre of Celtic Christianity, which, it is now generally acknowledged, generated the *Book of Kells*, 'the chief relic of the Western World'. This finest flower of Celtic art is now held in Dublin but some believe it to be the equivalent of the Elgin Marbles. North Argyll includes Morvern, possibly identified with Ossian's land of Fingal, and Ardnamurchan, the westernmost part of mainland Britain.

Next are Islay and Kintyre – a wedge-shaped area penetrating to the heart of the land of the Scots. Here the site with the richest heritage and cultural associations is probably Finlaggan on Islay. The Lords of the Isles had their administrative centre on an islet in a loch and dispensed justice where today others dispense Islay's famous malts.

According to the *Annals of Ulster* and their version of the history of the Scots, Lorn was a brother of Fergus Mac Erc, who took for himself that northern part of Dalriada and gave it his name. In this anthology we take Lorn to encompass the extensive area to the north of Mid-Argyll, which includes the east shore of the Firth of Lorn with Oban and Appin as well as Glencoe, and south again to the great bulk of Cruachan. Much of this was traditionally associated with the MacDougall followers of the Lord of Lorn himself. The area also includes the island of Lismore so deeply associated with the *Book of the Dean of Lismore* which 'contains the remains of an otherwise lost literature'.

As in any anthology the selection is no more than the summary of the editorial tastes and prejudices. We have included what interested, engaged or amused us, we have grouped material in fairly arbitrary ways and brought together some improbable bedfellows. We hope that this anthology will give pleasure to many and will awaken or reawaken affection for one of the loveliest places in the Celtic world.

Brian D. Osborne
Ronald Armstrong
Ronald Renton
May 2000

2
COWAL AND MID-ARGYLL
Introduction

This area of Argyll stretches from the southern shore of Loch Awe to the Clyde estuary and thus includes some of the most familiar areas of Argyllshire, beloved of generations of 'doon the watter' holidaymakers. The Cowal tourist centres of Dunoon, Kirn and Innellan were largely brought into being by the steamboat after the advent of Henry Bell's pioneering *Comet* in 1812. The reasonably swift and regular sailings of these early steamboats made, for the first time, tourism and commuting to the coast a practical possibility and led to the development of these communities and their outlying string of 'marine villas' – the country homes of Glasgow businessmen, engineers, ship owners and shipbuilders. However behind the coastal resorts lies a large and much less well-known hinterland stretching between Loch Long and Loch Fyne.

North of Loch Fyne lies Mid-Argyll. Here one of the main tourist attractions of Argyll – the Ducal seat of Inveraray – has for centuries provided a magnet for travellers and fertile soil for descriptive writers. Lord Cockburn, the early nineteenth-century Scottish judge whose *Circuit Journeys* contain perceptive observations of Scotland gleaned from his travels on Justiciary business, wrote of the Argyllshire sea-lochs:

> The boldness and beauty of their scenery, their strange, savage history, their wild language, and (till lately) their delightful inaccessibility, all give them a character of picturesque romance which nothing else in this country resembles.

In the midst of all this wildness the Dukes of Argyll rebuilt their stark ancestral fortress into an elegant eighteenth-century mansion and created a planned town to set off their new palace. An entire anthology could be filled with accounts of visitors to Inveraray who were able to enjoy the thrill of adventurous travel in the wild Highlands with the comfort of knowing that they were not too far from the pleasures of civilisation and the security of knowing that they were travelling in lands sympathetic to the Hanoverian succession and controlled by a family who were for long periods in the eighteenth century the effective rulers of Scotland. The pioneering traveller, Richard Pococke, Bishop of Meath, writing in 1760, expressed himself:

> ... most agreeably surprised with the sight of Inveraray, the grand castle built by the Duke of Argyll, and the beautiful hill to the north of the town [Duniquaich] with two heads, on one of which a turret is built ...

Inveraray does not, however, exhaust the charms and attractions of Mid-Argyll. Indeed if any single part of the county has the claim to this anthology's title of 'Cradle of the Scots' it is that part of Mid-Argyll lying around Kilmartin and Dunadd, with its awe-inspiring assembly of historic and pre-historic monuments.

Our south-western boundary for this section is the line of the Crinan Canal, which allows Ardrishaig just to squeeze into Mid-Argyll. Ardrishaig was, in the great days of the West Coast steamer services, the destination for the magnificent MacBrayne's steamer *RMS Columba* which, occasionally relieved by her consort, *Iona*, sailed daily from Glasgow's Bridge Wharf on the service which MacBrayne energetically promoted as 'The Royal Route' to the Highlands. As the Company's publicity in 1903 boasted:

> The Route has been called the ROYAL ROUTE ever since her late Majesty Queen Victoria traversed it in 1847. She thrice visited the Highlands and twice sailed on the Company's Steamers.
>
> In 1902 their Majesties King Edward and Queen Alexandra cruised through the Highlands on the Royal Yacht, and visited most of the scenes of interest on the Royal Route.

The *Columba* left Glasgow at 7.00 a.m. each day in the season and reached Ardrishaig at 12.40 where her passengers were transferred to the canal steamer *Linnet* for the journey through the Crinan Canal. At the western end of the canal the *Chevalier* awaited passengers for 'Oban and points north'.

'Dunadd'

from Argyll, the Enduring Heartland

MARION CAMPBELL OF KILBERRY (1919–)

*There can be few more evocative sights in all Argyll than the ancient
citadel rock of the Dalriadic Scots rising out of the moss of 'A'Mhoine
Mhor'. Dunadd, lying at the centre of one of the most remarkable
assemblages of standing stones, carved stones and other ancient remains in
Scotland, is indeed a place to fire the imagination. The mystery of its
inscriptions and carvings, the lost rites of kingship which were
undoubtedly enacted here, the feeling of being at the centre of a vanished
power structure, all contribute to this sense of the mysterious and
numinous. Dunadd, above all other places in Argyll, might truly be
described as 'the cradle of the Scots'.*

*Marion Campbell, a descendant of an ancient Argyll family who have
held Kilberry Castle near Tarbert for four centuries, has written historical
novels for children and adults and has contributed to archaeological works
on her native county.* Argyll, the Enduring Heartland, *first published in
1977, draws on her historical and archaeological knowledge and her
ability as a story-teller to give a personal view of the roots of Argyll and
the forces that have shaped it. Her chapter on Dunadd (and her title for it
'The Centre' accurately reflects the vast significance of this site in
Argyllshire and Scottish history) not only describes the fortress of Dunadd
but offers insights into the customs, beliefs and way of life of the vanished
people whose capital it was.*

The grey marsh is three miles wide, reclaimed in parts, elsewhere a
quaking salt-bog barely above the tidemark. A few low hillocks break it;
above them the grey geese wheel and the curlews cry. In summer rare
plants flower and salmon crowd upstream, but in winter the Big Moss is
desolate.

A'Mhòine Mhór – the name has the sough of winds in it. Veils of sleet
drive over withered grasses and hang in cold walls of glass around the
highest rock. It rises less than two hundred feet from the swamp, the first
enclosed fields at its feet, but in its setting it crouches like a great lion.

A causeway leads to it through the winter-sodden fields, a pot-holed farmtrack down which have gone the feet of spear-men, riding-ponies, pack-horses and royal chariots, for it was once the high road to a capital.

A steep path climbs to a rock-cleft a hundred feet above the plain. Here, within a massive girdling wall, is a green level strewn with hut-ruins and a well whose spring now supplies the farm below. A grass-grown stairway leads to higher terraces, the topmost of them still bearing part of a curved citadel-wall, and below it to the northward a bare sheet of rock.

There are six things to see on that rock: a deep basin, a faint barefoot print, the outline of some figure now indecipherable and beside it the clearcut shape of a wild boar, a hollowed footprint pointing to the far peak of Cruachan, and lastly some lines of writing in the Ogam script. The basin and barefoot print may be prehistoric; the deeper print and the incised drawings most probably belong with the Ogam to the years between AD 500 and 800, the years of Dunadd's glory. The writing should, in all reason, explain the rest – but it reveals nothing.

Ogam is a simple alphabet, and the long Dunadd inscription can be read with ease – read, but not interpreted, for it yields only a string of unpronounceable letters. A code, a spell, a magic formula – all these question-begging answers have been suggested. Once as I watched one of the greatest living authorities kneeling by it, baffled, I thought I heard a ghostly chuckle from the bare rock-boss behind me, a rock that forms no part of the defences and that may have served for other things – for sacrifice, or divination, or the composition of misleading epigraphs.

From the citadel one looks seaward over the marsh and across the linked channels of the Add. Where the crag runs out in smooth whalebacks on the southern side, below a second gate, local tradition claims that ships once berthed before the Moss was drained; and among the mass of excavation-finds there are scraps of the red Samian ware the Romans used – souvenirs of trade or of raiding – and sherds of Gaulish wine-jars. Adomnan's *Life of Columba* tells of French wine-ships coming to *caput regionis*, 'the head of the region', and it may be that these rocks felt the pull of their hawsers.

Look the other way, beyond the standing and the fallen stones of Bronze Age mystery, and you face the green levels of Kilmichael Glassary where a great market used to be held. It is well attested that the market was moved to that stance in the late Middle Ages from Loch Awe, when the main church of the parish was changed from Kilneuair to Kilmichael, and a new High Cross was carved to stand in the field beside the Inn; but it might be that the market was returning to an ancient site, and that in early days a great Fair was held under the protection of Dunadd like the prehistoric fairs of Carman or Tailtiu in Ireland, markets and meeting-places that were closely linked to the rituals of Irish kingship.

The crag in its marsh has been a refuge from the earliest times, like its sister-crag of Dunbarton where the British kings of Strathclyde held court; the excavation-finds span some thousands of years, but the one thing that legend affirms to have been here is here no longer. Once there was a boulder, a block with carrying-rings let into its ends, over which St Patrick prophesied and which later Christian legend averred to be Jacob's pillow. On that stone the first Christian kings in Britain were enthroned and, as their realm enlarged, the stone was borne from Dunadd to Dunstaffnage, to Forteviot, and to Scone.

St Patrick's prophecy was a blessing on the race of Fergus, son of Erc, a fifth-century sub-king in Ulster. Where the stone rested, the children of Fergus would reign; and so, when the sons of Erc left Ireland to seek their fortunes, they took their stone with them. Here at Dunadd they set up their stronghold; from here the brothers went out to gain their own share of the land – Loairn to give his name to Lorn, Comgall to Cowal – and here the kingdom of the Scotti of Dalriada gained its first precarious foothold on the hems of Alba and spread to give their name to the northern half of Britain.

At first they called their new territory Dalriada, after the tribal kingdom they had left. The area had already absorbed many immigrants from Ireland, and there were many links across the sea; the sons of Erc had not to conquer a hostile alien race but to assert their rule over earlier settlers. They were entering a land in turmoil; whoever was nominal ruler of western Argyll was most probably off on a raid into the former Roman province of Britannia, now bereft of its legionary defenders, or helping some eastern ally fight the Angles, or lifting cattle from Strathclyde. Old alliances had failed, new confederacies were forming, everywhere men were on the move – masterless men who had once followed the Eagles, runaway slaves, refugees, all the flotsam and jetsam of an empire's end.

Roman records tell of Angles and Saxons invading on the cast and *Picti*, *Scotti* and *Attacotti* swarming down the western seaboard before the legions left in AD 410. *Scotti* we have met; *Attacotti* were perhaps the men of Galloway; *Picti* were all the wild hillmen, the painted or tattooed barbarians of the north – fuzzy-wuzzies, to be held back by the two Walls or taught a lesson by the legions, until at last Rome could no longer carry the burden of Empire.

The late-Roman writers are confused and confusing about the Picts (the early writers do not mention them by name). Perhaps the simplest interpretation of various references is also the best – that there existed, at times and in places, a loose confederation of different tribes, a confederation that shifted and split and re-grouped. Some of these tribes, from Cape Wrath to the Forth–Clyde line, may well have been pre-Celtic; many of them seem to have had animal totems (and possibly worshipped the gods who shared these totems, Lugh, Taranos and the rest); some spoke a kind of p–Celtic like Welsh, some a sort of Gaelic, others a non-Celtic tongue now lost. Some were re-groupings of broken tribes, others may have been forcibly transplanted by the army of occupation.

The little we know of the Picts centres on two things – their stone-carvings (and the Dunadd boar is in a Pictish style), and their curious system of kingship. This system is not unlike the pre-republican Roman kingship; the kings of the Picts ascended their thrones not in father-to-son succession nor (like the Dalriadic Scots) by election, but through mother-right. If one may trust the fragmentary king-lists, the royal fathers were often foreigners; the royal women did not rule, as Boudicca and Cartimandua had ruled in southern Celtic kingdoms, but they transmitted the kingship to their sons.

Mother-right – matriliny – and exogamy, marriage outside the tribal group, both belong to a primitive social order. They have left traces among us to this day, in the way that a man may be known by his wife's or mother's name ('Katie Campbell's man' is her husband Robert MacDonald, 'Katie's Robbie' is her son) and even in Scots law, which cites a woman under both maiden and married name, 'Mrs Katherine Campbell or MacDonald'. Gaelic proverbs, too, assert the custom: 'I will not say "brother" save to the man my mother bore.' In the case of the Pictish kings, the system seems to have produced a succession of skilful war-leaders who were able to keep the Dalriadic invaders in their place, conquer them at times and make allies of them at others, until at last the balance of power was reversed and the Scots gained the mastery; but that did not come about until many years had passed.

The Dalriadic settlers brought their own laws and rules. In Ireland a dynasty reached extinction when it ended in an heiress. Irish kings were elected by spokesmen of their supporters, from a short-list of the royal kinship down to great-grandsons of any former king. This group, the *dearbh-fine* ('true kindred') formed the basic unit throughout society; an individual existed only as part of a *dearbh-fine* of whatever social standing, and the group was answerable for any misdeed committed by one of its members. There were other social groupings, larger and smaller, but the *dearbh-fine* composed of thirteen adult males was the most important.

Only a royal *dearbh-fine* could provide candidates for election to the throne; after four generations the group lost all chance of kingship unless some catastrophe wiped out nearer claimants. In practice the kingship swung between two or more branches of the royal house in turn, each branch trying to ensure a continuing claim. Again, any physical blemish disqualified a candidate (and might even, in early times, cause dethronement; kings had need of all their limbs and faculties to cope with their subjects and rivals). No doubt there was a highish accident-rate among princes, and plenty of skulduggery at election-time, but the system had a surprising strength, and it did allow the tribe to choose the man of the hour – warrior, lawgiver or peacemaker. The last traces of it lingered in Scotland to the Bruce–Balliol contest of 1291–2, and may even have stirred in men's minds in 1689.

There is no knowing what rituals took place at Dunadd when a king was chosen, but a strong presumption exists that the rock near the summit was the place of inauguration. Elsewhere in the Gaelic realms, primitive ceremonies survived into the Middle Ages; a twelfth-century king in Ireland went through a ritual that culminated in drinking the blood of a slaughtered white mare; still later, Lords of the Isles took office standing on a footprint-stone with the white rod of justice in their hands. Elizabethan spies in Ireland reported that a rebel Earl had 'gone to the Stone to be made', and in 1249 the child Alexander III of Scots was enthroned upon the Stone of Destiny, brought from Scone Abbey church to a green mound among the assembled people of his land.

The footprints of Dunadd are so placed that anyone who stands in them faces the distant crests of Cruachan; and at once it comes to mind that the portals of prehistoric cairns look towards some far peak. The deep rock-basin may have been lustral or may have held a sacrificial drink. The Boar may be a symbol of courage, or a totem, or even a mark of Pictish conquest; in the last case, it must seem odd that he was not defaced when the Pictish yoke was broken. He may have been recut, the bristling crest lowered into a meek hog's-back, the tusks erased; astern of him a cryptic design might perhaps be some counter-spell to dissolve his strength and drive him off to join the herds of porkers destined for the royal feastings.

However all that may be, it seems that here the first kings of Dalriada were inaugurated, on this high rock with their electors and law-men around them, the royal women perhaps excluded or perhaps watching from the upper citadel, and the bulk of their followers massed on the main level below. No less than fourteen hill-forts stand within sight of Dunadd today; one need not suppose that they were all in use simultaneously, but it is possible that from their walls the shields flashed in salute and the hilltop fires blazed out on Coronation night. It was sound Celtic custom to have the nominal centre of a kingdom as near as possible to the physical centre – no bad thing, as those who are ruled from a distant corner of another country might agree – and this custom may well have affected the choice of Dunadd as the head place, the *caput regionis*. Probably the king did not live there permanently; like later rulers, he would have to move throughout his kingdom with his judges and soldiers and huntsmen, if only because it was easier to go where the food was than to have it brought to a central palace. There is, however, plenty of evidence from the excavations that Dunadd had its permanent workshops, its bronzesmiths and ironsmiths who served the court.

Celtic kings were probably, like any other primitive king, half-divine; on their courage and integrity depended the health of the people and the fruitfulness of the land; but they were not absolute monarchs. They remained subject to the law (as indeed the Crown in Scotland is still under the law, and can be sued through its ministers), and the law was in the hands of a class of highly-trained jurists, the Brehons (*Breitheamhan*), men of the priestly caste which stood above the warrior-caste from which the kings were drawn. To reach the rank of Brehon they passed through a strenuous course of training.

First, they spent seven years of mastering metres and rhyme-schemes, and learning the lays which enshrined tribal history; from this stage they graduated as Poets, *Filidhean*, with all the skills that admitted them to the ranks of the *Aes Dana* with its liberties and its secret powers. A poet not only knew his history and genealogy, he could also compose an impromptu satire which might blast a reputation or even take a life; he could understand the language of birds and beasts, and command their obedience like Orpheus; and he stood on the boundary of magic, the dark world outside the safety of the tribe.

Next, another seven-year course made the Brehon, his memory charged with the ancient law. It could only be stored in his memory, for a deep prohibition forbade the recording of any part of the sacred learning. At the other end of the Indo-European world, the Brahmins observe the same ban.

There is no point in banning writing unless a system of writing exists; some Irish stories mention yew-wood tablets, and perhaps these were used in the schools and bore texts in Ogam – but none has survived. Again, as each Ogam letter bears the name of a tree, one might string leaves or twigs into a message, but there is no record that this was ever done. The laws have been saved for us, albeit in fragmentary form, by the intervention of St Patrick himself, who caused them to be collected and endorsed those that did not conflict with Christian ethics. The oldest surviving text is a seventh-century recension of his review, and its precision might seem suspect, an idealised theory of primitive justice, except that parallel laws are found in ninth-century Wales and medieval Scotland. They are disguised by a single clear principle applied to every aspect – the principle of contract.

Everything is reduced to a contract, overt or implied, between man and man, man and woman, tutor and pupil, master and servant, God and man. The principle was accepted by the Christians; one biblical text glosses Adam's sin as a breach of contract, for the fruit of the Tree of Knowledge had been expressly reserved in the lease of Eden, and 'the whole world died for one red apple'.

It follows that, though past cases may be cited, the law determines each cause on the basic rule, by identifying the contract involved and deciding whether or not it has been breached. There is no muddled thinking about intention and commission; it is the offence intended that is punishable, and murder is murder though the victim survives. He who aids a criminal – who is 'art and part', in modern Scots terminology – is guilty in proportion to the help he gave, and is to be judged and condemned with (but after) the principal offender.

Every breach is healed by compensation, assessed on a scale fixed by tribal status and weighted for special skills; a chief who wounds a craftsman pays compensation based on his own standing (for he should have known better), and on the injury inflicted and how it affects the workman's ability to ply his trade.

The compensation was reckoned in cattle as the basis of currency, and was levied upon the offender's kinsmen in set shares and distributed among the victim's *dearbh-fine* in the same proportions. (There was every incentive to collar one's drunken cousin before he got into a fight.) Failure to pay was backed by a single sanction: outlawry. To be driven out of the tribe, to dwell among strangers or lurk like a wolf in the wilderness – there was no more terrible fate, and no protection. *Cha dhuine duine 'n a aonar* – man alone is no man; the individual without a group was like a hermit-crab without its shell.

Finally, and beyond the Brehon's training, loomed the last seven-year course that led to the priesthood; and here the secrecy becomes impenetrable. Greek and Roman authors speak of the Celtic priests as Druids, and hint at divination, human sacrifice, weird ceremonials around oak-trees in deep forests. Later Irish tales which have passed through Christian hands present the Druids as elderly and incompetent magicians, sulking and fuming as some missionary-saint outwits them. What the

Druids really did and were remains a mystery. The towering edifice of legend that wreathes Bronze Age monoliths with mistletoe and sets old gentlemen circling them in nightshirts is simply legend, eked out with a good deal of vivid imagination in recent times. It is conceivable that some Celtic tribes adopted the religious customs they found in the lands they colonised as the Bronze Age reached its stormy end, and that here and there old rituals survived; but that is the nearest possible link between a standing-stone of 1500 BC and a priest of the third or fourth century AD.

Perhaps the Druids were beginning to lose ground before the Christian missionaries came to challenge them. Perhaps they were indeed an intellectual group of Deep Thinkers, dealing with ideas of transmigration of souls and working along parallel lines to the Pythagoreans (as some Greek writers believed), gradually becoming too erudite for common men's needs. Perhaps in the upheavals of Dalriadic thrust and Pictish counterattack the ordinary people turned to older ways, offering to trees or springs where kindly godlings lived and consulting the village Wise Woman for their ills and sorrows. Certainly the full force of a united and organised priesthood was not there to take the field against the new faith; many Druids actually joined the new order and brought their learning with them.

The fourth and fifth centuries are full of tumult, the sounds of war, the sound of running feet. Men with spears, men with the last of their household goods or with sacks of loot, men with belated offerings to angry altars, fill the mists; somewhere a child cries, a woman shrieks in terror. The Irish law-text names 'three periods when the world dies; the period of a plague, the period of a general war, the period of the dissolution of contracts'. Cold winds blow, the earth has turned to iron, the scheme of things has fallen apart.

And up through the cracks, like aconites through frozen ground, come points of light. It is time to look southward from Dunadd, towards the low brown woods on the ridge that thrusts across the Moss from Barrnakill; for there, hidden under the trees, a cross is cut on a rock-sheet, and there in a clearing within a little wall there once stood a stone with another cross upon it and a letter or two of a writing that is not Ogam.

Learned among the learned, exiles among exiles, the saints of Ireland are raising their sails to cross the sea to Alba.

Sir Neil Campbell and the Lamonts

from The Dewar Manuscripts

ANONYMOUS

The Dewar Manuscripts are a collection of Gaelic tales of the oral tradition collected in the West Highlands between 1862 and 1872 by John Dewar at the instigation of George Douglas Campbell, the 8th Duke of Argyll. Dewar was a forester on the Argyll estates at Rosneath, Dumbartonshire, and his collection was translated into English by Hector MacLean of Islay. The edition from which this extract comes was published in 1963.

Clan Campbell is so associated with Argyll that powerful clans who held sway in earlier centuries, before the rise of the Campbells, are often overlooked. The Lamonts of Cowal, with their headquarters at Castle Toward, are one clan who fell foul of the inexorable rise of the House of Argyll. The story of the Toward massacre of 1646 is well known – the Lamonts were besieged by the Campbells and, surrendering on terms of truce, were treacherously seized and taken to Dunoon where thirty-six leading men of the Lamonts were hung on the Castle Hill.

This account of another conflict between the two clans is a reminder that the Toward massacre was not an isolated example of bad blood between the Campbells and their neighbours.

Oddly enough the traditional burying place of the Campbell chiefs is Kilmun in the very heartland of the rival Lamonts. Neil Munro wrote:

> *It is an odd and unhappy termination to the career of each Argyll that he must find his place of sepulture in a mausoleum among strangers, a day's journey from his own home. The custom of nearly five hundred years compels it, and in all probability it may be another five hundred years before the house of Diarmaid arrives at the common conclusion of ordinary men – that one's ashes lie more appropriately, and one's memory remains the longer fresh and kindly, among familiar scenes.*

The origins of this tradition date back, as Munro suggests, to the fifteenth century, to the death of Celestin, son of Duncan Campbell, Black Knight of Lochow. Celestin died in the lowlands and it proved impossible, because of storm, to bring the body any nearer home. Seton Gordon gives the story in these words

> *. . . the Black Knight asked of Lamont that his son might be buried at Kilmun. The request was granted in these words 'I, Great Lamont of all Cowall, do grant unto thee, Black Knight of Lochow, a grave of flags, wherein to bury thy son in thy distress.*

The grateful Campbell endowed the church at Kilmun and in 1442
founded a collegiate church there and in 1453 was buried here himself.

When battles were fought between the Lamonts and the Campbells, the widow of the baron MacLachlan dwelt in Glaic at Strone Point, near the foot of Loch Striven. The baron MacLachlan had three farms; the name of one of them was Inverneil, of another Glaic, and of the third, the Corrie. When the baron died, the widow and her son were carrying on the farming in the best way they could.

She had a good crop of corn; and part of it was in the barn and the rest in stacks near it. The Lamonts were coming, thrashing the corn and carrying off the grain. They were wont to come in boats to the lower part of Glaic. They set a watch at a short distance from the place where the house of South Hall is now, in case any men should come from Sir Neil to succour the widow. After thrashing the corn they winnowed it on a hill, and then carried it off. The success of one party awoke emulation in others, who the next day went off to plunder the widow; so that, day after day, the number of plunderers increased.

One day they winnowed the corn so hurriedly that much remained in the chaff. After they had gone away the widow winnowed the chaff and obtained a sack full of corn from it; but the next day, when the Lamonts came, they searched the house and took from her that sackful along with the rest. The ensuing day again the Lamonts came in larger number, and began to deal in their usual manner with the corn, and every time they came young MacLachlan was obliged to hide himself.

When MacLachlan's widow perceived that they would leave her none of the corn, and that she should be ruined, she went to Sir Neil Campbell in Eilean Dearg, at the lower end of Loch Riddon, and complained of the manner in which she was used by the Lamonts.

Sir Neil listened to her and then said, 'Well, if they take their dinner from you, I will give them their supper.' She returned home, and Sir Neil assembled his tenantry, arming them with guns and swords. There was among his tenants a good soldier named Grey Lachlan; but as he was wont to be merciful when victorious, the command was given to a person called Mannach of the Big Boots, who was asked to give the Lamonts a good scourging, as they were themselves so cruel. The Lamonts had a watch on a hill near South Hall; but Mannach took the way of the moor with his men. When they were ascending the moor near a mountain dyke that was there, they saw a raven right above them that croaked thrice. Mannach of the Big Boots then said, 'Ha! Ha! Boys! That is a good sign! You shall draw blood before you return!'

They went forward behind the mountain dyke gliding along towards the Lamonts as if they had been stealthily advancing to a herd of deer to fire at them. As they reached the place above the houses of Glaic, one of the Lamonts was coming out of the widow's house eating a cake that he had taken from her. He was the same person who formerly had taken the sack of corn from her. He was ascending the brae above the house. The Campbells fired at him. He turned round to run down the moor. The widow said to him, 'Flee into my house and I will protect you.' 'I will not,' said he. 'Don't you remember what I did to you yesterday?' 'I would protect you today,' she said, 'when you are in danger of losing your life.'

He waited not for more talk but fled down the brae, and the next shot that was fired at him wounded him in the side. He applied a handkerchief to the wound to keep in the blood as he ran down the brae, but he fell in a hollow between the houses and the kyle. He was buried there, and the place was, thereafter, called Lag an Duine, the hollow of the man.

The Lamonts had their guns and swords with them. They armed themselves and the fight began. The Campbells fired down from the upper ground on the Lamonts, and the Lamonts fired upwards from the lower ground on the Campbells. As the Campbells were behind the mountain dyke, however, which was pretty high, they were well protected from the fire of the Lamonts.

They put up a gallows at the top of a rock, a little above Eilean Dearg, at the side of Loch Riddon, on which they hanged many of the Lamonts; and they threw their bodies from the rock into the loch. The Lamonts were so much harassed by the Campbells that the greater part of the former were obliged to flee altogether from Cowal. When the Campbells and Lamonts made peace with each other Lamont of Aird had not enough men to till his land, in consequence of which he found it necessary to get tenants from other places. At that time there came from Largs in the Lowlands Shearers, Mains and Lucases; and some of the descendants of those people are there yet in Cowal.

Is mairg dá ngalar an grádh
(Alas for him whose sickness is love)

from The Book of the Dean of Lismore
ISEABAL NÍ MHEIC CAILÉIN (fl. 1480?)
ISABEL, COUNTESS OF ARGYLL

TRANSLATION BY W.J. WATSON

Is mairg dá ngalar an grádh *appears in the* Book of the Dean of Lismore, *the most precious of all Gaelic literary manuscripts. It uniquely contains a wide range of Gaelic poems from the fourteenth to sixteenth century in genres as diverse as panegyric, satire, lament and courtly love lyric – as well as heroic poetry from the Ossianic cycle common to both Ireland and Scotland.*

The Book of the Dean of Lismore *was compiled mainly between 1512 and 1526 by James MacGregor and his brother Duncan who had inherited the task from their father Dugall. James MacGregor held the ecclesiastical post of Dean of Lismore, an island in the Firth of Lorn. He was also Vicar of Fortingall in west Perthshire and it was there that the brothers seem to have completed their manuscript. Since the anthology was compiled in Perthshire by MacGregors many of the poems concern the house of Macgregor but a very significant number also represent houses with deep roots in Argyll – Campbell, Macdonald, MacDugall of Dunollie, MacNeill of Gigha and MacSween of Castle Sween. Other poems cover the houses of Stewart of Rannoch, MacLeod of Lewis and MacLeod of Harris and Dunvegan – to say nothing of poems of Irish origin. The authors appear to range from highly trained bards to clan chiefs and other amateur writers.*

This manuscript is invaluable because it helps us to reconstruct how Gaelic culture operated in Scotland in the late Middle Ages; it shows us how bard and patron were linked and how Scottish and Irish Gaelic culture interacted. The text is thought to have been discovered in the course of the collecting tours (1760–1761) of James MacPherson of Ossian fame and is now in the National Library of Scotland.

Is mairg dá ngalar an grádh *is unusual as a Scottish example of the courtly love lyric. The majority of these in the collection are Irish. Iseabal Ní Mheic Cailéin was most probably the wife of Colin, the first Earl of Argyll (1457–1493).*

The translator, W.J. Watson, was professor of Celtic at the University of Edinburgh (1914–38). He was one of the outstanding Gaelic scholars of the twentieth century.

1. Is mairg dá ngalar an grádh,
gé bé fáth fá n-abrainn é;
deacair sgarachtainn ré pháirt;
truagh an cás i bhfeilim féin.

2. An grádh-soin tugas gan fhios,
ó's é mo leas gan a luadh,
mara bhfaigh mé furtacht tráth,
biaidh mo bhláth go tana truagh.

3. An fear-soin dá dtugas grádh,
's nach féadtar a rádh ós n-aird,
dá gcuireadh sé mise i bpéin,
gomadh dó féin bhus céad mairg.

ALAS FOR HIM WHOSE SICKNESS IS LOVE

1. Alas for him whose sickness is love, for what cause
soever I should say it; hard it is to be free of it;
sad is the plight in which I am myself.

2. That love which I have given in secret, since it profits
me to declare it not: if I find not quick relief, my
bloom will be slight and meagre.

3. He to whom I have given love, since I cannot speak
it openly, if me he should put in pain, may himself
have cause to say a hundred times, alas!

'Vanity of Vanities'

from Foirm na n-Urrnuidheadh

BISHOP JOHN CARSWELL (? 1520–72)

TRANSLATION BY MAGNUS MACLEAN

Built between 1565 and 1572 Carnassarie Castle stands on a ridge at the head of the Kilmartin valley. It is a building which shows architectural features of the Renaissance and on a lintel above the main doorway is the inscription 'Dia le Ua nDuibhne' which means 'God be with Ua Duibhne'. Ua Duibhne was Archibald Campbell, 5th Earl of Argyll, a committed Protestant and the patron of the builder and owner of the castle, Bishop John Carswell.

Carswell was a native of Kilmartin. He went on to graduate Master of Arts at the University of St Andrews in 1544. By 1551 he had been ordained a Catholic priest and become treasurer of the Cathedral of Lismore. He then became rector of Kilmartin in 1553 and after this rector of Southwick and Kingarth on Bute in 1558. Most importantly he became chaplain to the 5th Earl of Argyll and with his support he became a Protestant at the time of the Reformation. After the Reformation in 1560 Carswell was made one of the five superintendents responsible for the Reformed Church in Scotland and the district he was assigned was the equivalent of the old Catholic dioceses of Argyll and the Isles. In 1567 he was presented to the Protestant bishopric of the Isles. He died in 1572 and was buried in Ardchattan Priory.

Carswell's outstanding contribution to Gaelic culture and to religion was his book Foirm na n-Urrnuidheadh *which appeared in 1567. The title literally means 'The Form of the Prayers' and it is a translation of John Knox's* Book of Common Order, *a manual for the conduct of worship in the Reformed Church. It was the first printed book in Gaelic, appearing 90 years after Caxton's first printed book in England. It proved to be of vital importance for the future of the language. It used the Classical Gaelic of the Middle Ages, common to both Scotland and Ireland, and laid down the rules for spelling which would be adopted from then on. Furthermore Carswell had the Renaissance vision to see the tremendous advantage of the printed word. In his 'Epistle to the Reader' he complains that the Gaels of Scotland and Ireland have been disadvantaged by not having had their language or their history in print. Nor, indeed, had the Holy Bible been printed in Gaelic. (This was not to happen for another 200 years!) With the use of the printing press, he says, such desiderata could soon be achieved.*

For Carswell himself, of course, the main purpose of Foirm na n-Urrnuidheadh *was to spread and consolidate the doctrines of the Reformation throughout the Gaelic speaking area. As such it was effective and would have been used by ministers who like himself had been priests before the Reformation. Just, however, as the more zealous Reformers suppressed the arts in the Lowlands, so too did John Carswell, in his zeal to reform and to eradicate superstition, condemn the native tradition and oral literature of the Gael. In his 'Epistle to the Reader' he goes on:*

Agas is mōr an doille agas an dorchadas peacaidh agas aineōlais agas indtleachta do lucht deachtaidh agas sgrīobhtha agas chumhdaigh na Gaoidheilge gurab mó is mian léo agas gurab mó ghnāthuidheas siad eachtradha dīmhaoineacha buaidheartha brēgacha saoghalta, do cumadh ar Thuathaibh Dé Dhanond, agas ar Mhacaibh Mīleadh, agas ar na curadhaibh, agas ar Fhind mhac Cumhaill gona Fhianaibh, agas ar mhóran eile nach āirbhim agas nach indisim andso, do chumhdach agas do choimh-leasughagh, do chiond luadhuidheachta dīmhaoinigh an t-saoghail d'fhaghāil dōibh féin, iná briathra dīsle Dé agas slighthe foirfe na fīrinde do sgrīobhadh agas do dheachtadh agas do chumhdach. Oir is andsa leis an t-saoghal an bhrēg go mōr iná an fhīrinde. Dā dhearbhadh gurab fíor a n-abruim, do-bheirid daoine saoghalta ceandach ar an mbrēig, agas nī h-āil léo an fhīrinde dochluisdin a n-aisgidh. Cuid mhór eile dār n-ainbfios agas dār n-aineōlas, an drong-sa adubhramar romhaind, díth teagaisg fhīrindigh oraind agas leabhar maith, neoch do thuigfedīs cách go coitcheand as a mbriathruibh féin agas as a dteangaidh ghnāthaidh Ghaoidheilge.

VANITY OF VANITIES

And great is the blindness and sinful darkness and ignorance and perverseness of those who teach and write and compose in Gaelic, that with the view of obtaining for themselves the vain rewards of this world, they are more desirous, and more accustomed to preserve the vain, extravagant, false, and worldly histories concerning the Tuath de

Dananns and Milesians, Fionn, the son of Cumhail, and his heroes the Feinn, and many others, which I shall not here mention, nor attempt to examine, than they are to write, and to teach, and to compose the sincere words of God and the perfect way of truth. For the world loves falsehood more than the truth, and as a proof of it, worldly sinful men will pay for falsehood, and will not listen to the truth though they have it for nothing.

A great portion of the darkness and ignorance of such persons arises, too, from the aforesaid truths not being taught in good books, understood by all who speak the general language or habitual Gaelic tongue.

'Dugald Dalgetty visits the Marquis of Argyll'

from A Legend of the Wars of Montrose

WALTER SCOTT (1771–1832)

Walter Scott had a continuing and deep interest in the life and career of James Graham, 5th Earl and 1st Marquis of Montrose. Not only did the 'Great Marquis' feature in his short novel, first published in 1819, from which our extract is taken, but as Scott wrote in 1812 he owned:

> . . . a sword which was given to the great Marquis of Montrose by Charles I, and appears to have belonged to his father, our gentle King Jamie

The enigmatic figure of Montrose, Covenanter turned Royalist, was one which spoke to many of the contradictions and tensions in Scott's own personality.

The two historical figures who dominate A Legend of the Wars of Montrose, *set during the Civil War in 1644/45, are the Royalist commander Montrose and the commander of the Covenant forces, Archibald Campbell, 8th Earl and 1st Marquis of Argyll. Campbell, known throughout the Highlands as 'Gilleasbuig Gruamach' or Archibald the Grim, was by nature more of a politician than a war-leader and twice during Montrose's campaign ignominiously left his forces to fend for themselves. By the accident of history both of these leaders were to pay the supreme penalty for being on the losing side of this internal conflict. Montrose fled Scotland in 1645 after a defeat at Philiphaugh but returned in 1650, was captured and executed at the Mercat Cross in Edinburgh. Argyll watched his rival's execution, but, when Charles II was restored, was executed himself in 1661 for his compliance with the Cromwellian government. Today elaborate funerary monuments to the two men look out from opposite sides of St Giles, the High Kirk of Edinburgh.*

Scott's novel introduces the non-historical but entirely characteristic figure of Captain Dugald Dalgetty. Dalgetty, an impoverished bonnet-laird from Aberdeenshire, like many other Scots in the period took service as a mercenary soldier in the Europe of the Thirty Years War. His great hero-figure under whom he served in these wars (as he reminds his listeners at any opportunity) was the 'Lion of the North', Gustavus Adolphus King of Sweden – after whom Dalgetty has named his horse. One of the leading Covenanting commanders in the Civil War was Alexander Leslie, who like Dalgetty had served Gustavus Adolphus –

albeit as a Field Marshall rather than as a humble Captain or Ritt-master.

Dalgetty, like many other soldiers of fortune at this time, has returned from the Continent to the more promising military environment of Civil War Scotland with the intention of taking service with whichever side would prove to be the better paymaster. He falls in with a party of Royalists, including an incognito Montrose, is signed up by them, and promoted to Major to train an Irish regiment, which Alastair MacDonald of Colonsay, sometimes known as Colkitto, was bringing to join the Scottish Royalist forces. The Royalist leadership, meeting in a Perthshire castle, is visited by Sir Duncan Campbell of Ardenvohr, an emissary from the Marquis of Argyll. It is agreed that a messenger should be sent to parley with Argyll under a flag of truce and the dangerous duty falls on Dalgetty.

Our extract covers Dalgetty's journey to Inveraray, the seat of Argyll's power, and gives a good description of the old town of Inveraray (which Scott with proper attention to Gaelic pronunciation, if not orthography, writes as 'Inverara') and of the high state in which the Marquis resided in his castle surrounded by his servants and the gentlemen of Clan Campbell. The old castle and town would be swept away in an ambitious rebuilding programme by Gilleasbuig Gruamach's great-grandson, Archibald, 3rd Duke of Argyll, in the mid to late eighteenth century.

Scott's picture of the Marquis may be compared with that of a later historical novelist, Neil Munro, whose penetrating portrait of this enigmatic figure is a central feature in his novel John Splendid, *an extract from which also appears in this anthology.*

When Dalgetty mounted his steed, he found himself attended, or perhaps guarded, by five or six Campbells, well armed, commanded by one, who, from the target at his shoulder, and the short cock's-feather in his bonnet, as well as from the state which he took upon himself, claimed the rank of a Dunniewassel, or clansman of superior rank; and indeed, from his dignity of deportment, could not stand in a more distant degree of relationship to Sir Duncan, than that of tenth or twelfth cousin at furthest. But it was impossible to extract positive information on this or any other subject, inasmuch as neither this commander nor any of his party spoke English. The Captain rode and his military attendants walked; but such was their activity, and so numerous the impediments which the nature of the road presented to the equestrian mode of travelling, that far from being retarded by the slowness of their pace, his difficulty was rather in keeping up with his guides. He observed that they occasionally watched him with a sharp eye, as if they were jealous of some effort to escape; and once, as he lingered behind at crossing a brook, one of the gillies began to blow the match of his piece, giving him to understand that he would run some risque in case of an attempt to part company. Dalgetty did not augur much good from the close watch thus maintained upon his person; but there was no remedy, for an attempt to escape from his attendants in an impervious and unknown country, would have been little short of insanity. He therefore plodded patiently on through a waste and savage wilderness, treading paths which were only known to the shepherds and the cattle-drivers, and passing with much more of discomfort than satisfaction many of those sublime combinations of mountainous scenery, which now draw visitors from every corner of England to feast their eyes upon Highland grandeur, and mortify their palates upon Highland fare. At length they arrived on the southern verge of that noble lake upon which Inverara is situated; and a bugle, which the Dunniewassel winded till rock and greenwood rang, served as a signal to a well-manned galley, which, starting from a creek where it lay concealed, received the party on board, including Gustavus; which sagacious quadruped, an experienced traveller both by water and land, walked in and out of the boat with the discretion of a Christian.

Embarked on the bosom of Loch Fine, Captain Dalgetty might have admired one of the grandest scenes which nature affords. He might have noticed the rival rivers Aray and Shiray, which pay tribute to the lake, each issuing from its own dark and wooded retreat. He might have marked, on the soft and gentle slope which ascends from the shores, the noble old Gothic castle, with its varied outline, embattled walls, towers, and outer and inner courts, that, so far as the picturesque is concerned, presented an aspect much more striking than the present massive and uniform mansion. He might have admired those dark woods which for many a mile surrounded this strong and princely dwelling, and his eye might have dwelt on the picturesque peak of Duniquoich, starting abruptly from the lake, and raising its scathed brow into the mists of middle sky, while a solitary watch-tower, perched on its top like an eagle's nest, gave dignity to the scene by awakening a sense of possible danger. All these, and every other accompaniment of this noble scene, Captain Dalgetty might have marked, if he had been so minded. But, to confess the truth, the gallant captain, who had eaten nothing since day-break, was chiefly interested by the smoke which ascended from the castle chimnies, and the expectations which this seemed to warrant of his encountering an abundant stock of provant, as he was wont to call supplies of this nature.

The boat soon approached the rugged pier, which abutted into the loch from the little town of Inverara, then a rude asemblage of huts, with a very few stone mansions interposed, stretching upwards from the banks of Loch Fine to the principal gate of the castle, before which a scene presented itself that might easily have quelled a less stout heart, and turned a more delicate stomach, than those of Ritt-master Dugald Dalgetty, titular of Drumthwacket.

The village of Inverara, now a neat county town, then partook of the rudeness of the seventeenth century, in the miserable appearance of the houses, and the irregularity of the unpaved street. But a stronger and more terrible characteristic of the period appeared in the market-place, which was a space of irregular width, half way betwixt the harbour, or pier, and the frowning castle gate, which terminated with its gloomy arch-way, portcullis, and flankers, the upper end of the vista. Midway between was erected a rude gibbet, on which hung five dead bodies, two of which from their dress seemed to have been Lowlanders, and the other three corpses were muffled in their Highland plaids. Two or three women sate under the gallows, who seemed to be moaning and singing the coronach of the deceased, in a low voice. But the spectacle was apparently of too ordinary occurrence to have much interest for the inhabitants at large, who, while they thronged to look at the military figure, the horse of an unusual size, and the burnished panoply of Captain Dalgetty, seemed to bestow no attention whatever on the piteous spectacle which their own market-place afforded.

The envoy of Montrose was not quite so indifferent, and hearing a word or two of English escape from a Highlander of decent appearance, he immediately halted Gustavus and addressed him. 'The Provost Marshal has been busy here, my friend. May I crave of you what these delinquents have been justifed for?'

He looked towards the gibbet as he spoke, and the Gael compre-hending his meaning rather by his action than his words, immediately replied, 'Three gentlemen caterans, – God sain them (crossing himself) – twa Sassenach bits o' bodies, that wadna do something MacCallan More bade then.' And turning from Dalgetty with an air of indifference, away he walked, 'staying no further question.'

Dalgetty shrugged his shoulders and proceeded, for Sir Duncan Campbell's tenth or twelfth cousin had already shewn some signs of impatience.

At the gate of the Castle, another terrible spectacle of feudal power awaited him. Within a stockade or palisado, which seemed lately to have been added to the defences of the gate, and which was protected by two pieces of light artillery, was a small inclosure, where stood a huge block, on which lay an axe. Both were smeared with recent blood, and a quantity of saw-dust strewed around had partly retained and partly obliterated the marks of a very late execution.

As Dalgetty looked on this new object of terror, his principal guide suddenly twitched him by the skirt of his jerkin, and having thus attracted his attention, winked and pointed with his finger to a pole fixed on the stockade, which supported a human head, being that, doubtless, of the late sufferer. There was a leer on the Highlander's face, as he pointed to this ghastly spectacle, which seemed to his fellow-traveller ominous of nothing good.

Dalgetty dismounted from his horse at the gate-way, and Gustavus was taken from him without his being permitted to attend him to the stable according to his custom.

This gave the soldier a pang which the apparatus of death had not conveyed. 'Poor Gustavus,' said he to himself, 'if anything but good happens me, I had better have left him at Darnlinvarach than brought him here amongst those Highland salvages, who scarce know the head of a horse from his tail. But duty must part a man from his nearest and dearest –

> When the cannon are roaring, lads, and the colours are flying,
> The lads that seek honour must never fear dying;
> Then, stout cavaliers, let us toil our brave trade in,
> And fight for the Gospel and the bold King of Sweden.

Thus silencing his apprehensions with the butt-end of a military ballad, he followed his guide into a sort of guard-room, filled with Highland soldiers. It was intimated to him that he must remain here until his arrival was communicated to the Marquis. To make this annunciation the more intelligible, he gave to the Dunniewassel Sir Duncan Campbell's packet, desiring, as well as he could, by signs, that it should be delivered into the Marquis's own hand. His guide nodded and withdrew.

The Captain was left about half an hour in this place, to endure with indifference, or return with scorn, the inquisitive, and at the same time. the inimical glances of the armed Gael, to whom his exterior and equipage was as much subject of curiosity, as his person and country seemed matter of dislike. All this he bore with military nonchalance, until, at the expiry of the above period, a person dressed in black velvet, and wearing a gold chain like a modern magistrate of Edinburgh, but who was, in fact, steward of the household to the Marquis of Argyle, entered the apartment, and invited, with solemn gravity, the Captain to follow him to his master's presence.

The suite of apartments through which he passed, were filled with attendants or visitors of various descriptions, disposed, perhaps, with some ostentation, in order to impress the envoy of Montrose with an idea of the superior power and magnificence belonging to the rival house of Argyle. One anti-room was filled with lacqueys, arrayed in brown and yellow, the colours of the family, who, ranged in double file, gazed in silence upon Captain Dalgetty as he passed betwixt their ranks. Another was occupied by Highland gentlemen and chiefs of small branches, who were amusing themselves with chess, backgammon, and other games, which they scarce intermitted to gaze with curiosity upon the stranger. A third was filled with Lowland gentlemen and officers, who seemed also in attendance; and after all, the presence-chamber of the Marquis himself, shewed him attended by a levee which marked his high importance.

This apartment, the folding-doors of which were opened for the reception of Captain Dalgetty, was a long gallery, decorated with tapestry and family portraits, and having a vaulted ceiling of open wood-work, the extreme projections of the beams being richly carved and gilded. The gallery was lighted by long lanceolated Gothic casements, divided by heavy stone shafts and filled with painted glass, where the sunbeams glimmered dimly through boars-heads, and galleys, and batons, and swords, armorial bearings of the powerful house of Argyle, and emblems of the high hereditary offices of Justiciary of Scotland, and Master of the Royal Household, which they long enjoyed. At the upper end of this magnificent gallery stood the Marquis himself, the centre of a splendid circle of Highland and Lowland gentlemen, all richly dressed, among whom were two or three of the clergy, called in, perhaps, to be witnesses of his zeal for the Covenant.

The Marquis himself was dressed in the fashion of the period, which Vandyke has so often painted; but his habit was sober and uniform in colour, and rather rich than gay. His dark complexion, furrowed forehead, and downcast look, gave him the appearance of one frequently engaged in the consideration of important affairs, and who has acquired, by long habit, an air of gravity and mystery, which he cannot shake off even where there is nothing to be concealed. The cast with his eyes, which had procured him in the Highlands the nickname of Gillespie Grumach (or the grim), was less perceptible when he looked downward, which perhaps was one cause of his having adopted that habit. In person, he was tall and thin, but not without that dignity of deportment and manners which became his high rank. Something there was cold in his address and sinister in his look, although he spoke and behaved with the usual grace of a man of such quality. He was adored by his own clan, whose advancement he had greatly studied, although he was in proportion disliked by Highlanders of other septs, some of whom he had already stripped of their possessions, while others conceived themselves in danger from his future schemes, and all dreaded the height to which he was elevated.

We have already noticed, that in displaying himself amidst his councillors, his officers of the household, and his train of vassals, allies, and dependents, the Marquis of Argyle probably wished to make an impression on the nervous system of Captain Dugald Dalgetty. But that doughty person had fought his way, in one department or another, through the greater part of the Thirty Years War in Germany, a period when a brave and successful soldier was a companion for princes. The King of Sweden, and, after his example, even the haughty Princes of the Empire, had found themselves fain frequently to compound with their dignity, and silence when they could not satisfy the pecuniary claims of their soldiers, by admitting them to unusual privileges and familiarity. Captain Dugald Dalgetty had it to boast he had sate with princes at feasts made for monarchs, and therefore was not a person to be brow-beat even by the dignity which surrounded MacCallan More. Indeed, he was naturally by no means the most modest man of the world, but, on the contrary, had so good an opinion of himself, that into whatever company he chanced to be thrown, he was always proportionally elevated in his own conceit; so that he felt as much at ease in the most exalted society as among his own ordinary companions. In this high opinion of his own rank he was greatly fortified by his ideas of the military profession, which, in his phrase, made a valiant cavalier a cameradoe to an emperor.

When introduced, therefore, into the Marquis's presence-chamber, he advanced to the upper end with an air of more confidence than grace, and would have gone close up to Argyle's person before speaking, had not the latter waved his hand as a signal for him to stop short. Captain Dalgetty did so accordingly, and having made his military congee with easy confidence, he thus accosted the Marquis: 'Give you good morrow, my lord – or rather I should say, good even; *Beso a usted los manos*, as the Spaniard says.'

'Who are you, sir, and what is your business?' demanded the Marquis, in a tone which was intended to interrupt the offensive familiarity of the soldier.

'That is a fair interrogation, my lord,' answered Dalgetty, 'which I shall forthwith answer as becomes a cavalier, and that *peremptorie*, as we used to say at Mareschal College.'

'See who or what he is, Neal,' said the Marquis sternly to a gentleman who stood near him.

'I will save the honourable gentleman the labour of investigation,' continued the Captain. 'I am Dugald Dalgetty, of Drumthwacket that should be, late Ritt-master in various services, and now Major of I know not what or whose regiment of Irishes; and I am come with a flag of truce from a high and powerful lord, James Earl of Montrose, and other noble persons now in arms for his Majesty, and so God save King Charles.'

'Do you know where you are, sir, and the danger of dallying with us, sir,' again demanded the Marquis, 'that you reply to me as if I were a child or a fool? The Earl of Montrose is with the English Malignants, and I suspect you are one of those Irish runagates, who are come into this country to burn and slay, as they did under Sir Phelim O'Neale.'

'My lord,' replied Captain Dalgetty, 'I am no runagate, though a Major of Irishes, for which I might refer your lordship to the Invincible Gustavus Adolphus the Lion of the North, to Bannier, to Oxenstiern, to the warlike Duke of Saxe-Weimar, Tilly, Wallenstein, Piccolomini, and other great captains, both dead and living; and touching the noble Earl of Montrose, I pray your lordship to peruse this my full power for treating with you in the name of that right honourable commander.'

The Marquis looked slightly at the signed and sealed paper which Captain Dalgetty handed to him, and throwing it with contempt on a table, asked those around him what he deserved who came as the avowed envoy and agent of malignant traitors in arms against the state?

'A high gallows and a short shrift,' was the ready answer of one of the bye-standers.

'I will crave of that honourable cavalier who hath last spoken,' said Dalgetty, 'to be less hasty in forming his conclusions, and also of your lordship to be cautelous in adopting the same, in respect such threats are to be held out only to base bisognos, and not to men of spirit and action, who are bound to peril themselves as freely in services of this nature, as upon sieges, battles, or onslaughts of any sort. And albeit I have not with me a trumpet, or a white flag, in respect our army is not yet equipped with its full appointments, yet the honourable cavaliers and your lordship must concede unto me, that the sanctity of an envoy who cometh on matter of truce or parle, consisteth not in the fanfare of a trumpet, whilk is but a sound, or in the fluff of a white flag, whilk is but an auld rag in itself, but in the confidence reposed by the party sending, and the party sent, in the honour of those to whom the message is to be carried, and their full reliance that they will respect the *jus gentium* as weel as the law of arms in the person of the commissionate.'

'You are not come hither to lecture us upon the law of arms, sir,' said the Marquis, 'which neither does nor can apply to rebels and insurgents;

but to suffer the penalty of your insolence and folly for bringing a traitorous message to the Lord Justice General of Scotland, whose duty calls upon him to punish such an offence with death.'

'Gentlemen,' said the Captain, who began much to dislike the turn which his mission seemed about to take, 'I pray you to remember, that the Earl of Montrose will hold you and your possessions liable for whatever injury my person, or my horse, shall sustain by these unseemly proceedings, and that he will be justified in executing retributive vengeance on your persons and possessions.'

This menace was received with a scornful laugh, while one of the Campbells replied, 'It is a far cry to Lochow', a proverbial expression of the tribe, meaning that their ancient hereditary domains lay beyond the reach of an invading enemy. 'But, gentlemen,' further urged the unfortunate Captain, who was unwilling to be condemned, without at least the benefit of a full hearing, 'although it is not for me to say how far it may be to Lochow, in respect I am a stranger to those parts, yet what is more to the purpose, I trust you will advert that I have the guarantee of an honourable gentleman of your own name, Sir Duncan Campbell of Ardenvohr, for my safety on this mission; and I pray you to observe, that in breaking the truce towards me, you will highly prejudice his honour and fair fame.'

This seemed to be new information to many of the gentlemen, for they spoke aside with each other, and the Marquis's face, notwithstanding his power of suppressing all external signs of his passions, shewed impatience and vexation.

'Does Sir Duncan of Ardenvohr pledge his honour for this person's safety, my lord?' said one of the company, addressing the Marquis.

'I do not believe it,' answered the Marquis; 'but I have not yet had time to read his letter.'

'We will pray your lordship to do so,' said another of the Campbells; 'our name must not suffer discredit through the means of such a fellow as this.'

'A dead fly,' said a clergyman, 'maketh the ointment of the apothecary to stink.'

'Reverend sir,' said Captain Dalgetty, 'in respect of the use to be derived, I forgive you the unsavouriness of your comparison; and also remit to the gentleman in the red bonnet, the disparaging epithet of 'fellow' which he has discourteously applied to me, who am no way to be distinguished by the same, unless in as far as I have been called fellow-soldier by the great Gustavus Adolphus, the Lion of the North, and other choice commanders, both in Germany and in the Low Countries. But touching Sir Duncan's guarantee of my safety, I will gage my life upon his making my words good thereanent, when he comes hither to-morrow.'

'If Sir Duncan be so expected, my lord,' said one of the intercessors, 'it would be a pity to anticipate matters with this poor man.'

'Besides that,' said another, 'your lordship – I speak with reverence – should, at least, consult the Knight of Ardenvohr's letter, and learn the terms on which this Major Dalgetty, as he calls himself, has been sent hither by him.'

They closed around the Marquis, and conversed together in a low tone, both in Gaelic and English. The patriarchal power of the Chiefs was very great, and that of the Marquis of Argyle, armed with all his grants of hereditary jurisdiction, was particularly absolute. But there interferes some check of one kind or other even in the most despotic governments. That which mitigated the power of the Celtic Chiefs, was the necessity which they lay under of conciliating the kinsmen, who, under them, led out the lower orders to battle, and who formed a sort of council of the tribe in time of peace. The Marquis on this occasion thought himself under the necessity of attending to the remonstrances of this senate, or more properly *Couroultai*, of the name of Campbell, and, slipping out of the circle, gave orders for the prisoner to be removed to a place of security.

'Prisoner!' exclaimed Dalgetty, exerting himself with such force as well nigh to shake off two highlanders, who for some minutes past had waited the signal to seize him, and kept for that purpose close at his back. Indeed the soldier had so nearly attained his liberty, that the Marquis of Argyle changed colour, and stepped back two paces, laying, however, his hand on his sword, while several of his clan, with ready devotion, threw themselves betwixt him and the apprehended vengeance of the prisoner. But the highland guards were too strong to be shaken off, and the unlucky Captain, after having his weapons taken from him, was dragged off and conducted through several gloomy passages to a small side-door grated with iron, within which was another of wood. These were opened by a grim old highlander with a long white beard, and displayed a very steep and narrow flight of steps leading downward. The Captain's guards pushed him down two or three steps, then, unloosing his arms, left him to grope his way to the bottom as he could, a task which became much more difficult and even dangerous, when the two doors being successively locked, left the prisoner in total darkness.

Gillesbeg Gruamach

from John Splendid

NEIL MUNRO (1863–1930)

Neil Munro's John Splendid *deals, from an Inveraray perspective, with the same period and events as Walter Scott's* A Legend of the Wars of Montrose. *In both novels the most interesting character is Archibald Campbell, 8th Earl and 1st Marquis of Montrose – Gillesbeg Gruamach to give him his Gaelic by-name (which would be rendered in more modern Gaelic as Gilleasbuig Gruamach and in English as Archibald the Grim). This complex character was born into an age in which the head of the House of Argyll was still expected to act as a traditional Highland chief. His successors might well rule the Highlands and all Scotland with the pen, but the 1st Marquis lived in a warlike age. Twice, as Munro will relate, he failed to act in an appropriately chiefly manner; deserting his town of Inveraray when the forces of Montrose and MacDonald attacked it and later, at the Battle of Inverlochy, commanding his forces from a birlinn on Loch Linnhe and making good his escape when his army was crushed and many of his kinsmen and followers were slaughtered. Iain Aluinn – John Splendid – kinsman of the Marquis, who we meet in this extract, later reveals that he, at least, is in no doubt as to the reason for his chief's failings:*

> He has the stuff in him by nature, for none can deny Clan Diarmaid courage and knightliness, but for four generations court, closet and college have been taking the heart out of our chiefs.

Munro's portrayal of the Marquis is perhaps more nuanced and subtle than Scott's somewhat one-dimensional portrait. This may seem an unlikely verdict in view of the relative status and critical attention given to the two authors but would find support in the words of one critic (Lauchlan MacLean Watt) who observed of Munro that:

> ... in the matter of Celtic story and character he excelled Sir Walter because of his more deeply intimate knowledge of that elusive mystery.

Munro's fiction and short stories are indeed at their best when rooted in his native Argyll and in his home town of Inveraray. An obituary of Munro remarked that he was fortunate in his birthplace:

. . . for Inveraray was for more than a hundred years the centre of a political web of intrigue, which, woven primarily around clan antagonisms became ultimately entwined with the greater affairs of Scotland. Living in what had been the centre of that old web Munro was, as a poet, enabled to see with a just eye the intermingled fine and base elements of the strife of the clans.

John Splendid was Munro's first novel, published in 1898 to considerable critical acclaim. It tells of the return in 1644 from study and the foreign wars of Colin, 'Young Elrigmore', the heir to a small estate in Glen Shira, an ally but not a vassal of MacCailein Mór, the chief of Clan Campbell. Colin becomes caught up in the Civil War and the campaigns of Montrose and the Covenant Army and the intertwining ancient rivalry of Campbell and MacDonald.

Every land, every glen or town, I make no doubt, has its own peculiar air or atmosphere that one familiar with the same may never puzzle about in his mind, but finds come over him with a waft at odd moments like the scent of bog-myrtle and tansy in an old clothes-press. Our own air in Glen Shira had ever been very genial and encouraging to me. Even when a young lad, coming back from the low country or the scaling of school, the cool fresh breezes of the morning and the riper airs of the late afternoon went to my head like a mild white wine; very heartsome too, rousing the laggard spirit that perhaps made me, before, over-apt to sit and dream of the doing of grand things instead of putting out a hand to do them. In Glascow the one thing that I had to grumble most about next to the dreary hours of schooling was the clammy air of street and close; in Germanie it was worse, a moist weakening windiness full of foreign smells, and I've seen me that I could gaily march a handful of leagues to get a sniff of the salt sea. Not that I was one who craved for wrack and bilge at my nose all the time. What I think best is a stance inland from the salt water, where the mountain air, brushing over gall and heather, takes the sting from the sea air, and the two blended give a notion of the fine variousness of life. We had a herdsman once in Elrigmore, who could tell five miles up the glen when the tide was out on Loch Finne. I was never so keen-scented as that, but when I awakened next day in a camceiled room in Elrigmore, and put my head out at the window to look around, I smelt the heather for a second like an escapade in a dream.

Down to Ealan Eagal I went for a plunge in the linn in the old style, and the airs of Shira Glen hung about me like friends and lovers, so well acquaint and jovial.

Shira Glen, Shira Glen! If I was bard I'd have songs to sing to it, and all I know is one sculduddry verse on a widow that dwelt in Maam! There, at the foot of my father's house, were the winding river, and north and south the brown hills, split asunder by God's goodness, to give a sample of His bounty. Maam, Elrigmore and Elrigbeg, Kilblaan and Ben Bhuidhe – their steep sides hung with cattle, and below crowded the reeking homes of tacksman and cottar; the burns poured hurriedly to the flat beneath their borders of hazel and ash; to the south, the fresh water we call Dubh Loch, flapping with ducks and fringed with shelisters or water-flags and bulrush, and farther off the Cowal hills; to the north, the wood of Drimlee and the wild pass the red Macgregors sometimes took for a back-road to our cattle-folds in cloud of night and darkness. Down on it all shone the polished and hearty sun, birds chirmed on every tree, though it was late in the year; blackcock whirred across the alders, and sturdy heifers bellowed tunefully, knee-deep at the ford.

'Far have I wandered,' thought I to myself, 'warring other folk's wars for the humour of it and small wages, but here's the one place I've seen yet that was worth hacking good steel for in earnest!'

But still my heart was sore for mother, and sore, too, for the tale of changed times in Campbell country my father told me over a breakfast of braddan, fresh caught in a creel from the Gearron river, oaten bannock, and cream.

After breakfast I got me into my kilt for town. There are many costumes going about the world, but, with allowance for every one, I make bold to think our own tartan duds the gallantest of them all. The kilt was my wear when first I went to Glasgow College, and many a St Mungo keelie, no better than myself at classes or at English language, made fun of my brown knees, sometimes not to the advantage of his headpiece when it came to argument and neifs on the Fleshers' Haugh. Pulling on my old *breacan* this morning in Elrigmore was like donning a fairy garb, and getting back ten years of youth. We have a way of belting on the kilt in real Argile I have seen nowhere else. Ordinarily, our lads take the whole web of tartan cloth, of twenty ells or more, and coil it once round their middle, there belting it, and bring the free end up on the shoulder to pin with a brooch – not a bad fashion for display and long marches and for sleeping out on the hill with, but somewhat discommodious for warm weather. It was our plan sometimes to make what we called a philabeg, or little kilt, maybe eight yards long, gathered in at the haunch and hung in many pleats behind, the plain brat part in front decked off with a leather sporran, tagged with thong points tied in knots, and with no plaid on the shoulder. I've never seen a more jaunty and suitable garb for campaigning, better by far for short sharp tulzies with an enemy than the philamore or the big kilt our people sometimes throw off them in a skirmish, and fight (the coarsest of them) in their gartered hose and scrugged bonnets.

With my kilt and the memory of old times about me, I went walking down to Inneraora in the middle of the day. I was prepared for change from the complaints of my father, but never for half the change I found in the burgh town of MacCailein Mor. In my twelve foreign years the place was swamped by incomers, black unwelcome Covenanters from the shires of Air and Lanrick – Brices, Yuilles, Rodgers, and Riches – all brought up here by Gillesbeg Gruamach, Marquis of Argile, to teach his clans the arts of peace and merchandise. Half the folk I met between the arches and the Big Barns were strangers that seemingly never had tartan on their hurdies, but settled down with a firm foot in the place, I could see by the bold look of them as I passed on the plainstanes of the street. A queer town this on the edge of Loch Finne, and far in the Highlands! There were shops with Lowland stuffs in them, and over the doors signboards telling of the most curious trades for a Campbell burgh – horologers, cordiners, baxters, and such like mechanicks that I felt sure poor Donald had small call for. They might be incomers, but they were thirled to Gillesbeg all the same, as I found later on.

It was the court day, and his lordship was sitting in judgment on two Strathlachlan fellows, who had been brawling at the Cross the week before and came to knives, more in a frolic than in hot blood, with some of the town lads. With two or three old friends I went into the Tolbooth to see the play – for play it was, I must confess, in town Inneraora, when justice was due to a man whose name by ill-luck was not Campbell, or whose bonnet-badge was not the myrtle stem.

The Tolbooth hall was, and is to this day, a spacious, high-ceiled room, well lighted from the bay-side. It was crowded soon after we got in, with Cowalside fishermen and townpeople all the one way or the other – for or against the poor lads in bilboes, who sat, simple-looking enough, between the town officers, a pair of old *bodachs* in long scarlet coats and carrying *tuaghs*, Lochaber axes, or halberds that never smelt blood since they came from the smith.

It was the first time ever I saw Gillesbeg Gruamach sitting on the bench, and I was startled at the look of the man. I've seen some sour dogs in my day – few worse than Ruthven's rittmasters whom we met in

Swabia – but I never saw a man who, at the first vizzy, had the dour sour countenance of Archibald, Marquis of Argile and Lord of Lochow. Gruamach, or grim-faced, our good Gaels called him in a bye-name, and well he owned it, for over necklace or gorget I've seldom seen a sterner jowl or a more sinister eye. And yet, to be fair and honest, this was but the notion one got at a first glint; in a while I thought little was amiss with his looks as he leaned on the table and cracked in a humoursome laughing way with the pannelled jury.

He might have been a plain cottar on Glen Aora side rather than King of the Highlands for all the airs he assumed, and when he saw me, better put-on in costume than my neighbours in court, he seemingly asked my name in a whisper from the clerk beside him, and finding who I was, cried out in St Andrew's English –

'What! Young Elrigmore back to the Glens! I give you welcome, sir, to Baile Inneraora!'

I but bowed, and in a fashion saluted, saying nothing in answer, for the whole company glowered at me, all except the home-bred ones who had better manners.

The two MacLachlans denied in the Gaelic the charge the sheriff clerk read to them in a long farrago of English with more foreign words to it than ever I learned the sense of in College.

His lordship paid small heed to the witnesses who came forward to swear to the unruliness of the Strathlachlan men, and the jury talked heedlessly with one another in a fashion scandalous to see. The man who had been stabbed – it was but a jag at the shoulder, where the dirk had gone through from front to back with only some loss of blood – was averse from being hard on the panels. He was a jocular fellow with the right heart for a duello, and in his nipped burgh Gaelic he made light of the disturbance and his injury.

'Nothing but a bit play, my jurymen – MacCailein – my lordship – a bit play. If the poor lad didn't happen to have his dirk out and I to run on it, nobody was a bodle the worse.'

'But the law' – started the clerk to say.

'No case for law at all,' said the man. 'It's an honest brawl among friends, and I could settle the account with them at the next market-day, when my shoulder's mended.'

'Better if you would settle my account for your last pair of brogues, Alasdair M'Iver,' said a black-avised juryman.

'What's your trade?' asked the Marquis of the witness.

'I'm at the Coillebhraid silver-mines!' said he. 'We had a little too much drink, or these MacLachlan gentlemen and I had never come to variance.'

The Marquis gloomed at the speaker and brought down his fist with a bang on the table before him.

'Damn those silver-mines!' said he; 'they breed more trouble in this town of mine than I'm willing to thole. If they put a penny in my purse it might not be so irksome, but they plague me sleeping and waking, and I'm not a plack the richer. If it were not to give my poor cousin, John Splendid, a chance of a living and occupation for his wits, I would drown them out with the water of Cromalt Burn.'

The witness gave a little laugh, and ducking his head oddly like one taking liberties with a master, said, 'We're a drouthy set, my lord, at the mines, and I wouldn't be saying but what we might drink them dry again of a morning, if we had been into town the night before.'

His lordship cut short his sour smile at the man's fancy, and bade the officers on with the case.

'You have heard the proof,' he said to the jury when it came to his turn to charge them. 'Are they guilty, or not? If the question was put to me I should say the Laird of MacLachlan – arrant Papist! – should keep his men at home to Mass on the other side of the loch instead of loosing them on honest, or middling honest, Campbells, for the strict virtue of these Coillebhraid miners is what I am not going to guarantee.'

Of course the fellows were found guilty – one of stabbing, the other of art and part – for MacLachlan was no friend of MacCailein Mor, and as little friend to the merchant burghers of Inneraora, for he had the poor taste to buy his shop provand from the Lamont towns of Low Cowal.

'A more unfriendly man to the Laird of MacLachlan might be for hanging you on the gibbet at the town-head,' said his lordship to the prisoners, spraying ink-sand idly on the clean page of a statute-book as he spoke; 'but our three trees upbye are leased just now to other tenants – Badenoch hawks a trifle worse than yourselves, and more deserving.'

The men looked stupidly about them, knowing not one word of his lordship's English, and he was always a man who disdained to converse much in Erse. He looked a little cruelly at them and went on.

'Perhaps clipping your lugs might be the bonniest way of showing you what we think of such on-goings in honest Inneraora; or getting the Doomster to bastinado you up and down the street. But we'll try what a fortnight in the Tolbooth may do to amend your visiting manners. Take them away, officers.'

'*Abair moran taing* – say "many thanks" to his lordship,' whispered one of the red-coat halberdiers in the ear of the bigger of the two prisoners. I could hear the command distinctly where I sat, well back in the court, and so no doubt could Gillesbeg Gruamach, but he was used to such obsequious foolishness and he made no dissent or comment.

'*Taing! Taing!*' said one spokesman of the two MacLachlans in his hurried Cowal Gaelic, and his neighbour, echoing him word for word in the comic fashion they have in these parts; '*Taing! Taing!* I never louted to the horseman that rode over me yet, and I would be ill-advised to start with the Gruamach one!'

The man's face flushed up as he spoke. It's a thing I've noticed about our own poor Gaelic men: speaking before them in English or Scots, their hollow look and aloofness would give one the notion that they lacked sense and sparkle; take the muddiest-looking among them and challenge him in his own tongue, and you'll find his face fill with wit and understanding.

I was preparing to leave the court-room, having many people to call on in Inneraora, and had turned with my two friends to the door, when a fellow brushed in past us – a Highlander, I could see, but in trews – and he made to go forward into the body of the court, as if to speak to his lordship, now leaning forward in a cheerful conversation with the Provost of the burgh, a sonsy gentleman in a peruke and figured waistcoat.

'Who is he, this bold fellow?' I asked one of my friends, pausing with a foot on the door-step, a little surprised at the want of reverence to MacCailein in the man's bearing.

'Iain Aluinn – John Splendid,' said my friend. We were talking in the Gaelic, and he made a jocular remark there is no English for. Then he added, 'A poor cousin of the Marquis, a McIver Campbell (*on the wrong side*), with little schooling, but some wit and gentlemanly parts. He has gone through two fortunes in black cattle, fought some fighting here and there, and now he manages the silver-mines so adroitly that Gillesbeg Gruamach is ever on the brink of getting a big fortune, but never done launching out a little one instead to keep the place going. A decent soul, the Splendid! Throughither a bit, and better at promise than performance, but at the core as good as gold, and a fellow you would never weary of though you tramped with him in a thousand glens. We call him Splendid, not for his looks but for his style.'

The object of my friend's description was speaking into the ear of MacCailein Mor by this time, and the Marquis's face showed his tale was interesting, to say the least of it.

We waited no more, but went out into the street. I was barely two closes off from the Tolbooth when a messenger came running after me, sent by the Marquis, who asked if I would oblige greatly by waiting till he made up on me. I went back, and met his lordship with his kinsman and mine-manager coming out of the court-room together into the lobby that divided the place from the street.

'Oh, Elrigmore!' said the Marquis, in an offhand jovial and equal way; 'I thought you would like to meet my cousin here – McIver of the Barbreck; something of a soldier like yourself, who has seen service in Lowland wars.'

'In the Scots Brigade, sir?' I asked McIver, eyeing him with greater interest than ever. He was my senior by about a dozen years seemingly, a neat, well-built fellow, clean-shaven, a little over the middle height, carrying a rattan in his hand, though he had a small sword tucked under the skirt of his coat.

'With Lumsden's regiment,' he said. 'His lordship here has been telling me you have just come home from the field.'

'But last night. I took the liberty while Inneraora was snoring. You were before my day in foreign service, and yet I thought I knew by repute every Campbell that ever fought for the hard-won dollars of Gustavus even before my day. There were not so many of them from the West Country.'

'I trailed a pike privately,' laughed McIver, 'and for the honour of Clan Diarmaid I took the name Munro. My cousin here cares to have none of his immediate relatives make a living by steel at any rank less than a cornal's, or a major's at the very lowest. Frankfort, and Landsberg, and the stark field of Leipzig were the last I saw of foreign battles, and the God's truth is they were my bellyful. I like a bit splore, but give it to me in our old style, with the tartan instead of buff, and the target for breastplate and taslets. I came home sick of wars.'

'Our friend does himself injustice, my dear Elrigmore,' said Argile, smiling; 'he came home against his will, I have no doubt, and I know he brought back with him a musketoon bullet in the hip, that couped him by the heels down in Glassary for six months.'

'The result,' McIver hurried to exclaim, but putting out his breast with a touch of vanity, 'of a private *rencontre*, an affair of my own with a Reay gentleman, and not to be laid to my credit as part of the war's scaith at all.'

'You conducted your duello in odd style under Lumsden, surely,' said I, 'if you fought with powder and ball instead of steel, which is more of a Highlander's weapon to my way of thinking. All our affairs in the Reay battalion were with claymore – sometimes with targe, sometimes wanting.'

'This was a particular business of our own,' laughed John Splendid (as I may go on to call McIver, for it was the name he got oftenest behind and before in Argile). 'It was less a trial of valour than a wager about which had the better skill with the musket. If I got the bullet in my groin, I at least showed the Mackay gentleman in question that an Argile man could handle arquebus as well as *arme blanche* as we said in the France. I felled my man at one hundred and thirty paces, with six to count from a ritt-master's signal. Blow, present, God sain Mackay's soul! But I'm not given to braggadocio.'

'Not a bit, cousin,' said the Marquis, looking quizzingly at me.

'I could not make such good play with the gun against a fort gable at so many feet,' said I.

'You could, sir, you could,' said John Splendid in an easy, offhand, flattering way, that gave me at the start of our aquaintance the whole key to his character. 'I've little doubt you could allow me half-a-dozen paces and come closer on the centre of the target.'

By this time we were walking down the street, the Marquis betwixt the pair of us commoners, and I to the left side. Lowlanders and Highlanders quickly got out of the way before us and gave us the crown of the causeway. The main part of them the Marquis never let his eye light on; he kept his nose cocked in the air in the way I've since found peculiar to his family. It was odd to me that had in wanderings got to look on all honest men as equal (except Camp-Master Generals and Pike Colonels), to see some of his lordship's poor clansmen cringing before him. Here indeed was the leaven of your low-country scum, for in all the broad Highlands wandering before and since I never saw the like! 'Blood of my blood, brother of my name!' says our good Gaelic old-word: it made no insolents in camp or castle, yet it kept the poorest clansmen's head up before the highest chief. But there was, even in Baile Inneraora, sinking in the servile ways of the incomer, something too of honest worship in the deportment of the people. It was sure enough in the manner of an old woman with a face peat-tanned to crinkled leather who ran out of the Vennel or lane, and, bending to the Marquis his lace wrist-bands, kissed them as I've seen Papists do the holy duds in Notre Dame and Bruges Kirk.

This display before me, something of a stranger, a little displeased Gillesbeg Gruamach. 'Tut, tut!' he cried in Gaelic to the *cailleach*, 'thou art a foolish old woman!'

'God keep thee, MacCailein!' said she, 'thy daddy put his hand on my head like a son when he came back from his banishment in Spain, and I keened over thy mother dear when she died. The hair of Peggy Bheg's head is thy door-mat, and her son's blood is thy will for a foot-bath.'

'Savage old harridan!' cried the Marquis, jerking away; but I could see he was not now unpleased altogether that a man new from the wide world and its ways should behold how much he was thought of by his people.

He put his hands in a friendly way on the shoulders of us on either hand of him, and brought us up a bit round turn, facing him at a standstill opposite the door of the English kirk. To this day I mind well the rumour of the sea that came round the corner.

'I have a very particular business with both you gentlemen,' he said. 'My friend here, McIver, has come hot-foot to tell me of a rumour that a body of Irish banditty under Alasdair MacDonald, the MacColkitto as we call him, has landed somewhere about Kinlochaline or Knoydart. This portends damnably, if I, an elder ordained of this kirk, may say so. We have enough to do with the Athole gentry and others nearer home. It means that I must on with plate and falchion again, and out on the weary road for war I have little stomach for, to tell the truth.'

'You're able for the best of them, MacCailein,' cried John Splendid, in a hot admiration. 'For a scholar you have as good judgment on the field and as gallant a seat on the saddle as any man ever I saw in haberschone and morion. With your schooling I could go round the world conquering.'

'Ah! Flatterer, flatterer! Ye have all the guile of the tongue our enemies give Clan Campbell credit for, and that I wish I had a little more of. Still and on, it's no time for fair words. Look! Elrigmore. You'll have heard of our kittle state in this shire for the past ten years, and not only in this shire but all over the West Highlands. I give you my word I'm no sooner with the belt off me and my chair pulled in to my desk and papers than its some one beating a point of war or a piper blowing the warning under my window. To look at my history for the past few years any one might think I was Dol' Gorm himself, fight and plot, plot and fight! How can I help it – thrust into this hornet's nest from the age of sixteen, when my father (*beannachd leis!*) took me out warring against the islesmen, and I only in the humour for playing at shinty or fishing like the boys on the moor-lochs behind the town. I would sooner be a cottar in Auchnagoul down there, with porridge for my every meal, than constable, chastiser, what not, or whatever I am, of all these vexed Highlands. Give me my book in my closet, or at worst let me do my country's work in a courtier's way with brains, and I would ask no more.'

'Except Badenoch and Nether Lochaber – fat land, fine land, MacCailein!' said John Splendid, laughing cunningly.

The Marquis's face flamed up.

'You're an ass, John,' he said, 'picking up the countryside's gossip. I have no love for the Athole and Great Glen folks as ye ken; but I could long syne have got letters of fire and sword that made Badenoch and

Nether Lochaber mine if I had the notion. Don't interrupt me with your nonsense, cousin; I'm telling Elrigmore here, for he's young and has skill of civilised war, that there may, in very few weeks, be need of every arm in the parish or shire to baulk Colkitto. The MacDonald and other malignants have been robbing high and low from Lochow to Loch Finne this while back; I have hanged them a score a month at the town-head there, but that's dealing with small affairs, and I'm sore mistaken if we have not cruel times to come.'

'Well, sir' I said, 'what can I do?'

The Marquis bit his moustachio and ran a spur on the ground for a little without answering, as one in a quandary, and then he said, 'You're no vassal of mine, Baron' (as if he were half sorry for it), 'but all you Glen Shira folk are well disposed to me and mine, and have good cause, though that Macnachtan fellow's a Papisher. What I had in my mind was that I might count on you taking a company of our fencible men, as John here is going to do, and going over-bye to Lorn with me to cut off those Irish blackguards of Alasdair MacDonald's from joining Montrose.'

For some minutes I stood turning the thing over in my mind, being by nature slow to take on any scheme of high emprise without some scrupulous balancing of chances. Half-way up the closes, in the dusk, and in their rooms, well back from the windows, or far up the street, all aloof from his Majesty MacCailein Mor, the good curious people of Inneraora watched us. They could little guess the pregnancy of our affairs. For me, I thought how wearily I had looked for some rest from wars, at home in Glen Shira after my years of foreign service. Now that I was here, and my mother no more, my old father needed me on hill and field, and Argile's quarrel was not my quarrel until Argile's enemies were at the foot of Ben Bhuidhe or coming all boden in fier of war up the pass of Shira Glen. I liked adventure, and a captaincy was a captaincy, but –

'Is it boot and saddle at once, my lord?' I asked.

'It must be that or nothing. When a viper's head is coming out of a hole, crunch it incontinent, or the tail may be more than you can manage.'

'Then, my lord,' said I, 'I must cry off. On this jaunt at least. It would be my greatest pleasure to go with you and my friend McIver, not to mention all the good fellows I'm bound to know in rank in your regiment, but for my duty to my father and one or two other considerations that need not be named. But – if this be any use – I give my word that should MacDonald or any other force come this side the passes at Accurach Hill, or anywhere east Lochow, my time and steel are yours.'

MacCailein Mor looked a bit annoyed, and led us at a fast pace up to the gate of the castle that stood, high towered and embrasured for heavy pieces, stark and steeve above town Inneraora. A most curious, dour, and moody man, with a mind roving from key to key. Every now and then he would stop and think a little without a word, then on, and run his fingers through his hair or fumble nervously at his leathern buttons, paying small heed to the Splendid and I, who convoyed him, so we got into a crack about the foreign field of war.

'Quite right, Elrigmore, quite right!' at last cried the Marquis, pulling up short, and looked me plump in the eyes. 'Bide at hame while bide ye may. I would never go on this affair myself if by God's grace I was not Marquis of Argile and son of a house with many bitter foes. But, hark ye! A black day looms for these our homelands if ever Montrose and those Irish dogs get through our passes. For twenty thousand pounds Saxon I would not have the bars off the two roads of Accurach! And I thank you, Elrigmore, that at the worst I can count on your service at home. We may need good men here on Loch Finne-side as well as farther afield, overrun as we are by the blackguardism of the North and the Papist clans around us. Come in, friends, and have your meridian. I have a flagon of French brown brandy you never tasted the equal of in any town you sacked in all Low Germanie.'

Rug eadrain
(He hath made an intervention)
BARD OF THE MACEWEN FAMILY
TRANSLATION W.J. WATSON

He hath made an intervention *is a fine example of a bardic praise poem and demonstrates the relationship between the bard and his patron. The poem is dedicated to Gillesbeg Gruamach, Marquis of Argyll, referred to here also as lord of the race of Duibhne (the ancient name for Clan Campbell). The poet is very probably a member of the bardic family of MacEwen who were attached to the House of Argyll. He appears to have been deprived of part of his patrimony which would have been situated at Kilchoan on Loch Melfort. He seeks by obsequious flattery to persuade his chief to restore to him his father's heritage and compares him very favourably with ancient classical heroes like Hector and Caesar – even with the Greek philosopher Aristotle! – and with the great Celtic warriors Oscar, Conall Cearnach and Cú Chullain. In return his chief will receive the bard's praise which brings the most lasting fame of all. The poem was written some time between 1641, the year Gillesbeg was made Marquis, and February, 1645, the date of the battle of Inverlochy. After his cowardly behaviour on that occasion he is unlikely to have received praise for heroism.*

1. Rug eadrain ar iath nAlban,
    ón decair í d'ionnarbadh,
fear cabhra Gaoidheal is Gall,
    saoirfhear gan labhra ar leatram.

2. Ársaidh ar ccríoch do chosnamh,
    ar mionn óir, ar n-árasbhrugh;
lámh Osgair a n-am feadhma,
    ar ccrann fosguidh fíneamhna.

3. Madh síoth madh cogadh do chách,
   MacCailín is é ar n-ursgáth;
lámh leantar mar thuinn ttoruidh,
   Eachtair an fhuinn Albanuigh.

4. Poimpe maighe mhaicne Duibhne,
   Cato a ccruth a ríoghchuimhne,
Sésar le sénuibh ccatha,
   's é go mbésuibh mbuan-fhlatha.

5. Fear ar ccoimhéid-ne a ccúirt ríogh,
   chonmhas síoth 's nach ob eisíoth;
fuilngidh soin créchtfhoghuil ccuim,
   mar Choin ccédfadhuigh cCulainn.

6. Leómhan léimneach tar gach toigh,
   triath chothuighthe a ccreidimh;
a n-iath Alban 'n a phosda triath,
   go n-ardbhladh n-eaglasda.

7. Go bhfuil 'n a Mharcus ar méd,
   tré itche cliar da choimhéd;
dóigh le cách tuaith is theas
   gur 'n a thráth fuar gach flaitheas.

8. Do bhéir tré chomhrádh ccunnail
   aimsir eile ar th'agalluimh,
a mhéin ríoghdha, a sgiath sgaoilte,
   a thriath dhíona an Duibhnaicme.

9. Ní chreidim nach cuala sibh
   gur aomadar mic Mílidh
cur na bfileadh tar sál soir
   gan dligheadh tar Chlár Conghail.

10. A h-ucht a n-ainbhreithe féin
    as do h-ionnarbadh iadséin,
cliar Bhanbha na mbreath ccoimheach,
    a dhearc amhra ionnsoigheach.

11. Ní h-ionann dóibh is damhsa,
    ní bhead is cách codarsna,
áros an ghrianfhuinn ghuirmghil,
    ort gé iarruinn athchuinge.

12. Do fosdadh le Coin na ccleas
    tré oineach an t-ord éigeas,
mar dhearbhthar ar bheithir Bhreagh,
    do neamhthoil cheithre ccóigeadh.

13. Gá córa do Choin cCulainn
    iomchar uilc is anfhulaing,
a dhonnabhruigh shaoir gan tsal,
    ná daoibh d'ollamhnuibh Alban?

14. Da mhó th'ainm ar aoi ngarma,
    mó th'inmhe, as fearr th'athardha,
iná Cú comhluinn na ccleas
    anú a bfoghluim 'sa bflaitheas.

15. A Mhic MhicCailín, éisdidh inn;
    déna dhamhsa bhur ndichioll;
bi ar mo shon ag labhra libh,
    adhbhar dom chur a ccéimibh.

16. A chodhnuigh chloinne Duibhne,
    an tan-sa éisd m' orfhuighle;
gabh 'na thráth m'égnach at ucht,
    a chédrath, a bhláth bheannacht.

17. Léigidh dhamh dúthchas m'athar,
    a n-onóir na h-ealadhan,
a ghég tarla fá thoradh,
    do mhéd th'anma is adhmholadh.

18. Tuig féin, a sgeallán na sgol,
    's a rélta eoil na n-ollamh,
ó's tú is coimhdhe dod chinneadh,
    nach dú oirne th' aindligheadh.

19. Cíos na n-aithreach ór fhás mé,
　　díghruis gráidh, cruas a cceirde,
caidhe mál as buaine bladh,
　　a lámh as cruaidhe a ccogadh?

20. Ní h-ór, ní h-ionmhus eile,
　　do ghéibha uaim d'áiridhe,
ní cána no comha cruidh,
　　acht rogha ar ndána dheacruigh.

21. Mairidh a sein-leabhruibh suadh,
　　's a ndíoghluim ar ndréacht bhfionnuar,
gach maith da ndiongantur dhamh,
　　a bhraithfhionn ardghlan iarladh.

22. Níor thuill th'athair, gá tám dhó,
　　sul tarraidh sé ainm iarla,
a choillbhile is tiogh toradh,
　　oirbhire ó fhior ealadhan.

23. A thriath oirdheirc fhóid Abha,
　　a sdiúrthóir chóig ccédfatha,
a bhile thairtheach ós tráigh,
　　a chridhe chaithmheach conáigh.

24. A thaobh tláith go tlacht ccuilce,
　　mo chúis ar do chomairce;
a throim-meanmhna nach beag bladh,
　　a léag loinneardha lóghmhar.

25. A cheannlaoch Locha Fíne,
　　a chraobh óir na h-airdríghe,
a fhir nár dhonnadh le dáimh,
　　ná sir ar th'ollamh éadáil.

26. A Chonaill Chearnaigh ar ghoil,
　　a fhoghluim Arasdotuil,
ó do chneasghuin ní dú dradh,
　　a chnú chleasruidh an chomhruig.

HE HATH MADE AN INTERVENTION

1. He hath made an intervention on Scotland's soil, whence it may not lightly be expelled, he who helps Gael and Gall, that noble of unbiassed utterance.

2. He is a veteran to defend our bounds, he is our diadem of gold, our abiding mansion; his hand is like Oscar's in hour of action, he is our sheltering vine.

3. Whether others be at peace or at war, MacCailín is our firm defence; his hand is followed as a wave of fruitfulness; he is the Hector of the land of Scotland.

4. He is the Pompey of the plain of Duibhne's race, he is as Cato in the fashion of his royal memory; like Caesar with omens of victory in battle; he has the traits of a lasting prince.

5. He is our guardian in the king's court, who maintains peace and who refuses not dispeace; he endureth war-wounding of his body like the intrepid Hound of Culann.

6. He is a lion that leaps over every house; he is a lord who defends the faith; in Scotland's land he is a pillar of lords, whose fame is high within the Church.

7. He is a Marquis in degree, through the prayers of churchmen for his safe-keeping; all men, north and south, deem all his honours won when due.

8. I will with talk discreet take further time for addressing thee, thou of royal mind, thou wide-spread shield, thou lord that shelterest the race of Duibhne.

9. Methinks thou must have heard how the sons of Míl once inclined to send the poets eastwards over the sea, unlawfully, across the Plain of Conghal.

10. It was from their own injustice that those were being expelled, Banha's poets of strange dooms, thou of the wondrous warlike eye.

11. Unlike their case is mine; I shall not be perverse as those others; thou abode of the resplendent bright sunny soil, even if I ask a petition of thee.

12. By the Hound of feats the poet order was retained, through his generosity, as is proved of Bregia's champion, despite the reluctance of four provinces.

13. How was it meeter for Cu Chulainn to endure ill and suffering, thou brown-browed noble without spot, than it is for thee for the sake of Scotland's poets?

14. In as much as thy name is greater as regards thy style, greater thy position, better thy patrimony than those of the warlike Hound of feats this day in point of learning and of princely rule.

15. Thou son of MacCailín, hearken to me; do thou thy best in my behalf; be favourable to me when thou dost speak, be thou the cause of raising my degree.

16. Thou lord of the children of Duibhne, at this time hearken to my appeal; do thou receive kindly my plaint in its due time, thou who art first of fortune, thou bloom of blessings.

17. Restore to me my father's heritage in honour of mine art, thou branch laden with fruit, according to the greatness of thy name and of thy praises.

18. Wot thou, thou darling of the schools and guiding star of poets, since it is thou art lord for thy kin, that wrong from thee to me is unmeet.

19. The tribute of my fathers from whom I am sprung, fervour of love, rigour in art, what tax brings more lasting fame than these, thou whose hand is hardest in warfare?

20. Not gold nor other treasure wilt thou get from me in special, not cess nor gift of cattle, but the choicest of our hard-wrought poems.

21. In the ancient books of the learned and in the gleanings of our refreshing poems each good deed that shall be done to me remains on record, thou fair-judging bright and lofty earl.

22. Thy father, in one word, ere ever he had won the name of earl, deserved not reproach from man of art, thou forest tree thick of fruit.

23. Thou illustrious lord of the sod of Awe, thou who dost guide the five senses, thou tall tree of fruit above the strand, thou heart of wealth and bounty.

24. Thou tender of side, with grace as of a reed, I lay my case on thy protection; thou of deep mind, not small of fame, thou glittering precious jewel;

25. Thou chief warrior of Loch Fyne, thou golden bough of the kingdom, thou who art unsmirched by poet band, seek not to make spoil of thy poet.

26. Thou who art as Conall Cearnach for valour, thou who hast the learning of Aristotle, trouble from wound at thy hand were unbefitting, thou without peer in feats of battle.

'Loch Fyne Herring'

from A Tour in Scotland, 1769

THOMAS PENNANT (1726–98)

Thomas Pennant, born into a land-owning family in Flintshire, studied at Queen's College, Oxford and built up a reputation as a significant zoologist as well as one of the classic British travel writers. Elected a Fellow of the Royal Society for his British Zoology, *he made two substantial tours in the Highlands and Islands of Scotland and wrote of his experiences in two highly regarded and very popular books. The account of his first 1769 tour, from which our extract comes, went through five editions by 1790 and inspired many other travellers. That acute critic, Dr Samuel Johnson, observed while on his own tour in the Hebrides in 1773 that:*

> Pennant has greater variety of enquiry than almost any man, and has told us more than perhaps one in ten thousand could have done, in the time that he took

and years later he wrote to Boswell:

> Pennant seems to have seen a great deal which we did not see: when we travel again let us look better about us.

Pennant's enquiry in this extract is devoted to what a later writer would describe as 'a great, great, mystery' – the Loch Fyne Herring. The detailed description of both the techniques and the economics of the herring fishery is typical of Pennant's style and the concluding note about the gulls feasting on a surface shoal of herring serves as a reminder that natural history was his first love.

Sadly the herring fishing of Loch Fyne is no longer on the scale described by Pennant – a massive fishery whose description is echoed almost a century and half later by Neil Munro, whose Inveraray puffer skipper Para Handy reminisces of the good old days:

> The herrin' wass that thick in Loch Fyne in them days, that sometimes you couldna get your anchor to the ground, and the quality wass chust sublime.

The busy scene of the herring-fishery gave no small improvement to the magnificent environs of *Inveraray*. Every evening some hundreds of boats in a manner covered the surface of *Loch-Fine*, an arm of the sea, which, from its narrowness and from the winding of its shores, has all the beauties of a fresh-water lake: on the week-days, the chearfull noise of the bagpipe and dance echoes from on board: on the sabbath, each boat approaches the land, and psalmody and devotion divide the day; for the common people of the North are disposed to be religious, having the example before them of a gentry untainted by luxury and dissipation, and the advantage of being instructed by a clergy, who are active in their duty, and who preserve respect, amidst all the disdvantages of a narrow income.

The length of *Loch-Fine* from the eastern end to the point of *Lamond*, is above thirty *Scotch* miles; but its breadth scarce two measured: the depth from sixty to seventy fathoms. It is noted for the vast shoals of herrings that appear here in *July* and continue till *January*. The highest season is from *September* to *Christmas*, when near six hundred boats with four men in each, are employed. A chain of nets is used (for several are united) of an hundred fathoms in length. As the herrings swim at very uncertain depths, so the nets are sunk to the depth the shoal is found to take: the success therefore depends much on the judgment or good fortune of the fishers, in taking their due depths; for it often happens that one boat will take multitudes, while the next does not catch a single fish, which makes the boatmen perpetually enquire of each other about the depth of their nets. These are kept up by buoys to a proper pitch; the ropes that run through them fastened with pegs, and by drawing up, or letting out the rope (after taking out the pegs) they adjust their situation, and then replace them. Sometimes the fish swim in twenty fathom water, sometimes in fifty, and oftentimes even at the bottom.

It is computed that each boat gets about £40 in the season. The fish are either salted, and packed in barrels for exportation, or sold fresh to the country people, two or three hundred horses being brought every day to the water side from very distant parts. A barrel holds 500 herrings, if they are of the best kind; at a medium, 700: but if more, for sometimes a barrel will hold 1000, they are reckoned very poor. The present price £1 4s. *per* barrel; but there is a drawback of the duty on salt for those that are exported.

The great rendezvous of vessels for the fishery off the western isles is at *Cambeltown*, in *Cantyre*, where they clear out on the 12th of *September*, and sometimes three hundred busses are seen there at a time: they must return to their different ports by *January* 13th, where they ought to receive the præmium of £2 10s. *per* tun of herrings; but it is said to be very ill paid, which is a great discouragement to the fishery.

The herrings of *Loch-Fine* are as uncertain in their migration as they are on the coast of *Wales*. They had for numbers of years quitted that water; but appeared again there within these dozen years. Such is the case with the lochs on all this western coast, not but people despair too soon of finding them, from one or two unsuccessfull tryals in the beginning of the season; perhaps from not adjusting their nets to the depth the fish happen then to swim in: but if each year a small vessel or two was sent to make a thorough tryal in every branch of the sea on this coast, they would undoubtedly find shoals of fish in one or other.

Tunnies, called here *Mackrel-Sture*, are very frequently caught in the herring season, which they follow to prey on. They are taken with a strong iron hook fastened to a rope and baited with a herring: as soon as hooked lose all spirit, and are drawn up without any resistance: are very active when at liberty, and jump and frolick on the surface of the water.

Crossed over an elegant bridge of three arches upon the *Aray*, in front of the castle, and kept riding along the slide of the Loch for about seven miles: saw in one place a shoal of herrings, close to the surface, perfectly piled on one another, with a flock of Gulls, busied with this offered booty.

'Inveraray'

from A Journey through England and Scotland to the Hebrides in 1784

BARTHÉLEMY FAUJAS DE SAINT FOND (1741–1819)

Barthélemy Faujas de Saint Fond was born to a wealthy land-owning family in the Rhone valley, trained as a lawyer at Grenoble but devoted his life to the study of geology and natural history.

Faujas was a significant and influential part of the wave of scientifically motivated travellers to the West Highlands of Scotland in the late eighteenth century. His account of his travels has many digressions into geological commentary, and indeed the object of his travels was to reach the island of Staffa, with its remarkable formations of columnar basalt. However he was an acute and entertaining travel writer; both in describing the general scenery of Argyll – such as his description of the Rest and Be Thankful and Hell's Glen, which formed his introduction to Argyll and with which our extract opens; and in his accounts of the people he meets on his journey.

Although as a gentleman traveller Faujas went equipped with letters of introduction to the nobility and gentry of the area – such as the Duke of Argyll – the hazards and inconveniences of travel in eighteenth century Scotland were not entirely eliminated. On his way up Loch Lomondside to Argyll, Faujas and his postillions had been unable to find shelter in Luss Inn, due to it being entirely taken over by a judge of the High Court of Justiciary on his way to hold the circuit criminal court at Inveraray. Later, at a dinner in the magnificent surroundings of the relatively new Inveraray Castle he meets the judge:

> . . . a good loyal Scot, worthy of all the respect that has been paid to him, for
> he filled his office with justice and humanity

and the travellers make their peace, with the judge assuring the French traveller that on another occasion he would not have to sleep in a shed. The judge (though Faujas does not name him) can be identified from the Justiciary Court duty roster as the famous Robert McQueen, Lord Braxfield, later to become Lord Justice-Clerk of Scotland. Faujas's comment on Braxfield's 'justice and humanity' is of interest in the light of later criticisms of his behaviour.

Faujas was an acute observer of manners. In his description, for

*example, of the style of dinner enjoyed by the Duke of Argyll – down to
the type of knives and forks used and the chamber pots conveniently
placed in the corners of the room – Faujas de St Fond gives a fine
illustration of the potential for aristocratic enjoyment of life in eighteenth-
century Argyll.*

But let us proceed upon our journey. I soon found a contrast to the
delightful scenes we left. They were succeeded by deserts and dismal
heaths. We entered a narrow pass between two chains of high mountains,
which appear to have, at a very remote period, formed only one ridge, but
which some terrible revolution has torn asunder throughout its length.

This defile is so narrow, and the mountains are so high and steep, that
the rays of the sun can scarcely reach the place and be seen for the space of
an hour in the twenty-four. For more than ten miles, which is the length of
this pass, there is neither house nor cottage, nor living creature except a
few fishes in a small lake, about half way. I do not mention the flocks of
sheep that feed on the heights, because they are at so great an elevation,
and among heathery slopes so steep, that as neither their shape nor their
movements can be distinguished, they may be taken to be stones rather
than living animals; but they can be made out when one watches them
with glasses.

We travelled thus for nearly six hours in this dismal traverse, through
which the roads are neither metalled nor kept in repair, until at last we
suddenly debouched on the shore of Loch Fyne, in Argyllshire. The first
village met with at the end of this lake is Cairndow. Going round this point
of the lake, which forms a kind of fork, we arrived at Inverary, the capital of
Argyllshire. It must not be imagined that this chief place is a town; it is
merely what would be called a village in France; but a village pleasantly
situated upon the side of the beautiful Loch Fyne, which may be navigated
by large vessels, and abounds with herring at the proper season. This
fishery yields a considerable revenue to the country. On one side, there is
the view of pasture-grounds and some trees in the valley, which ends in a
fine park; on the other, diversified gardens, meadows covered with flocks,
and hills planted with green trees, at the bottom of which a superb and vast
habitation, in the Gothic style, gives life to this fine landscape. This is the
castle of the Duke of Argyll, about a mile from Inverary.

We were standing at the door of the only inn in the village, whence we were enjoying this fine prospect; our carriages were already within the yard, when the landlord came to tell us, very politely, that we could not be received, as every room in his house was either engaged, or already occupied. It was again the lord-judge who was expected here, and for whom the best room had very properly been reserved: the jurymen were in possession of the rest of the house.

We had letters of recommendation to the Duke of Argyll,* and we knew that he had come to pass the autumn in this beautiful country; but we did not wish to wait upon him until after having procured quarters elsewhere, as we should have been sorry to abuse any kindness that might be shewn us.

The inflexibility of our host, however, cruelly embarrassed us. He would not let us have our luggage detached, nor set foot in his house. No other hostelry existed in the place. Our only alternative was to push on to Dalmally, about fifteen miles from Inverary; but it was already too late to undertake the journey, and we should have been obliged to travel during a part of the night by very bad roads. Besides, we should thus have lost the opportunity of seeing the Duke of Argyll, delivering our letters, and receiving from him information respecting the country, and the difficult route we had still to pursue through such a desert region before we could arrive at the port of Oban.

These considerations induced us to ask the innkeeper if he would permit us to step into a room, and write a letter to the Duke of Argyll. This name was held in such esteem that instantly every thing we wished for was granted. We stated our situation to the Duke, informing him at the same time our desire to present our respects to him and expressing our reluctance to give him any trouble on that account. To this billet we joined our letters of recommendation. An express was dispatched with the packet, and a reply was promptly brought to us by a French painter, who was working at the Castle, and who came to tell us, that we were eagerly expected, and to beg us to come just us we were, as the family would not sit down to dinner till we arrived. Servants were, at the same time, sent to take care of our carriages.

On our way, we saw the Duke's son† who came to meet us with manifestations of the frankest politeness and the most gracious affability. We were received at the house with every mark of friendship in the midst of a numerous company and an amiable family, who, joined to the most polished manners those prepossessing dispositions which are the natural

* John, 5th Duke of Argyll, born 1723, died 1806.
† This was George William (1766–1839) who afterwards became 6th Duke of Argyll.

dowry of sensitive and well-born minds. After the first compliments, we placed ourselves at the dinner-table, and as every thing pleased and interested me in this house, which was pervaded, if I may use the expression, with a kindly sympathy, I said to myself – 'The good woman of Tarbet was right. Here is indeed a charming family.' French was spoken at this table with as much purity as in the most polished circles of Paris. They did not fail to enquire the object of our journey to a country so little visited as this remote part of Scotland; but they were not at all surprised when they heard that our purpose was to go to the Isle of Staffa, with its Cave of Fingal, which had now a great reputation in the country.

If I recollect aright, they told us that Sir William Hamilton, Ambassador at Naples, and his nephew Lord Greville, had come here with the same intention, without having found a day favourable for the short passage between the mainland and Staffa. As this cliff-girt island has neither harbour nor anchorage, and can only be reached in very small boats, settled weather and a calm sea are absolutely necessary. These conditions, however, are extremely rare upon this coast, strewn as it is with islands, washed by currents, and exposed to impetuous winds.

To shorten the passage by sea, we were advised to make for Oban and coast thence up the Sound of Mull to the island of that name: to cross the whole breadth of the island to Torloisk, where we should find the house of Mr McLean, a very worthy gentleman, to whom the Duke of Argyll promised us letters of recommendation. From Torloisk to Staffa the crossing and return can be made in one day, by setting off in the morning early, and getting back somewhat late. But even for this little voyage the traveller must have one of those fine days which we had little reason to expect at a season already too far advanced. We were told, however, that the autumn might chance to have some of these fine days; and that moreover, we should not have been better off had we come sooner, seeing that the sea had been stormy for some months.

The Duke of Argyll kindly said that he wished to have the pleasure of detaining us for at least a few weeks, that we might have an opportunity of becoming well acquainted with the country, and such of the neighbouring mountains as were particularly worthy of note. But, pressed for time, we thought that three days, well employed, would suffice to enable us to see what was most remarkable around the castle of Inverary, particularly some rather high hills and some open quarries, and that if we began our work early in the morning, we might devote part of the evening to the duties of society and to the pleasure of becoming more intimately acquainted with a family so unaffected, so well informed, and so worthy of respect.

We remained, then, three whole days in this delightful retreat, devoting the mornings to natural history, and the evenings to music or conversation. As the gentle and amiable manners of the master and mistress of the house strongly interested me, as well as the friendly tone of his children, who were clever and had a thirst for knowledge; and as, besides, I saw here some customs connected with Scottish frankness and hospitality, I shall give a rapid sketch of my observations and remarks. These naturally ought to precede what I have to say on the natural history of the environs of Inverary.

Inverary Castle is entirely built of squared blocks of a grey-coloured *lapis ollaris*, soft to the touch, capable of taking a fine polish, as well as every form that the chisel can give it: though tender, it resists the weather, at least as well as the most durable marble.

One is at first sight surprised that a castle, in appearance so ancient, should show not the slightest mark of decay: every part is so well dressed, the angles are so clean and perfect, and the colour of the stone is so equal, that the building seems to have just come from the hand of the workman.*

My astonishment on this subject, however, soon ceased, when, after crossing some draw-bridges, and passing through a gateway, as Gothic as that of the time of Charlemagne, I arrived at a fine vestibule, which led to a staircase in the Italian style, with double balusters, of the best taste and the most perfect architecture.

This vestibule was ornamented with large bronze vases, of antique shape, placed on their pedestals, between the columns. These vases served, at the same time, as stoves to warm the air of the vestibule and the staircase.

The whole enclosure of this staircase is magnificent, tastefully decorated, and skilfully lighted. The steps are covered with elegant carpets; every thing here proclaims a love of the greatest neatness. There appears, however, to have been a desire to recall even here some reminiscences of the Gothic, for in the perspective of the staircase, a large niche, ornamented with groups of Gothic columns, has had placed in it a large organ-case: which gives an imposing and religious air to the place. This contrast may appear somewhat odd in theory, but it has been done with a certain charm, which is not without merit.

The rest of the house is laid out in a manner equally elegant and

---

* Inverary Castle was built (1744–1761) of stone obtained from quarries in the nieghbourhood, and had not been finished more than about twenty-three years at the time of the author's visit.

commodious, and can accommodate a large company. As ought always to be the case in the country, much more attention has here been paid to the luxury of simplicity, and the extreme of neatness, than to the display of gilding, and sumptuous furniture.

Notwithstanding its antique appearance, this castle is quite a modern building. The Gothic style was selected, coupled with the best design for the interior, because buildings of the tenth century look well amidst woods, and at the foot of hills. They recall ideas of chivalry connected with the bravery and gallant adventures of those romantic times. These recollections diffuse a kind of charm over the scene: they embellish it, and make it impressive. We are all a little fond of romance.

The parks, planted with foreign trees side by side with those of the country, are of great extent and have the finest effect. Open spaces, covered with the most beautiful verdure, have been carefully left and are traversed by roads and foot-paths which lead to gardens, green-houses, sheep-folds, and sequestered woods, on the sides of hills, the banks of rivulets, or towards the shore of an arm of the sea.*

There were staying in the castle, at this time, the Duke of Argyll, one of the best of men, who had travelled in Italy and in France; the Duchess, who was first married to the Duke of Hamilton, and after his death, to the Duke of Argyll: she passes, and justly, for having been one of the most beautiful women in Great Britain: she is certainly one of the best informed;† the Countess of Derby, the Duchess's daughter, by her first marriage: this lady had travelled a great deal, and speaks French with so much ease and so little accent, that she might be taken for a native of Paris: there are few women more amiable or more beautiful. The children of the Duke were at home. The eldest daughter sings exceedingly well, and plays admirably on the piano-forte, and she, as well as her younger sister, has the sweetest and most lovely expression. The Duke's son, about sixteen or seventeen [actually eighteen] years of age, has the courtesy and kindness of his father, and already shews much skill in drawing. A

* Knox, who was at Inverary two years after me, in speaking of that place, says: 'Inverary has become of some importance, by the care of the family of Argyll, who have a magnificent house there, surrounded with more than a million of trees, which occupy several miles square.' *Tour through the Highlands of Scotland and the Hebride Isles*, Vol. I.

† This was the celebrated Elizabeth Gunning, daughter of an Irish country gentleman, and one of the greatest beauties at the court of George III. She had two sons and a daughter by the Duke of Hamilton. Her family by the Duke of Argyll consisted of three sons and two daughters. The eldest son had died in infancy, and the second, now the heir to the title, was only eighteen years of age at the time of the author's visit.

physician and chaplain formed the rest of the family circle. There were also several visitors in the house, among whom was a member of Parliament, a man of much intelligence, who had travelled, with advantage, in almost every part of Europe.

I must not omit to mention, that on the second day after our arrival, the lord-judge, who had ousted us so often, came to dine at the castle. He was already advanced in years, but a good loyal Scot, worthy of all the respect that had been paid to him, for he filled his office with justice and humanity. We made our peace with him in the midst of toasts; and he assured us, with great good nature, that he would have shared his lodging with us, if he had known what passed, and that we might be assured that we should not sleep in the shed, if he had the pleasure of meeting us another time upon the road.

Such was the quiet and kindly way in which we spent our time in Inverary castle. Compare it with life in towns! Each person rose in the morning at any hour he pleased. Some took a ride, others went to the chase. I started off at sunrise to examine the natural history of the neighbourhood.

At ten o'clock a bell gives warning that it is breakfast-time: we then repair to a large room, ornamented with historical pictures of the family; among which there are some by Battoni, Reynolds and other eminent Italian and English painters. Here we find several tables, covered with tea-kettles, fresh cream, excellent butter, rolls of several kinds, and in the midst of all, bouquets of flowers, newspapers, and books. There are besides, in this room, a billiard-table, pianos, and other musical instruments.

After breakfast, some walk in the parks, others employ themselves in reading or in music, or return to their rooms until half-past four, when the bell makes itself heard to announce that dinner is ready; we all go to the dining-room, where the table is usually laid for twenty-five or thirty covers. When every one is seated, the chaplain, according to custom, makes a short prayer, and blesses the food, which is eaten with pleasure, for the dishes are prepared after the manner of an excellent French cook; every thing is served here as in Paris, except some courses in the English style, for which a certain predilection is preserved; but this makes a variety, and thus gives the epicures of every country an opportunity of pleasing their palates.

I was particularly pleased to see napkins on the table, as well as forks of the same kind as those used in France. I do not like to prick my mouth or my tongue with those little sharp steel tridents which are generally used in England, even in houses where very good dinners are given. I know that this kind of forks, which are sometimes placed in a knife handle, are only intended for seizing and fixing the pieces of meat while they are cut, and that the English knives being very large and rounded at the point, serve the same purpose to which forks in France are applied; that is, to carry food to the mouth[!]. But, I must confess, that I use the knife very awkwardly in this way. As it is well, however, to take account of the usages of different countries, it seems to me that at table, as well as elsewhere, the English calculate better than we do.

In England, the fork, whether of steel or even of silver, is always held in the left hand and the knife in the right. The fork seizes, the knife cuts, and the pieces may be carried to the mouth with either. The motion is quick and precise. The manœuvres at an English dinner are founded upon the same principle as the Prussian tactics – not a moment is lost.

In France, the first manœuvre is similar to that of the English; but when the meat is cut in pieces, the knife is laid down idle on the right side of the plate, while the fork on the other hand passes from left to right which makes the first loss of time; the right hand seizes it and lifts the morsel to the mouth, thus making a threefold mandœuvre. The English plan is better, but it necessitates large blunt knives rounded at the point. Well! What harm is there in that? It would mean one weapon less in the hands of fools or villains.

How many beings in illness or in despair have made use of sharp-pointed knives against themselves? How many monsters have made a cruel use of them against others? The list would, doubtless, be long; and, if this useful instrument had not in Italy, Spain, and most other countries taken the form of a stilletto, it is probable that such crimes would be less frequently committed. Experience has long since proved that great effects may spring from very trivial causes.

But I am forgetting that the knives and forks at the Duke of Argyll's table are used in eating very excellent things. The entrées, the rôti, the entremets are all served as in France with the same variety and abundance. If the poultry be not so juicy as in Paris, one eats here in compensation hazel-hens, and above all moorfowl, delicious fish, and vegetables, the quality of which maintains the reputation of the Scottish gardeners who grow them.

At the dessert, the scene changes; the cloth, the napkins, and every thing vanish. The mahogany table appears in all its lustre; but it is soon covered with brilliant decanters, filled with the best wines; comfits, in fine porcelain or crystal vases; and fruits of different kinds in elegant baskets. Plates are distributed together with many glasses; and in every object elegance and conveniency seem to rival each other. I was surprised, however, to see on the same table, in so cold a climate, and in the middle of the month of September, beautiful peaches, very good grapes, apricots, prunes, figs, cherries, and raspberries, though the figs could hardly be called juicy by a person born in the south of France. It is probable, however, that the greater part of these fruits were produced with much care and expense in hot-houses.

Towards the end of the dessert, the ladies withdrew to a room destined for the tea-table. I admit that they were left alone a little too long; but the Duke of Argyll informed me that he had preserved this custom in the country, in order that the people of the district might not be offended by the breach of an ancient practice to which they had always been accustomed. Although the ceremony of toasts lasts for at least three-quarters of an hour, no person is made uncomfortable, and every one drinks as he pleases. This, however, does not prevent a great number of healths being drunk with pleasure and good grace. Wines are the great luxury of the table in England, where they drink the best and dearest that grow in France and Portugal. If the lively champagne should make its diuretic influence felt, the case is foreseen, and in the pretty corners of the room the necessary convenience is to be found. This is applied to with so little ceremony, that the person who has occasion to use it, does not even interrupt his talk during the operation. I suppose this is one of the reasons why the English ladies, who are exceedingly modest and reserved, always leave the company before the toasts begin.

At last we proceed to the drawing-room, where tea and coffee abound, and where the ladies do the honours of the table with much grace and ceremony; the tea is always excellent, but it is not so with the coffee. Now, since the coffee is not good in a house like this, where no expense is spared, and where I presume it is not brought, already roasted and ground, from the nearest town, in which it is sold by privileged shops, as in London, it cannot be expected to be good any where else in the country. I should imagine that the English attach no importance to the perfume and flavour of good coffee; for it seems to be all one to them what kind they drink, provided they have four or five cupfuls of it. Their coffee is always weak and bitter, and has completely lost its aromatic odour. Thus they are deprived of an excellent beverage, which would be a thousand times better for their health than tea. Kæmpfer, who resided long in Japan, and who has published some very curious observations upon tea and the shrub that bears it, remarks that it contains something of a narcotic nature.

After tea those who wished retired to their rooms; those who preferred conversation or music remained in the drawing-room; others went out to walk. At ten o'clock supper was served, and those attended it who pleased. I find that as a rule people eat a great deal more in England than in France. I do not know that they are more healthy for it; I doubt if they are; but this I know, that Dumoulin, one of the most celebrated physicians of Paris, declared that he had never been called in the night to attend any person who had not supped.

Epigram

ROBERT BURNS (1759–96)

These two verses by Burns arose from a visit the poet and a friend paid to Inveraray in June 1787. Calling at the inn they found the inn-keeper entirely preoccupied with a party of visitors who were in the town to pay a call on the Duke of Argyll at Inveraray Castle. Burns was irritated by the discourtesy of the inn-keeper but being a poet was able to take lasting revenge in these memorable lines.

Who'er he be that sojourns here,
I pity much his case,
Unless he comes to wait upon
The Lord their God, his Grace.

There's naething here but Highland pride,
And Highland scab and hunger;
If Providence has sent me here,
'Twas surely in an anger.

'Inveraray'

from collections of a Tour made in Scotland AD 1803

DOROTHY WORDSWORTH (1771–1855)

Nineteen years after Barthélemy Faujas de St Fond visited Inveraray on his Highland Tour, Dorothy Wordsworth and her poet brother William called in on the capital of Mid-Argyll in their six-week long tour of Scotland. Their travelling companion, Coleridge, had left them at Arrochar and our extract commences with the travellers entering Argyll at the head of Loch Long on 29th August. They ascend Glen Croe to the stone seat marked 'Rest and Be Thankful' and descend to Loch Fyne to find shelter for the night in the Inn at Cairndow. Unlike a later poetic traveller, John Keats, the Wordsworths were well enough briefed to know that 'Rest and Be Thankful' was merely an inscription. The unfortunate Keats, travelling in Scotland with his friend Charles Brown in July 1818, wrote:

> We were up at 4 this morning and have walked to breakfast 15 miles through two tremendous Glens – at the end of the first there is a place called rest and be thankful which we took for an Inn – fit was nothing but a Stone and so we were cheated into 5 more Miles to Breakfast.

This spot produced in William Wordsworth a later sonnet reflecting on the effort needed to reach the Rest and on the physical journey as an allegory of the journey of the soul:

> Doubling and doubling with laborious walk,
> Who, that has gained at length the wished-for Height,
> This brief this simple wayside Call can slight,
> And rests not thankful? Whether cheered by talk
> With some loved friend, or by the unseen hawk
> Whistling to clouds and sky-born streams that shine,
> At the sun's outbreak, as with light divine,
> Ere they descend to nourish root and stalk
> Of valley flowers. Nor, while the limbs repose,
> Will we forget that, as the fowl can keep
> Absolute stillness, poised aloft in air,
> And fishes front, unmoved, the torrent's sweep –
> So may the Soul, through powers that Faith bestows,
> Win rest, and ease, and peace, with bliss that Angels share.

Descending from the mountains, Dorothy, however greatly she might have been impressed with the setting and indeed the general view of Inveraray, found much in the town to trouble her on a closer inspection – describing it as 'a doleful example of Scotch filth'. The problem seems to have been with the residents rather than the planned town created by the Dukes of Argyll to complement their new castle. 'The windows and door-steads', Dorothy remarks, 'were as dirty as in a dirty by-street of a large town, making a most unpleasant contrast with the comely face of the buildings towards the water'.

Unlike the aristocratic Faujas de St Fond, travelling with introductions to the Ducal family, the Wordsworths were less favoured and had they wished to visit the Castle would have gone through the usual procedure for respectable but otherwise unconnected travellers in the period before stately homes were regularly opened to the general public for a fee:

> *Travellers who wish to view the inside of the Castle send in their names, and the Duke appoints the time of their going . . .*

However the Wordsworths were not sufficiently excited by the Castle's attractions – 'there being no pictures', and its modernity – 'has not been built above half a century'. A very different reaction to that of the indomitable Dr Samuel Johnson, who called at Inveraray with James Boswell in 1773 and remarked of the new Castle 'What I admire here is the total defiance of expence' – although Johnson, who could often find fault with Scotland and the Scots, thought the castle too low and would have wished it a storey higher.

The Wordsworths left Inveraray by way of Glen Aray, heading for Dalmally and Kilchurn Castle on Loch Aweside. As they did so they noted one of the three waterfalls on the River Aray, though sadly they seem to have missed the most impressive and certainly the most eloquently named of these – the Lenach Gluthin, the 'angry slurp', which Louis Stott's Waterfalls of Scotland *describes as 'having a good claim to be the most aesthetically satisfying in the West of Scotland'.*

Dorothy's descriptions of the scenery of Argyllshire are vivid and effective – the poetic imagination in the Wordsworth line was not confined to William.

Our road – the same along which the carriages had come – was directly under the mountains on our right hand, and the lake was close to us on our left, the waves breaking among stones overgrown with yellow sea-weed; fishermen's boats, and other larger vessels than are seen on fresh-water lakes were lying at anchor near the opposite shore; seabirds flying overhead; the noise of torrents mingled with the beating of the waves, and misty mountains enclosed the vale; – a melancholy but not a dreary scene. Often have I, in looking over a map of Scotland, followed the intricate windings of one of these sea-lochs, till, pleasing myself with my own imaginations, I have felt a longing, almost painful, to travel among them by land or by water.

This was the first sea-loch we had seen. We came prepared for a new and great delight, and the first impression which William and I received, as we drove rapidly through the rain down the lawn of Arrochar, the objects dancing before us, was even more delightful than we had expected. But, as I have said, when we looked through the window, as the mists disappeared and the objects were seen more distinctly, there was less of sheltered valley-comfort than we had fancied to ourselves, and the mountains were not so grand; and now that we were near to the shore of the lake, and could see that it was not of fresh water, the wreck, the broken sea-shells, and scattered sea-weed gave somewhat of a dull and uncleanly look to the whole lake, and yet the water was clear, and might have appeared as beautiful as that of Loch Lomond, if with the same pure pebbly shore. Perhaps, had we been in a more cheerful mood of mind we might have seen everything with a different eye. The stillness of the mountains, the motion of the waves, the streaming torrents, the sea-birds, the fishing-boats were all melancholy; yet still, occupied as my mind was with other things, I thought of the long windings through which the waters of the sea had come to this inland retreat, visiting the inner solitudes of the mountains, and I could have wished to have mused out a summer's day on the shores of the lake. From the foot of these mountains whither might not a little barque carry one away? Though so far inland, it is but a slip of the great ocean: seamen, fishermen, and shepherds here find a natural home. We did not travel far down the lake, but, turning to the right through an opening of the mountains, entered a glen called Glen Croe.

Our thoughts were full of Coleridge, and when we were enclosed in the narrow dale, with a length of winding road before us, a road that seemed to have insinuated itself into the very heart of the mountains – the brook, the road, bare hills, floating mists, scattered stones, rocks, and herds of black cattle being all that we could see – I shivered at the thought of his being sickly and alone, travelling from place to place.

The Cobbler, on our right, was pre-eminent above the other hills; the singular rocks on its summit, seen so near, were like ruins – castles or watch-towers. After we had passed one reach of the glen, another opened out, long, narrow, deep, and houseless, with herds of cattle and large stones; but the third reach was softer and more beautiful, as if the mountains had there made a warmer shelter, and there were a more gentle climate. The rocks by the river-side had dwindled away, the mountains were smooth and green, and towards the end, where the glen sloped upwards, it was a cradle-like hollow, and at that point where the slope became a hill, at the very bottom of the curve of the cradle, stood one cottage, with a few fields and beds of potatoes. There was also another house near the roadside, which appeared to be a herdsman's hut. The dwelling in the middle of the vale was a very pleasing object. I said within myself, How quietly might a family live in this pensive solitude, cultivating and loving their own fields! But the herdsman's hut, being the only one in the vale, had a melancholy face; not being attached to any particular plot of land, one could not help considering it as just kept alive and above ground by some dreary connexion with the long barren tract we had travelled through.

The afternoon had been exceedingly pleasant after we had left the vale of Arrochar; the sky was often threatening, but the rain blew off, and the evening was uncommonly fine. The sun had set a short time before we had dismounted from the car to walk up the steep hill at the end of the glen. Clouds were moving all over the sky – some of a brilliant yellow hue, which shed a light like bright moonlight upon the mountains. We could not have seen the head of the valley under more favourable circumstances.

The passing away of a storm is always a time of life and cheerfulness, especially in a mountainous country; but that afternoon and evening the sky was in an extraordinary degree vivid and beautiful. We often stopped in ascending the hill to look down the long reach of the glen. The road, following the course of the river as far as we could see, the farm and cottage hills, smooth towards the base and rocky higher up, were the sole objects before us. This part of Glen Croe reminded us of some of the dales of the north of England – Grisdale above Ulswater, for instance; but the length of it, and the broad highway, which is always to be seen at a great distance, a sort of centre of the vale, a point of reference, gives to the whole of the glen, and each division of it, a very different character.

At the top of the hill we came to a seat with the well-known inscription, 'Rest and be thankful'. On the same stone it was recorded that the road had been made by Col. Wade's regiment. The seat is placed so as to command a full view of the valley, and the long, long road, which, with the fact recorded, and the exhortation, makes it an affecting resting-place. We called to mind with pleasure a seat under the braes of Loch Lomond on which I had rested, where the traveller is informed by an inscription upon a stone that the road was made by Col. Lascelles' regiment. There, the spot had not been chosen merely as a resting-place, for there was no steep ascent in the highway, but it might be for the sake of a spring of water and a beautiful rock, or, more probably, because at that point the labour had been more than usually toilsome in hewing through the rock. Soon after we had climbed the hill we began to descend into another glen, called Glen Kinglas. We now saw the western sky, which had hitherto been hidden from us by the hill – a glorious mass of clouds uprising from a sea of distant mountains, stretched out in length before us, towards the west – and close by us was a small lake or tarn. From the reflection of the crimson clouds the water appeared of a deep red, like melted rubies, yet with a mixture of a grey or blackish hue: the gorgeous light of the sky, with the singular colour of the lake, made the scene exceedingly romantic; yet it was more melancholy than cheerful. With all the power of light from the clouds, there was an overcasting of the gloom of evening, a twilight upon the hills.

We descended rapidly into the glen, which resembles the lower part of Glen Croe, though it seemed to be inferior in beauty; but before we had passed through one reach it was quite dark, and I only know that the steeps were high, and that we had the company of a foaming stream; and many a vagrant torrent crossed us, dashing down the hills. The road was bad, and, uncertain how we should fare, we were eager and somewhat uneasy to get forward; but when we were out of the close glen, and near to Cairndow, as a traveller had told us, the moon showed her clear face in the sky, revealing a spacious vale, with a broad loch and sloping corn fields; the hills not very high. This cheerful sight put us into spirits, and we thought it was at least no dismal place to sit up all night in, if they had no beds, and they could not refuse us a shelter. We were, however, well received, and sate down in a neat parlour with a good fire.

Tuesday, August 30th. – Breakfasted before our departure, and ate a herring, fresh from the water, at our landlord's earnest recommendation – much superior to the herrings we get in the north of England. Though we rose at seven, could not set off before nine o'clock; the servants were in bed; the kettle did not boil – indeed, we were completely out of patience; but it had always been so, and we resolved to go off in future without breakfast. Cairndow is a single house by the side of the loch, I believe resorted to by gentlemen in the fishing season: it is a pleasant place for such a purpose; but the vale did not look so beautiful as by moonlight – it had a sort of sea-coldness without mountain grandeur. There is a ferry for foot passengers from Cairndow to the other side of the water, and the road along which all carriages go is carried round the head of the lake, perhaps a distance of three miles.

After we had passed the landing-place of the ferry opposite to Cairndow we saw the lake spread out to a great width, more like an arm of the sea or a great river than one of our lakes; it reminded us of the Severn at the Chepstow pasage; but the shores were less rich and the hills higher. The sun shone, which made the morning cheerful, though there was a cold wind. Our road never carried us far from the lake, and with the beating of the waves, the sparkling sunshiny water, boats, the opposite hills, and, on the side on which we travelled, the chance cottages, the coppice woods, and common business of the fields, the ride could not but be amusing. But what most excited our attention was, at one particular place, a cluster of fishing-boats at anchor in a still corner of the lake, a small bay or harbour by the wayside. They were overshadowed by fishermen's nets hung out to dry, which formed a dark awning that covered them like a tent, overhanging the water on each side, and falling in the most exquisitely graceful folds. There was a monastic pensiveness, a funereal gloom in the appearance of this little company of vessels, which was the more interesting from the general liveliness and glancing motions of the water, they being perfectly still and silent in their sheltered nook.

When we had travelled about seven miles from Cairndow, winding round the bottom of a hill, we came in view of a great basin or elbow of the lake. Completely out of sight of the long track of water we had coasted, we seemed now to be on the edge of a very large, almost circular, lake, the town of Inverary before us, a line of white buildings on a low promontory right opposite, and close to the water's edge; the whole landscape a showy scene, and bursting upon us at once. A traveller who was riding by our side called out, 'Can that be the Castle?' Recollecting the prints which we had seen, we knew it could not; but the mistake is a natural one at that distance: it is so little like an ordinary town, from the mixture of regularity and irregularity in the buildings. With the expanse of water and pleasant mountains, the scattered boats and sloops, and those gathered together, it had a truly festive appearance. A few steps more brought us in view of the Castle, a stately turreted mansion, but with a modern air, standing on a lawn, retired from the water, and screened behind by woods covering the sides of high hills to the top, and still beyond, by bare mountains. Our road wound round the semicircular shore, crossing two bridges of lordly archictecture. The town looked pretty when we drew near to it in connexion with its situation, different from any place I had ever seen, yet exceedingly like what I imaged to myself from representations in raree-shows, or pictures of foreign places – Venice, for example – painted on the scene of a play-house, which one is apt to fancy are as cleanly and gay as they look through the magnifying-glass of the raree-show or in the candle-light dazzle of a theatre. At the door of the inn, though certainly the buildings had not that delightful outside which they appeared to have at a distance, yet they looked very pleasant. The range bordering on the water consisted of little else than the inn, being a large house, with very large stables, the county gaol, the opening into the main street into the town, and an arched gateway, the entrance into the Duke of Argyle's private domain.

We were decently well received at the inn, but it was over-rich in waiters and large rooms to be exactly to our taste, though quite in harmony with the neighbourhood. Before dinner we went into the Duke's pleasure-grounds, which are extensive, and of course command a variety of lively and interesting views. Walked through avenues of tall beech-trees, and observed some that we thought even the tallest we had ever seen; but they were all scantily covered with leaves, and the leaves exceedingly small – indeed, some of them, in the most exposed situations, were almost bare, as if it had been winter. Travellers who wish to view the inside of the Castle send in their names, and the Duke appoints the time of their going; but we did not think that what we should see would repay us for the trouble, there being no pictures, and the house, which I believe has not been built above half a century, is fitted up in the modern style. If there had been any reliques of the ancient costume of the castle of a Highland chieftain, we should have been sorry to have passed it.

Sate after dinner by the fireside till near sunset, for it was very cold, though the sun shone all day. At the beginning of this our second walk we passed through the town, which is but a doleful example of Scotch filth. The houses are plastered or rough-cast, and washed yellow – well built, well sized, and sash-windowed, bespeaking a connexion with the Duke, such a dependence as may be expected in a small town so near to his mansion; and indeed he seems to have done his utmost to make them comfortable, according to our English notions of comfort: they are fit for the houses of people living decently upon a decent trade; but the windows and door-steads were as dirty as in a dirty by-street of a large town, making a most unpleasant contrast with the comely face of the buildings towards the water, and the ducal grandeur and natural festivity of the scene. Smoke and blackness are the wild growth of a Highland hut: the mud floors cannot be washed, the door-steads are trampled by cattle, and if the inhabitants be not very cleanly it gives one little pain; but dirty people living in two-storied stone houses, with dirty sash windows, are a melancholy spectacle anywhere, giving the notion either of vice or the extreme of wretchedness.

Returning through the town, we went towards the Castle, and entered the Duke's grounds by a porter's lodge, following the carriage-road through the park, which is prettily scattered over with trees, and slopes gently towards the lake. A great number of lime-trees were growing singly, not beautiful in their shape, but I mention them for the resemblance to one of the same kind we had seen in the morning, which formed a shade as impenetrable as the roof of any house. The branches did not spread far, nor any one branch much further than another; on the outside it was like a green bush shorn with shears, but when we sate upon a bench under it, looking upwards, in the middle of the tree we could not perceive any green at all; it was like a hundred thousand magpies' nests clustered and matted together, the twigs and boughs being so intertwined that neither the light of the mid-day sun nor showers of hail or rain could pierce through them. The lime-trees on the lawn resembled this tree both in shape and in the manner of intertwisting their twigs, but they were much smaller, and not an impenetrable shade.

The views from the Castle are delightful. Opposite is the lake, girt with mountains, or rather smooth high hills; to the left appears a very steep rocky hill, called Duniquoich Hill, on the top of which is a building like a watch-tower; it rises boldly and almost perpendicular from the plain, at a little distance from the river Arey, that runs through the grounds. To the right is the town, overtopped by a sort of spire or pinnacle of the church, a thing unusual in Scotland, except in the large towns, and which would often give an elegant appearance to the villages, which, from the uniformity of the huts, and the frequent want of tall trees, they seldom exhibit.

In looking at an extensive prospect, or travelling through a large vale, the Trough of the Clyde for instance, I could not help thinking that in England there would have been somewhere a tower or spire to warn us of a village lurking under the covert of a wood or bank, or to point out some particular spot on the distant hills which we might look at with kindly feelings. I well remember how we used to love the little nest of trees out of which Ganton spire rose on the distant Wolds opposite to the windows at Gallow Hill. The spire of Inverary is not of so beautiful a shape as those of the English churches, and, not being one of a class of buildings which is understood at once, seen near or at a distance, is a less interesing object; but it suits well with the outlandish trimness of the buildings bordering on the water; indeed, there is no one thing of the many gathered together in the extensive circuit of the basin or vale of Inverary, that is not in harmony with the effect of the whole place. The Castle is built of a beautiful hewn stone, in colour resembling our blue slates. The author-tourists have quarrelled with the architecture of it, but we did not find much that we were disposed to blame. A castle in a deep glen, overlooking a roaring stream, and defended by precipitous rocks, is, no doubt, an object far more interesting; but, dropping all ideas of danger or insecurity, the natural retinue in our minds of an ancient Highland chieftain – take a Duke of Argyle at the end of the eighteenth century, let him have his house in Grosvenor Square, his London liveries, and daughters glittering at St James's, and I think you will be satisfied with his present mansion in the Highlands, which seems to suit with the present times and its situation, and that is indeed a noble one for a modern Duke of the mountainous district of Argyleshire, with its bare valleys, its rocky coasts, and sea lochs.

There is in the natural endowments of Inverary something akin to every feature of the general character of the county; yet even the very mountains and the lake itself have a kind of princely festivity in their appearance. I do not know how to communicate the feeling, but it seemed as if it were no insult to the hills to look on them as the shield and enclosure of the ducal domain, to which the water might delight in bearing its tribute. The hills near the lake are smooth, so smooth that they might have been shaven or swept; the shores, too, had somewhat of the same effect, being bare, and having no roughness, no woody points; yet the whole circuit being very large, and the hills so extensive, the scene was not the less cheerful and festive, rejoicing in the light of heaven. Behind the Castle the hills are planted to a great height, and the pleasure-grounds extend far up the valley of Arey. We continued our walk a short way along the river, and were sorry to see it stripped of its natural ornaments, after the fashion of Mr Brown,* and left to tell its tale – for it would not be silent like the river at Blenheim – to naked fields and the planted trees on the hills. We were disgusted with the stables, outhouses, or farm-houses in different parts of the grounds behind the Castle: they were broad, out-spreading, fantastic, and unintelligible buildings.

Sate in the park till the moonlight was perceived more than the light of day. We then walked near the town by the water-side. I observed that the

* 'Capability' Brown.

children who were playing did not speak Erse, but a much worse English than is spoken by those Highlanders whose common language is the Erse. I went into the town to purchase tea and sugar to carry with us on our journey. We were tired when we returned to the inn, and went to bed directly after tea. My room was at the very top of the house – one flight of steps after another! – but when I drew back the curtains of my window I was repaid for the trouble of panting up-stairs by one of the most splendid moonlight prospects that can be conceived: the whole circuit of the hills, the Castle, the two bridges, the tower on Duniquoich Hill, and the lake with many boats – fit scene for summer midnight festivities! I should have liked to have seen a bevy of Scottish ladies sailing, with music, in a gay barge. William, to whom I have read this, tells me that I have used the very words of Browne of Ottery, Coleridge's fellow-townsman: –

> As I have seen when on the breast of Thames
> A heavenly bevy of sweet English dames,
> In some calm evening of delightful May,
> With music give a farewell to the day,
> Or as they would (with an admired tone)
> Greet night's ascension to her ebon throne.
>
> Browne's *Britannia's Pastorals*

Wednesday, August 31st. – We had a long day's journey before us, without a regular baiting-place on the road, so we breakfasted at Inverary, and did not set off till nine o'clock, having, as usual, to complain of the laziness of the servants. Our road was up the valley behind the Castle, the same we had gone along the evening before. Further up, though the plantations on the hills are noble, the valley was cold and naked, wanting hedgerows and comfortable houses. We travelled several miles under the plantations, the vale all along seeming to belong almost exclusively to the Castle. It might have been better distinguished and adorned, as we thought, by neater farm-houses and cottages than are common in Scotland, and snugger fields with warm hedgerows, at the same time testifying as boldly its adherence to the chief.

At that point of the valley where the pleasure-grounds appear to end, we left our horse at a cottage door, and turned a few steps out of the road to see a waterfall, which roared so loud that we could not have gone by without looking about for it, even if we had not known that there was one near Inverary. The waterfall is not remarkable for anything but the good taste with which it has been left to itself, though there is a pleasure-road from the Castle to it. As we went further up the valley the roads died away, and it became an ordinary Scotch glen, the poor pasturage of the hills creeping down into the valley, where it was little better for the shelter, I mean little greener than on the hill-sides; but a man must be of a churlish nature if, with a mind free to look about, he should not find such a glen a pleasing place to travel through, though seeing little but the busy brook, with here and there a bush or tree, and cattle pasturing near the thinly-scattered dwellings. But we came to one spot which I cannot forget, a single green field at the junction of another brook with the Arey, a peninsula surrounded with a close row of trees, which overhung the streams, and under their branches we could just see a neat white house that stood in the middle of the field enclosed by the trees. Before us was nothing but bare hills, and the road through the bare glen. A person who has not travelled in Scotland can scarcely imagine the pleasure we have had from a stone house, though fresh from the workmen's hands, square and sharp; there is generally such an appearance of equality in poverty through the long glens of Scotland, giving the notion of savage ignorance – no house better than another, and barns and houses all alike. This house had, however, other recommendations of its own; even in the fertile parts of Somersetshire it would have been a delicious spot; here, ''Mid mountain wild set like a little nest', it was a resting-place for the fancy, and to this day I often think of it, the cottage and its green covert, as an image of romance, a place of which I have the same sort of knowledge as of some of the retirements, the little valleys, described so livelily by Spenser in his Fairy Queen.

We travelled on, the glen now becoming entirely bare. Passed a miserable hut on a naked hill-side, not far from the road, where we were told by a man who came out of it that we might refresh ourselves with a dram of whisky. Went over the hill, and saw nothing remarkable till we came in view of Loch Awe, a large lake far below us, among high mountains – one very large mountain right opposite, which we afterwards found was called Cruachan. The day was pleasant – sunny gleams and a fresh breeze; the lake – we looked across it – as bright as silver, which made the islands, three or four in number, appear very green. We descended gladly, invited by the prospect before us, travelling downwards, along the side of the hill, above a deep glen, woody towards the lower part near the brook; the hills on all sides were high and bare, and not very stony: it made us think of the descent from Newlands into Buttermere, though on a wider scale, and much inferior in simple majesty.

Suaicheantas na h-Alba
(The Thistle of Scotland)
EVAN MACCOLL (1808–1898)
TRANSLATION BY MALCOLM MACFARLANE

Eòghan MacColla, Bard Loch Fìne, Evan MacColl, the Bard of Loch Fyne, as he is known in Argyll, was born in the beautiful planned fishing village of Kenmore a few miles south of Inveraray. His parents ensured that he was educated to read and write Gaelic at a time when steps were being taken at his own school to extirpate the language. He was attracted to writing poetry from his youth and when his family decided to emigrate to Canada in 1831 he chose to remain in Scotland until he had published his first book of poems. This he did in 1836 with the volume of Gaelic poems Clàrsach nam Beann *(The Harp of the Hills) and this was soon followed by his volume of English poems* The Mountain Minstrel. *Although like many writers he was not at first appreciated in his own locality, he did enjoy the friendship of such major figures as Hugh Miller of Cromarty and the aristocrat, folklorist and polymath John Francis Campbell (Iain Og Ile) through whose good offices he obtained the post of clerk at the Customs House in Liverpool. His health, however, deteriorated and in 1850 he went to visit his family in Canada and decided to settle there. He worked again with the Customs in Kingston, Ontario, and later in 1890 moved to Toronto where he died at the age of 89.*

Evan MacColl wrote a long series of love poems and, although some of these are rather conventional and stylised, several of them, like Mo Chaileag Shuaineartach (My Sunart Girl) *and* Ròsan an Leth-Bhaile (Rose of the Half-Town) *are still very popular today. He also describes the Argyllshire landscape in poems about Glen Aray and Glendaruel and one of his finest works* Moladh Abhainn Ruaile (Praise of the River Ruel) *displays fine observation without sentimentality and interesting and skilfully controlled use of metre. There is also a sharp political dimension to MacColl's work. He was outraged by the Clearances as his* Tuireadh nan Eilthireach (Lament for the Exiles) *bears witness. He also contributed to that surge of nationalism which was to lead to the establishment of the National Association for the Vindication of Scottish Rights in 1853. The song* Suaicheantas na h-Alba *(The Thistle of Scotland) is the most famous of his works in this genre. This translation by Malcolm MacFarlane*

(*Calum MacPhàrlain*), *of Loch Aweside and Paisley, was revived in the 1950s by singers like Kenneth MacKellar and became for a while a minor Scottish anthem.*

Séist
'Se Foghnan na h-Alba lus ainmeil nam buadh;
Lus grinn nan dos calgach thug dearbh air bhi cruaidh;
Sean shuaicheantas mòrail tìr bhòidhich mo luaidh;
'S tric dh'fhadaich a dheagh cliù tein' eibhinn 'nam ghruaidh.

Lus deas nam meur cròcach nach leònar le stoirm;
Ged's ionann teachd geàrr air 's laoch dàna fo airm,
'S leis clòimh tha cho maoth-gheal ri faoileig na tràigh,
'S bàrr-ghucan cho ciùin-ghorm ri suilean mo ghràidh.

Mo dhùthaich, chan iognadh mòr chliù air thighinn uait,
'Sa liuthad buaidh-làraich 's deagh gnàth tha ris fuaight';
An cian is le Albainn luchd seanachais no bàrd,
Bidh meas air an dealbh anns gach gorm-bhonaid àird.

Sluagh borb, le droch rùn da, 's tric bhrùchd air a nuas;
'S tric bhrùchd, ach, gun taing dhoibh, a cheann chum e suas,
'N uair shaoil iad bhi buadhach, 's ann fhuair iad fath bròin.
Feuch! a'cinn thar an uaighean an cluaran gun leòn.

Mo bheannachd gu bràth air! Có'n Gaidheal no'n Gall
Nach seasadh gu bàs e, g' theàrnadh o chall!
Có ìosal no uasal, bheir clùas do mo dhàn,
Nach òladh leam 'buaidh leis' o chuachana làn!

THE THISTLE OF SCOTLAND

Chorus
O, the Thistle of Scotland was famous of auld,
Wi' its toorie sae snod and its bristles sae bauld;
'Tis the badge o' my country, it's aye dear tae me;
And the thoucht o' them baith brings the licht tae my e'e.

Its strength and its beauty the storm never harms;
It stan's on its guard like a warrior in arms;
Yet its down is as saft as the gull's on the sea,
And its tassle as bricht as my Jeannie's blue e'e.

O my country, what wonder yer fame's gane afar;
For yer sons hae been great baith in peace and in war:
While the sang and the tale live they'll win respect,
The lads neath the bonnets wi' thistles bedeckt.

Langsyne the invaders cam owre to our shore,
And fiercely our thistle they scutched and they tore;
When they maist thocht it deid, 'twas then it up bore,
And it bloomed on their graves quite as strong as before.

My blessings be yours! Is there Scotsman ava
Wad stan' by and see ony harm on ye fa'?
Is there gentle or semple wha lives in our land
Wad refuse to drink health to the thistle so grand?

Dark Dunoon

THOMAS LYLE (1792–1859)

Thomas Lyle was born in Paisley, trained as a doctor at Glasgow University, practising in Airth, Stirlingshire and later in Glasgow. He is now perhaps best remembered for the popular lyric Let us haste to Kelvin Grove, bonnie lassie, O.

The 'distant beacon's revolving light' referred to in verse 2 is presumably the Cloch Lighthouse on the opposite, Renfrewshire, coast which was erected in 1797.

See the glow-worm lits her fairy lamp,
From a beam of the rising moon;
On the heathy shore at evening fall,
Twixt Holy-Loch and dark Dunoon;
Her fairy lamp's pale silvery glare,
From the dew-clad, moorland flower,
Invite my wandering footsteps there,
At the lonely twilight hour.

When the distant beacon's revolving light
Bids my lone steps seek the shore,
There the rush of the flow-tide's rippling wave
Meets the dash of the fisher's oar;
And the dim-seen steamboat's hollow sound,
As she seaward tracks her way.
All else are asleep in the still calm night,
And robed in the misty gray.

When the glow-worm lits her elfin lamp,
And the night breeze sweeps the hill,
It's sweet on thy rock-bound shores, Dunoon,
To wander at fancy's will.
Eliza, with thee in this solitude,
Life's cares would pass away,
Like the fleecy clouds over gray Kilmun,
At the wake of early day.

O Love that wilt not let me go

GEORGE MATHESON (1842–1906)

Behind this, one of the finest and best-loved Scottish hymns of the nineteenth century, lies a story of remarkable triumph over adversity. Its author, George Matheson, went blind at the age of eighteen but completed his studies at Glasgow University and went on to a career in the ministry of the Church of Scotland, being appointed to Innellan in 1868 where he served until he was translated to Edinburgh, St Bernard's in 1886. Contemporary accounts record that visitors to Innellan often did not realise that Matheson was blind as he conducted the Service, expounded the Scriptures from memory and preached.

This hymn of personal faith and resignation was composed in the Manse of Innellan on 6th June 1882 in a few minutes under the stress of what Matheson later described as 'the most severe mental suffering'. One later minor alteration suggested by the editors of the Church of Scotland Hymnary – the substitution of 'trace' for 'climb' in verse three – was all the revision it received or required.

O Love that wilt not let me go,
I rest my weary soul in thee:
I give thee back the life I owe,
That in thine ocean depths its flow
   May richer, fuller be.

O Light that followest all my way,
I yield my flickering torch to thee:
My heart restores its borrowed ray,
That in thy sunshine's blaze its day
   May brighter, fairer be.

O Joy that seekest me through pain,
I cannot close my heart to thee:
I trace the rainbow through the rain,
And feel the promise is not vain,
   That morn shall tearless be.

O Cross that liftest up my head,
I dare not ask to fly from thee:
I lay in dust life's glory dead,
And from the ground there blossoms red
  Life that shall endless be.

The Hills of Ruel

'FIONA MACLEOD' (1855–1905)

William Sharp, Paisley-born novelist and poet, created an alternative, female, Celtic persona in the shape of 'Fiona Macleod'. Sharp elaborately maintained the fiction of her existence and publicly denied any connection with 'Macleod' who went on to publish novels and poetry on Highland themes. Her knowledge of Gaelic and Highland culture was, however, questioned at the time, Neil Munro writing that it was obvious that:

> *. . . the topographical knowledge displayed in the stories was merely as much as could be got from a few trips on the 'Claymore' or 'Clansman'; and that a Gaelic dictionary and a 'Guide to Gaelic Conversation' were responsible for all the Gaelic phrases with which the books were recklessly interlarded to maintain the illusion that here was the voice of the veritable Gael.*

Nonetheless the work of 'Fiona Macleod' was a significant part of the 'Celtic Revival' at the end of the nineteenth century.

The two parallel personalities of Sharp and 'Macleod' went much deeper, and are more psychologically interesting, than simply being an author using a pseudonym for part of his output. In a symposium on Neil Munro's John Splendid *published in the London magazine* The Bookman *in 1898 'Fiona Macleod' and William Sharp contributed separate essays (and presumably collected separate fees).*

This poem, set in Glendaruel in Cowal, is typical of the author's preoccupation with fantasy and fairies, and although perhaps somewhat 'fey' for modern tastes is redeemed by a strong rhythmic pulse.

'Over the hills and far away' –
That is the tune I heard one day
When heather-drowsy I lay and listened
And watched where the stealthy sea-tide glistened.
Beside me there on the Hills of Ruel
An old man stooped and gathered fuel –
And I asked him this: if his son were dead,
As the folk in Glendaruel all said,

How could he still believe that never
Duncan had crossed the shadowy river?

Forth from his breast the old man drew
A lute that once on a rowan-tree grew:
And, speaking no words, began to play
'Over the hills and far away.'

'But how do you know,' I said, thereafter,
'That Duncan has heard the fairy laughter?
How do you know he has followed the cruel
Honey-sweet folk of the Hills of Ruel?'
'How do I know?' the old man said,
'Sure I know well my boy's not dead:
For late on the morrow they hid him, there
Where the black earth moistens his yellow hair,
I saw him alow on the moor close by,
I watched him low on the hillside lie,
An' I heard him laughin' wild up there,
An' talk, talk, talkin' beneath his hair –
For down o'er his face his long hair lay
But I saw it was cold and ashy grey,
Ay, laughin' and talkin' wild he was,
An' that to a Shadow out on the grass,
A Shadow that made my blood go chill,
For never its like have I seen on the hill,
An' the moon came up, and the stars grew white,
An' the hills grew black in the bloom o' the night,
An' I watched till the death star sank in the moon
And the moonmaid fled with her flittermice shoon,
Then the Shadow that lay on the moorside there
Rose up and shook its wildmoss hair,
And Duncan he laughed no more, but grey
As the rainy dust of a rainy day,
Went over the hills and far away.'

'Over the hills and far away' –
That is the tune I heard one day.
O that I too might hear the cruel
Honey-sweet folk of the Hills of Ruel.

The Provost and the Queen

from Lunderston Tales

ROBIN JENKINS (1912–)

Although born in Cambuslang, Lanarkshire, Robin Jenkins has long been settled in Cowal and a number of his most effective and powerful novels such as The Cone Gatherers *are set in the Highlands. Having spent much of his working life abroad many of his novels are set in Asia. Jenkins's range also includes works set in a Central Scotland milieu, for example his fine study of the impact of football on an urban community –* The Thistle and the Grail. *His* Lunderston Tales *(published in 1996) seem ostensibly to be set in a fictitious small town of that name in Ayrshire but many readers might well suspect that the true setting and the spirit of this richly comic episode owes as much to Jenkins's home in Dunoon as to any location to be found on the southern shores of the Firth of Clyde.*

For hundreds of years before the recent lamentable restructuring of local government in the interests of the false gods efficiency and economy Lunderston, like all the burghs in Scotland, had its own town council and its own provost. In those homelier days you saw a councillor in the street every day and could have it out with him man-to-man concerning any grievance you might have had or any municipal improvement you were keen to advocate. It was a family affair. In these so-called efficient and economical times of district councils that meet in distant places decisions regarding your own town are taken by a gaggle of councillors from other towns, men and women you've never set eyes on. It was strangers like these who not long ago voted to close Lunderston's public lavatories during the off-season, in spite of the protests of the two Lunderston councillors who pointed out that their town being by the sea suffered from chilly winds in winter and had a large proportion of elderly citizens with weak bladders.

There was the Provost's chain of office, worn round his neck at all council functions. In Lunderston's case it had been more brass than gold but kept well polished it had a ducal look. More venerable than the chain and more historical was the Lunderston Missal, as it was called, the Toon's Ain Buik, about the size of a family Bible, in which were inscribed the signatures of famous people who had visited the town; among them were Mary, Queen of Scots, and the present monarch Queen Elizabeth. Its batters were of red leather faded and scuffed with age. Engraved on the front was the town's emblem, a seagull with in its beak a fish that had in its mouth a smaller fish; and the town's motto, found in documents going back to the time of Robert the Bruce, 'Naething Wasted'. It was kept in a glass case in the burgh chambers, on a piece of red velvet. It was said that there had also been a quill pen, the one used by Mary Stuart, but this had got lost or stolen or perhaps had just crumbled with age.

The last provost but two before the dissolution of the office was John Golspie, the most notorious in the town's history, guilty of what in many townspeople's opinion was worse than rape or murder. He arrived in the town one cold December, a hulking glowering young man, wearing a thick black coat with a fur collar, and carrying a bag stuffed with money. So the story went anyway. How he got it and where he had come from were never established. Even then when he was not yet thirty he was not a man to pester with inconvenient questions. Big, over six feet, and heavy, over fourteen stones, he had a low brow and coarse red face, hands like a navvy's, and a voice that could be heard, it was claimed, from within the council chambers by folk strolling on the promenade half a mile away.

At first Big Jock, as he soon came to be called, lived in a two-roomed cottage in the slum district known as the Vennel. There, so slyly that it was some time before people were aware of what he was up to, he carried on his business. He bought up dilapidated tenements cheaply, refurbished them at little cost, and then rented them at high rents. He also snapped up plots of vacant land all over the town, at that time, just after the War, going for low prices to anyone with ready cash. As a sideline he lent money to carefully chosen clients, at scandalous rates of interest.

Even in those early days he had his heart set on being Provost, not because of the honour or because he was eager to serve the community, but because he wanted to be top man. When he first put himself up as a candidate for the council he had no difficulty in finding the required number of sponsors from among those in his financial clutches, but at the election, which of course was by secret ballot, the people of the ward he had chosen showed what they thought of him by giving him 51 votes out of a total of 875. One of the questions put to him by hecklers was: 'During the War, Mr Golspie, were you ever in uniform?' Not a bit fashed, he replied that unfortunately he had been rejected on medical grounds, but he had served his country in other capacities; he refused to say what these were. Then, with a brazenness not commonly found among petitioners for votes, he challenged his baiters to stand up and tell what heroic exploits *they* had won their VCs for. Thus it was learned that there was a new kind of politician active in the town, one who did not hesitate to show his contempt for those whose votes he was seeking. At that time all candidates stood as Independents, though they were really Tories, some more reactionary than others. Big Jock described himself as a free-thinking, honest-speaking individualist. 'I'm a bigger man physically, and in any other way you like to mention, than any other man in this town. I'm going to be the most famous Provost you ever had. What I'll do I'll do for myself, let me be frank about that, but the town will benefit too. Just you wait.'

Well, they waited, for nearly twenty years, and sure enough he did become Provost. He had got himself elected councillor for the Ardgartan Ward which included within its boundaries the fine big villas along the East Bay. In the pubs where the poorer sort drank no one was surprised that Big Jock had got the well-to-do to elect him. Though they deplored his vulgarity they had decided that he was their man. They knew that he was a crook, but their kind of crook, who could be depended on to protect their privileges.

Though it would have been hard to find anyone who had a good word for him Big Jock became the most powerful man in town. He was re-elected councillor with bigger and bigger majorities, and in due course the two lamp-posts, with the town's coat-of-arms painted on the glass, appeared in the street outside his house, by which it was made known to all the world that therein dwelled the Provost of Lunderston.

It was not of course the two-roomed cottage with the outside toilet, in the Vennel; that area had long since been demolished. It was one of the villas in the East Bay. They were large and built of the same grey stone as churches, solid, dignified, and commanding respect. Their owners had allowed themselves some individuality in the colour with which the woodwork was painted, but all had agreed, without ever discussing it, that a discreet colour like dark-blue or dark-green would be appropriate. The stone was left untouched. The result was a row of houses of quiet distinction. Not only were their owners proud of them; so was the whole town.

Big Jock had been Provost only three weeks when he had his villa painted a bright pink, front, back, gables, and chimneys. He bought two life-size china lions – God knew from where – to be placed on either side of his front door. These too he had painted pink, with their noses and the tips of their tails golden.

The town was aghast. Why had he done it? There were many conjectures.

It was to affront his neighbours. They voted for him but they didn't invite him to their homes, nor did they accept invitations to his.

It was to make it known to passengers on planes coming down to land at Prestwick a few miles away, and to passing yachtsmen on the Firth, that there lived Big Jock Golspie, Provost of Lunderston.

He had been given the paint free. Like all money-lenders he was tight-fisted.

So far as anybody knew he had never been to sunny lands like Italy and Spain where houses were brightly painted, but perhaps he had seen them in pictures.

He really thought he was brightening up the East Bay, which to a person of his crude taste might seem rather drab.

It was while they were joking among themselves, grimly, about his pink house, that the townsfolk realised as never before how solitary Big Jock was. He had no friends or confidants who could be consulted as to his motive, or who could have advised him against such a monstrosity of bad taste. He neither smoked nor drank, out of meanness many people thought, but it could have been principle of some kind, though he went to church only as Provost, wearing his chain, never as himself. He had never married; indeed, so far as was known, he had never had a woman friend. That he preferred celibacy was his business and only rude boozers in the pubs were ribald about it, but if he had had a wife or even a mistress, she would surely have prevented him from making so ghastly a mistake, unless of course she had the same vulgar taste as himself, which wasn't unlikely, for he wouldn't have chosen any other kind of woman.

But what emphasised his loneliness most of all was that there wasn't one person in the whole of Lunderston who felt close enough to him or liked him well enough to ask: For God's sake, Jock, why pink? He seemed to have no relatives. What were his hobbies, how did he pass his private hours, what possessions gave him most pleasure, what secret regrets did he have? No one knew.

* * *

Glowering at the top of the table, with his fists pounding it like hammers and his roars heard in the street outside, Big Jock had all his councillors cowed. They complained to their wives that he turned up at the meetings not just with the chain round his neck but dressed in striped breeks, black jacket, and stiff white collar, as if he was Prime Minister, while the rest of them looked so common, in lounge suits and pullovers. They had thought of wearing formal dress themselves in retaliation but the absurdity of it and the cost of it deterred them.

Though among the citizens in general he was far from popular he had nevertheless won the reputation of getting things done, in contrast to the fushionlessness of the rest of the council. If tinkers parked their van too near your hotel, to the annoyance of your guests, it was no use your protesting to the police, they just mumbled that they had been given orders not to harass the travelling people. What you did then, whether or not you lived in Big Jock's ward, was lift the telephone and ask his help. Within a couple of hours the police would arrive in force and the nuisances would be moved on. Similarly if a new washer was wanted on a tap in your council house and you had complained to the Clerk of Works several times without his bothering to do anything about it, you just let Big Jock know and there were two workmen, let alone one, at your door within an hour. He did it by the force of his physical presence, for as he got older he got more massive, and by the volume of his voice, but there had to be something else. He had no doubt himself what it was; he was a big man among little men. If you had said a pike among minnows he would have nodded.

But for his insulting behaviour towards the Queen his obituary, when it came to be written, would have had to be grudgingly laudatory, but even the few republicans in the town thought he disgraced himself then beyond recovery. Not, to be fair, that he ever admitted that he had done anything wrong, and he claimed to have witnesses who would have spoken in his defence, the Queen herself and Prince Philip.

During his term of office as Provost the building of the new conference hall was begun and completed. It had been proposed years before but he could certainly claim credit for bringing it about. Whether or not he had insisted on alterations to the architect's plans, as was alleged, the result was, alas, a dreary, unlikeable building inside and out. What ought to have been an embellishment to the town was an eyesore. Appalled and disappointed, the ratepayers' only consolation was that it had cost a great deal of money. No one could say that it had been ruined by cheapness.

Big Jock himself thought it magnificent, so much so that only one person in the land was fit to declare it open. He meant the Queen. For God's sake, Jock, muttered the councillors, in embarrassment, you can't expect Her Majesty to find the time to come to Lunderston to open a mere conference hall. They shuddered as they thought what Prince Philip, a forthright critic, would say about the building. Big Jock scowled but was not dissuaded. He went personally to discuss it with the Lord Lieutenant, who liked the idea. They were lucky. The Queen's advisers, looking at Lunderston on the map and finding it close to seditious and republican Glasgow, must have seen the propaganda value in her paying it a visit. The royal yacht could anchor off Lunderston on its way up round Pentland to Aberdeen, and the Queen could disembark for an hour or so to declare open the hall or whatever it was, with television cameras present, and hundreds of school children supplied with little Union Jacks. In such a douce and loyal town there would be no danger of loutish demonstrators. Therefore, in due course, an important-looking letter came from Buckingham Palace saying that Her Majesty had graciously consented. Big Jock, remover of tinkers' vans and mender of leaky taps, had brought off the supreme triumph of his life.

When he announced it to his councillors they were thunder-struck. Men who despised him babbled apologies. Their fear of Prince Philip's ridicule was forgotten. No one actually knelt down and kissed Big Jock's shoes but their submission was just as abject as if they had. They havered among themselves that they ought to do something to show not just their appreciation of his bringing upon the burgh the greatest honour in its history – the visit of Mary, Queen of Scots, was too far distant for comparison – but also their contrition at having so meanly under-estimated him. One even suggested having a statue of him erected in front of the town hall; after all, he'd pay for it himself.

When it was made public in the *Lunderston Gazette* that the Queen was going to open the new Conference Hall everybody was astonished and delighted. It did not need the editor to remind them that this wonderful honour to the town had been achieved by their Provost, Mr John Golspie. They all knew it. Big Jock might be a vulgar, arrogant, ignorant brute, but he could get things done. Old ladies stopped him in the street and congratulated him. Letters to the *Gazette* sternly reminded the townspeople that they had not in the past shown sufficient gratitude to Mr Golspie for all his endeavours on their behalf. This must be remedied forthwith. No doubt the Queen would award him an OBE, but he must also be made a freeman of the town. When his term of office as Provost expired he must, as a special privilege, be permitted to keep the two lamp-posts outside his house; the custom being to take one away, to distinguish between present and past provosts. There were some people, said one letter, who had condemned Mr Golspie's painting of his house pink. They should at once withdraw that criticism. Mr Golspie deserved that his house be a vivid landmark. Indeed, once he was no longer with us, ought not the burgh to buy the house and so ensure that it remained gloriously pink?

So high was his standing in the town that there were some people, that day in June, who gave Big Jock the credit for the blue skies and warm sunshine, especially as the day before had been overcast and rainy. In his pink mansion what magic had he evoked? When the *Britannia* came sailing round Cumbrae and anchored off Lunderston pier, sounding its siren in salutation, there was such a brightness in the air, such a purity and clarity, that everything seemed newly created for the occasion, from the pebbles on the beach to the hills of Arran in the distance. Few people could remember so splendid a day. There were only two words to describe it, royal and heavenly. Some there thought, secretly, with catches of their breaths, as they saw the Queen waving to the children, that she was not just greeting them, she was blessing them too. She was dressed in blue, the Madonna's colour, and had pearls round her neck.

As she stepped on to the pier, which was covered with red carpet, she was bowed to first by the Lord Lieutenant with his feathered hat and then by the Provost representing the town, with his gray lum hat in his hand and his chain of office glinting in the sun. His citizens saw with pride how, knowing his place, he stood respectfully back. Prince Philip, in naval uniform, chatted to him amiably, though it must have been difficult for them to hear each other, such a din was being made by the pipe band, the seagulls, and the cheering children.

The official party, with the Provost and the Lord Lieutenant accompanying the royal couple, was driven in Jimmy Paterson's funereal Rolls Royces, through streets crammed with spectators, to the conference hall three hundred yards away.

The ceremony of unveiling the plaque and declaring the hall open was to be followed by a brief tour of the building, during which the Queen was to sign the Lunderston Missal. All the councillors and town officials and their wives were in attendance. Afterwards they were to be ferried out to the royal yacht for afternoon tea. Promptly at four they would be ferried back, so that Her Majesty would be able to continue her voyage towards the Hebrides. Nervous, for they had never before been in such exalted company, the councillors kept looking to their Provost for example and courage.

Afterwards accounts differed as to how he had done it. The councillors and town officials were keyed up and there was a screen of equerries, ladies-in-waiting, and bodyguards between them and the royal visitors, but the account generally accepted was that at one point in the tour of the hall, with the Provost acting as her guide, he produced a large handsome album with red leather covers and invited the Queen to sign it. (It was jaloused that he must have had it planked in readiness, with the connivance of some workman.) In any case the Queen, though surprised, for she probably expected a little more ceremony, signed it with the gold fountain pen that the Provost handed her. She was even more surprised when, minutes later, in the room specially prepared, she was asked to sign again, this time in the authentic book. It appeared that she said something to the Provost, perhaps reminding him that she had already signed. He made some reply, whereupon, with a glance at Prince Philip and a smile to herself, she signed. Then, minutes later, up to time, they were all out of the building and on their way to the pier. The deed of shame had been done and there was its perpetrator, looking mightily pleased with himself.

According to Councillors Grant and Donaldson they were approached on the yacht by Prince Philip, who seemed half-indignant and half-amused. Could they tell him what the big fellow with the top hat and red face had been up to, with the two town Missals? Surely it was unusual to have two. Was it an insurance against one of them being devoured by mice or rotted with damp? Or had one of them belonged to the big chap himself? If so then he had a damned cheek. Did they agree or were they all in it? Miserably but earnestly they assured him that it was all the Provost's doing. No one had known that he was going to do it. An explanation would be demanded.

They had to admit afterwards that the Prince had not seemed all that offended and had given the impression that he and the Queen when they were alone would enjoy a laugh at the extraordinary impudence of the Provost of Lunderston.

No one in the town laughed. They were all shocked and shamed.

Behind the Provost's back the councillors sought the advice of the town clerk, who was a lawyer. Could the Provost be charged with degrading his office? There was no such offence. Could he be dismissed, with ignominy, before his term was expired? It wouldn't be easy, for he would fight them all the way up to the Court of Session. Well, couldn't a vote of censure be passed, after which surely he wouldn't have the effrontery to remain, not only in the Provost's chair but in the town itself? Such a vote was up to the council, said the town clerk, but he sounded as if he didn't think they had the necessary resolution. In any case if the Provost chose to ignore it, as he doubtless would, that would be the end of it. The councillors were incensed. They could name countries which had found it easier to get rid of kings or presidents.

The meeting took place at which the Provost was to be censured and asked to resign. The public gallery was full. People had queued for hours to get in. Others waited out in the street, in the rain. Every councillor was present, even one who had risen from his death bed; he died three days later.

One of the bailies put the charge and the other called upon the Provost to make some amends by apologising to the town and then leaving it for good. 'Russia's the place for you,' one councillor muttered. Other councillors stood up and spoke, supporting the motion. Big Jock sat in silence, sucking peppermints, with his big fists resting on the table. Now and then he rifted. It was noticed how white hair that made other men look venerable made him look villainous. They were disgusted with themselves for having elected as their Provost such a coarse brute. They ought to have known that he would disgrace them. It broke their hearts to see him wearing the chain.

When they had had their say they waited for him to respond. If he had broken down and wept and flung himself upon their mercy they would have been embarrassed and uncertain, for some of them had known him for over thirty years and like themselves he was an old man. If he had committed murder and was about to be hanged they might for auld lang syne's sake have pitied him in the condemned cell and shaken his hand; but what he had done was worse than murder, though they couldn't have said exactly what it was.

At last he spoke or rather growled, 'I don't know what all the fuss is about. What happened was between me and Her Majesty. She didn't object, so why should you? No man in this room or in this town honours her more than me, but, dammit, she's not God Almighty. That's all I'm going to say on the subject.'

And in spite of their clamour he kept his word.

Of course it wasn't enough. In fact he had added to the insult to the Queen by saying she wasn't God Almighty. They hadn't needed the big clown to tell them that. They had all been to school. They knew that her ancestors Jamie the Saxt and Charles had got into trouble by claiming divine right; the latter had had his head chopped off. All that had been fought over and settled long ago. In the Queen's presence people did humble themselves more than they did before the Moderator of the Church of Scotland or the Archbishop of Canterbury (though not more than Catholics did before the Pope) but that was because she represented the grandeur and majesty of the State, not because they took her for God. They knew all that, but they shouldn't be made to say it openly because a big ignoramus had been discourteous and disrespectful, if not quite blasphemous.

No one was sorry for him. Afterwards as he walked down the main street people stepped into the gutter so as not to rub shoulders with him. Many for whom he had done favours crossed the street to avoid him. One old lady, Mrs McDougall, who lived in an East Bay villa, stopped him once but it was to slap his face. Those who saw it said that he just glowered and strode on. At the next election he did not put himself forward as a candidate. One of the lamp-posts outside his house was removed with all haste. In retaliation, it was thought, he had his house repainted, a brighter pink than before.

When he died, aged seventy-five, the general opinion, privately whispered, was good riddance. In his obituary in the *Gazette* the episode of the fraudulently obtained autograph was mentioned. 'It was the most curious episode in a curious man's career. No one knew why he did it. He offered no explanation. For forty years he was one of the most familiar figures in the town and yet no one ever knew him.'

After the abolition of the town council the Lunderston Missal went missing. It happened at a time of acrimonious argument as to its rightful owners, whether the burgh, which really was no longer a burgh but simply a part of the district, or the District Council. If, muttered the townspeople, some loyal Lunderstonian had purloined it to save it from falling into the hands of outsiders, and if he was preserving it till the day that Lunderston would be a burgh again, running its own affairs, then good luck to him.

Ironically, among the relics of the town later gathered into a kind of museum in the old burgh hall, the most revered was Provost Golspie's album, containing the Queen's signature.

3
MULL AND NORTH ARGYLL
Introduction

This area of Argyll has some of the wildest and most beautiful scenery on the whole of the West Coast, with some modern holiday centres like Tobermory, as well as two heritage sites which can fairly be said to be among the most celebrated tourist destinations anywhere.

Fourteen centuries after it became a lamp of learning and cradle of Celtic Christianity for all of Scotland and beyond, Iona continues to radiate a kind of glamour (to use an old Scots word) which assures its position as a World Heritage Site. It is beautiful, too. Iona is a low-lying island, with one of the Hebrides' best examples of the fertile grassland known as the 'machair' which grows on the western, Atlantic side of those islands' beaches of shell sand. W.H. Murray describes the machair of a shore such as 'The Bay at the Back of the Ocean' on Iona:

> Protected from erosion by the marram grass belt, the machair is developed by a first colonisation of flowering plants like the clovers and trefoils, which fix nitrogen and create the conditions that allow seventy or eighty different plants to strike root. Until a man has seen good machair, like that of . . . Tiree, he may find it hard to realise that although the crofters call it 'gress' it grows not grass but flowers. Among the most common of the four-score plants are buttercups, red and white clover, daisy, blue speedwell, dandelion, eyebright, birdsfoot trefoil, hop trefoil, harebell, wild thyme, yellow and blue pansy, and silverweed.

Poets such as 'Fiona Macleod' are inspired by the space and light associated with this merging of seascape and landscape. The call of the corncrake can still be heard beside the road that winds past the island's township to the Abbey. The historic links which Iona has with Columban monasticism, with the Norse raiders who broke the chain of civilisation for a while, with Somerled and various dynasties and lordships including the Kings of Scots themselves, are often described and remarked upon in our and others' literature. The roots are deep –

even Shakespeare knew about Iona or Colmekill:

> Ross: Where is Duncan's body?
> Macduff: Carried to Colmekill,
> The sacred storehouse of his predecesors
> And guardian of their bones.
>
> *Macbeth* Act I scene III

The last quote is a reminder that the island's burial place of kings, contains tombs of Norse as well as Scots, Irish and French Kings, lords and assorted princelings. In our own day a famous politician has also been interred on Iona.

Staffa is the other little island which has attracted vast numbers of visitors – although not so many in recent years, since the MacBrayne's steamer ceased to call. In the nineteenth century, certainly, a call at Staffa was an obligatory part of the Scottish tour for such as Scott, Wordsworth, Keats, Turner, Tennyson and Jules Verne. That is, if the weather permitted a call on the rocky shores of the basalt island which drew many to gaze at its unique geological formation – it is entirely made from columnar or vertical jointing with hexagonal cross-section. It was given its name, 'Stave Island', by the Vikings as a reminder of their own houses which were built from logs set vertically. The other major 'draw' of Staffa was its association with the legendary Ossian and in particular the great sea-cave called after Ossian's 'King of Morven', Fingal. The craze for visiting Fingal's Cave obviously dates from the 1770s, just after a visiting group of scientists had first brought it to the attention of outside world, since that was when enthusiasm for Ossian – or at least the version of Ossian as presented by James Macpherson – was at its height. Another distinguished European tourist that we instantly think of in connection with Staffa and Fingal's Cave is of course Felix Mendelssohn. The occasion of the German composer's inspiration, is described here by his biographer:

> It is said that this was the manner in which the overture, *The Hebrides*, took its rise: Mendelssohn's sisters asked him to tell them something about the Hebrides. 'It cannot be told, only played,' he said. No sooner spoken than he seated himself at the piano and played the theme which afterwards grew into the overture.

The attention paid to those tiny islands Iona and Staffa may seem disproportionate to their significance in other ways – Iona has a population around a hundred and Staffa has been uninhabited since the nineteenth century. We have also said nothing about Iona as a place of pilgrimage and about the work of the Iona Community. Even so, the cultural significance of these islands, especially Iona, remains immense and the extent to which they have inspired writers as well as composers is incalculable.

The much larger island of Mull has a great variety of scenery and character, from the feeling of the Outer Hebrides that you get down at the tip of the Ross of Mull – that tautologous headland in the south-west – to the bare slopes of Ben More at the island's centre. Tobermory is a capital with much charm and the scatter of habitation at Calgary Bay attracts many curious visitors from Alberta looking for the prototype of their own city.

Mull has a great scatter of satellite islands. These include the line of low basalt platforms, in line astern like a battle fleet of dreadnoughts, the Treshnish Islands. Slightly larger is Ulva, once famous for its kelp industry, which at its peak employed 600 people, and for the people who made a way for themselves in the world, once they had left Ulva. These include Lachlan Macquarie, the so-called 'Father of Australia' and David Livingstone's father.

Coll and Tiree are the real outliers of Argyll and serve as stopping places for shipping on its way to the Outer Isles. Tiree's name comes from *Tir Iodh* or 'Land of Corn' (today it is better known for cattle-raising) and it is extremely low-lying – it has another Gaelic name which means the land 'whose heights are lower than the waves'. The high winds on this low platform of an island are a constant feature of life, and conservation measures have been taken, such as the planting of marram grass on the western dunes, in order to save what soil there is. The Dukes of Argyll at one time made this a condition of a lease. Agriculture in the Hebrides has always been a precarious business and we can understand what Dr Johnson meant when he observed, while on Mull:

> Your country consists of two things, stone and water. There is indeed, a little earth above the stone in some places, but a very little; and the stone is always appearing. It is like a man in rags; the naked skin is still peeping out.

On the mainland of Argyll (though not officially part of it since the 1970s), across the Sound of Mull, bulk the great hilly wildernesses of Morvern, Ardgour and the more oceanic peninsula of Ardnamurchan. Ardgour and Morvern have tiny populations and the little settlements like Kinlochaline have a romantic air, perhaps symbolised by the latter's honour of being the birthplace of Dougie the Mate in the *Para Handy* tales. Ardnamurchan's past and heritage is beautifully described in this anthology, in prose but by a poet, Alasdair Maclean. He gives a clear-eyed view of what it is like to live in remote places such as these:

> There are no concert halls, theatres, cinemas or libraries. If by chance you find yourself a little depressed one day and decide that a grilled chop for supper might offer solace – forget it. You will discover neither restaurant nor butcher on the corner. There is no corner.

'The Saint on Iona'

from Life of St Columba

ADOMNAN (c. 7th CENTURY)

These extracts are taken from Adomnan's Life of the Saint whose exploits built the foundations of the Celtic church in Scotland, and to a large extent in Ireland too. Although Christianity already had a foothold in Scotland when Columba crossed on his fabled journey from Dalriada, the impact of his arrival was political as well as religious, not least because of his status as a prince of the Ui Neill. Iona, as an island base, was well suited for missionary work on the heavily indented west coast and among the Scots of the new Dalriada. Iona became a beacon of civilisation and learning, and although many of Adomnan's stories strain credulity, it represents an ideal of a Celtic church which survived centuries of strife and even today retains a special place in Scotland's spiritual life.

Of the arrival of the abbot Saint Cainnech, which Saint Columba had prophetically foretold

At another time, in the island of Io, on a day of crashing storm and unendurably high waves, when the saint, sitting in the house and giving orders to the brothers, said: 'Prepare the guest-house quickly, and draw water for washing the feet of guests', one of the brothers then said: 'On this very windy and too perilous day, who can cross in safety even the narrow strait?' Hearing him, the saint spoke thus: 'To one holy and chosen man, who will reach us before the evening, the Omnipotent has granted calm, though in the midst of storm.'

And behold, on the same day, a ship that the brothers had for some time awaited and in which Saint Cainnech was, arrived according to the saint's prophecy. The saint with the brothers went to meet him, and honourably and hospitably received him. And the sailors who were in the ship with Cainnech, when asked by the brothers what kind of voyage they had had, replied in exact agreement with what Saint Columba had earlier foretold of storm and calm together, by God's dispensation, in the same sea and at the same hours, but miraculously separated; and they declared that they had not felt the storm, which they had seen far off.

Of the peril of the bishop Saint Colmán
mocu Sailni in the sea near the island that is
called Rechru [Rathlin]

In like manner on another day, Saint Columba, while he was living in his mother church, suddenly exclaimed, with a smile: 'Colmán, Beogna's son, has begun to sail over to us, and is now in great danger in the surging tides of the whirlpool of Brecán; and sitting in the prow he raises both hands to heaven, and blesses the troubled and very terrible sea. But the Lord terrifies him thus, not in order that the ship in which he sits may be overwhelmed by the waves in shipwreck, but rather to rouse him to more fervent prayer that with God's favour he may reach us after passing through the danger.'

Adiutor Laborantium
(Helper of Workers)

ST COLUMBA (521–97)

TRANSLATED BY THOMAS OWEN CLANCY AND GILBERT MÁRKUS

The Latin poem Adiutor Laborantium *(Helper of Workers) is attributed to St Columba himself. It is a prayer to God the Father. The first half of the poem reads rather like a litany, listing many titles of God which show both His power and His mercy. In the second half of the poem Columba makes a petition using an image very appropriate to the sea-girt monastery of Iona and one which is employed later by his biographer Adomnan. The saint pictures himself as an insignificant, frail human rowing against the storm and asks God to bring him safe to the harbour of heaven. Even to the reader who has no Latin this poem is metrically interesting and skilful. Each line consists of eight syllables and ends with the rhyming syllable '-um'. Furthermore, each of the first 24 lines begins with a successive letter of the Latin alphabet except for lines 10 and 11 where, there being no K in the Latin alphabet, the poet begins with the letter C and then chooses to repeat this practice in the next line. In line 22 the X is treated as the equivalent of the Greek letter Chi which is pronounced 'ch', a common practice in medieval Latin writing.*

Adiutor laborantium
Bonorum rector omnium,
Custos ad propugnaculum,
Defensorque credentium,
Exaltator humilium,
Fractor superbientium,
Gubernator fidelium,
Hostis inpoenitentium,
Iudex cunctorum iudicum,
Castigator errantium,

Casta vita viventium,
Lumen et pater luminum,
Magna luce lucentium,
Nulli negans sperantium
Opem atque auxilium,
Precor ut me homunculum
Quassatum ac miserrimum
Remigantem per tumultum
Saeculi istius infinitum
Trahat post se ad supernum
Vitae portum pulcherrimum
Xristus; . . . infinitum
Ymnum sanctum in seculum
Zelo subtrahas hostium
Paradisi in gaudium.
    Per te, Christe Ihesu,
    qui vivis et regnas.

HELPER OF WORKERS

O helper of workers,
ruler of all the good,
guard on the ramparts
and defender of the faithful,
who lift up the lowly
and crush the proud,
ruler of the faithful,
enemy of the impenitent,
judge of all judges,
who punish those who err,
pure life of the living,
light and Father of lights
shining with great light,
denying to none of the hopeful
your strength and help,
I beg that me, a little man
trembling and most wretched,

rowing through the infinite storm
of this age,
Christ may draw after Him to the lofty
most beautiful haven of life
. . . an unending
holy hymn forever.
From the envy of enemies you lead me
into the joy of paradise.
   Through you, Christ Jesus,
   who live and reign.

'Mull and Iona'

from Journal of a Tour to the Hebrides

JAMES BOSWELL (1740–95)

In the autumn of 1773 James Boswell, advocate, traveller, writer and heir to an Ayrshire estate, set off on a tour of the Highlands and Islands of Scotland with his friend, hero and father-figure, Dr Samuel Johnson, poet, essayist, lexicographer and controversialist. The two travellers had a variety of experiences and some rough accommodation on their adventure into these little-known and seldom-travelled regions. In less than thirty years since the collapse of the last Jacobite rising little had been done to open up the Highlands and only a few adventurous travellers like Pennant had crossed the Highland Line. Boswell was in the prime of life at thirty three, although given to dissipation, while Johnson, who celebrated his sixty-fourth birthday on the tour and had suffered from ill health all his life, might have been thought rather old for such arduous journeys by land and sea.

Both of the travellers wrote accounts of the tour or 'jaunt'. Johnson's Journey to the Western Islands *appeared the following year with considerable success. Boswell's version of events was not published until 1785 and is much racier and more personal, with, in this extract, some typically Boswellian reflections on memory. We also include Boswell's account of the famous visit they paid to Iona, although he, not surprisingly, chooses to quote at some length Johnson's 'strength of thought and energy of language'.*

Thursday, 14th October

When Dr Johnson awaked this morning, he called, '*Lanky!*' having, I suppose, been thinking of Langton; but corrected himself instantly, and cried, '*Bozzy!*' He has a way of contracting the names of his friends. Goldsmith feels himself so important now, as to be displeased at it. I remember one day, when Tom Davies was telling that Dr Johnson said, 'We are all in labour for a name to *Goldy*'s play,' Goldsmith cried, ' I have often desired him not to call me *Goldy*.'

Between six and seven we hauled our anchor, and set sail with a fair breeze; and, after a pleasant voyage, we got safely and agreeably into the harbour of Tobermorie, before the wind rose, which it always has done, for some days, about noon.

Tobermorie is an excellent harbour. An island lies before it, and it is surrounded by a hilly theatre. The island is too low, otherwise this would be quite a secure port; but, the island not being a suffficient protection, some storms blow very hard here. Not long ago, fifteen vessels were blown from their moorings. There are sometimes sixty or seventy sail here: to-day there were twelve or fourteen vessels. To see such a fleet was the next thing to seeing a town. The vessels were from different places; Clyde, Campbelltown, Newcastle, &c. One was returning to Lancaster from Hamburgh. After having been shut up so long in Col, the sight of such an assemblage of moving habitations, containing such a variety of people, engaged in different pursuits, gave me much gaiety of spirit. When we had landed, Dr Johnson said, 'Boswell is now all alive. He is like Antæus; he gets new vigour whenever he touches the ground.' – I went to the top of a hill fronting the harbour, from whence I had a good view of it. We had here a tolerable inn. Dr Johnson had owned to me this morning, that he was out of humour. Indeed, he shewed it a good deal in the ship; for when I was expressing my joy on the prospect of our landing in Mull, he said, he had no joy, when he recollected that it would be five days before he should get to the main land. I was afraid he would now take a sudden resolution to give up seeing Icolmkill. A dish of tea, and some good bread and butter, did him service, and his bad humour went off. I told him, that I was diverted to hear all the people whom we had visited in our Tour, say *'Honest man! he's pleased with every thing; he's always content!'* – 'Little do they know,' said I. He laughed, and said, 'You rogue!'

* * *

We saw the island of Staffa, at no very great distance, but could not land upon it, the surge was so high on its rocky coast.

Sir Allan, anxious for the honour of Mull, was still talking of its *woods*, and pointing them out to Dr Johnson, as appearing at a distance on the skirts of that island, as we sailed along. – *Johnson.* 'Sir, I saw at Tobermorie what they called a wood, which I unluckily took for *heath*. If you shew me what I shall take for *furze*, it will be something.'

In the afternoon we went ashore on the coast of Mull, and partook of a cold repast, which we carried with us. We hoped to have procured some rum or brandy for our boatmen and servants, from a publick-house near where we landed; but unfortunately a funeral a few days before had exhausted all their store. Mr Campbell however, one of the Duke of Argyle's tacksmen, who lived in the neighbourhood, on receiving a message from Sir Allan, sent us a liberal supply.

We continued to coast along Mull, and passed by Nuns' Island, which, it is said, belonged to the nuns of Icolmkill, and from which, we were told, the stone for the buildings there was taken. As we sailed along by moon-light, in a sea somewhat rough, and often between black and gloomy rocks, Dr Johnson said, 'If this be not *roving among the Hebrides*, nothing is.' – The repetition of words which he had so often previously used, made a strong impression on my imagination; and, by a natural course of thinking, led me to consider how our present adventures would appear to me at a future period.

I have often experienced, that scenes through which a man has passed, improve by lying in the memory: they grow mellow. *Acti labores sunt jucundi.* This may be owing to comparing them with present listless ease. Even harsh scenes acquire a softness by length of time; and some are like very loud sounds, which do not please, or at least do not please so much, till you are removed to a certain distance. They may be compared to strong coarse pictures, which will not bear to be viewed near. Even pleasing scenes improve by time, and seem more exquisite in recollection, than when they were present; if they have not faded to dimness in the memory. Perhaps, there is so much evil in every human enjoyment, when present – so much dross mixed with it, that it requires to be refined by time; and yet I do not see why time should not melt away the good and the evil in equal proportions; – why the shade should decay, and the light remain in preservation.

After a tedious sail, which, by our following various turnings of the coast of Mull, was extended to about forty miles, it gave us no small pleasure to perceive a light in the village at Icolmkill, in which almost all the inhabitants of the island live, close to where the ancient buildings stood. As we approached the shore, the tower of the cathedral, just discernible in the air, was a picturesque object.

When we had landed upon the sacred place, which, as long as I can remember, I had thought on with veneration, Dr Johnson and I cordially embraced. We had long talked of visiting Icolmkill; and, from the lateness of the season, were at times very doubtful whether we should be able to effect our purpose. To have seen it, even alone, would have given me great satisfaction; but the venerable scene was rendered much more pleasing by the company of my great and pious friend, who was no less affected by it than I was; and who has described the impressions it should make on the mind, with such strength of thought, and energy of language, that I shall quote his words, as conveying my own sensations much more forcibly than I am capable of doing:

'We were now treading that illustrious Island, which was once the luminary of the Caledonian regions, whence savage clans and roving barbarians derived the benefits of knowledge, and the blessings of religion. To abstract the mind from all local emotion would be impossible, if it were endeavoured, and would be foolish, if it were possible. Whatever withdraws us from the power of our senses, whatever makes the past, the distant, or the future, predominate over the present, advances us in the dignity of thinking beings. Far from me, and from my friends, be such frigid philosophy as may conduct us indifferent and unmoved over any ground which has been dignified by wisdom, bravery, or virtue. That man is little to be envied, whose patriotism would not gain force upon the plain of *Marathon*, or whose piety would not grow warmer among the ruins of *Iona*!'

'The Isle of Earraid'

from Kidnapped

ROBERT LOUIS STEVENSON (1850–94)

Stevenson's most famous Scottish novel, Kidnapped, was finished in 1886 while he was living quietly for the sake of his health in Bournemouth. However distant in miles Stevenson's links to his homeland remained strong. Symbolic of these links was his choice of names for his Bournemouth villa – 'Skerryvore' – after the great rock lighthouse built by the Stevensons on a rock reef off Tiree. As a younger man Stevenson had travelled round Scotland's west coast and visited the tidal island of Earraid, off Mull, which was the supply base for the Skerryvore light and, at the time of his visit, the construction base for the equally spectacular Dubh Heartach light. This explains the poem of dedication for the villa:

> *For love of lovely words, and for the sake*
> *Of those, my kinsmen and my countrymen,*
> *Who, early and late in the windy ocean toiled*
> *To plant a star for seamen, where was then*
> *The surfy haunt of seals and cormorants:*
> *I, on the lintel of this cot, inscribe*
> *The name of a strong tower.*

The extract from Kidnapped tells how the young hero, David Balfour, is cast up on Earraid after a shipwreck and is temporarily separated from his new acquaintance, Alan Breck Stewart. Here we see Stevenson making use of his youthful experiences to evoke a Hebridean isle.

With my stepping ashore I began the most unhappy part of my adventures. It was half-past twelve in the morning, and though the wind was broken by the land, it was a cold night. I dared not sit down (for I thought I should have frozen), but took off my shoes and walked to and fro upon the sand, barefoot, and beating my breast, with infinite weariness. There was no sound of man or cattle; not a cock crew, though it was about the hour of their first waking; only the surf broke outside in the distance, which put me in mind of my perils and those of my friend. To walk by the sea at that hour of the morning, and in a place so desert-like and lonesome, struck me with a kind of fear.

As soon as the day began to break I put on my shoes and climbed a hill – the ruggedest scramble I ever undertook – falling, the whole way, between big blocks of granite or leaping from one to another. When I got to the top the dawn was come. There was no sign of the brig, which must have lifted from the reef and sunk. The boat, too, was nowhere to be seen. There was never a sail upon the oean; and in what I could see of the land, was neither house nor man.

I was afraid to think what had befallen my shipmates, and afraid to look longer at so empty a scene. What with my wet clothes and weariness, and my belly that now began to ache with hunger, I had enough to trouble me without that. So I set off eastward along the south coast, hoping to find a house where I might warm myself, and perhaps get news of those I had lost. And at the worst, I considered the sun would soon rise and dry my clothes.

After a little, my way was stopped by a creek or inlet of the sea, which seemed to run pretty deep into the land; and as I had no means to get across, I must needs change my direction to go about the end of it. It was still the roughest kind of walking; indeed the whole, not only of Earraid, but of the neighbouring part of Mull (which they call the Ross) is nothing but a jumble of granite rocks with heather in among. At first the creek kept narrowing as I had looked to see; but presently to my surprise it began to widen out again. At this I scratched my head, but had still no notion of the truth; until at last I came to a rising ground, and it burst upon me all in a moment that I was cast upon a little, barren isle, and cut off on every side by the salt seas.

Instead of the sun rising to dry me, it came on to rain, with a thick mist; so that my case was lamentable.

I stood in the rain, and shivered, and wondered what to do, till it occurred to me that perhaps the creek was fordable. Back I went to the narrowest point and waded in. But not three yards from shore, I plumped in head over ears; and if ever I was heard of more it was rather by God's grace than my own prudence. I was no wetter (for that could hardly be) but I was all the colder for this mishap; and having lost another hope, was the more unhappy.

And now, all at once, the yard came in my head. What had carried me through the roost, would surely serve me to cross this little quiet creek in safety. With that I set off, undaunted, across the top of the isle, to fetch and carry it back. It was a weary tramp in all ways, and if hope had not buoyed me up, I must have cast myself down and given up. Whether with the sea salt, or because I was growing fevered, I was distressed with thirst, and had to stop as I went, and drink the peaty water out of the hags.

I came to the bay at last, more dead than alive; and at the first glance, I thought the yard was something further out than when I left it. In I went, for the third time, into the sea. The sand was smooth and firm and shelved gradually down; so that I could wade out till the water was almost to my neck and the little waves splashed into my face. But at that depth my feet began to leave me and I durst venture in no further. As for the yard, I saw it bobbing very quietly some twenty feet in front of me.

I had borne up well until this last disappointment; but at that I came ashore, and flung myself down upon the sands and wept.

The time I spent upon the island is still so horrible a thought to me, that I must pass it lightly over. In all the books I have read of people cast away, they had either their pockets full of tools, or a chest of things would be thrown upon the beach along with them, as if on purpose. My case was very different. I had nothing in my pockets but money and Alan's silver button; and being inland bred, I was as much short of knowledge as of means.

I knew indeed that shell-fish were counted good to eat; and among the rocks of the isle I found a great plenty of limpets, which at first I could scarcely strike from their places, not knowing quickness to be needful. There were, besides, some of the little shells that we call buckies; I think periwinkle is the English name. Of these two I made my whole diet, devouring them cold and raw as I found them; and so hungry was I, that at first they seemed to me delicious.

Perhaps they were out of season, or perhaps there was something wrong in the sea about my island. But at least I had no sooner eaten my first meal than I was seized with giddiness and retching, and lay for a long time no better than dead. A second trial of the same food (indeed I had no other) did better with me and revived my strength. But as long as I was on the island, I never knew what to expect when I had eaten; sometimes all was well, and sometimes I was thrown into a miserable sickness; nor could I ever distinguish what particular fish it was that hurt me.

All day it streamed rain; the island ran like a sop; there was no dry spot to be found; and when I lay down that night, between two boulders that made a kind of roof, my feet were in a bog.

The second day I crossed the island to all sides. There was no one part of it better than another; it was all desolate and rocky; nothing living on it but game birds which I lacked the means to kill, and the gulls which haunted the outlying rocks in a prodigious number. But the creek, or straits, that cut off the isle from the mainland of the Ross, opened out on the north into a bay, and the bay again opened into the sound of Iona; and it was the neighbourhood of this place that I chose to be my home; though if I had thought upon the very name of home in such a spot, I must have burst out weeping.

I had good reasons for my choice. There was in this part of the isle a little hut of a house like a pig's hut, where fishers used to sleep when they came there upon their business; but the turf roof of it had fallen entirely in; so that the hut was of no use to me, and gave me less shelter than my rocks. What was more important, the shell-fish on which I lived grew there in great plenty; when the tide was out I could gather a peck at a time: and this was doubtless a convenience. But the other reason went deeper. I had become in no way used to the horrid solitude of the isle, but still looked round me on all sides (like a man that was hunted) between fear and hope that I might see some human creature coming. Now, from a little up the hillside over the bay, I could catch a sight of the great, ancient church and the roofs of the people's houses in Iona. And on the other hand, over the low country of the Ross, I saw smoke go up, morning and evening, as if from a homestead in a hollow of the land.

I used to watch this smoke, when I was wet and cold, and had my head half turned with loneliness; and think of the fireside and the company, till my heart burned. It was the same with the roofs of Iona. Altogether, this sight I had of men's homes and comfortable lives, although it put a point on my own sufferings, yet it kept hope alive, and helped me to eat my raw shell-fish (which had soon grown to be a disgust) and saved me from the sense of horror I had whenever I was quite alone with dead rocks, and fowls, and the rain, and the cold sea.

I say it kept hope alive; and indeed it seemed impossible that I should be left to die on the shores of my own country, and within view of a church tower and the smoke of men's houses. But the second day passed; and though as long as the light lasted I kept a bright look-out for boats on the Sound or men passing on the Ross, no help came near me. It still rained; and I turned in to sleep, as wet as ever and with a cruel sore throat, but a little comforted, perhaps, by having said good night to my next neighbours, the people of Iona.

Charles the Second declared a man could stay out-doors more days in the year in the climate of England than in any other. This was very like a king with a palace at his back and changes of dry clothes. But he must have had better luck on his flight from Worcester than I had on that miserable isle. It was the height of the summer; yet it rained for more than twenty-four hours, and did not clear until the afternoon of the third day.

This was the day of incidents. In the morning I saw a red deer, a buck with a fine spread of antlers, standing in the rain on the top of the island; but he had scarce seen me rise from under my rock, before he trotted off upon the other side. I supposed he must have swum the straits; though what should bring any creature to Earraid, was more than I could fancy.

A little after, as I was jumping about after my limpets, I was startled by a guinea-piece, which fell upon a rock in front of me and glanced off into the sea. When the sailors gave me my money again, they kept back not only about a third of the whole sum, but my father's leather purse; so that from that day out, I carried my gold loose in a pocket with a button. I now saw there must be a hole, and clapped my hand to the place in a great hurry. But this was to lock the stable door after the steed was stolen. I had left the shore at Queensferry with near on fifty pounds; now I found no more than two guinea-pieces and a silver shilling.

It is true I picked up a third guinea a little after, where it lay shining on a piece of turf. That made a fortune of three pounds and four shillings, English money, for a lad, the rightful heir of an estate and now starving on an isle at the extreme end of the wild Highlands.

This state of my affairs dashed me still further; and indeed my plight on that third morning was truly pitiful. My clothes were beginning to rot; my stockings in particular were quite worn through, so that my shanks went naked; my hands had grown quite soft with the continual soaking; my throat was very sore, my strength had much abated and my heart so turned against the horrid stuff I was condemned to eat, that the very sight of it came near to sicken me.

And yet the worst was not yet come.

There is a pretty high rock on the north-west of Earraid, which (because it had a flat top and overlooked the Sound) I was much in the habit of frequenting; not that ever I stayed in one place, save when asleep, my misery giving me no rest. Indeed I wore myself down with continual and aimless goings and comings in the rain.

As soon, however, as the sun came out, I lay down on the top of that rock to dry myself. The comfort of the sunshine is a thing I cannot tell. It set me thinking hopefully of my deliverance, of which I had begun to despair; and I scanned the sea and the Ross with a fresh interest. On the south of my rock, a part of the island jutted out and hid the open ocean, so that a boat could thus come quite near me upon that side, and I be none the wiser.

Well, all of a sudden, a coble with a brown sail and a pair of fishers aboard of it, came flying round that corner of the isle, bound for Iona. I shouted out, and then fell on my knees on the rock and reached up my hands and prayed to them. They were near enough to hear – I could even see the colour of their hair; and there was no doubt but they observed me, for they cried out in the Gaelic tongue, and laughed. But the boat never turned aside, and flew on, right before my eyes, for Iona.

I could not believe such wickedness, and ran along the shore from rock to rock, crying on them piteously; even after they were out of reach of my voice, I still cried and waved to them; and when they were quite gone, I thought my heart would have burst. All the time of my troubles I wept only twice. Once, when I could not reach the yard; and now, the second time, when these fishers turned a deaf ear to my cries. But this time I wept and roared like a wicked child, tearing up the turf with my nails and grinding my face in the earth. If a wish would kill men, those two fishers would never have seen morning, and I should likely have died upon my island.

When I was a little over my anger, I must eat again, but with such loathing of the mess as I could now scarce control. Sure enough, I should have done as well to fast, for my fishes poisoned me again. I had all my first pains; my throat was so sore I could scarce swallow; I had a fit of strong shuddering which clucked my teeth together; and there came on me that dreadful sense of illness which we have no name for either in Scotch or English. I thought I should have died, and made my peace with God, forgiving all men, even my uncle and the fishers; and as soon as I had thus made up my mind to the worst, clearness came upon me: I observed the night was falling dry; my clothes were dried a good deal; truly, I was in a better case than ever before, since I had landed on the isle; and so I got to sleep at last, with a thought of gratitude.

The next day (which was the fourth of this horrible life of mine) I found my bodily strength run very low. But the sun shone, the air was sweet, and what I managed to eat of the shell-fish agreed well with me and revived my courage.

I was scarce back on my rock (where I went always the first thing after I had eaten) before I observed a boat coming down the Sound, and with her head, as I thought, in my direction.

I began at once to hope and fear exceedingly; for I thought these men might have thought better of their cruelty and be coming back to my assistance. But another disappointment, such as yesterday's, was more than I could bear. I turned my back, accordingly, upon the sea, and did not look again till I had counted many hundreds. The boat was still heading for the island. The next time I counted the full thousand, as slowly as I could, my heart beating so as to hurt me. And then it was out of all question. She was coming straight to Earraid!

I could no longer hold myself back, but ran to the sea side and out, from one rock to another, as far as I could go. It is a marvel I was not drowned; for when I was brought to a stand at last, my legs shook under me, and my mouth was so dry, I must wet it with the sea-water before I was able to shout.

All this time the boat was coming on; and now I was able to perceive it was the same boat and the same two men as yesterday. This I knew by their hair, which the one had of a bright yellow and the other black. But now there was a third man along with them, who looked to be of a better class.

As soon as they were come within easy speech, they let down their sail and lay quiet. In spite of my supplications, they drew no nearer in, and what frightened me most of all, the new man tee-hee'd with laughter as he talked and looked at me.

Then he stood up in the boat and addressed me a long while, speaking fast and with many wavings of his hand. I told him I had no Gaelic; and at this he became very angry, and I began to suspect he thought he was talking English. Listening very close, I caught the word 'whateffer' several times; but all the rest was Gaelic, and might have been Greek and Hebrew for me.

'Whatever,' said I, to show him I had caught a word.

'Yes, yes – yes, yes,' says he, and then he looked at the other men, as much as to say, 'I told you I spoke English,' and began again as hard as ever in the Gaelic.

This time I picked out another word 'tide'. Then I had a flash of hope. I remembered he was always waving his hand towards the mainland of the Ross.

'Do you mean when the tide is out – ?' I cried, and could not finish.

'Yes, yes,' said he. 'Tide.'

At that I turned tail upon their boat (where my adviser had once more begun to tee-hee with laughter), leaped back the way I had come, from one stone to another, and set off running across the isle as I had never run before. In about half an hour I came out upon the shores of the creek; and, sure enough, it was shrunk into a little trickle of water, through which I dashed, not above my knees, and landed with a shout on the main island.

A sea-bred boy would not have stayed a day on Earraid; which is only what they call a tidal islet, and except in the bottom of the neaps, can be entered and left twice in every twenty-four hours, either dryshod, or at the most by wading. Even I, who had the tide going out and in before me in the bay and even watched for the ebbs, the better to get my shell-fish –

even I (I say) if I had sat down to think, instead of raging at my fate, must have soon guessed the secret, and got free. It was no wonder the fishers had not understood me. The wonder was rather that they had ever guessed my pitiful illusion, and taken the trouble to come back. I had starved with cold and hunger on that island for close upon one hundred hours. But for the fishers, I might have left my bones there, in pure folly. And even as it was, I had paid for it pretty dear, not only in past sufferings, but in my present case; being clothed like a beggar-man, scarce able to walk, and in great pain of my sore throat.

I have seen wicked men and fools, a great many of both; and I believe they both get paid in the end; but the fools first.

Staffa

JOHN KEATS (1795–1821)

In 1818, three years before he died of consumption in Rome, John Keats spent the months of July and August in Scotland with his friend Charles Armitage Brown. Like many before him, such as the Wordsworths and Coleridge, Keats found inspiration in Scotland's wildness and rugged grandeur. He used the experience in attempting his great epic poem 'Hyperion', of which only fragments were completed, and in this astonishing poem in which he pictures Fingal's Cave as the refuge of the drowned Lycidas, the subject of John Milton's elegy for his friend Edward King. Staffa's fantastic geological formations made a great impression on Keats and he compares the cave to a 'cathedral of the sea' where Oceanus's 'mighty waters play, hollow organs all the day'. Keats came to Staffa from Iona and wrote to his brother in London:

> *The old Schoolmaster is an ignorant little man but reckoned very clever, showed us these things (the tombs of the kings) – he is a Macklean and as much above 4 foot as he is under 4 foot 3 inches – he stops at one glass of wiskey unless you press another and at the second unless you press a third.*

Not Aladdin magian
Ever such a work began;
Not the wizard of the Dee
Ever such a dream could see;
Not St John, in Patmos' Isle,
In the passion of his toil,
When he saw the churches seven,
Golden aisl'd, built up in heaven,
Gaz'd at such a rugged wonder.
As I stood its roofing under,
Lo! I saw one sleeping there,
On the marble cold and bare.
While the surges wash'd his feet,
And his garments white did beat

Drench'd about the sombre rocks;
On his neck his well-grown locks,
Lifted dry above the main,
Were upon the curl again.
'What is this? and what art thou?'
Whispered I, and touched his brow;
'What art thou? and what is this?'
Whispered I, and strove to kiss
The spirit's hand, to wake his eyes;
Up he started in a trice:
'I am Lycidas,' said he,
'Fam'd in funeral minstrelsy!
This was architectur'd thus
By the great Oceanus! –
Here his mighty waters play
Hollow organs all the day;
Here, by turns, his dolphins all,
Finny palmers, great and small,
Come to pay devotion due, –
Each a mouth of pearls must strew.
Many a mortal of these days,
Dares to pass our sacred ways;
Dares to touch audaciously
This cathedral of the sea!
I have been the pontiff-priest
Where the waters never rest,
Where a fledgy sea-bird choir
Soars for ever! Holy fire
I have hid from mortal man;
Proteus is my Sacristan!
But the dulled eye of mortal
Hath passed beyond the rocky portal;
So for ever will I leave
Such a taint, and soon unweave
All the magic of the place.'

So saying, with a spirit's glance
He dived!

'Staffa'

from Circuit Journeys

HENRY COCKBURN (1779–1854)

Henry Cockburn was born far from Argyll, in a house in the Old Parliament Close of Edinburgh, and in the course of his education spent 'about nine years at two dead languages' to little effect. At any rate he was called to the Bar, ultimately became Solicitor-General for Scotland, then a lord of justiciary, and was largely responsible for drafting the Scottish Reform Act of 1832 which secured, as he claimed in his Diaries, 'the regeneration of Scotland'.

This extract comes from Circuit Journeys, *not published till 1888, and is part of a record he kept of a tour in the West in the summer of 1840. The description of Fingal's Cave on the isle of Staffa is particularly interesting. So too, for different reasons, are his comments about the beggars he witnessed on Iona and the remarks about the ducal house of Argyll. Cockburn was a well known Whig, but even so he evidently did not intend that his remarks should ever reach the public's gaze.*

The paddle steamer Brenda *on which he and his legal companions cruised around '120 miles of islands' was running that year on the Crinan to Oban route. She had been built in Dumbarton for Robert Napier's Gareloch service and had also provided the service from Crinan to Oban that later became known as 'The Royal Route'.*

Lochgilphead, Tuesday Night, 1st September 1840. – Well! I have actually had my piety warmed by musing over the ruins of Iona, and my faith in Ossian excited by being in Fingal's Cave.

Francis, Elizabeth, and I left Oban yesterday morning in the Brenda, a rumbling steamer, at six o'clock, and were relanded there, after a prosperous voyage round the Island of Mull, at eight in the evening, going by the south end and returning by the Sound. Consequently we not only saw Iona and Staffa, but about 120 miles of islands, and nature never produced a better day.

I saw little after the tenth or twelfth mile till I reached Iona, for my very unmaritime stomach was rebellious, and for about four hours I lay abusing my folly, and vowing that this should be my last voyage. In this state I was landed on that island, but my infirmity instantly ceased, and, getting into water like glass, it never came over me again during the day.

The ruins greatly surpassed my expectation. I thought that all I was to see was the mere stools of buildings, whereas I found as many legible old inscriptions, carved tombstones, and standing walls, as in most very ancient, fallen edifices. Being walked round by the Captain, and only an hour allowed, and a whole cargo of travellers to be satiated, it was not a visit that could do more than leave a general idea of the appearance of the place, and enable one to know hereafter what people are speaking about when they speak of Iona. Were it not absurd, after all that has been said and written, it would be irresistible for any one of ordinary sense or feeling to indulge in the visions which this remote and deserted little island is so well fitted to inspire. They came across me, and the recollection of the scene will now for ever suggest them more easily and vividly.

I must confess that my contemplations of the past were greatly marred by the reality of the present. A more wretched set of creatures than those that crawled around us I doubt if even Ireland could exhibit. Certainly no other part of the world that I have ever read of could exceed it. It might have been accounted for by supposing that Argyleshire had sent its most humiliating destitution to affect the visitors of Iona, had it not been for the sad truth, that the naked and diseased dirt which greets and follows the tourists there, will meet and follow him in many other islands of the Hebrides. My sensibility has perhaps been too little blunted by the past reality of such spectacles, for I doubt if I was ever on one of the western islands before, but it is dreadful to think that these poor creatures are not only human, but countrymen. Yet they have an infants' school, which I saw in action, and a church where the Sacrament was dispensed the day before. So easy is it to combine the forms of religion and education with the degradation of human habits, if not the prostration of the human character. They are the better of the church and the school, but still are about as brutish in the economy of life as their very nasty cows and swine are.

But what can be expected, though they had all the churches and schools in Christendom, of people who live in the constant view of these still more brutally kept monuments and temples. What a disgrace to their owners! who I understand are the Argyles. All the waters of Loch Fyne will not cleanse them from the shame of these neglected solemn ruins. They are the most interesting relics in the British Empire, and might, by mere attention, and with very little expenditure, have been protected for centuries; the flat, carved tombstones might have had their venerable letters saved from being worn out by regardless feet; and the grass might have been kept as smooth and pure as the turf at any of the Oxford colleges; but no foul beast ever trod a pearl in the dirt so unconsciously as these titled men have, for many ages, but particularly during the last hundred years, deliberately allowed fragments, that have been the wonder of thinking men, to be reduced to a worse condition than most pigstyes. If proprietors who behave so had all the apology of bankruptcy, this might be a consolation, for a well-disposed mind could not fail to consider this as God's punishment for their crime. But every one of them wastes yearly, on contemptible importance, what would be quite sufficient to transmit these sacred gifts of a former age to succeeding ones, and in such a condition that they might be admired, as they descend, without having the veneration they inspire marred by unnecessary disgust. Even the Argyle is diminished in my sight.

We landed easily on Staffa, and I was one of four who went to the very innermost recess of the cave. It is one of the very few much-spoken-of wonders to which my fancy had not come up. And I cannot say that my expectation had been lowered by the opinion of Serjeant Talfourd, who told me, two years ago, that he thought Staffa 'contemptible', a crotchet to be ascribed, no doubt, to the poet's stomach not having come to its senses so soon as mine had. It is one of nature's great geological feats. No thunder is more awful than the roar of the wave as it breaks along the sides, and on the inner end of the cavern. And then there is nothing human about it. It is all pure nature. Not a single ass has even painted its name upon it. The solitude and storminess of its position greatly enhance its interest.

On the whole, I have rarely been more gratified than by at last beholding these two sights, one of the wonder of nature, the other of man. I had been anxious to see them almost all my life, and the recollection will now be more exciting than the fancy of them was.

The rest of the sail was delightful. We moved over a sea nearly of glass, past places, but particularly past islands and points, and other things called castles, the names of which were familiar, and where the mere surprise of seeing what one had so often heard of was a pleasure. In their present state there is very little beauty in any one place along that coast, and not a single old building of any architectural interest. The great want is of wood, even of larch, which, however, for scenery, is rarely wood. Nor is it true that wood would not grow on these tempest-beaten and foam-washed spots. A thousand small and exposed, but still oak-clad islands, and promontories, and bays, and knolls, and ravines, but especially islands which are most in the way of the spray and the wind, attest that, even though not planted in great masses, the whole of the Hebrides might be adorned and warmed by trees. It is sheep and poverty, not the ocean or the storm, that keep them hard and uniform. What an Archipelago it would be had it only due summer!

As it is, the charm of the region consists in the picturesque grouping of the features of the scenery, particularly of the hills, in the barbarous history, and above all, in the desolation that seems to prevail over everything. We did not see two dozen of vessels, including boats, throughout the whole day, no town, or even village, except Tobermory, very few, and very insignificant houses, and no people; we heard no sounds except the oars of the few boats that came alongside for passengers; everything was silent, hard, and still, under the impressiveness of which one sails along, amidst scenes which time had been incapable of changing, and which seem as if they had been preserved merely that they might be the localities of old stories.

The two finest prospects are, a little after leaving Aros, when the whole of Ben Cruachan, and a little after leaving Ardtornish, when the Appin mountains stand before us, both as we saw them, blazing with the setting sun, and contrasted with the shaded, and almost black groups behind us.

I suspect that had I seen Tobermory first, I should have said of it all I have said of Oban, which it is very like. Tobermory has the advantages of a steeper immediate background, fringed with scattered wood; of a high and low town, the one on the summit of the cliff seeming to stand on the top of the houses on the beach; and of a church with a sort of a spire peering out from among the trees amidst the upper buildings. Our twenty-five passengers, or so, were mostly English, and all of them were struck with its resemblance to Torquay in its primitive condition.

The number of foreign, but chiefly of English, travellers is extraordinary. They fill every conveyance, and every inn, attracted by scenery, curiosity, superfluous time and wealth, and the fascination of Scott, while, attracted by grouse, the mansion-houses of half of our poor devils of Highland lairds are occupied by rich and titled Southrons. Even the students of Oxford and Cambridge come to the remote villages of Scotland in autumn to study! I found ten of them three years ago, with two tutors, in lodgings at Callander; and a party, also with the tutor and the Greek books, at Inverary last time I was there; and I found both English and Irish youths established now at Oban. The quantity of Greek imbibed, even by the dominie, I can only conjecture, but they can do nothing better for their minds or bodies than breathe such air, in such scenes.

'Skerry Vhor to Ulva'

from The Voyage of the Pharos

WALTER SCOTT (1771–1832)

Some years before Cockburn, in the late summer of 1814 Walter Scott took advantage of the long court recess (he was at that time Sheriff-Depute of Selkirkshire) to sail around Scotland as a guest of the Commissioners of the Northern Lights on board the Lighthouse Yacht Pharos, *on its regular inspection cruise. He resolved to keep a diary throughout the six week voyage and the diary, from which we take this extract, reveals a relaxed Scott with an unusually light humorous touch. At the same time, his journal is a valuable document in which we see the Highlands and Islands of Scotland at a period of significant change and social upheaval. It was also a period when Britain was at war with the United States (this explains the special mention of 'the American' ship). American privateers were taking prizes in Scottish waters and twice the* Pharos *narrowly avoided encounters with them. This extract makes an interesting comparison with the piece by Cockburn, also written by someone with a legal background.*

On the cruise with Scott was Robert Stevenson, engineer to the Commissioners, designer of the famous Bell Rock Lighthouse, founder of the Stevenson dynasty of lighthouse engineers, and, of course, grandfather of Robert Louis Stevenson. One of the highlights of the voyage was the visit to Skerryvore (or Skerry Vhor), the low-lying rock surrounded by dangerous reefs off Tiree, where Stevenson planned to build a lighthouse. His nephew Alan eventually completed it in 1844 from Mull granite. As mentioned earlier in this chapter, Stevenson called it 'the noblest of all extant deep-sea lights' and in verse described the challenge faced by the 'Lighthouse Stevensons':

> *To plant a star for seamen, where was then*
> *The surfy haunt of seals and cormorants.*

27th August, 1814. – The wind, to which we resigned ourselves, proves exceedingly tyrannical, and blows squally the whole night, which, with the swell of the Atlantic, now unbroken by any islands to windward, proves a means of great combustion in the cabin. The dishes and glasses in the steward's cupboards become locomotive-portmanteaus and writing-desks are more active than necessary – it is scarce possible to keep one's self within bed, and impossible to stand upright if you rise. Having crept upon deck about four in the morning, I find we are beating to windward off the Isle of Tyree, with the determination on the part of Mr Stevenson that his constituents should visit a reef of rocks called *Skerry Vhor*, where he thought it would be essential to have a lighthouse. Loud remonstrances on the part of the Commissioners, who one and all declare they will subscribe to his opinion, whatever it may be, rather than continue this infernal buffeting. Quiet perseverance on the part of Mr S., and great kicking, bouncing, and squabbling upon that of the Yacht, who seems to like the idea of Skerry Vhor as little as the Commissioners. At length, by dint of exertion, come in sight of this long ridge of rocks (chiefly under water), on which the tide breaks in a most tremendous style. There appear a few low broad rocks at one end of the reef, which is about a mile in length. These are never entirely under water, though the surf dashes over them. To go through all the forms, Hamilton, Duff, and I resolve to land upon these bare rocks in company with Mr Stevenson. Pull through a very heavy swell with great difficulty, and approach a tremendous surf dashing over black pointed rocks. Our rowers, however, get the boat into a quiet creek between two rocks, where we contrive to land well wetted. I saw nothing remarkable in my way, excepting several seals, which we might have shot, but, in the doubtful circumstances of the landing, we did not care to bring guns. We took possession of the rock in name of the Commissioners, and generously bestowed our own great names on its crags and creeks. The rock was carefully measured by Mr S. It will be a most desolate position for a lighthouse – the Bell Rock and Eddystone a joke to it, for the nearest land is the wild island of Tyree, at fourteen miles' distance. So much for the Skerry Vhor.

Came on board proud of our achievement; and, to the great delight of all parties, put the ship before the wind, and run swimmingly down for Iona. See a large square-rigged vessel, supposed an American. Reach Iona about five o'clock. The inhabitants of the isle of Columba, understanding their interest as well as if they had been Deal boatmen, charged two guineas for Pilotage which Captain W. abridged into fifteen shillings, too much for ten minutes' work. We soon got on shore, and landed in the bay of Martyrs, beautiful for its white sandy beach. Here all dead bodies are still landed, and laid for a time upon a small rocky eminence, called the Sweyne, before they are interred. Iona, the last time I saw it, seemed to me to contain the most wretched people I had anywhere seen. But either they have got better since I was here, or my eyes, familiarized with wretchedness of Zetland and the Harris, are less shocked with that of Iona. Certainly their houses are better than either, and the appearance of the people not worse. This little fertile isle contains upwards of 400 inhabitants, all living upon small farms, which they divide and subdivide as their families increase, so that the country is greatly over-peopled, and in some danger of a famine in case of a year of scarcity. Visit the nunnery and Reilig Oran, or burial-place of St Oran, but the night coming on we return on board.

28th August, 1814. – Carry our breakfast ashore – take that repast in the house of Mr Maclean, the schoolmaster and cicerone of the island – and resume our investigation of the ruins of the cathedral and the cemetery. Of these monuments, more than of any other, it may be said with propriety,

> You never tread upon them but you set
> Your feet upon some ancient history.

I do not mean to attempt a description of what is so well known as the ruins of Iona. Yet I think it has been as yet inadequately performed, for the vast number of carved tombs containing the reliques of the great, exceeds credibility. In general, even in the most noble churches, the number of the vulgar dead exceed in all proportion the few of eminence who are deposited under monuments. Iona is in all respects the reverse; until lately the inhabitants of the isle did not presume to mix their vulgar dust with that of chiefs, reguli, and abbots. The number, therefore, of carved and inscribed tombstones is quite marvellous, and I can easily credit the story told by Sacheverell, who assures us that 300 inscriptions had been collected, and were lost in the troubles of the 17th century. Even now, many more might be deciphered than have yet been made public, but the rustic step of the peasants and of Sassenach visitants is fast destroying these faint memorials of the valiant of the isles. A skilful antiquary remaining here a week, and having (or assuming) the power of raising the half-sunk monuments, might make a curious collection. We could only gaze and grieve; yet had the day not been Sunday, we would have brought our seamen ashore, and endeavoured to have raised some of these monuments. The celebrated ridges called *Jomaire na'n Righrean*, or Graves of the Kings, can now scarce be said to exist, though their site is still pointed out. Undoubtedly, the thirst of spoil, and the frequent custom of burying treasures with the ancient princes, occasioned their early violation; nor am I any sturdy believer in their being regularly ticketed off by inscriptions into the tombs of the Kings of Scotland, of Ireland, of Norway, and so forth. If such inscriptions ever existed, I should deem them the work of some crafty bishop or abbot, for the credit of his diocese or convent. Macbeth is said to have been the last King of Scotland here buried; sixty preceded him, all doubtless as powerful in their day, but now unknown – *carent quia vate sacro*. A few weeks' labour of Shakespeare, an obscure player, has done more for the memory of Macbeth than all the gifts, wealth, and monuments of this cemetery of princes have been able to secure to the rest of its inhabitants. It also occurred to me in Iona (as it has on many similar occasions) that the traditional recollections concerning the monks themselves are wonderfully faint, contrasted with the beautiful and interesting monuments of architecture which they have left behind them. In Scotland particularly, the people have frequently traditions wonderfully vivid of the persons and achievements of ancient warriors, whose towers have long been levelled with the soil. But of the monks of Melrose, Kelso, Aberbrothock, Iona, etc. etc. etc., they can tell nothing but that such a race existed, and inhabited the stately ruins of these monasteries. The quiet, slow, and uniform life of those recluse beings glided on, it may be, like a dark and silent stream, fed from unknown resources, and vanishing from the eye without leaving any marked trace of its course. The life of the chieftain was a mountain torrent thundering over rock and precipice, which, less deep and profound in itself, leaves on the minds of the terrified spectators those deep impressions of awe and wonder which are most readily handed down to posterity.

Among the various monuments exhibited at Iona is one where a Maclean lies in the same grave with one of the Macfies or Macduffies of Colonsay, with whom he had lived in alternate friendship and enmity during their lives. 'He lies above him during death,' said one of Maclean's followers, as his chief was interred, 'as he was above him during life.' There is a very ancient monument lying among those of the Macleans, but perhaps more ancient than any of them; it has a knight riding on horseback, and behind him a minstrel playing on a harp; this is conjectured to be Reginald Macdonald of the Isles, but there seems no reason for disjoining him from his kindred who sleep in the cathedral. A supposed ancestor of the Stewarts called Paul Purser, or Paul the Purse-bearer (treasurer to the King of Scotland), is said to lie under a stone near the Lord of the Isles. Most of the monuments engraved by Pennant are still in the same state of preservation, as are the few ancient crosses which are left. What a sight Iona must have been, when 360 crosses, of the same size and beautiful workmanship, were ranked upon the little rocky ridge of eminences which form the background to the cathedral! Part of the tower of the cathedral has fallen since I was here. It would require a better architect than I am, to say anything concerning the antiquity of these ruins, but I conceive those of the nunnery and of the *Reilig nan Oran*, or Oran's chapel, are decidedly the most ancient. Upon the cathedral and buildings attached to it there are marks of repairs at different times, some of them at late date, being obviously designed not to enlarge the buildings but to retrench them. We take a reluctant leave of Iona, and go on board.

The haze and dulness of the atmosphere seem to render it dubious if we can proceed, as we intended, to Staffa to-day – for mist among these islands is rather unpleasant. Erskine reads prayers on deck to all hands, and introduces a very apt allusion to our being now in sight of the first Christian Church from which Revelation was diffused over Scotland and all its islands. There is a very good form of prayer for the Lighthouse Service, composed by the Rev. Mr Brunton. A pleasure vessel lies under our lee from Belfast, with an Irish party related to Macneil of Colonsay. The haze is fast degenerating into downright rain, and that right heavy-verifying the words of Collins –

> And thither where beneath the showery west
> The mighty Kings of three fair realms are laid.

After dinner, the weather being somewhat cleared, sailed for Staffa, and took boat. The surf running heavy up between the island and the adjacent rock, called Booshala, we landed at a creek near the Cormorant's cave. The mist now returned so thick as to hide all view of Iona, which was our landmark; and although Duff, Stevenson, and I had been formerly on the isle, we could not agree upon the proper road to the cave. I engaged myself, with Duff and Erskine, in a clamber of great toil and danger, and which at length brought me to the *Cannonball*, as they call a round granite stone moved by the sea up and down in a groove of rock, which it has worn for itself, with a noise resembling thunder. Here I gave up my research, and returned to my companions, who had not been more fortunate. As night was now falling, we resolved to go aboard and postpone the adventure of the enchanted cavern until next day. The yacht came to an anchor with the purpose of remaining off the island all night, but the hardness of the ground, and the weather becoming squally, obliged us to return to our safer mooring at Y-Columb-Kill.

29th August, 1814. – Night squally and rainy – morning ditto – we weigh, however, and return toward Staffa, and, very happily, the day clears as we approach the isle. As we ascertained the situation of the cave, I shall only make this memorandum, that when the weather will serve, the best landing is to the lee of Booshala, a little conical islet or rock, composed of basaltic columns placed in an oblique or sloping position. In this way, you land at once on the flat causeway, formed by the heads of truncated pillars, which leads to the cave. But if the state of tide renders it impossible to land under Booshala, then take one of the adjacent creeks; in which case, keeping to the left hand along the top of the ledge of rocks which girdles the isle, you find a dangerous and precipitous descent to the causeway aforesaid, from the table. Here we were under the necessity of towing our Commodore, Hamilton, whose gallant heart never fails him, whatever the tenderness of his toes may do. He was successfully lowered by a rope down the precipice, and proceeding along the flat terrace or causeway already mentioned, we reached the celebrated cave. I am not sure whether I was not more affected by this second, than by the first view of it. The stupendous columnar side walls – the depth and strength of the ocean with which the cavern is filled – the variety of tints formed by stalactites dropping and petrifying between the pillars, and resembling a sort of chasing of yellow or cream-coloured marble filling the interstices of roof – the corresponding variety below, where the ocean rolls over a red, and in some places a violet-coloured rock, the basis of the basaltic pillars – the dreadful noise of those august billows so well corresponding with the grandeur of the scene – are all circumstances elsewhere unparalleled. We have now seen in our voyage the three grandest caverns in Scotland, Smowe, Macallister's cave, and Staffa; so that, like the Troglodytes of yore, we may be supposed to know something of the matter. It is, however, impossible to compare scenes of natures so different, nor, were I compelled to assign a preference to any of the three, could I do it but with reference to their distinct characters, which might affect different individuals in different degrees. The characteristic of the Smowe cave may in this case be called the terrific, for the difficulties which oppose the stranger are of a nature so uncommonly wild as, for the first time at least, convey an impression of terror – with which the scenes to which he is introduced fully correspond. On the other hand, the dazzling whiteness of the incrustations in Macallister's cave, the elegance of the entablature, the beauty of its limpid pool, and the graceful dignity of its arch, render its leading features those of severe and chastened beauty. Staffa, the third of these subterraneous wonders, may challenge sublimity as its principal characteristic. Without the savage gloom of the

Smowe cave, and investigated with more apparent ease, though, perhaps, with equal real danger, the stately regularity of its columns forms a contrast to the grotesque imagery of Macallister's cave, combining at once the sentiments of grandeur and beauty. The former is, however, predominant, as it must necessarily be in any scene of the kind.

We had scarce left Staffa when the wind and rain returned. It was Erskine's object and mine to dine at Torloisk on Loch Tua, the seat of my valued friend Mrs Maclean Clephane, and her accomplished daughters. But in going up Loch Tua between Ulva and Mull with this purpose,

> So thick was the mist on the ocean green,
> Nor cape nor headland could be seen.

It was late before we came to anchor in a small bay presented by the little island of Gometra, which may be regarded as a continuation of Ulva. We therefore dine aboard, and after dinner, Erskine and I take the boat and row across the loch under a heavy rain. We could not see the house of Torloisk, so very thick was the haze, and we were a good deal puzzled how and where to achieve a landing; at length, espying a cart-road, we resolved to trust to its guidance, as we knew we must be near the house. We therefore went ashore with our servants, *à la bonne aventure*, under a drizzling rain. This was soon a matter of little consequence, for the necessity of crossing a swollen brook wetted me considerably, and Erskine, whose foot slipped, most completely. In wet and weary plight we reached the house, after a walk of a mile, in darkness, dirt, and rain, and it is hardly necessary to say that the pleasure of seeing our friends soon banished all recollection of our unpleasant voyage and journey.

Lord Ullin's Daughter

THOMAS CAMPBELL (1777–1844)

Although a Glasgow man by birth and a poet who spent much of his time as a professional writer in England, Thomas Campbell had Argyll connections, as will be guessed from his surname. He was descended from the Campbells of Kirnan, in Glassary.

Rather like James Boswell did with Corsica, Campbell took up the cause of Polish nationalism and expressed his feelings in his first successful long poem 'The Pleasures of Hope' in 1799. His shorter patriotic poems like 'The Battle of the Baltic', 'Hohenlinden' and 'Ye Mariners of England' were based on observations he was able to make on a trip to Europe – he had, for example, the experience of seeing the British fleet which had recently won the battle of Copenhagen. These poems with a martial theme were astonishingly popular for many years and even won him a government pension.

'Lord Ullin's Daughter' is another popular much anthologised early poem, the atmosphere of which he doubtless gathered during the time he spent working as a tutor in Mull and Lochgilphead. The unnamed chieftain, who is eloping with Lord Ullin's child (Ullin is a name from the Ossianic epics), is the chief of Ulva, an island off Mull's west coast. The poem is in ballad metre – Scott, whom Campbell much admired, had published the ballads of The Minstrelsy of the Scottish Border *in 1802. Palgrave, of* Golden Treasury *fame, wrote:*

> *'Lord Ullin's Daughter' has all the four qualities which Matthew Arnold found to be the main characteristics of Homer, rapidity, plainness of thought, plainness of diction, and within its compass nobility. There can scarcely be higher praise for a ballad.*

A Chieftain to the Highlands bound
Cries 'Boatman, do not tarry!
And I'll give thee a silver pound
To row us o'er the ferry!'

'Now who be ye, would cross Lochgyle,
This dark and stormy water?'
'O I'm the chief of Ulva's isle,
And this, Lord Ullin's daughter.

'And fast before her father's men
Three days we've fled together,
For should he find us in the glen,
My blood would stain the heather.

'His horsemen hard behind us ride –
Should they our steps discover,
Then who will cheer my bonnie bride,
When they have slain her lover?'

Out spoke the hardy Highland wight,
'I'll go, my chief, I'm ready:
It is not for your silver bright,
But for your winsome lady: –

'And by my word! the bonny bird
In danger shall not tarry;
So though the waves are raging white
I'll row you o'er the ferry.'

By this the storm grew loud apace,
The water-wraith was shrieking;
And in the scowl of Heaven each face
Grew dark as they were speaking.

But still as wilder blew the wind,
And as the night grew drearer,
Adown the glen rode arméd men,
Their trampling sounded nearer.

'O haste thee, haste!' the lady cries,
'Though tempests round us gather;
I'll meet the raging of the skies,
But not an angry father.'

The boat has left a stormy land,
A stormy sea before her, –
When, oh! too strong for human hand
The tempest gather'd o'er her.

And still they row'd amidst the roar
Of waters fast prevailing:
Lord Ullin reach'd that fatal shore –
His wrath was changed to wailing.

For, sore dismay'd, through storm and shade
His child he did discover: –
One lovely hand she stretched for aid,
And one was round her lover.

'Come back! come back!' he cried in grief,
'Across this stormy water:
And I'll forgive your Highland chief,
My daughter! – Oh, my daughter!'

'Twas vain: the loud waves lash'd the shore,
Return or aid preventing:
The waters wild went o'er his child,
And he was left lamenting.

'Travellers in Argyll'

from Humphry Clinker

TOBIAS SMOLLETT (1721–71)

Humphry Clinker *has been accepted as the best of Tobias Smollett's novels ever since it appeared in 1771, the year of his death. He wrote it during the period 1768 to 1770, mostly while staying in the hills near the Italian resort of Leghorn, where he had gone in a vain attempt to regain his health. As in much of his work, Smollett incorporates autobiographical material, and this is obviously the case with the Scottish section of the novel. This includes a brief tour made by the group of fictional characters, including the eponymous Clinker, to Edinburgh, then to Argyll and finally to Glasgow by way of Loch Lomond and the Vale of Leven, the birthplace of Smollett himself.*

He was born at Dalquhurn near Renton in Dumbartonshire and as a surgeon's apprentice served with the Navy at Cartagena – an experience which he also made use of in his writing. He favoured a fairly loose episodic and picaresque structure but added to this tremendous vitality and a flair for storytelling. Humphry Clinker, *like other early novels in English, is in epistolary form and in the letter from which our extract comes we read of some of the impressions of Scotland, and in particular of Argyll, which are gained by Jerry Melford and Matthew Bramble. Smollett has a nice humorous touch, as when he includes himself as a character, somewhat in the Hitchcockian manner. He tells us of the famous Mull shipwreck of the* Florida, *a ship of the Armada, 'blown up by one of Mr Smollett's ancestors'. (See also Neil Munro's* Treasure Trove.)

'JERRY MELFORD'S LETTER'

The Highlanders, on the contrary, despise this liquor, and regale themselves with whisky; a malt spirit, as strong as geneva, which they swallow in great quantities, without any signs of inebriation. They are used to it from the cradle, and find it an excellent preservative against the winter cold, which must be extreme on these mountains – I am told that it is given with great success to infants, as a cordial in the confluent smallpox, when the eruption seems to flag, and the symptoms grow unfavourable – The Highlanders are used to eat much more animal food than falls to the share of their neighbours in the Low-country – They delight in hunting; have plenty of deer and other game, with a great number of sheep, goats, and black-cattle running wild, which they scruple not to kill as venison, without being much at pains to ascertain the property.

Inverary is but a poor town, though it stands immediately under the protection of the duke of Argyle, who is a mighty prince in this part of Scotland. The peasants live in wretched cabins, and seem very poor; but the gentlemen are tolerably well lodged, and so loving to strangers, that a man runs some risque of his life from their hospitality – It must be observed that the poor Highlanders are now seen to disadvantage – They have been not only disarmed by act of parliament, but also deprived of their ancient garb, which was both graceful and convenient; and what is a greater hardship still, they are compelled to wear breeches; a restraint which they cannot bear with any degree of patience: indeed, the majority wear them, not in the proper place, but on poles or long staves over their shoulders – They are even debarred the use of their striped stuff called Tartane, which was their own manufacture, prized by them above all the velvets, brocades, and tissues of Europe and Asia. They now lounge along in loose great coats, of coarse russet, equally mean and cumbersome, and betray manifest marks of dejection – Certain it is, the government could not have taken a more effectual method to break their national spirit.

We have had princely sport in hunting the stag on these mountains – These are the lonely hills of Morven, where Fingal and his heroes enjoyed the same pastime; I feel an enthusiastic pleasure when I survey the brown heath that Ossian wont to tread; and hear the wind whistle through the bending grass – When I enter our landlord's hall, I look for the suspended harp of that divine bard, and listen in hopes of hearing the aerial sound of his respected spirit – The poems of Ossian are in every mouth – A famous antiquarian of this country, the laird of Macfarlane, at whose house we dined a few days ago, can repeat them all in the original Gallick, which has a great affinity to the Welch, not only in the general sound, but also in a great number of radical words; and I make no doubt that they are both sprung from the same origin. I was not a little surprised, when asking a Highlander one day, if he knew where we should find any game? he replied, 'hu niel Sassenagh', which signifies no English: the very same answer I should have received from a Welchman, and almost in the same words. The Highlanders have no other name for the people of the Low-country, but Sassenagh, or Saxons; a strong presumption, that the Lowland Scots and the English are derived from the same stock – The peasants of these hills strongly resemble those of Wales in their looks, their manners, and habitations; every thing I see, and hear, and feel, seems Welch – The mountains, vales, and streams; the air and climate; the beef, mutton, and game, are all Welch – It must be owned, however, that this people are better provided than we in some articles – They have plenty of red deer and roebuck, which are fat and delicious at this season of the year – Their sea teems with amazing quantities of the finest fish in the world; and they find means to procure very good claret at a very small expence.

'MATTHEW BRAMBLE'S LETTER'

It cannot be expected, that the gentlemen of this country should execute commercial schemes to render their vassals independent; nor, indeed, are such schemes suited to their way of life and inclination; but a company of merchants might, with proper management, turn to good account a fishery established in this part of Scotland – Our people have a strange itch to colonize America, when the uncultivated parts of our own island might be settled to greater advantage.

After having rambled through the mountains and glens of Argyle, we visited the adjacent islands of Ila, Jura, Mull, and Icolmkill. In the first, we saw the remains of a castle, built in a lake, where Macdonald, lord or king of the isles, formerly resided. Jura is famous for having given birth to one Mackcrain, who lived one hundred and eighty years in one house, and died in the reign of Charles the Second. Mull affords several bays, where there is safe anchorage: in one of which, the Florida, a ship of the Spanish armada, was blown up by one of Mr Smollett's ancestors – About forty years ago, John duke of Argyle is said to have consulted the Spanish registers, by which it appeared, that this ship had the military chest on board – He employed experienced divers to examine the wreck; and they found the hull of the vessel still entire, but so covered with sand, that they could not make their way between decks; however, they picked up several pieces of plate, that were scattered about in the bay, and a couple of fine brass cannon.

Icolmkill, or Iona, is a small island which St Columba chose for his habitation – It was respected for its sanctity, and college or seminary of ecclesiastics – Part of its church is still standing, with the tombs of several Scottish, Irish, and Danish sovereigns, who were here interred – These islanders are very bold and dexterous watermen, consequently the better adapted to the fishery: in their manners they are less savage and impetuous than their countrymen on the continent; and they speak the Erse or Gaelick in its greatest purity.

Having sent round our horses by land, we embarked in the distinct of Cowal, for Greenock, which is a neat little town, on the other side of the Frith, with a curious harbour formed by three stone jetties, carried out a good way into the sea – Newport-Glasgow is such another place, about two miles higher up – Both have a face of business and plenty, and are supported entirely by the shipping of Glasgow, of which I counted sixty large vessels in these harbours – Taking boat again at Newport, we were in less than an hour landed on the other side, within two short miles of our head-quarters, where we found our women in good health and spirits – They had been two days before joined by Mr Smollett and his lady, to whom we have such obligations as I cannot mention, even to you, without blushing.

To-morrow we shall bid adieu to the Scotch Arcadia, and begin our progress to the southward, taking our way by Lanerk and Nithsdale, to the west borders of England. I have received so much advantage and satisfaction from this tour, that if my health suffers no revolution in the winter, I believe I shall be tempted to undertake another expedition to the Northern extremity of Caiththness, unencumbered by those impediments which now clog the heels of,

Yours,
MATT. BRAMBLE

Leanabh an Aigh
(Child in a Manger)

MARY MACDONALD (1817–c. 1890)

TRANSLATION BY LACHLAN MACBEAN (1853–1931)

Leanabh an Aigh *(literally* Child of Joy*) is one of the best known Gaelic hymns. It is more easily recognised in its English version by Lachlan MacBean* – Child in a Manger. *Its tune, Bunessan, is now also sung to the words* Christ Be Beside Me *and, of course, Cat Stevens took the same tune for his now internationally famous* Morning has Broken. *'Leanabh an Aigh' was written by Mary MacDonald who came from Brolas on the Ross of Mull. Her family were Baptists and her brother Duncan MacDougall founded the Baptist Church on Tiree. He too composed hymns and published them in the volume* Laoidhean Spirodail a chum cuideachadh le crabhadh nan Gael *(Glasgow) 1841. Lachlan Macbean (1853–1931) whose English version is given here was a journalist from Kiltarlity in Inverness-shire who wrote a number of hymns and songs.*

Leanabh an àigh, an leanabh aig Màiri
Rugadh san stàball, Rìgh nan Dùl;
Thàinig don fhàsach, dh'fhuiling nar n-àite –
Son' iad an àireamh bhitheas dhà dlùth!

Cha b'ionnan 's an t-Uan thàinig gur fuasgladh –
Iriosal, stuama ghluais e'n tùs;
E naomh gun truailleachd, Cruithfhear an t-sluaigh,
Dh'èirich e suas le buaidh on ùir.

Leanabh an àigh, mar dh'aithris na fàidhean;
'S na h-àinglean àrd', b'e miann an sùl;
'S E 's airidh air gràdh 's air urram thoirt dhà-
Sona an àireamh bhitheas dhà dlùth.

CHILD IN A MANGER

Child in a manger, infant of Mary;
Outcast and stranger, Lord of all;
Child who inherits all our transgressions,
All our demerits on him fall.

Once the most holy child of salvation
Gently and lowly lived below;
Now as our glorious mighty Redeemer,
See him victorious o'er each foe.

Prophets foretold him, infant of wonder:
Angels behold him on his throne;
Worthy our Saviour of all their praises;
Happy for ever are his own.

An t-Eilean Muileach
(The Isle of Mull)

DUGALD MACPHAIL (1819–1887)

TRANSLATION BY MALCOLM MACFARLANE

The song An t-Eilean Muileach *or* The Isle of Mull *is one of the most popular of all Gaelic songs. It is frequently sung at ceilidhs and is undoubtedly the anthem of Mull. Not a great deal is known about Dugald MacPhail, its composer. He was born at Strathcoil at the head of Loch Spelve in the south east of the island. Like so many nineteenth-century Gaelic songs this is a song of exile and longing, written when the poet was working in distant Newcastle. The river Lussa ('shining river'), Ben Varnick (shown as Beinn Bhearnach on maps and meaning 'limpet shaped mountain') and Durry-Cooling (Doire a'Chuillin, 'the holly copse') which the composer nostalgically associates with his childhood and youth in stanzas 2 and 3 are all close to his birthplace. A handsome monument to his memory has been erected there on which are engraved the opening words of the song. Other songs by Dugald MacPhail were published in Archibald Sinclair's collection of Gaelic songs* An t-Oranaiche (The Gaelic Songster) *in 1879.*

Séist
An t-Eilean Muileach, an t-eilean àghmhor,
An t-eilean grianach mu'n iath an sàile;
Eilean buadhmhor nam fuar-bheann àrda,
Nan coilltean uaine, 's nan cluaintean fàsail.

Ged tha mi 'm fhògarrach cian air m'aineol,
'Sa'Chaisteal Nuadh, 'san taobh tuath de Shasunn,
Bidh tìr mo dhùthchais a'tighhin fainear dhomh,
An t-Eilean Muileach bu lurach beannaibh.

B'fhallain, cùbhraidh 'bu réidh an t-àilean,
Le' bhlàthan maoth-bog bu chaoine fàileadh;
Bu ghlan na bruachan mu'n d'fhuair mi m'àrach
An Doire-'Chuilinn aig bun Beinn-bhàirneach.

Air Lusa chaisleach nan stac 's nan cuartag,
Bhiodh bradain thàrr-geal nam meanbh-bhall ruadh-bhreac,
Gu beò-bhrisg, siùbhlach, le sùrd ri lùth-cleas
'Na cuislibh dù-ghorm gun ghrùid, gun ruadhan.

Bu chulaidh-shùgraidh do dh'òg-fhir uallach,
Le gathan trì-mheurach, rinneach, cruaidh-glan,
Air caol-chroinn dhìreach, gun ghniamh, gun chnuac-mheòir,
'Bhi toirt nan làn-bhreac gu tràigh mu' bruachan.

B e'n sòlas-intinn leam a bhi 'g éisdeachd
Ri coisir bhinn-ghuthach, grinn a'Chéitein
A'seinn gu sunndach an dlùths nan geugan –
A' choill' fo liath-dhealt', 's a'ghrian ag éirigh!

Chlaon gach sòlas dhiubh sud mar bhruadar,
'S mar bhristeadh builgean air bhàrr nan stuadh-thonn:
Ach soraidh slàn leis gach loinn is buaidh
A bh'air eilean àghmhor nan àrd-bheann fuara.

THE ISLE OF MULL

Chorus
The Isle of Mull is of isles the fairest,
Of ocean's gems 'tis the first and rarest;
Green grassy island of sparkling fountains,
Of waving woods and high towering mountains.

Tho' far from hame I am now a ranger,
In grim Newcastle a doleful stranger,
The thought of thee stirs my heart's emotion
And deeper fixes its fond devotion.

Oh! fresh and fair are thy meadows blooming,
With fragrant blossoms the air perfuming,
Where boyhood's days I've oft spent in fooling,
Around Ben Varnick and Durry-Cooling.

Where Lussa's stream through the pools come whirling,
Or o'er the clear pebbly shallows swirling,
The silvery salmon is there seen playing,
And in the sunbeams his hues displaying.

There might young manhood find fit enjoyment,
In healthy, vigorous, rare employment;
With three-pronged spear on the margin standing,
And with quick dart the bright salmon landing.

How pleasant 'twas in the sweet May morning,
The rising sun thy gay fields adorning;
The feathered songsters their lays were singing,
While rocks and woods were with echoes ringing.

But gone are now all those joys forever,
Like bubbles bursting on yonder river:
Farewell, farewell to thy sparkling fountains,
Thy waving woods and high towering mountains!

Treasure Trove

from The Complete Para Handy

NEIL MUNRO (1863–1930)

In 1905, when he was preparing his Clyde, River and Firth, *Neil Munro first delighted readers of his 'Looker-On' column in the* Glasgow Evening News *with the adventures of Para Handy and the crew of the steam lighter or puffer,* Vital Spark, *'the smertest boat in the coastin' tred'. Munro continued to record the adventures of Para Handy in the* News *for close on twenty years. The stories have never been out of print and their west coast setting, charm, humour and wry social comment have continued to attract readers from every generation.*

Both in newspaper and book form, Munro's creation has become one of the enduring comic characters – as long-lasting as Bertie Wooster, as evergreen as Jerome's Three Men in a Boat. *The stories have been successfully translated into the television medium and stage plays and inspired the 1954 film* The Maggie.

The story chosen for this anthology is one of many dealing with Argyll, most of which are set in Para's (and Munro's) beloved Loch Fyne. In this instance, however, the setting is Tobermory Bay, on Mull, and the story about a beached whale on Calve Island. The title and the name the crew give to the whale, 'The Tobermory Treasure', tells us that Munro is making a wry reference to the perennial interest in the possibility that a bullion ship of the Spanish Armada lies wrecked under the waters of the bay.

The Claymore, *whose passengers mistake the smell of the whale for ozone, was a famous steamer built by William Denny & Bros at Dumbarton in 1881 for David MacBrayne's West Highland services.*

Sunny Jim proved a most valuable acquisition to the *Vital Spark*. He was a person of humour and resource, and though they were sometimes the victims of his practical jokes, the others of the crew forgave him readily because of the fun he made. It is true that when they were getting the greatest entertainment from him, they were, without thinking it, generally doing his work for him – for indeed he was no sailor, only a Clutha mariner – but at least he was better value for his wages than The Tar, who could neither take his fair share of the work nor tell a baur. Sunny Jim's finest gift was imagination; the most wonderful things in the world had happened to him when he was on the Cluthas – all intensely interesting, if incredible: and Para Handy, looking at him with admiration and even envy, after a narrative more extraordinary than usual, would remark, 'Man! it's a peety listenin' to such d — d lies iss a sin, for there iss no doobt it iss a most pleeasant amuusement!'

Macphail the engineer, the misanthrope, could not stand the new hand. 'He's no' a sailor at a'!' he protested; 'he's a clown; I've see'd better men jumpin' through girrs at a penny show.'

'Weel, he's maybe no' aawful steady at the wheel, but he hass a kyind, kyind he'rt!' Dougie said.

'He's chust sublime!' said Para Handy. 'If he was managed right there would be money in him!

Para Handy's conviction that there was money to be made out of Sunny Jim was confirmed by an episode at Tobermory, of which the memory will be redolent in Mull for years to come.

The *Vital Spark*, having discharged a cargo of coal at Oban, went up the Sound to load with timber, and on Calve Island, which forms a natural breakwater for Tobermory harbour, Dougie spied a stranded whale. He was not very much of a whale as whales go in Greenland, being merely a tiny fellow of about five-and-twenty tons, but as dead whales here are as rarely to be seen as dead donkeys, the *Vital Spark* was steered close in to afford a better view, and even stopped for a while that Para Handy and his mate might land with the punt on the islet and examine the unfortunate cetacean.

'My Chove! he's a whupper!' was Dougie's comment, as he reached up and clapped the huge mountain of sea-flesh on its ponderous side. 'It wass right enough, I can see, Peter, aboot yon fellow Jonah; chust look at the accommodation!'

'Chust waste, pure waste,' said the skipper; 'you can make a meal off a herrin', but whales iss only lumber, goin' aboot ass big as a land o' hooses, blowin' aal the time, and puttin' the fear o' daith on aal the other fushes. I never had mich respect for them.'

'If they had a whale like that aground on Clyde,' said Dougie, as they returned to the vessel, 'they would stick bills on't; it's chust thrown away on the Tobermory folk.'

Sunny Jim was enchanted when he heard thc whale's dimensions. 'Chaps,' he said with enthusiasm, 'there's a fortune in't; right-oh! I've see'd them chargin' tuppence to get into a tent at Vinegar Hill, whaur they had naethin' fancier nor a sea-lion or a seal.'

'But they wouldna be deid,' said Para Handy; 'and there's no' mich fun aboot a whale's remains. Even if there was, we couldna tow him up to Gleska, and if we could, he wouldna keep.'

'Jim'll be goin' to embalm him, rig up a mast on him, and sail him up the river; are ye no', Jim?' said Macphail with irony.

'I've a faur better idea than that,' said Sunny Jim. 'Whit's to hinder us clappin' them tarpaulins roon' the whale whaur it's lyin', and showin' 't at a sixpence a heid to the Tobermory folk? Man! ye'll see them rowin' across in hunners, for I'll bate ye there's no much fun in Tobermory in the summer time unless it's a Band o' Hope soiree. Give it a fancy name – the "Tobermory Treasure"; send the bellman roond the toon, sayin' it's on view to-morrow from ten till five and then goin' on to Oban; Dougie'll lift the money, and the skipper and me'll tell the audience a' aboot the customs o' the whale when he's in life. Macphail can stand by the ship at Tobermory quay.'

'Jist what I said a' alang,' remarked Macphail darkly. 'Jumpin' through girrs! Ye'll need a big drum and a naphtha lamp.'

'Let us first paause and consider,' remarked Para Handy, with his usual caution; 'iss the whale oors?'

'Wha's else wad it be?' retorted Sunny Jim. 'It was us that fun' it, and naebody seen it afore us, for it's no' mony oors ashore.'

'Everything cast up on the shore belangs to the Crown; it's the King's whale,' said Macphail.

'Weel, let him come for 't,' said Sunny Jim; 'by the time he's here we'll be done wi't.'

The presumption that Tobermory could be interested in a dead whale proved quite right; it was the Glasgow Fair week, and the local boat-hirers did good business taking parties over to the island where an improvised enclosure of oars, spars, and tarpaulin and dry sails concealed the 'Tobermory Treasure' from all but those who were prepared to pay for admission. Para Handy, with his hands in his pockets and a studied air of indifference, as if the enterprise was none of his, chimed in at intervals with facts in the natural history of the whale, which Sunny Jim might overlook in the course of his introductory lecture.

The biggest whale by three feet that's ever been seen in Scotland,' Sunny Jim announced. 'Lots o' folk thinks a whale's a fish, but it's naething o' the kind; it's a hot-blooded mammoth, and couldna live in the watter mair nor a wee while at a time withoot comin' up to draw its breath. This is no' yin of thae common whales that chases herrin', and goes pechin' up and doon Kilbrannan Sound; it's the kind that's catched wi' the harpoons and lives on naething but roary borealises and icebergs.'

'They used to make umbrella-rubs wi' this parteecular kind,' chimed in the skipper diffidently; 'forbye, they're full o' blubber. It's an aawful useful thing a whale, chentlemen.' He had apparently changed his mind about the animal, for which the previous day he had said he had no respect.

'Be shair and tell a' your friends when ye get ashore that it's maybe gaun on to Oban to-morrow,' requested Sunny Jim. 'We'll hae it up on the Esplanade there and chairge a shillin' a heid; if we get it the length o' Gleska, the price 'll be up to hauf a-croon.'

'Is it a "right" whale?' asked one of the audience in the interests of exact science.

'Right enough, as shair's onything; isn't it, Captain?' said Sunny Jim.

'What else would it be?' said Para Handy indignantly. 'Does the chentleman think there iss onything wrong with it? Perhaps he would like to take a look through it; eh, Jum? Or maybe he would want a doctor's certeeficate that it's no a dromedary.'

The exhibition of the 'Tobermory Treasure' proved so popular that its discoverers determined to run their entertainment for about a week. On the third day passengers coming into Tobermory with the steamer *Claymore* sniffed with appreciation, and talked about the beneficial influence of ozone; the English tourists debated whether it was due to peat or heather. In the afternoon several yachts in the bay hurriedly got up their anchors and went up Loch Sunart, where the air seemed fresher. On the fourth day the residents of Tobermory overwhelmed the local chemist with demands for camphor, carbolic powder, permanganate of potash, and other deodorants and disinfectants; and several plumbers were telegraphed for to Oban. The public patronage of the exibition on Calve Island fell off.

'If there's ony mair o' them wantin' to see this whale,' said Sunny Jim, 'they'll hae to look slippy.'

'It's no' that bad to windward,' said Para Handy. 'What would you say to coverin' it up wi' more tarpaulins?'

'You might as weel cover't up wi' crape or muslin,' was Dougie's verdict. 'What you would need iss armour-plate, the same ass they have roond the cannons in the man-o'-wars. If this wind doesn't change to the west, half the folk in Tobermory'll be goin' to live in the cellar o' the Mishnish Hotel.'

Suspicion fell on the 'Tobermory Treasure' on the following day, and an influential deputation waited on the police sergeant, while the crew of the Vital Spark, with much discretion, abandoned their whale, and kept to their vessel's fo'c'sle. The sergeant informed the deputation that he had a valuable clue to the source of these extraordinary odours, but that unfortunately he could take no steps without a warrant from the Sheriff, and the Sheriff was in Oban. The deputation pointed out that the circumstances were too serious to permit of any protracted legal forms and ceremonies; the whale must be removed from Calve Island by its owners immediately, otherwise there would be a plague. With regret the police sergeant repeated that he could do nothing without authority, but he added casually that if the deputation visited the owners of the whale and scared the life out of them, he would be the last man to interfere.

'Hullo, chaps! pull the hatch efter yez, and keep oot the cold air!' said Sunny Jim, as the spokesman of the deputation came seeking for the crew in the fo'c'sle. 'Ye'd be the better o' some odecolong on your hankies.'

'We thought you were going to remove your whale to Oban before this,' said the deputation sadly.

'I'm afraid,' said Para Handy, 'that whale hass seen its best days, and wouldna be at aal popular in Oban.'

'Well, you'll have to take it out of here immediately anyway,' said the deputation. 'It appears to be your property.'

'Not at aal, not at aal!' Para Handy assured him, 'it belongs by right to His Majesty, and we were chust takin' care of it for him till he would turn up, chairgin' a trifle for the use o' the tarpaulins and the management. It iss too great a responsibility now, and we've given up the job; aren't we, Jum?'

'Right-oh!' said Sunny Jim, reaching for his melodeon; 'and it's time you Tobermory folk were shiftin' that whale.'

'It's impossible,' said the deputation, 'a carcase weighing nearly thirty tons – and in such a condition!'

'Indeed it is pretty bad,' said Para Handy, 'perhaps it would be easier to shift the toon o' Tobermory.'

But that was, luckily, not necessary, as a high tide restored the 'Tobermory Treasure' to its natural element that very afternoon.

Oran nam Prìosonach
(Song about the Prisoners)

JOHN MACLEAN (1827–95)

TRANSLATION BY DONALD E. MEEK

The work of John MacLean from Balemartin in Tiree is very well known, so much so that he is still referred to by his popular title of Bàrd Bhaile Mhàrtainn, the Bard of Balemartin. He wrote love songs and satires and his Calum Beag, *a witty 'send up' of his neighbour of that name, is still frequently sung at ceilidhs. He also wrote political songs and, having involved himself significantly in the land agitation of the 1880s, he became in effect the bard of the local branch of the Land League in Tiree.*

Oran nam Prìosanach *is an example of his political verse. It opens with an idyllic picture of the island which stands in sharp contrast to the rest of the poem (stanzas 5–13) where MacLean vents his anger at the injustices which Highlanders and his people in particular have been subjected to. George, 8th Duke of Argyll owned Tiree. Ducal land policy of creating bigger crofts, almost the size of small farms, was far from popular with a large section of the community because it led to evictions and emigration. The immediate stimulus for this poem was the expiry of a farm lease at Grianal in 1886. Many local people wished it to be divided up into smaller crofts. It was not. The local branch of the Land League, therefore, occupied it by grazing their own animals on it. The Duke was enraged and both police and military were called in to deal with the crisis. On 7th August six islanders were arrested and later charged with trespass and deforcement of the messenger-at-arms and sent to prison in Inveraray jail. They were quickly released on bail – paid by Lachlan MacQuarrie, shopkeeper on Tiree. Charges against three of the men were later dropped. In September a further five men were arrested. All eight were convicted at the High Court in Edinburgh and given custodial sentences ranging from four to sixth months. As a result of public outcry, however, they were all released early in the New Year of 1887.*

The translator, Donald E. Meek, is himself a native of Tiree. He is Professor of Celtic in the University of Aberdeen and is one of the foremost authorities on The Book of the Dean of Lismore *and nineteenth-century Gaelic poetry.*

'S ro fhada tha mi gu tosdach, sàmhach,
Mun eilean ghràdhach a dh'àraich òg mi,
Bhon chaidh a' Bhànrighinn 's an Diùc le chèile
A chur 'na h-èiginn tìr rèidh an eòrna.

An t-eilean uaine tha torrach, snuadhmhor,
'S e 's balla-cuain dha na tonnan mòra;
'S cho fada siar e ri Barraidh 's Ile,
Làn lusan rìomhach, 's e ìosal còmhnard.

Sa mhadainn shamhraidh nuair chinneas seamrag,
'S i geal is dearg air a' mhachair chòmhnard,
Is lurach, blàthmhor a lusan sgiamhach,
Fo dhriùchd na h-iarmailt 's a' ghrian gan òradh.

Tha muran, luachair is biolair uaine
'Na lagain uaigneach far 'n goir an smeòrach;
Is tric a fhuair sinn a' mhil sna bruachan
Bho sheillean luaineach breac-ruadh a' chrònain.

Mun tàinig Diùc ann, no aon de shinnsir,
No Deòrsa rìoghail à rìoghachd Hanòbhair,
Bha 'n t-eilean ìosal, bu lìonmhor àirigh,
Aig clann nan Gàidheal 'na àite còmhnaidh.

Gach eilean ìosal no beanntan àrda,
'S gach gleann bha 'g àrach nan Gàidheal còire,
Tha mòran fàs dhiubh, gun duin' ach cìobair,
O Mhaol Chinntìre gu Taigh Iain Ghròta.

Tìr nan gaisgeach 's nam breacan rìomhach;
B' e uaill na rìoghachd iad ged chaidh am fògar;
Bu lìonmhor àirigh is bà air buaile,
Le ceòl nan gruagach mu bhruachaibh Mòirbheinn.

Chùm iad Cèasar as le chuid lèigion,
Fir Lochlainn ghèill iad do Chaledònia;
Aig blàr na Leirge chaidh ruaig air Hàcon;
'S e meud a thàmailt thug bàs ri bròn dha.

Is tha luchd-àiteachaidh an eilein ìosail
Fo ghrunnan millteach, gun àite còmhnaidh,
'S e 'n-diugh 'na fhàsach aig luchd am mìoruin
A chuir sa phrìosan ar gillean òga.

An Inbhir-aora, toll dubh a' chruadail,
Gun dhùnadh suas iad a Luan 's a Dhòmhnach;
Ach bha de dh' uaisle an com MhicGuaire
Nach biodh iad uair ann nam fuasgladh òr iad.

Theich na tràillean bho chùis na h-aimhreit
Mar nì an t-aingidh gun aon an tòir air;
Gun deach an tilleadh; cha robh ach breugan
An cùirt Dhun Eideann; bu lèir siud dhòmhsa.

B' iad sin na saighdearan smearail, lùthmhor,
A thighinn don dùthaich bho Chrùn Rìgh Deòrsa;
Gach fear ma seach dhiubh toirt eachdraidh ghàbhaidh
Air each MhicPhàidein bha 'n àite còirneil.

Chaidh sinne bhuaireadh le luchd an tuaileis,
Ach sheasadh suas leinn airson na còrach,
Gu fearail, cliùiteach, air chùl nan Gàidheal,
Mar rinn ar càirdean san Eilean Cheòthmhor.

SONG ABOUT THE PRISONERS

For too long I have been quiet and silent
about the much-loved island which reared me,
since the Queen and the Duke have collaborated
to reduce to desperation the level-surfaced land of barley.

This green, productive, pleasant island
is surrounded by an ocean-wall formed by great breakers;
it lies as far west as Barra and Islay,
and is full of pretty flowers – a low-lying expanse.

On a summer morning when the shamrock grows
white and red on the level machair,
its beautiful flowers are many-coloured and attractive
under the dew of the sky, as the sun gilds them.

Marram-grass, rushes and green water-cress
adorn its secluded hollows where the thrush sings;
frequently we discovered honey in the banks,
deposited by the restless, brown-speckled,
    humming bee.

Before the Duke arrived there or any of his ancestors,
or royal George of the family of Hanover,
the low-lying island with its many shielings
belonged to Highlanders as a dwelling-place.

All low-lying islands and high mountains
and every glen which reared the hospitable Highlanders
are, in most cases, deserted, with nobody but a shepherd,
from the Mull of Kintyre to John O'Groats.

This is the land of fine tartans and heroes
who were the pride of the nation, though now exiled;
it had many shielings and cows in cattle-folds,
with maidens' songs around the banks of Morven.

They kept out Caesar and all his legions,
the Norsemen surrendered to Caledonia;
at the Battle of Largs Haakon was routed;
he was so deeply humiliated that he died in grief.

The inhabitants of the low-lying island,
in subjection to a destructive minority, have no
    place to live;
today it has been laid waste by those who despise us,
who have put in prison our young lads.

In Inveraray, that black hole of hardship,
they were incarcerated Monday and Sabbath;
but there was sufficient nobleness in MacQuarrie's breast
to ensure that they would not be there one hour, if gold
    could release them.

The wretches fled from the scene of the confrontation,
as the wicked flees when no man pursues him;
they were driven back; there was nothing but lies
in the Edinburgh court; that was clear to me.

What clever, strong soldiers those were
to come to the island by order of the Crown of King George;
every one in turn was telling a terrifying story
about MacFadyen's horse,[1] that took the place
    of a colonel.

We have been troubled by scandal-mongers,
but we stood up for what was just,
in a manly, honourable manner, supporting our
    fellow Highlanders,
as did our kinspeople in the Misty Isle.[2]

[1] MacFadyen's horse: this is a reference to the horse of Alan MacFadyen who owned the Scarinish hotel. MacFadyen was accompanying the sheriff when his horse became a danger to a crowd of children and had to be restrained by the protesters.
[2] The Misty Isle: the Isle of Skye.

Oran Luaidh
(Waulking Song)

COLLECTED AND TRANSLATED BY

ALEXANDER CARMICHAEL (1832–1912)

An 'òran luaidh' or 'waulking song' is a rhythmic work song which used to be sung by women when they were fulling cloth. Modern folk groups and bands have often adapted waulking songs to help generate a modern musical idiom that has authentic roots in the folk tradition.

This particular waulking song was collected by Alexander Carmichael on the island of Coll and published in his Carmina Gadelica. *In it the woman blames the Campbells for the loss of her lover whom she wished to marry. The 'stìom' or 'snood' was a headband worn by unmarried women. The 'bréid' or 'kertch' was a head-dress, made of a square of fine linen, which was worn by married women.*

Hó haoi ri hó ro

Mhic Fhir Shórasdail, mo rùn ort!
'S oil liom fhéin a chuir air chùl thu,
Is air-san a chall a dhùthcha;
Gun tig siod fhathast gu cunntas,
Gum bi Caimbeulaich 'gan sgiùrsadh,
Sgabadh air prasgan an t-sùghain.

'S truagh gun mi 's mo rogha céile
Anns a' choill ud thall ag éirigh;
Gur math a nighinn do léine,
Thiormaichinn i air bharr nan geugan,
Bheirinn glan an làimh do phéid i.

'S truagh nach robh mis 's an t-òg gasd
Air mullach nam beann geura casa,
Gun duine beò bhith 'gar faicinn.
Thigeamaid gu cliùiteach dhachaigh,
Reachadh an stìom dhearg am pasgadh,
Reachadh am bréid beannd san fhasan.

WAULKING SONG

Ho haoi ri ho ro

My love is to thee, son of the laird of Sórasdal!
I hate the man who has cast thee down,
And against him who destroyed his country;
That will yet come to be reckoned,
The Campbells will be driven out,
And the rabble of the sowens scattered.

Sad that I and my chosen love
Were not in yonder wood arising;
Well would I wash thy shirt,
I would dry it on the tips of the boughs,
I would set it clean in thy page's hand.

Sad that I and the splendid youth
Were not on the summit of the sharp steep peaks,
With no living man beholding us.
In good repute we would come home,
The red snood would be folded by,
The peaked kertch would come into fashion.

'The Free Church Yacht'

from The Cruise of the Betsey

HUGH MILLER (1802–56)

Hugh Miller, geologist, journalist, Free Churchman and folklorist, was born in Cromarty in 1802. A wild and fiercely independent boy, he took to wandering the beaches of Easter Ross in preference to attending school and indeed his formal schooling came to an abrupt end after a fight with his schoolmaster. Those early experiences of the land and the time he spent apprenticed to a stonemason gave him an interest in geology which he translated into three best-selling books, The Old Red Sandstone, Footprints of the Creator *and* The Testimony of the Rocks. *It also informed a number of articles for the* Witness *newspaper and the book from which this extract is taken,* The Cruise of the Betsey, *or* A Summer Ramble among the Fossiliferous Deposits of the Hebrides, *which was published posthumously in 1857, the year after he killed himself during a bout of overworking and stress. The book's editor phrased it thus: 'Naturalists of every class know too well how Hugh Miller died – the victim of an overworked brain; and how that bright and vigorous spirit was abruptly quenched for ever'.*

The Betsey *was indeed a yacht used by a Free Church minister as 'a home on the sea beside his island charge' (the Small Isles). This cruise took place in 1844, the year after the Disruption, and the minister in question would have lost his manse when he left the 'Auld Kirk', as part of that great upheaval in Presbyterianism.*

The sun-light was showering its last slant rays on island and loch, and then retreating upwards along the higher hills, chased by the shadows, as our boat quitted the bay of Oban, and stretched northwards, along the end of green Lismore, for the Sound of Mull. We had just enough of day left as we reached mid sea, to show us the gray fronts of the three ancient castles – which at this point may be at once seen from the deck – Dunolly, Duart, and Dunstaffnage; and enough left us as we entered the Sound, to show, and barely show, the Lady Rock, famous in tradition, and made classic by the pen of Campbell, raising its black back amid the tides, like a belated porpoise. And then twilight deepened into night, and we went snorting through the Strait with a stream of green light curling off from either bow in the calm, towards the high dim land, that seemed standing up on both sides like tall hedges over a green lane. We entered the Bay of Tobermory about midnight, and cast anchor amid a group of little vessels. An exceedingly small boat shot out from the side of a yacht of rather diminutive proportions, but tautly rigged for her size, and bearing an outrigger astern. The water this evening was full of phosphoric matter, and it gleamed and sparkled around the little boat like a northern aurora around a dark cloudlet. There was just light enough to show that the oars were plied by a sailor-like man in a Guernsey frock and that another sailor-like man – the skipper, mayhap – attired in a cap and pea-jacket, stood in the stern. The man in the Guernsey frock was John Stewart, sole mate and half the crew of the Free Church yacht *Betsey*; and the skipper-like man in the pea-jacket was my friend the minister of the Protestants of Small Isles. In five minutes more I was sitting with Mr Elder beside the little iron stove in the cabin of the *Betsey*; and the minister, divested of his cap and jacket, but still looking the veritable skipper to admiration, was busied in making us a rather late tea.

The cabin – my home for the greater part of the three following weeks, and that of my friend for the greater part of the previous twelvemonth – I found to be an apartment about twice the size of a common bed, and just lofty enough under the beams to permit a man of five feet eleven to stand erect in his nightcap. A large table, lashed to the floor, furnished with tiers of drawers of all sorts and sizes, and bearing a writing desk bound to it a-top, occupied the middle space, leaving just room enough for a person to pass between its edges and the narrow coffin-like beds in the sides, and space enough at its fore-end for two seats in front of the stove. A jealously-barred skylight opened above; and there depended from it this evening a close lanthorn-looking lamp, sufficiently valuable, no doubt, in foul weather, but dreary and dim on the occasions when all one really wished from it was light. The peculiar furniture of the place gave evidence to the mixed nature of my friend's employment. A well-thumbed chart of the Western Islands lay across an equally well-thumbed volume of Henry's *Commentary*. There was a Polyglot and a spy-glass in one corner, and a copy of Calvin's *Institutes*, with the latest edition of *The Coaster's Sailing Directions* in another; while in an adjoining state-room, nearly large enough to accommodate an arm-chair, if the chair could have but contrived to get into it, I caught a glimpse of my friend's printing-press and his case of types, canopied overhead by the blue ancient of the vessel, bearing in stately six-inch letters of white bunting, the legend, 'FREE CHURCH YACHT'. A door opened which communicated with the forecastle; and John Stewart, stooping very much to accommodate himself to the low-roofed passage, thrust in a plate of fresh herrings, splendidly toasted, to give substantiality and relish to our tea. The little rude forecastle, a considerably smaller apartment than the cabin, was all a-glow with the bright fire in the coppers, itself invisible: we could see the chain-cable dangling from the hatchway to the floor, and John Stewart's companion, a powerful-looking, handsome young man, with broad bare breast, and in his shirt sleeves, squatted full in front of the blaze, like the household goblin described by Milton, or the 'Christmas Present' of Dickens. Mr Elder left us for the steamer, in which he prosecuted his voyage next morning to Skye; and we tumbled in, each to his narrow bed – comfortable enough sort of resting-places, though not over soft; and slept so soundly, that we failed to mark Mr Elder's return for a few seconds, a little after daybreak. I found at my bedside, when I awoke, a fragment of rock which he had brought from the shore, charged with Liasic fossils; and a note he had written, to say that the deposit to which it belonged occurred in the trap immediately above the village-mill; and further, to call my attention to a house near the middle of the village, built of a mouldering red sandstone which had been found *in situ* in digging the foundations. I had but little time for the work of exploration in Mull, and the information thus kindly rendered enabled me to economize it.

The village of Tobermory resembles that of Oban. A quiet bay has its secure island-breakwater in front; a line of tall, well-built houses, not in the least rural in their aspect, but that seem rather as if they had been transported from the centre of some stately city entire and at once, sweeps round its inner inflection like a bent bow; and an amphitheatre of mingled rock and wood rises behind. With all its beauty, however, there hangs about the village an air of melancholy. Like some of the other western-coast villages, it seems not to have grown piecemeal, as a village ought, but to have been made wholesale, as Frankenstein made his man; and to be ever asking, and never more incessantly than when it is at its quietest, why it should have been made at all? The remains of the *Florida*, a gallant Spanish ship, lie off its shores, a wreck of the Invincible Armada, 'deep whelmed', according to Thomson,

> What time,
> Snatched sudden by the vengeful blast,
> The scattered vessels drove, and on blind shelve,
> And pointed rock that marks th' indented shore,
> Relentless dashed, where loud the northern main
> Howls through the fractured Caledonian isles.

Macculloch relates, that there was an attempt made, rather more than a century ago, to weigh up the Florida, which ended in the weighing up of merely a few of her guns, some of them of iron greatly corroded; and that, on scraping them, they became so hot under the hand that they could not be touched, but that they lost this curious property after a few hours' exposure to the air. There have since been repeated instances elsewhere, he adds, of the same phenomenon, and chemistry has lent its solution of the principles on which it occurs; but in the year 1740, ere the riddle was read, it must have been deemed a thoroughly magical one by the simple islanders of Mull. It would seem as if the guns, heated in the contest with Drake, Hawkins, and Frobisher, had again kindled, under some supernatural influence, with the intense glow of the lost battle.

* * *

We weighed anchor about two o'clock, and beat gallantly out the Sound in the face of an intermittent baffling wind and a heavy swell from the sea. I would fain have approached nearer the precipices of Ardnamurchan, to trace along their inaccessible fronts the strange reticulations of trap figured by Macculloch; but prudence and the skipper forbade our trusting even the docile little *Betsey* on one of the most formidable lee shores in Scotland, in winds so light and variable, and with the swell so high. We could hear the deep roar of the surf for miles, and see its undulating strip of white flickering under stack and cliff. The scenery here seems rich in legendary association. At one tack we bore into Bloody Bay, on the Mull coast – the scene of a naval battle between two island chiefs; at another, we approached, on the mainland, a cave inaccessible save from the sea, long the haunt of a ruthless Highland pirate. Ere we rounded the headland of Ardnamurchan, the slant light of evening was gleaming athwart the green activities of Mull, barring them with long horizontal lines of shadow, where the trap terraces rise step beyond step, in the characteristic stair-like arrangement to which the rock owes its name; and the sun set as we were bearing down in one long tack on the Small Isles. We passed the Isle of Muck, with its one low hill; saw the pyramidal mountains of Rum looming tall in the offing; and then, running along the Isle of Eigg, with its colossal Scuir rising between us and the sky, as if it were a piece of Babylonian wall, or of the great wall of China, only vastly larger, set down on the ridge of a mountain, we entered the channel which separates the island from one of its dependencies, Eilean Chaisteil, and cast anchor in the tideway about fifty yards from the rocks. We were now at home, – the only home which the proprietor of the island permits to the islanders' minister; and, after getting warm and comfortable over the stove and a cup of tea, we did what all sensible men do in their own homes when the night wears late – got into bed.

'The Scots and Ireland'

from The Poems of Ossian

JAMES MACPHERSON (1736–96)

A Highland schoolmaster; a colonial officer in Florida; an MP for a Cornwall constituency; a noted libertine of Boswellian proportions; buried at his own expense in Westminster Abbey – all of these are descriptions of James Macpherson, who achieved superstardom with the translations (or authorship) of the Gaelic verse epics, Fingal *and* Temora. *He had fans as diverse as Napoleon Bonaparte and Thomas Jefferson. Even Goethe, who later recanted or perhaps saw through Macpherson, had been at one time so overwhelmed by his discovery of 'Ossian' that he included a huge chunk in his own sensationally successful* Sorrows of Young Werther. *Morven is the name given to the land of Fingal – it seems to refer to much of the west of Scotland rather than simply the Morvern of today.*

This extract is not from the poetic works but from A Dissertation *which Macpherson wrote as a preamble to* Temora. *In this he seeks to validate the distinctness of the third-century epic poems which he claimed to have discovered and translated, and does so by maintaining that the Scots were not people from Ireland, but native to Scotland. It followed that the Ossianic epics were more Scottish than anything. The controversy has continued since the 1760s right up to the present day. Interestingly, Dr Ewan Campbell, an archaeologist at the University of Glasgow, has recently published a book,* Saints and Sea Kings, *which appears to endorse some at any rate of Macpherson's contentions. Campbell is quoted as saying:*

> *The indigenous people of Argyll (based on Dunadd) assimilated their neighbours, the Picts and Anglo-Saxons, to produce their own distinctive culture... The archaeological evidence is convincing that it was the Scots themselves who were responsible for the flowering of culture in early medieval Scotland.*

Ossian has not only preserved the history of the first migration of the Caledonians into Ireland, he has also delivered some important facts, concerning the first settlement of the *Firbolg*, or *Belgœ of Britain*, in that kingdom, under their leader Larthon, who was ancestor to Cairbar and Cathmor, who successively mounted the Irish throne, after the death of Cormac, the son of Artho. I forbear to transcribe the passage, on account of its length. It is the song of Fonar, the bard; towards the latter end of the seventh book of Temora. As the generations from Larthon to Cathmor, to whom the episode is addressed, are not marked, as are those of the family of Conar, the first king of Ireland, we can form no judgment of the time of the settlement of the Firbolg. It is, however, probable, it was some time before the *Caël*, or Caledonians, settled in Ulster. – One important fact may be gathered from this history of Ossian, that the Irish had no king before the latter end of the first century. Fingal lived, it is certain, in the third century; so Conar, the first monarch of the Irish, who was his grand-uncle, cannot be placed farther back than the close of the first. The establishing of this fact, lays, at once, aside the pretended antiquities of the Scots and Irish, and cuts off the long list of kings which the latter give us for a millennium before.

Of the affairs of Scotland, it is certain, nothing can be depended upon, prior to the reign of Fergus, the son of Erc, who lived in the fifth century. The true history of Ireland begins somewhat later than that period. Sir James Ware, who was indefatigable in his researches after the antiquities of his country, rejects, as mere fiction and idle romance, all that is related of the antient Irish, before the time of St Patrick, and the reign of Leogaire. It is from this consideration, that he begins his history at the introduction of christianity, remarking, that all that is delivered down, concerning the times of paganism, were tales of late invention, strangely mixed with anachronisms and inconsistencies. Such being the opinion of Ware, who had collected with uncommon industry and zeal, all the real and pretendedly antient manuscripts, concerning the history of his country, we may, on his authority, reject the improbable and self-condemned tales of Keating and O'Flaherty. Credulous and puerile to the last degree, they have disgraced the antiquities they meant to establish. It is to be wished, that some able Irishman, who understands the language and records of his country, may redeem, ere it is too late, the genuine antiquities of Ireland, from the hands of these idle fabulists.

By comparing the history preserved by Ossian with the legends of the Scots and Irish writers, and, by afterwards examining both by the test of the Roman authors, it is easy to discover which is the most probable. Probability is all that can be established on the authority of tradition, ever dubious and uncertain. But when it favours the hypothesis laid down by contemporary writers of undoubted veracity, and, as it were, finishes the figure of which they only drew the out-lines, it ought, in the judgment of sober reason, to be preferred to accounts framed in dark and distant periods, with little judgment, and upon no authority.

Concerning the period of more than a century, which intervenes between Fingal and the reign of Fergus, the son of Erc or Arcath, tradition is dark and contradictory. Some trace up the family of Fergus to a son of Fingal of that name, who makes a considerable figure in Ossian's poems. The three elder sons of Fingal, Ossian, Fillan, and Ryno, dying without issue, the succession, of course, devolved upon Fergus, the fourth son and his posterity. This Fergus, say some traditions, was the father of Congal, whose son was Arcath, the father of Fergus, properly called the first king of Scots, as it was in his time the *Caël*, who possessed the western coast of Scotland, began to be distinguished, by foreigners, by the name of *Scots*. From thence forward, the Scots and Picts, as distinct nations, became objects of attention to the historians of other countries. The internal state of the two Caledonian kingdoms has always continued, and ever must remain, in obscurity and fable.

It is in this epoch we must fix the beginning of the decay of that species of heroism, which subsisted in the days of Ossian. There are three stages in human society. The first is the result of consanguinity, and the natural affection of the members of a family to one another. The second begins when property is established, and men enter into associations for mutual defence, against the invasions and injustice of neighbours. Mankind submit, in the third, to certain laws and subordinations of government, to which they trust the safety of their persons and property. As the first is formed on nature, so, of course, it is the most disinterested and noble. Men, in the last, have leisure to cultivate the mind, and to restore it, with reflection, to a primæval dignity of sentiment. The middle state is the region of compleat barbarism and ignorance. About the beginning of the fifth century, the Scots and Picts were advanced into the second stage, and, consequently, into those circumscribed sentiments, which always distinguish barbarity. – The events which soon after happened did not at all contribute to enlarge their ideas, or mend their national character.

About the year 426, the Romans, on account of domestic commotions, entirely forsook Britain, finding it impossible to defend so distant a frontier. The Picts and Scots, seizing this favourable opportunity, made incursions into the deserted province. The Britons, enervated by the slavery of several centuries, and those vices, which are inseparable from an advanced state of civility, were not able to withstand the impetuous, though irregular attacks of a barbarous enemy. In the utmost distress, they applied to their old masters, the Romans, and (after the unfortunate state of the Empire could not spare aid) to the Saxons, a nation equally barbarous and brave, with the enemies of whom they were so much afraid. Though the bravery of the Saxons repelled the Caledonian nations for a time, yet the latter found means to extend themselves, considerably, towards the South. It is, in this period, we must place the origin of the arts of civil life among the Scots. The seat of government was removed from the mountains to the plain and more fertile provinces of the South, to be near the common enemy, in case of sudden incursions. Instead of roving through unfrequented wilds, in search of subsistance, by means of hunting, men applied to agriculture, and raising of corn. This manner of life was the first means of changing the national character. – The next thing which contributed to it was their mixture with strangers.

In the countries which the Scots had conquered from the Britons, it is probable that most of the old inhabitants remained. These incorporating with the conquerors, taught them agriculture, and other arts, which they themselves had received from the Romans. The Scots, however, in number as well as power, being the most predominant, retained still their language, and as many of the customs of their ancestors, as suited with the nature of the country they possessed. Even the union of the two Caledonian kingdoms did not much affect the national character. Being originally descended from the same stock, the manners of the Picts and Scots were as similar as the different natures of the countries they possessed permitted.

What brought about a total change in the genius of the Scots nation, was their wars, and other transactions with the Saxons. Several counties in the south of Scotland were alternately possessed by the two nations. They were ceded, in the ninth age, to the Scots, and, it is probable, that most of the Saxon inhabitants remained in possession of their lands. During the several conquests and revolutions in England, many fled, for refuge, into Scotland, to avoid the oppression of foreigners, or the tyranny of domestic usurpers; in so much, that the Saxon race formed perhaps near one half of the Scottish kingdom. The Saxon manners and language daily gained ground, on the tongue and customs of the antient Caledonians, till, at last, the latter were entirely relegated to inhabitants of the mountains, who were still unmixed with strangers.

It was after the accession of territory which the Scots received, upon the retreat of the Romans from Britain, that the inhabitants of the Highlands were divided into clans. The king, when he kept his court in the mountains, was considered, by the whole nation, as the chief of their blood. Their small number, as well as the presence of their prince, prevented those divisions, which, afterwards, sprung forth into so many separate tribes. When the seat of government was removed to the south, those who remained in the Highlands were, of course, neglected. They naturally formed themselves into small societies, independent of one another. Each society had its own *regulus*, who either was, or in the succession of a few generations, was regarded as chief of their blood. – The nature of the country favoured an institution of this sort. A few valleys, divided from one another by extensive heaths and impassible mountains, form the face of the Highlands. In these valleys the chiefs fixed their residence. Round them, and almost within sight of their dwellings, were the habitations of their relations and dependents.

The seats of the Highland chiefs were neither disagreeable nor inconvenient. Surrounded with mountains and hanging woods, they were covered from the inclemency of the weather. Near them generally ran a pretty large river, which, discharging itself not far off, into an arm of the sea, or extensive lake, swarmed with variety of fish. The woods were stocked with wild-fowl; and the heaths and mountains behind them were the natural seat of the red deer and roe. If we make allowance for the backward state of agriculture, the valleys were not unfertile; affording, if not all the conveniencies, at least the necessaries of life. Here the chief lived, the supreme judge and law-giver of his own people; but his sway was neither severe nor unjust. As the populace regarded him as the chief of their blood, so he, in return, considered them as members of his family. His commands therefore, though absolute and decisive, partook more of the authority of a father, than of the rigor of a judge. – Though the whole territory of the tribe was considered as the property of the chief, yet his vassals made him no other consideration for their lands than services, neither burdensome nor frequent. As he seldom went from home, he was at no expence. His table was supplied by his own herds, and what his numerous attendants killed in hunting.

In this rural kind of magnificence, the Highland chiefs lived, for many ages. At a distance from the seat of government, and secured, by the inaccessibleness of their country, they were free and independent. As they had little communication with strangers, the customs of their ancestors remained among them, and their language retained its original purity. Naturally fond of military fame, and remarkably attached to the memory of their ancestors, they delighted in traditions and songs, concerning the exploits of their nation, and especially of their own particular families. A succession of bards was retained in every clan, to hand down the memorable actions of their forefathers. As the æra of Fingal, on account of Ossian's poems, was the most remarkable, and his chiefs the most renowned names in tradition, the bards took care to place one of them in the genealogy of every great family. – That part of the poems, which concerned the hero who was regarded as ancestor, was preserved, as an authentic record of the antiquity of the family, and was delivered down, from race to race, with wonderful exactness.

The bards themselves, in the mean time, were not idle. They erected their immediate patrons into heroes, and celebrated them in their songs. As the circle of their knowledge was narrow, their ideas were confined in proportion. A few happy expressions, and the manners they represent, may please those who understand the language; their obscurity and inaccuracy would disgust in a translation. – It was chiefly for this reason, that I kept wholly to the compositions of Ossian, in my former and present publication. As he acted in a more extensive sphere, his ideas are more noble and universal; neither has he so many of those peculiarities, which are only understood in a certain period or country. The other bards have their beauties, but not in that species of composition in which Ossian excels. Their rhimes, only calculated to kindle a martial spirit among the vulgar, afford very little pleasure to genuine taste. This observation only regards their poems of the heroic kind; in every other species of poetry they are more successful. They express the tender melancholy of desponding love, with irresistible simplicity and nature. So well adapted are the sounds of the words to the sentiments, that, even without any knowledge of the language, they pierce and dissolve the heart. Successful love is expressed with peculiar tenderness and elegance. In all their compositions, except the heroic, which was solely calculated to animate the vulgar, they give us the genuine language of the heart, without any of those affected ornaments of phraseology, which, though intended to beautify sentiments, divest them of their natural force. The ideas, it is confessed, are too local, to be admired, in another language; to those who are acquainted with the manners they represent, and the scenes they describe, they must afford the highest pleasure and satisfaction.

Soraidh Slàn le Fionnairidh
(Farewell to Fiunary)

REV. DR NORMAN MACLEOD (1783–1862)

TRANSLATION BY ARCHIBALD SINCLAIR

Norman MacLeod is a major figure in the history of Highland society. For the massive work he did to relieve poverty in the 1830s and 40s and for his sterling work in promoting the Church of Scotland's scheme for education for the Highlands and Islands (which included the publication of a quarto edition of the Gaelic Bible) he earned the soubriquet 'Caraid nan Gaidheal' (Friend of the Gaels), the name by which he is referred to by Highlanders to this day.

Among his many written works his two periodicals An Teachdaire Gaelach *(1829–1831) and* Cuairtear nan Gleann *(1840–1843) were most influential. Before this there was no tradition of popular prose writing in Gaelic and in these periodicals MacLeod sought to make available to Gaels in their own language articles on topics such as history, current affairs, science, geography and religious matters whilst also including short stories of a homiletic nature. A selection of his prose writings was published under the title* Caraid nan Gaidheal *by his son-in-law Rev. Archibald Clerk in 1867. MacLeod is very much the father of modern Gaelic prose.*

MacLeod was born and brought up in the manse of Fiunary in Morvern where his father Norman was the parish minister. Like so many Gaels, however, he had to leave home for education and work and this song which he wrote in English (and which was later translated into Gaelic by Archibald Sinclair) depicts feelings of exile and nostalgia which are to be found so often in Gaelic songs and poems. It is interesting also to note the references to Ossian and Fingal. Morvern had been the setting for the famous prose poems Fingal *and* Temora *of James MacPherson (1736–1796).*

Tha'n latha math, s'an soirbheas ciùin;
Tha'n uine 'ruith, 's an t-àm dhuinn dlùth,
Tha'm bàt' 'gam fheitheamh fo a siùil,
     Gu'm thoirt a null a Fionnairidh.

Séist
Eirich agus tiugainn O,
Eirich agus tiugainn O,
Eirich agus tiugainn O,
     Mo shoraidh slàn le Fionnairidh.

Tha ioma mìle ceangal blàth,
Mar shaighdean annam fèin an sàs,
Mo chridhe 'n impis a bhi sgàinnt'
     A chionn bhi 'fàgail Fhionnairidh.

Bu tric a ghabh mi sgrìob leam fhèin
Mu'n chuairt air lùchairt Fhinn an trèin;
'S a dh'éisd mi sgeulachdan na Fèinn'
     'Gan cur an cèill am Fionnairidh.

Bu tric a sheall mi feasgar Màirt
Far am biodh Oisean 'seinn a dhàin;
A'coimhead grèin aig ioma tràth
     'Dol seach gach là 's mi 'm Fionnairidh.

Beannachd le beanntaibh mo ghaoil
Far am faigh mi'm fiadh le 'laogh, –
Gu ma fad' an coileach-fraoich
     A' glaodhaich ann am Fionnairidh.

Ach cha'n iad glinn 'us beanntan àrd'
A lot mo chrìdh' 's a rinn mo chràdh,
Ach an diugh na tha fo phràmh
     An teach mo ghràidh am Fionnairidh.

Beannachd le athair mo ghràidh;
Bidh mi 'cuimneach ort gu bràth;
Ghuidhinn sonas agus àgh
     Do'n t-sean fhear bhàn am Fionnairidh.

Am feum mi siubhal uait gun dàil?
Na siùil tha togte ris a bhàt' –
Soraidh slàn, le tir mo ghràidh,
    'Us slàn, gu bràth le Fionnairidh!

FAREWELL TO FIUNARY

The wind is fair, the day is fine,
And swiftly swiftly runs the time;
The boat is floating on the tide,
    That wafts me off from Fiunary.

Chorus
We must up and be away!
We must up and be away!
We must up and be away!
    Farewell, farewell to Fiunary.

A thousand, thousand tender ties –
Accept this day my plaintive sighs;
My heart within me almost dies
    At thought of leaving Fiunary.

With pensive steps I've often strolled
Where Fingal's castle stood of old,
And listened while the shepherds told
    The legend tales of Fiunary.

I've often paused at close of day
Where Ossian sang his martial lay,
And viewed the sun's departing ray,
    When wand'ring o'er Dun Fiunary.

Farewell ye hills of storm and snow
The wild resorts of deer and roe;
In peace the heath-cock long may crow
    Along the banks of Fiunary.

'Tis not the hills or woody vales
Alone my joyless heart bewails;
A mournful group this day remains
   Within the manse of Fiunary.

Can I forget Glenturret's name?
Farewell, dear father, best of men:
May heaven's joys with thee remain
   Within the Manse of Fiunary.

Oh must I leave those happy scenes?
See, they spread the flapping sails,
Adieu! adieu! my native plains;
   Farewell, farewell to Fiunary!

'Ardnamurchan Story'

from Night Falls on Ardnamurchan

ALASDAIR MACLEAN (1926–94)

The poet Alasdair Maclean produced Night Falls on Ardnamurchan *as a memoir of his parents who had been crofters at remote Sanna on this, the westernmost part of the mainland of Britain. After his father's death Maclean discovered that for around twenty years he had kept a diary which gave a graphic account of the unimaginably hard life endured by crofters on Ardnamurchan. He originally intended to have the journal published in its entirety, but then decided to choose extracts and link them with his own commentary and reflections. The result is a wonderful book, full of poetic insight mixed with the immediacy of descriptions like the one which tells of the high winds that blow in that part of Argyll, winds so high that at times a man has to crawl around the croft on all fours. Our extract is, however, taken from the introduction to the book which gives a fascinating account of the history and character of Ardnamurchan.*

Doctor Johnson and James Boswell did not include Ardnamurchan on their 1773 tour of the Highlands and Islands, but the area is mentioned when the Laird of Lochbuie on Mull asks about the Doctor's origins. Boswell reports:

> *Being told that Dr Johnson did not hear well, Lochbuy bawled out to him, 'Are you of the Johnstons of Glencro, or of Ardnamurchan?' – Dr Johnson gave him a significant look, but made no answer; and I told Lochbuy that he was not Johnston, but Johnson, and that he was an Englishman.*

For most of its long life Ardnamurchan has lain as far off the beaten track in history as it does in geography. The great tides that surged to and fro across Scotland, tossing plumes and pennants in their midst and drowning the screams of the dying in their wake, made but a ripple or two here. The Norsemen came and conquered but eventually went. Various feudal chieftains debated the overlordship with one another, when they were not being overwhelmed by the superior rhetoric of the Stuart kings and their mighty vassals, the Campbell Dukes of Argyll. James IV visited Mingary

Castle at Kilchoan, in 1493, to pretend that he was receiving the submission of the unruly Hebridean chiefs. Much good it did him, for he was back two years later on the same fruitless errand. After that he turned his attention to the English, who unfortunately were never much interested in pretenders and who were shortly to demonstrate their superior grasp of reality at Flodden. Ardnamurchan slumbered on.

It came to life briefly in 1519 when the Lord of the Isles decided that he might as well add the place to his territories, it being undoubtedly Hebridean and for all practical purposes an isle. The Lord of Ardnamurchan objected and the two met to settle their differences on the flat ground below Craig an Airgid, which is a hill overlooking the present road, halfway between Sanna and Kilchoan. A skirmish only, the engagement rates no mention in the history books, yet it was deadly enough. One wonders in passing how much blood has been spilled up and down the land, unrewarded even by the parrot cries of schoolboys because there were but ninety-nine gallons of it lost at a time, instead of a hundred. On this occasion the Lord of the Isles proved the better butcher. The Lord of Ardnamurchan, however, retained possession of a small part of the field, some six feet by six, being sufficient to cover himself and his two sons. There he lies still, if our new bounty hunters, with their clickety-click machines have not dug him up. Where the ordinary men of Ardnamurchan, who fell in their common heaps around these luminaries, have their burial is not recorded. Perhaps they awaited the attentions of those earlier bounty hunters, the Highland ravens, who also went 'clickety-click' as they whetted their great black bills.

Pretending had another of its periodic Highland efflorescences in the eighteenth century, so beloved of Scottish historians. How satisfying it is to be able to write down merely 'the 15' or 'the 45' and have all men know instantly what you refer to! Here's romance for you, here's fame! Such an internationally-understood shorthand is not often permitted our parchments. It gives one the feeling of being a member of a cosy club, where the password is a mystic number.

Ardnamurchan was hardly a member of this club, for all that Charles Stuart landed nearby. Passing through the area he patted a little girl, who had been brought out from her home to see him, on the head. She was a grandmother of mine, several times great and was ever afterwards known by a Gaelic designation meaning 'the girl who was singled out by the Prince'. There is no record in my family that she became any wiser or richer or more beautiful. The Prince went on to Edinburgh, where the girls were bigger and the patting adjusted to correspond.

Later in the same century Ardnamurchan was to come under the spotlight once more, and finally, when Cruikshank discovered at Strontian a mineral which he named strontianite and from which was later extracted strontium. And much good that did him, or anybody else either.

While all this was going on superficially, as a scum on the surface, no doubt the old compact between man and the land was elsewhere being renewed each spring. One imagines the people of Ardnamurchan, when they could avoid the recruiting sergeant, beginning the slow process of trying to take possession of their birthright. It was a process that was never to reach fruition. Like crofters everywhere we of present-day Ardnamurchan still live on and walk over land that others own, go we north, south, east or west, and still we find that generations of back-breaking toil and starvation have brought no more than a quasi-legal sufferance.

As the nineteenth century approached, then, a pattern of crofting began to emerge in these parts. Slowly the townships took form and filled with men and women crudely sheltered, workers of two or three dyked-off acres, possessors of a cow if they were lucky and a potato patch and perhaps a corn patch; burners of peat; cobblers and weavers of their own rough wear; of a self-sufficiency that was due to the emptiness of their pockets rather than the generosity of nature; essentially tenant farmer in minuscule but without the security of even a quarterly agreement; more accurately, indeed, squatters, though they squatted on land that was theirs if it were anyone's; above all, bitterly, bitterly poor.

The Church, almost the only source of charity, did what it could to alleviate hardship, though it exacted its own peculiar return. The Session Records of those days, still extant for the Parish of Ardnamurchan, make harrowing reading. On 26 November 1789, for instance, the minister and elders, in Session, found themselves to be in possession of six pounds seven shillings in Church funds. They retained one pound for emergencies and distributed the rest among forty-one of their poorest parishioners. John Henderson of Achnaha, aged seventy-seven, received five shillings, for example. Mary MacColl of the same hamlet received two and sixpence and Duncan MacLauchlan (described factually and bluntly as 'a Changeling'; one of several so called) had three shillings. 1790 sees a long list of three- and four-shilling distributions. In 1797 one notes that John Henderson of Achnaha, by now aged eighty-one, was allowed eleven shillings 'because his wife, Anne Macdonald, aged eighty-three, was equally frail and destitute'.

Sometimes the charity was in kind instead of cash. In 1779 the then owner of Ardnamurchan – and how strange that sounds when one considers it, though as a rule we recognize such strangeness only when we magnify the occasion and talk about, say, the owner of Britain – the then owner, Sir James Miles Riddell, empowered the distribution of twenty bolls of meal among the poor. Archibald MacArthur of Sanna got four stones but Christy Henderson of Swordle only two. One wonders how much deprivation went into qualifying as a four-stone person. One pictures the great day when the Factor's horse and cart arrived to begin the distribution: 'Four-stone people on the left, two-stone on the right.'

The Church paid for funerals, too, when the relatives were unable to do so and regularly among the accounts for this period one sees three shillings for a coffin and one shilling for the accompanying bottle of whisky. The latter item might scandalize some readers. 'How can you claim poverty for these people yet tell us that they splashed liquor around at their funerals?' I have wondered about the whisky myself. Was it perhaps doled out among the grieving relations along the lines of the strong drink that used to be recommended for patients having teeth out? One gulp equals one gap? But, no; one bottle in a crowd of men – a sip a-piece – would ensure neither anaesthesia nor licence nor yet serve as the simple stimulant it was later to become. The whisky was surely ritual, and age-old at that; time was when it would have been poured into the ground.

The income of the Church derived from various sources. There were the fines imposed by the Session for moral lapses: non-attendance at divine service or sexual relations outside wedlock. These ranged from one pound to three pounds and in the case of sexual misbehaviour seem to have been imposed jointly; evidently the view taken was that both parties were equally guilty. On 19 July 1837, Duncan Maclachlan, Glendrian and Christy Henderson, Achnaha, for instance, were jointly fined three pounds for illicit sex. She was his late wife's sister.

What nonsense! How better, I should like to know, might one assuage one's grief than in the arms of the next nearest and dearest? For God's sake, what could be more natural or more seemly? And is not three pounds a savage price to pay for a moment's closeness to another human being, bearing in mind that as an object of charity rather than a reluctant benefactor you would be lucky to receive a tenth of that sum?

The Church in Ardnamurchan inherited, too, the interest on a few small legacies and there were also, of course, the usual Sunday collecting boxes. Income from the latter, as might be expected, was pitifully small; a penny-halfpenny was a common total at Kilchoan and a penny at Kilmory.

Fornication was not the only crime that might cost one money then, nor was the Church the only levier of fines outside the civil authority. There was also the Factor to be reckoned with, the right-hand man of the estate owner, serving as his bailiff and his thumbscrews. The Factor, indeed, was essentially the civil law in a place as remote as Ardnamurchan. (It was like being 'West of the Pecos' in early Texas, and under the dominion of that brigand and self-styled judge – Roy Bean.) On the 19 July 1837, for example, the Ardnamurchan Factor fined 'a son of James Henderson' and 'a son of John MacGlashan', both of Achnaha, the sum of five shillings for 'spoiling a horse's tail'. (Horse hair had a number of uses, such as providing 'gut' for a fishing line, and if you did not have a horse yourself you might try, as these lads did, to sever a few strands from the tail of one of the estate horses. At five shillings, however – possibly two years' income if you were a charitable case – your fish would be dearly bought.) Again, on 13 January 1838, Alexander MacKenzie of Sanna was fined twelve and sixpence by the Factor for 'cutting saplings in the enclosure at Coirevulin'. (This man, finding himself evicted and shelterless, had returned to his former home to cut roof timbers for a new house. I suppose that few Ardnamurchan cottages were worth twelve and sixpence lock, stock and barrel.)

Estate owners – Proprietors as they were generally called then – came and went and if they ordered their comings and goings entirely without reference to their living chattels it is fair to add that not all of them were ogres by any means. The best of them, however, came up against a problem that all along bedevilled humane and well-meaning landlords in the Highlands (e.g. Lord Lever, the soap manufacturer, who was willing to spend a fortune on his Island tenants). This was the problem of helping a people whose one huge and overriding wish was to be left alone. Ardnamurchan had its own Lord Lever in the shape of a Victorian magnate called Rudd, a former partner of Cecil Rhodes and a very wealthy man in his own right. Across the bay from Sanna lies a hamlet called Portuairk, a classically-marginal West Highland crofting community, huddled on a few poor acres of half-cultivable land between mountains and sea. Rudd once offered to translate the entire village over the hill to better ground where he would provide new houses and new crofts. He was turned down cold and retired baffled to his castle in Glenborrodale.

It may not be desirable or lovable to be stiff-necked to such a degree but there are worse attitudes to have. Were Rudd to make that offer to some present-day Ardnamurchan crofters he would find not merely his new houses grabbed but would be lucky if his castle were not demanded into the bargain.)

One gets the impression of a people of complex character, pushing independence up to and a little beyond whatever limit was available to them at a particular time, yet utterly lacking that fierce pride to be found in, say, the Plains Amerindians or the Pathan tribesmen. Rather than the latter we see a people gentle and dreamy, biddable – despite their independence – to the point of a fatalistic passivity. The most astonishing thing about the notorious Highland Clearances of the nineteenth century, given their widespread nature, the large numbers of crofters cleared and the frequent callousness and brutality involved, is surely the almost complete absence of resistance. Yet the men who allowed themselves to be thus herded off their land, in the same fashion as the sheep that replaced them were herded on to it, albeit with somewhat less granted them in the way of consideration, were the grandsons, many of them, of the men who charged with hand weapons the English field artillery on Culloden Moor.

Passive suffering is not necessarily an endearing trait. Faced with a man who accepts a savagely unjust burden without complaint, one's reaction is often to add an item or two to his load. At times it seemed that nature itself was becoming irritated with the Highlander. One indication of this came with the devastating epidemics such as smallpox that swept up from the south, creating unimaginable havoc in a folk whose blood cells were as unsophisticated as their minds. There still exists in Sanna, below the present little church, a pond, *Lochan Cuilc* (the Pool of the Reeds), where in 1830 a man called Neil Macdonald, of Portuairk, a man with a freak immunity to the then current epidemic and the only 'old wife' available, used to strip and bathe on his way home after laying out the latest batch of Sanna corpses.

Another such portent came with the mid-nineteenth-century failure of the potato crop, the Great Hunger. Yet none of these plagues became as enshrined in Gaelic legend as did the Clearances, though their effect, even considered severally, was much more severe. No doubt they were somewhat less amenable to the folk-song treatment or sounded less pathetically glamorous when trotted out with the whisky at the evening ceilidh. You would have to be a dull raconteur indeed not to be able to draw a tear or two with the story of how your great-granny was rifle-butted by the soldiers and had her rafters burned above her head. It is harder to make capital out of pustules and diarrhoea.

Of the Clearances themselves, the restocking of the great Highland estates with profitable sheep and deer and the forced resettling on still more marginal land of the unprofitable crofters, too much has already been written. Clearances certainly took place in Ardnamurchan. Sanna, for example, though people had dwelt there at least since neolithic times, was settled in its present form about 1830 by crofters who were evicted from further up the peninsula, from villages like Swordle. But the

Ardnamurchan clearances seem to have been more for non-payment of rent than because the Proprietor had discovered a better use for his land. A year's notice was given and there was no burning of houses and no physical force. Perhaps in the long run the evicted crofters were no worse off, in the harsh sense that they went from being dirt poor to being dirt poor. In Sanna, certainly, new houses had to be built and new crofts hacked out of a bog and patiently coaxed into something resembling fertility. At least the incomers had the grim satisfaction of reaching the end of the road: literally, for having been driven to the very tip of the peninsula they could be driven no further; and financially, for having been robbed of all they owned they could not be robbed again. A more positive benefit occurred when the international outcry over the genuinely bloody-minded and occasionally bloody Sutherland clearances at last brought crofters everywhere what security of tenure they now possess.

To blame the Clearances for all the ills of the Highlands or even for most of them is a belief so distorted as to bear no resemblance to reality, though it is a belief that seems to hold a fatal charm for many Highlanders. There is something in the Celtic character continually seeking to draw a perverted nourishment from dwelling on disaster, continually fostering in the dark of the mind a lovely sense of betrayal. Your Highlander is your scab-picker extraordinary. Truly, one might almost say that if the Clearances had not taken place it would have been necessary to institute them. Of course, they provided readily identifiable villains and an easy short-cut to the emotions – of natives and pseudo-natives – and that is a lot simpler than thinking hard about the problem of the Highlands and evolving a complex solution in which you yourself might have to shoulder part of the blame.

Ardnamurchan reached its apotheosis as a crofting area as the twentieth century dawned. People were still very poor but it was not exactly the grinding and deadly grub-in-the-fields-for-roots poverty of the previous two hundred years. Not quite. Paying work was obtainable – mostly elsewhere, it is true, but communications and transport had improved to the point where a man could go off for a year or two to earn some money. Most crofters now owned a brace of cows and a scattering of poultry. Crofts and the art of working them had reached their final perfected form. Families were large; there were bodies enough and to spare for both private and communal endeavour. Young folk remained in their villages; there was a pool of potential mates and potential child-bearers. Education was freely available and good; in the width and depth of their knowledge and in the extent of their thirst for it crofters of my father's generation could put many school-leavers of today to shame. Tourism, that *ignis fatuus* of the modern Highlands, had not yet begun to lead astray those it purported to be guiding. Bureaucracy had not yet strangled initiative nor initiative become so lacking in taste and so self-centred as to require bureaucratic check. It was a late flowering and while the blossom was still opening the rot was creeping up the stem.

It is difficult to say what happened. Part of the answer is suggested in the body of this book and implied in the above paragraph. Findings might be subsumed under some such heading as 'The Onward March of Time'. Ardnamurchan has suffered a bad attack of history. There was never anything immutable about the old West Highland way of life; like much else of interest and nobility it came, achieved its hour and passed. Crofts and crofters evolved in response to a specific set of circumstances; those circumstances have now altered out of all recognition. If they come round again, as well they may, I shall not see it. But when I reflect that I knew that way of life, even in the yellow leaf, I am filled with pride and love.

I have always looked on the ferry that crosses the Narrows of the Linnhe Loch at Corran as a kind of mobile decompression chamber where various kinds of pollution were drained from the blood and I was fitted to breathe pure air again. On the far side lay Ardgour, with its jetty and its huddle of white houses. Once across one was in the *echt* Highlands. The road turns west at Ardgour, or the best part of it does; if not yet within sight of the Hebrides, the heart of Gaeldom on earth, one is at least within reach of their spell. To go on is to be protected and fed; if one is lucky enough and receptive enough, touched with goodness.

That road winds down through Strontian and Salen and Glenborrodale and Kilchoan and at last trickles to a halt on the *machair* at Sanna. Beyond land, here at land's end, lie only a handful of islands and Labrador. Electricity arrived two years ago. Most of the houses now have piped water and septic tank sewage. There is even a weekly refuse collection. Yet the nearest shop and the nearest post office are six miles off, in Kilchoan, the nearest policeman and doctor thirty, in Strontian, the nearest town and the nearest hospital fifty, at Fort William. If you include bookshops among your necessities, as I do, you have a hundred and twenty miles to go, to Inverness.

In the small hours of one night my father had a heart attack. A nurse had first of all to be summoned (six miles). She inspected him and authorized the rousing of a doctor (thirty miles). The doctor came, made an examination and called out an ambulance (fifty miles). It was decided to take the patient to the better-equipped hospital at Inverness (a hundred and twenty miles). By the time Father was at last stretchered away from Sanna it was well on in the forenoon. The initial thirty miles of his journey were over a single-track road notorious for its roughness. He lasted as far as Salen (twenty-five miles). Still in the ambulance he had a second and massive thrombosis and died.

Respect and admiration for the past do not always balance the difficulties of the present. If, like my crofting ancestors, you have no choice about where you live or the means by which you encompass your living, that is one thing. Choosing such a life of your own free will is another. There is no spiritual value in poverty or in isolation in themselves, or if there is I was too busy being hungry and lonely to find it. I am rendered ill at ease by luxury but I have never seen why one should deliberately elect bone-bare circumstances when one might own a modest degree of comfort, and I am all in favour of combining the best of both worlds in this world, if it can be managed, since I do not count greatly on the world to come. There exists today, among certain of those who forsake the town for the country, a cult of the spartan, a notion that – for instance – where electricity is available and can be paid for it yet should be rejected in favour of oil lamps. I have no sympathy with such thinking. Living in Ardnamurchan offers consolations many and sweet, some of which I hope emerge in my pages, but it is not all scenery and skittles, even for those of us who can afford to stay indoors when the gales blow. Television reception in Sanna is poor and, such as it is, requires special and expensive equipment. Radio reception, even on VHF, is equally bad and the best programmes are the hardest to get. Obtaining the better newspapers varies from difficult to impossible. There are no concert halls, theatres, cinemas or libraries. If by chance you find yourself a little depressed one day and decide that a grilled chop for supper might offer solace – forget it. You will discover neither restaurant nor butcher on the corner. There is no corner. Extract what joy you can from a tin of beans.

And if these things do not matter to you, reader, then you are fortunate; they matter a good deal to me. Of Sanna I may not be the reluctant lover quite, but I reckon myself a clear-eyed and clear-headed one. Above all, I am not in the business of creating glamour where none exists. It is here, perhaps more than most places, a question of deciding how you want to live – and why.

4

KINTYRE AND ISLAY
Introduction

We have used Kintyre and Islay as a shorthand description for all that part of Argyll south of the Crinan Canal. We thus include, with due apologies to their residents, the equally interesting district of Knapdale and the islands of Jura, Colonsay and Gigha.

This long peninsula and its adjacent islands is perhaps one of the lesser known areas of Argyll, although in scenic beauty and historic interest it equals any other. Part of the reason for this relative unfamiliarity is a modern preoccupation with land transport which makes Campbeltown a remote and isolated community. In earlier days, when the Lords of the Isles ruled a sea-kingdom from Finlaggan on Islay, the sea was a uniting, not a dividing feature and the sea-girt communities of Argyll were more easily linked the one to the other and across the narrow channel to Ireland.

The narrow neck of land at Tarbert, separating Knapdale from Kintyre, was of course the scene of that most famous of Viking exploits when, in 1098, the splendidly named Magnus Barelegs had himself dragged overland in a Viking longship, thus enabling him to claim that as he had sailed round it, Kintyre was an island and so rightfully part of his Hebridean kingdom. This exploit was, if Walter Scott's *The Lord of the Isles* is to believed, repeated by the Highland forces joining Bruce in the War of Independence:

> Ever the breeze blows merrily,
> But the galley ploughs no more the sea,
> Lest, rounding wild Cantyre, they meet
> The southern foeman's watchful fleet.
> They held unwonted way; –
> Up Tarbat's western lake they bore,
> Then dragg'd their bark the isthmus o'er,

As far as Kilmaconnel's shore,
Upon the eastern bay.

Kilmaconnel, or Kilcalmonell, being still the name of the parish in which
the Royal Burgh of Tarbert is located.

Further south at Campbeltown, or Kilkerran as it was formerly known
before the House of Argyll asserted its dominance over this part of the
world, the traveller Thomas Pennant observed, with some distaste, the
local distilling industry. After noting the amount of barley or bere raised
locally he comments:

> ... there is often a sort of dearth; the inhabitants being mad enough to
> convert their bread into poison, distilling annually six thousand bolls of
> grain into whisky ...
>
> The Duke of Argyle, the principal proprietor of this country, takes great
> pains in discouraging this pernicious practice; and obliges all his tenants to
> enter into articles, to forfeit five pounds and the still, in case they are
> detected in making this *liqueur d'enfer*, but the trade is so profitable that
> many persist in it to the great neglect of manufactures.

So important was the 'infernal liquor' to Campbeltown's economy that
at the time of the Second Statistical Account there were 25 licensed
distilleries in the burgh and the individual character of Campbeltown
malt whisky is still recognised by its separate identity alongside
Highland, Island, Islay and Lowland malts in the classification of whisky.
Sadly, the industry in Campbeltown has now shrunk almost to vanishing
point with only the great names of Springbank and Scotia remaining.

A resident of Campbeltown, appearing in court before Lord Cockburn
in 1838, gave a curious account of her daily routine:

> For about twenty-five years she has scarcely ever been in bed after five. The
> first thing she does after dressing is, to go to a rock about a mile off, and to
> take a large draught of sea water. She then proceeds about another mile, in a
> different direction, where she washes the taste of this out by a large draught
> of fresh water, after which she proceeds home, and about half past six puts
> on the tea-kettle and breakfasts. This is a healthy and romantic seeming
> morning. And therefore I regret to add that it was proved that three or four
> times a week the rest of the day is given to whisky ...

Whether the Campbeltown seamstress was enabled to continue in her
whisky drinking by this curious regime does not emerge from the learned
judge's remarks.

Islay's place in Scottish history is secure with its many associations
with the Lords of the Isles – its neighbour, Jura's, place in world literature

is equally secure. It was at the remote farmhouse of Barnhill in the north end of Jura, that George Orwell lived from May 1947 to December 1948, while finishing what must be seen as one of the defining works of the twentieth century, the bleak portrait of life under the all-seeing gaze and rule of Big Brother, *Nineteen Eighty-Four*. In between revising his last masterpiece, Orwell, suffering from the tuberculosis that would kill him in January 1950, explored the island and had an alarmingly close encounter with the Corrievreckan whirlpool.

Nì h-éibhneas gan Chlainn Domhnaill
(It is no joy without Clan Donald)

GIOLLA COLUIM MAC AN OLLAIMH (fl. c. 1490)

TRANSLATION BY W. J. WATSON

Nì h-éibhneas gan Chlainn Domhnaill (It is no joy without Clan Donald) *was written by the bard Giolla Coluim Mac an Ollàimh and appears in the Book of the Dean of Lismore. This fine poem is written in the bardic tradition of panegyric. It extols the virtues and generosity of Clan Donald in great detail in the traditional bardic manner and at the same time laments the disintegration of the Lordship of the Isles.*

In 1140 Somerled, Thane of Argyll and progenitor of the clan to which his grandson Donald gave his name, led a Gaelic resurgence against the Viking occupation of the Hebrides. His descendants maintained their independence and Angus Og MacDonald's support for Robert Bruce in the Scottish Wars of Independence ensured that they were allowed to maintain their hold on their by now extensive territories in the highlands and islands. From 1350 to 1493 (the period of the Lordship of the Isles) the lands of Clan Donald had extended to cover the Inner and Outer Hebrides and the territories along the whole West Highland coastline. The Lordship operated as an independent state administered by the Lord of the Isles and his Council which met at Finlaggan on Islay. The castle at Ardtornish in Morvern on the Sound of Mull was also a favourite residence. The Lords of the Isles were frequently in conflict with the lowland Kings of Scots and their governments and often sought to oppose them by making alliances with disaffected Scottish factions and with the English. Indeed, John the fourth and last Lord of the Isles was forfeited in 1475 and, although he was restored on this occasion, finally in 1493, after his nephew Alexander's invasion of Ross, the Scottish Parliament forfeited him again. He was deprived of estates and title. In 1494 he came to Edinburgh and made formal resignation of the Lordship to King James IV. The decline in the fortunes of Clan Donald with the demise of the Lordship made way for the hegemony in Argyll of their great rivals, Clan Campbell.

Nì h-éibhneas gan Chlainn Domhnaill is clearly inspired by the misfortunes which befell the ruling family of the Isles in the last quarter of the fifteenth century. Its author, Giolla Coluim Mac an Ollàimh, was a highly trained court bard of the ruling house of the Isles. He was a member of a learned bardic family, almost certainly the MacMhuirichs, the most distinguished in Scotland. He has two other deftly wrought poems in the Book of the Dean of Lismore. *One of these is a lament for Angus Og (the illegitimate son of John, the fourth Lord of the Isles) who was murdered in 1488 and with whom, as confidant and generous patron, the poet clearly enjoyed a good relationship.*

1. Ní h-éibhneas gan Chlainn Domhnaill,
      ní comhnairt bheith 'na n-éagmhais,
an chlann dob fhearr san gcruinne:
      gur dhíobh gach duine céatach.

2. Clann as saoire dár dealbhadh,
      i roibh eangnamh is ághas;
clann dárbh umhail na tíorain,
      i roibh críonnacht is crábhadh.

3. Clann chunnail chalma chródha,
      clann ba teódha i n-am troda;
clann ba mhíne i measg bantracht,
      agus ba chalma i gcogadh.

4. Clann ba líonmhoire eireacht,
      dob fhearr eineach is áireamh;
clann nár chathuigh ar eaglais,
      clann lérbh eagail a gcáineadh.

5. Uaithne ána Alban uaine,
      clann as cruaidhe ghabh bhaisteadh;
'gá roibh treas gacha tíre,
      seabhaig Íle ar ghaisgeadh.

6. Clann ba mhó is ba mhire,
      clann ba ghrinne is ba réidhe;
clann dob fhairsinge croidhe,
      dob fhearr foidhide is féile.

7. Meic ríogh nár thuill a n-aoradh,
   i roibh daonnacht is truime;
fir allta uaisle fhonnmhor,
   i roibh bronntacht is buige.

8. Clann dob fhearr feidhm is faisgeadh,
   clann dob fhearr gaisgeadh láimhe;
olc liom giorrad a h-íorna,
   'n bhé lér sníomhadh a snáithe.

9. Níorbh iad na droichfhir bhodhra,
   ná na fir lobhra laga;
ré dol i n-ionad bhuailte
   fir nach cruaidhe na craga.

10. Clann gan uabhar gan éagcáir,
    nár ghabh acht éadáil chogaidh;
'gar mheanmnach daoine uaisle,
    is agar bhuaine bodaigh.

11. Mairg ó rugadh an fheadhain,
    mairg do dheadhail ré gcaidreabh;
gan aonchlann mar Chlainn Domhnaill,
    saorchlann ba chomhnairt aigneadh.

12. Gan áireamh ar a n-urdail,
    gan chuntadh ar a nduaisibh;
gan chrích gan tús gan deireadh
    ar eineach agá n-uaislibh.

13. I dtosach Clainne Domhnaill
    do bhí foghlaim 'gá fáithneadh,
agus do bhí 'na ndeireadh
    feidhm is eineach is náire.

14. Ar bhrón agus ar thuirse
    do thréigeas tuigse is foghlaim;
gach aoinní ortha thréigeas:
    ní h-éibhneas gan Chlainn Domhnaill.

15. Dobadh tréan gaoth ag tíorain
      fán aicme chríonna chomhnairt:
 gé táid i ndiu fá dhímheas,
      ní h-aoibhneas gan Chlainn Domhnaill.

16. Na slóigh as fearr san gcruinne
      a muirn a mire a bhfoghnamh;
ní comhnairt bheith 'na bhféagmhais:
      ní h-éibhneas gan Chlainn Domhnaill.

17. Macán láimhe [   ]
      dár saoradh ar gach doghrainn:
gé tá sé dhúinne díleas,
      ní h-aoibhneas gan Chlainn Domhnaill.

IT IS NO JOY WITHOUT CLAN DONALD

1. It is no joy without Clan Donald; it is no strength to be without them; the best race in the round world; to them belongs every goodly man.

2. The noblest race of all created, in whom dwelt prowess and terribleness; a race to whom tyrants bowed, in whom dwelt wisdom and piety.

3. A race kindly, mighty, valorous; a race the hottest in time of battle; a race the gentlest among ladies, and mightiest in warfare.

4. A race whose assembly was most numerous, the best in honour and in esteem; a race that made no war on church, a race whose fear it was to be dispraised.

5. Brilliant pillars of green Alba, a race the hardiest that received baptism; a race who won fight in every land, hawks of Islay for valour.

6. A race the greatest and the most active; a race the comeliest and calmest of temper; a race the widest of heart, the best in patience and in liberality.

7. Sons of kings, who deserved not satire, in whom were manliness and dignity; men untamed, noble, hearty, who were open-handed and generous.

8. A race the best for service and for shelter; a race the best for valour of hand; ill I deem the shortness of her skein, by whom their thread was spun.

9. Not they the miserly men and deaf, nor yet men weak and feeble; to go where blows were struck they were men than whom the rocks were not harder.

10. A race without arrogance, without injustice, who seized naught save spoil of war; whose nobles were men of spirit, and whose common men were most steadfast.

11. Alas for those who have lost that company; alas for those who have parted from their society; for no race is as Clan Donald, a noble race, strong of courage.

12. There was no counting of their bounty; there was no reckoning of their gifts; their nobles knew no bound, no beginning, no end of generosity.

13. In the van of Clan Donald learning was commanded, and in their rear were service and honour and self-respect.

14. For sorrow and for sadness I have forsaken wisdom and learning; on their account I have forsaken all things: it is no joy without Clan Donald.

15. Mighty was the blast of tyrants against that tribe wise and strong; though to-day they are unhonoured, it is no joy without Clan Donald.

16. The best people in the round world – their joyousness, their keenness, their effectiveness; without them is no strength; it is no joy without Clan Donald.

17. The Babe of the hand [   ], may He save us from every evil; though He to us is dear, it is no joy without Clan Donald.

Jura and Islay

from A Description of the Western Islands of Scotland

MARTIN MARTIN (c.1660–1719)

Martin Martin's book was first published in 1703 and among its claims to fame is the fact that it was one of the inspirations behind Samuel Johnson's decision to visit the Hebrides and a copy of the first edition accompanied Johnson and Boswell on their travels. Despite this, Dr Johnson thought little of Martin's literary style, however much the vivid descriptions of this almost unknown region provoked his interest and curiosity.

Martin was born near Duntulm in Skye, graduated as Master of Arts from Edinburgh University in 1681 and worked as a tutor or 'governor' to various Skye families. In later life he followed the long established Scots tradition of going overseas to study, in his case at Leiden in the Netherlands, where he graduated as Doctor of Medicine. He died in London in 1719.

His account of the Western Isles is the first significant work on the subject, written by a native of the region, since the Description *compiled by Donald Monro, the Dean of the Isles in 1549.*

Martin's description of these two islands is slightly curious in that he devotes more space to Jura than to Islay, despite the latter island's immense historical significance as the seat of the Lordship of the Isles. His description of the remarkable healthiness of Jura – a veritable island paradise where gout and agues were not known, nobody suffered from insanity, and death in childbirth had not occurred for 34 years – does lead one to wonder why the Lords of the Isles had not established their residence and courts there. Perhaps as a result of this healthiness he tells of Gillouir MacCrain who 'lived to have kept one hundred and eighty Christmasses in his own house'. His information on these matters comes of course from the residents and Martin had the great advantage that travellers such as Pennant, Johnson and Faujas de St Fond lacked, of being able to speak to the islanders in their own tongue.

Martin also produced an important account of a voyage to St Kilda. This book, published in 1698, is a key work on this remote island group.

The isle of Jura is by a narrow channel of about half a mile broad separated from Islay. The natives say that Jura is so called from Dih and Rah, two brethren, who are believed to have been Danes, the names Dih and Rah signifying as much as without grace or prosperity. Tradition says that these two brethren fought and killed one another in the village Knock–Cronm, where there are two stones erccted of 7 feet high each, and under them, they say, there are urns, with the ashes of the two brothers; the distance between them is about 60 yards. The isle is mountainous along the middle, where there are four hills of a considerable height. The two highest are well known to sea-faring men by the name of the Paps of Jura. They are very conspicuous from all quarters of sea and land in those parts.

This isle is twenty-four miles long, and in some places six or seven miles in breadth. It is the Duke of Argyll's property, and part of the Sheriffdom of Argyll.

The mould is brown and greyish on the coast, and black in the hills, which are covered with heath and some grass that proves good pasturage for their cattle, which are horses, cows, sheep, and goats. There is variety of land and water-fowl here. The hills ordinarily have about three hundred deer grazing on them, which are not to be hunted by any without the steward's licence. This isle is perhaps the wholesomest plot of ground either in the isles or continent of Scotland, as appears by the long life of the natives and their state of health, to which the height of the hills is believed to contribute in a large measure, by the fresh breezes of wind that come from them to purify the air; whereas Islay and Gigha, on each side this isle, are much lower, and are not so wholesome by far, being liable to several diseases that are not here. The inhabitants observe that the air of this place is perfectly pure, from the middle of March till the end or middle of September. There is no epidemical disease that prevails here. Fevers are but seldom observed by the natives, and any kind of flux is rare. The gout and agues are not so much as known by them, neither are they liable to sciatica. Convulsions, vapours, palsies, surfeits, lethargies, megrims, consumptions, rickets, pains of the stomach, or coughs, are not frequent here, and none of them are at any time observed to become mad. I was told by several of the natives that there was not one woman died of childbearing there these 34 years past. Blood-letting and purging are not used here.

If any contract a cough, they use brochan only to remove it. If after a fever one chance to be taken ill of a stitch, they take a quantity of ladywrack, and half as much of red-fog, and boil them in water. The patients sit upon the vessel, and receive the fume, which by experience they find effectual against this distemper. Fevers and the diarrhoeas are found here only when the air is foggy and warm, in winter or summer.

The inhabitants for their diet make use of beef and mutton in the winter and spring, as also of fish, butter, cheese, and milk. The vulgar take brochan frequently for their diet during the winter and spring; and brochan and bread used for the space of two days restores lost appetite.

The women of all ranks eat a lesser quantity of food than the men. This and their not wearing anything strait about them is believed to contribute much to the health of both the mothers and children.

There are several fountains of excellent water in this isle. The most celebrated of them is that of the mountain Beinbrek in the Tarbat, called Toubir ni Lechkin, that is, the well in a stony descent. It runs easterly, and they commonly reckon it to be lighter by one half than any other water in this isle; for though one drink a great quantity of it at a time, the belly is not swelled, or any ways burdened by it. Natives and strangers find it efficacious against nauseousness of the stomach and the stone. The river Nissa receives all the water that issues from this well, and this is the reason they give why salmon here are in goodness and taste far above those of any other river whatever. The river of Crockbreck affords salmon also, but they are not esteemed so good as those of the river Nissa.

Several of the natives have lived to a great age. I was told that one of them, called Gillouir MacCrain, lived to have kept one hundred and eighty Christmasses in his own house. He died about fifty years ago, and there are several of his acquaintances living to this day, from whom I had this account.

Bailiff Campbell lived to the age of one hundred and six years; he died three years ago; he passed the thirty-three last years before his death in this isle. Donald MacNamill, who lives in the village of Killearn at present, is arrived at the age of ninety years.

A woman of the Isle of Scarba, near the north end of this isle, lived seven score years, and enjoyed the free use of her senses and understanding all her days; it is now two years since she died.

There is a large cave, called King's Cave on the west side of the Tarbat, near the sea; there is a well at the entry which renders it the more convenient for such as may have occasion to lodge in it.

About two miles further from the Tarbat, there is a cave at Corpich which hath an altar in it; there are many small pieces of petrified substance hanging from the roof of this cave.

There is a place where vessels used to anchor on the west side of this island, called Whitfarlan, about 100 yards north from the porter's house.

About four leagues south from the north end of this isle, lies the bay

Da'l Yaul, which is about half a mile in length; there is a rock on the north side of the entry, which they say is five fathom deep, and but three fathom within.

About a league further to the south, on the same coast, lies the small isles of Jura, within which there is a good anchoring-place; the south entry is the best: island Nin Gowir must be kept on the left hand; it is easily distinguished by its bigness from the rest of the isles. Conney Isle lies to the north of this island. There are black and white spotted serpents in this isle; their head being applied to the wound, is by the natives used as the best remedy for their poison. Within a mile of the Tarbat there is a stone erected about eight feet high. Loch-Tarbat on the west side runs easterly for about five miles, but is not a harbour for vessels, or lesser boats, for it is altogether rocky.

The shore on the west side affords coral and coralline. There is a sort of dulse growing on this coast, of a white colour.

Between the north end of Jura, and the isle Scarba, lies the famous and dangerous gulf, called Cory Vrekan, about a mile in breadth; it yields an impetuous current, not to be matched anywhere about the isle of Britain. The sea begins to boil and ferment with the tide of flood, and resembles the boiling of a pot; and then increases gradually, until it appears in many whirlpools, which form themselves in sort of pyramids, and immediately after spout up as high as the mast of a little vessel, and at the same time make a loud report. These white waves run two leagues with the wind before they break; the sea continues to repeat these various motions from the beginning of the tide of flood, until it is more than half-flood, and then it decreases gradually until it hath ebbed about half an hour, and continues to boil till it is within an hour of low water. This boiling of the sea is not above a pistol-shot distant from the coast of Scarba Isle, where the white waves meet and spout up: they call it the Kaillach, *i.e.*, an old hag; and they say that when she puts on her kerchief, *i.e.*, the whitest waves, it is then reckoned fatal to approach her. Notwithstanding this great ferment of the sea, which brings up the least shell from the ground, the smallest fisher-boat may venture to cross this gulf at the last hour of the tide of flood, and at the last hour of the tide of ebb.

This gulf hath its name from Brekan, said to be son to the King of Denmark, who was drowned here, cast ashore in the north of Jura, and buried in a cave, as appears from the stone, tomb, and altar there.

The natives told me that about three years ago an English vessel happened inadvertently to pass through this gulf at the time when the sea began to boil; the whiteness of the waves, and their spouting up, was like the breaking of the sea upon a rock; they found themselves attracted irresistibly to the white rock, as they then supposed it to be: this quickly obliged them to consult their safety, and so they betook themselves to the small boat with all speed, and thought it no small happiness to land safe in Jura, committing the vessel under all her sails to the uncertain conduct of tide and wind. She was driven to the opposite continent of Knapdale, where she was no sooner arrived than the tide and wind became contrary to one another, and so the vessel was cast into a creek, where she was safe; and then the master and crew were, by the natives of this isle, conducted to her, where they found her as safe as they left her, though all her sails were still hoisted.

The natives gave me an account, that some years ago a vessel had brought some rats hither, which increased so much that they became very uneasy to the people, but on a sudden they all vanished; and now there is not one of them in the isle.

There is a church here called Killearn, the inhabitants are all Protestants, and observe the festivals of Christmas, Easter, and Michaelmas; they do not open a grave on Friday, and bury none on that day, except the grave has been opened before.

The natives here are very well proportioned, being generally black of complexion and free from bodily imperfections. They speak the Irish language, and wear the plaid, bonnet, etc., as other islanders.

The isle of Islay lies to the west of Jura, from which it is separated by a narrow channel; it is twenty-four miles in length from south to north, and eighteen from east to west; there are some little mountains about the middle on the east side. The coast is for the most part heathy and uneven, and by consequence not proper for tillage; the north end is also full of heaths and hills. The south-west and west is pretty well cultivated, and there is six miles between Kilrow on the west, and Port Escock in the east, which is arable and well inhabited. There is about one thousand little hills on this road, and all abound with limestone; among which there is lately discovered a lead mine in three different places, but it has not turned to any account as yet. The corn growing here is barley and oats.

There is only one harbour in this isle, called Loch-Dale; it lies near the north end, and is of a great length and breadth; but the depth being in the middle, few vessels come within half a league of the land side.

There are several rivers in this isle affording salmon. The fresh-water lakes are well stocked with trouts, eels, and some with salmons: as Loch-Guirm, which is four miles in circumference, and hath several forts built on an island that lies in it.

Loch-Finlagan, about three miles in circumference, affords salmon, trouts, and eels: this lake lies in the centre of the isle. The isle Finlagan, from which this lake hath its name, is in it. It is famous for being once the court in which the great Macdonald, King of the Isles, had his residence; his houses, chapel, etc., are now ruinous. His guards *de corps*, called Lucht-taeh, kept guard on the lake side nearest to the isle; the walls of their houses are still to be seen here.

The High Court of Judicature, consisting of fourteen, sat always here; and there was an appeal to them from all the Courts in the isles: the eleventh share of the sum in debate was due to the principal judge. There was a big stone of seven feet square, in which there was a deep impression made to receive the feet of Macdonald; for he was crowned King of the Isles standing in this stone, and swore that he would continue his vassals in the possession of their lands, and do exact justice to all his subjects; and then his father's sword was put into his hand. The Bishop of Argyll and seven priests anointed him king, in presence of all the heads of the tribes in the isles and continent, and were his vassals; at which time the orator rehearsed a catalogue of his ancestors, etc.

There are several forts built in the isles that are in fresh-water lakes, as in Ilan Loch-Guirn, and Ilan Viceain; there is a fort called Dunnivag in the south-west side of the isle, and there are several caves in different places of it. The largest that I saw was in the north end, and is called Vah Vearnag; it will contain 200 men to stand or sit in it. There is a kill for drying corn made on the east side of it; and on the other side there is a wall built close to the side of the cave, which was used for a bed-chamber; it had a fire on the floor, and some chairs about it, and the bed stood close to the wall. There is a stone without the cave door, about which the common people make a tour sunways.

A mile on the south-west side of the cave is the celebrated well called Toubir in Knahar, which in the ancient language is as much as to say, the well that sallied from one place to another: for it is a received tradition among the vulgar inhabitants of this isle, and the opposite isle of Colonsay, that this well was first in Colonsay, until an imprudent woman happened to wash her hands in it, and that immediately after, the well being thus abused, came in an instant to Islay, where it is like to continue, and is ever since esteemed a catholicon for diseases by the natives and adjacent islanders; and the great resort to it is commonly every quarter-day.

It is common with sick people to make a vow to come to the well, and after drinking, they make a tour sunways round it, and then leave an offering of some small token, such as a pin, needle, farthing, or the like, on the stone cover which is above the well. But if the patient is not like to recover, they send a proxy to the well, who acts as above-mentioned, and carries home some of the water to be drank by the sick person.

There is a little chapel beside this well, to which such as had found the benefit of the water, came back and returned thanks to God for their recovery.

There are several rivers on each side this isle that afford salmon. I was told by the natives that the Brion of Islay, a famous judge, is according to his own desire, buried standing on the brink of the river Laggan, having in his right hand a spear, such as they use to dart at the salmon.

There are some isles on the coast of this island, as island Texa on the south-west, about a mile in circumference; and island Ouirsa, a mile likewise in circumference, with the small isle called Nave.

The Names of the Churches in this Isle are as follows:

Kil-Chollim Kill, St Columbus his church near Port Escock, Kil-Chovan in the Rins, on the west side the isle; Kil-Chiaran in Rins, on the west side Nerbols in the Rins, St Columbus his church in Laggan, a chapel in island Nave, and Kilhan Alen, north-west of Kilrow. There is a cross standing near St Columbus's or Port Escock side, which is ten feet high. There are two stones set up at the east side of Loch-Finlagan, and they are six feet high. All the inhabitants are Protestants; some among them observe the festivals of Christmas and Good Friday. They are well proportioned and indifferently healthful. The air here is not near so good as that of Jura, from which it is but a short mile distant; but Islay is lower and more marshy, which makes it liable to several diseases that do not trouble those of Jura. They generally speak the Irish tongue; all those of the best rank speak English; they use the same habit and diet with those of Jura. This isle is annexed to the Crown of Scotland. Sir Hugh Campbell of Caddell is the King's steward there, and has one half of the island. This isle is reckoned the furthest west of all the isles in Britain. There is a village on the west coast of it called Cul, i.e., the back part; and the natives say it was so called because the ancients thought it the back of the world, as being the remotest part on that side of it. The natives of Islay, Colonsay, and Jura say that there is an island lying to the south-west of these isles, about the distance of a day's sailing, for which they have only a bare tradition. Mr MacSwen, present minister in the isle Jura, gave me the following account of it, which he had from the master of an English vessel that happened to anchor at that little isle, and came afterwards to Jura, which is thus:

As I was sailing some thirty leagues to the south-west of Islay, I was becalmed near a little isle, where I dropped anchor and went ashore. I found it covered all over with long grass. There was abundance of seals lying on the rocks and on the shore; there is likewise a multitude of sea-fowls in it; there is a river in the middle, and on each side of it I found great heaps of fish bones of many sorts; there are many planks and boards cast up upon the coast of the isle, and it being all plain, and almost level with the sea, I caused my men (being then idle) to erect a heap of the wood about two stories high; and that with a design to make the island more conspicuous to seafaring men. This isle is four English miles in length, and one in breadth. I was about thirteen hours sailing between this isle and Jura. Mr John MacSwen, above mentioned, having gone to the isle of Colonsay some few days after, was told by the inhabitants that from an eminence near the monastery in a fair day they saw as it were the top of a little mountain in the south-west sea, and that they doubted not but it was land, though they never observed it before. Mr MacSwen was confirmed in this opinion by the account above-mentioned; but when the summer was over, they never saw this little hill, as they called it, any more; the reason which is supposed to be this, that the high winds in all probability had cast down the pile of wood that forty seamen had erected the preceding year in that island, which, by reason of the description above recited, we may aptly enough call the Green Island.

By Islay's Shores

WILLIAM BLACK (1841–1898)

A once highly popular and successful novelist who specialised in novels with a Highland setting, such as In Far Lochaber *or* A Princess of Thule *– in which a Lewis laird's daughter is swept off south by a London artist. Born in Glasgow, Black was a central part of the 'Celtic Revival', together with 'Fiona Macleod'. However his work has attracted mockery for overwritten descriptions of Hebridean sunsets.*

This poem, simpler and more affecting, tells the story of one of the many Highland women whose man has gone off to battles far away – in this case to die at Minden in Germany, where a battle of the Seven Years War was fought in 1759.

By Islay's shores she sat and sang:
   'O winds come blowing o'er the sea,
And bring me back my love again
   That went to fight in Germanie!'

And all the live-long day she sang,
   And nursed the bairn upon her knee:
'Balou, balou, my bonnie bairn,
   Thy father's far in Germanie,

'But ere the summer days are gane,
   And winter blackens bush and tree,
Thy father will be welcome hame
   Frae the red wars in Germanie.'

O dark the nicht fell, dark and mirk;
   A wraith stood by her icily:
'Dear wife, I'll never more win hame,
   For I am slain in Germanie.'

'On Minden's field I'm lying stark,
   And heaven is now my far countrie;
Farewell, dear wife, farewell, farewell,
   I'll ne'er win hame frae Germanie.'

And all the year she came and went,
   And wandered wild frae sea to sea:
'O neighbours, is he ne'er come back,
   My love that went to Germanie?'

Port Ellen saw her many a time;
   Round by Port Askaig wandered she:
'Where is the ship that's sailing in
   With my dear love frae Germanie?'

But when the darkened winter fell:
   'It's cold for baith my bairn and me;
Let me lie down and rest awhile:
   My love's away frae Germanie.

'O far away and away he dwells;
   High Heaven is now his fair countrie;
And there he stands – with arms outstretched –
   To welcome hame my bairn and me!'

Fios chun a'Bhàird
(A Message for the Poet)

WILLIAM LIVINGSTON (1808–1870)

TRANSLATION BY DONALD E. MEEK

William Livingston (Uilleam MacDhun-lèibhe) was born in Killarrow on the island of Islay. He became a tailor and spent most of his life in Glasgow, living latterly in the Tradeston district. He was intensely interested in Scottish history and also taught himself a modicum of Greek, Latin, Hebrew, French and Welsh. Perhaps influenced by James MacPherson's Ossian he tried his hand at epic poems purporting to deal with the conflict between Norseman and Gael. These were rather unsuccessful, lacking strong delineation of character and sureness of plot. Much more successful was his vivid historical poem on the battle which took place at Traigh Ghruineart in Islay between the MacLeods of Mull and the MacDonalds of Islay in 1598.

An ardent Scottish nationalist, Livingston is at his most sustained and powerful when roused by the injustices of the Highland Clearances. Cuimhneachan Bhraid-Alba (Memorial of Breadalbane) is full of bitterness at the perpetrators of the clearance and full of anguish for the displaced whilst Eirinn a'Gull (Ireland Weeping) shows sympathy for the similar plight of the Irish. Fios chun a'Bhàird (A Message for the Poet) continues in this vein. It was probably written shortly after James Ramsay of Kildalton had orchestrated major clearances of the Oa district of Islay in 1862 and 1863, sending many of the inhabitants to Canada on emigrant ships. (The Rinns, the Glen and the Oa were the areas of Islay which suffered the most severe depopulation.) It achieves much of its effect from being in the form of a dramatic monologue in which the speaker appears to be sending a message to the poet telling him how she sees the state of things in Islay. The speaker, indeed, is intended to be the mother of the poet's editor, the Rev. Robert Blair, and the poem has the alternative title Oran Bean Dhonnachaidh, The Song of Duncan's Wife. (Bean Dhonnachaidh was the name by which Blair's mother was known locally.) At first the poem seems to be a very competent nature poem extolling an idyllic island scene. But this is a deception for at exactly half way through (at line 57 out of 112 lines) the mood alters dramatically and we are confronted with the human desolation which now pervades the island.

Sheep have replaced humans and uninhabited ruins of homes abound. The idyllic opening has been skilfully used to emphasise the human tragedy. This point is further emphasised in the second last stanza by the vivid picture of the coiled adder 'lying on the floors where once there grew the big men that I saw there'. And the urgency of the whole situation is hammered home by the speaker's repeated refrain 'take this message to the poet'.

Tha a' mhadainn soilleir grianach,
'S a' ghaoth 'n iar a' ruith gu réidh;
Tha an linne sleamhainn sìochail
On a chiùinich strì nan speur;
Tha an long 'na h-èideadh sgiamhach,
'S cha chuir sgìos i dh'iarraidh tàmh;
Mar a fhuair 's a chunnaic mise,
A' toirt an fhios seo chun a' Bhàird.

Seo crùnadh mais' a' mhìos
San tèid don dìthreabh treudan bhò,
Do ghlinn nan lagan uaigneach
Anns nach cuir 's nach buainear pòr,
Leab-innse buar nan geum –
Cha robh mo roinn diubh 'n-dè le càch;
Mar a fhuair 's a chunnaic mise,
Thoir am fios seo chun a' Bhàird.

Tha mìltean sprèidh air faichean,
'S caoraich gheal' air creachain fhraoich,
'S na fèidh air stùcan fàsail,
Far nach truaillear làr na gaoith;
An sìolach fiadhaich neartmhor
Fliuch le dealt na h-oiteig thlàith;
Mar a fhuair 's a chunnaic mise,
Thoir am fios seo chun a' Bhàird.

Tha an còmhnard 's coirean garbhlaich,
Còrs na fairg' 's gach gràinseach rèidh,
Le buaidhean blàths na h-iarmailt

Mar a dh'iarramaid gu lèir;
Tha 'n t-seamair fhiadhain 's neòinean
Air na lòintean feòir fo bhlàth;
Mar a fhuair 's a chunnaic mise,
Thoir am fios seo chun a' Bhàird.

Na caochain fhìor-uisg' luath
A' tighinn a-nuas o chùl nam màm
Bho lochain ghlan' gun ruadhan
Air na cruachan fad' on tràigh;
Far an òl am fiadh a phailteas,
'S bòidheach ealtan lach gan snàmh;
Mar a fhuair 's a chunnaic mise,
Thoir am fios seo chun a' Bhàird.

Tha bogha mòr an t-sàile
Mar a bha le reachd bithbhuan,
Am mòrachd maise nàdair
'S a cheann-àrd ri tuinn a' chuain –
A rìomball geal seachd mìle,
Gainmhean sìobt' o bheul an làin;
Mar a fhuair 's a chunnaic mise,
Thoir am fios seo chun a' Bhàird.

Na dùilean, stèidh na cruitheachd,
Blàths is sruthan 's anail neul,
Ag altram lusan ùrail
Air an laigh an driùchd gu sèimh,
Nuair a thuiteas sgàil na h-oidhche
Mar gum b' ann a' caoidh na bha;
Mar a fhuair 's a chunnaic mise,
Thoir am fios seo chun a' Bhàird.

Ged a roinneas gathan grèine
Tlus nan speur ri blàth nan lòn,
'S ged a chìthear sprèidh air àirigh,
Is buailtean làn de dh'àlach bhò,
Tha Ile 'n-diugh gun daoine,
Chuir a' chaor' a bailtean fàs;
Mar a fhuair 's a chunnaic mise,
Thoir am fios seo chun a' Bhàird.

Ged thig ànrach aineoil
Gus a' chaladh 's e sa cheò,
Chan fhaic e soills' on chagailt
Air a' chladach seo nas mò;
Chuir gamhlas Ghall air fuadach
Na tha bhuainn 's nach till gu bràth;
Mar a fhuair 's a chunnaic mise,
Thoir am fios seo chun a' Bhàird.

Ged a thogar feachd na h-Alb',
As cliùiteach ainm air faich' an àir,
Bithidh bratach fhraoich nan Ileach
Gun dol sìos ga dìon le càch;
Sgap mìorun iad thar fairge,
'S gun ach ainmhidhean balbh 'nan àit';
Mar a fhuair 's a chunnaic mise,
Thoir am fios seo chun a' Bhàird.

Tha taighean seilbh na dh'fhàg sinn
Feadh an fhuinn 'nan càrnan fuar;
Dh'fhalbh 's cha till na Gàidheil;
Stad an t-àiteach, cur is buain;
Tha stèidh nan làrach tiamhaidh
A' toirt fianais air 's ag ràdh,
'Mar a fhuair 's a chunnaic mise,
Leig am fios seo chun a' Bhàird.'

Cha chluinnear luinneag òighean,
Sèisd nan òran air a' chlèith,
'S chan fhaicear seòid mar b' àbhaist
A' cur bàir air faiche rèidh;
Thug ainneart fògraidh uainn iad;
'S leis na coimhich buaidh mar 's àill;
Leis na fhuair 's a chunnaic mise,
Biodh am fios seo aig a' Bhàrd.

Chan fhaigh an dèirceach fasgadh
No 'm fear-astair fois o sgìos,
No soisgeulach luchd-èisdeachd;
Bhuadhaich eucoir, Goill is cìs;
Tha an nathair bhreac 'na lùban

Air na h-ùrlair far an d'fhàs
Na fir mhòr' a chunnaic mise;
Thoir am fios seo chun a' Bhàird.

Lomadh ceàrn na h-Oa,
An Lanndaidh bhòidheach 's Roinn MhicAoidh;
Tha 'n Learga ghlacach ghrianach
'S fuidheall cianail air a taobh;
Tha an Gleann na fhiadhair uaine
Aig luchd-fuath gun tuath, gun bhàrr;
Mar a fhuair 's a chunnaic mise,
Thoir am fios seo chun a' Bhàird.

A MESSAGE FOR THE POET

The morning is clear and sunny
and the west wind gently blows;
the firth shimmers peacefully,
with the strife of skies now calm;
the ship is beautifully rigged,
and weariness will not make her seek rest,
just as I found and as I saw,
taking this message to the Poet.

This is the crowning beauty of the month
when herds of cattle go to the wilderness,
to the glens of lonely hollows
where the seed will not be sown or reaped,
the grazing-bed of lowing beasts –
my portion was not with the others yesterday;
just as I found and as I saw,
take this message to the Poet.

There are thousands of cattle on fields
and white sheep on heathery upper slopes,
and the deer on desolate tops
where the wind's base is unpolluted;

their wild, powerful offspring
are wet with the dew of the gentle breeze;
just as I found and as I saw,
take this message to the Poet.

The level plain and rough-land corries,
the ocean shoreline and every smooth cornfield
are reacting to the effects of the skies' warmth
as we would all desire;
the wild shamrock and the daisy
are in flower on fields of grass;
just as I found and as I saw,
take this message to the Poet.

The swift streams of pure water
descend from behind the rounded hills,
from lochs that are clean and scumless
on the eminences far from the shore;
where the deer will drink his fill,
beautiful flocks of wild duck swim;
just as I found and as I saw,
take this message to the Poet.

The great bow of the ocean
remains as before by an eternal decree,
in the majestic greatness of nature's beauty,
with its head high towards the waves;
its white arc extends seven miles,
its sands swept smooth from the tide's mouth;
just as I found and as I saw,
take this message to the Poet.

The elements, the foundation of creation,
warmth and streams and breath of clouds,
nurture fresh vegetation
on which the dew lies gently
as the shadow of night falls,
as if it were mourning what has gone;
just as I found and as I saw,
take this message to the Poet.

Although the shafts of sunlight impart
the gentleness of the skies to the meadows' hue,
and the cattle can be seen on the shieling,
and its folds are full of cattle's offspring,
Islay is today devoid of people;
the sheep has laid waste its townships;
just as I found and as I saw,
take this message to the Poet.

Although a poor lost wretch should come
to the harbour in a mist,
he will see no glimmer from a hearth
on this shore for ever more;
the bad feeling of the Foreigners has banished
those who have left us and will never return;
just as I found and as I saw,
take this message to the Poet.

Although the army of Scotland should be raised,
with its great reputation on the battlefield,
the heather banner of the Islaymen
will not advance to protect it with the others;
ill-will has scattered them over the sea,
and only dumb beasts have replaced them;
just as I found and as I saw,
take this message to the Poet.

The houses once owned by those who have left us
lie in cold heaps throughout the land;
the Gaels have gone, and they will never return;
cultivation, sowing and reaping have ceased;
the foundations of the sad ruins
bear witness to this and say,
'Just as I found and as I saw
let the Poet have this message'.

The spirited ditty of maidens will not be heard,
with a chorus of songs at the waulking-board,
and strong fellows will not be seen as before
driving home a goal on a smooth field;
the oppression of eviction has taken them from us;

the strangers have won, just as they wanted;
with all that I have found and seen,
let the Poet have this message.

The beggar will not find shelter
nor will the traveller get rest from his weariness,
nor will a gospel preacher find an audience;
injustice, Foreigners and taxes have triumphed;
the speckled adder is lying in coils
on the floors where once there grew
the big men that I saw there;
take this message to the Poet.

The district of the Oa has been stripped bare,
the beautiful Lanndaidh[1] and MacKay's Rinns;
sunny Largie[2] with its many hollows
has a pathetic remnant on its slope;
the Glen[3] has become a green wilderness,
owned by men of hatred without tenants or crops;
just as I found and as I saw,
take this message to the Poet.

---

[1] An Lanndaidh: an old district of Islay near the Rinns. Today it is often used as a poetic name for the whole island.
[2] Largie: an old district, probably between the Oa and the Glen.
[3] The Glen: an area stretching from Bridgend to Ballygrant.

Ursgeul na Feannaig
(The Tale of the Hoodie)

EDITOR: JOHN FRANCIS CAMPBELL (1822–85)

From Popular Tales of the West Highlands Vol. 1

TRANSLATION BY JOHN FRANCIS CAMPBELL

John Francis Campbell (1822–1885), still frequently referred to in Gaelic circles as Iain Og Ile (literally, Young John of Islay) was a truly remarkable person. As well as an aristocrat, civil servant and courtier, he was also a scientist, lawyer and brilliant linguist. Most of all, however, he will be remembered for his massive contribution to the study of the folklore and oral tradition of the West Highlands. He was brought up on the family estate on Islay and would, indeed, have become the Laird of Islay had the family not been forced to put the island up for sale against a massive debt. Unlike most aristocratic families Campbell's parents encouraged their son to talk to and befriend the ordinary island people and to learn Gaelic – things which Campbell did supremely well. As he himself said, 'I got to know a good deal about the ways of Highlanders by growing up as a Highlander myself.'

After the sale of the island in 1847 the family had to leave and John Francis went to London where he was to become Private Secretary to his cousin, George, 8th Duke of Argyll in 1854. In 1859, inspired by the work of the brothers Grimm and their famous Kinder und Hausmärchen *and, more directly, by the scholar of Norse folklore, his friend Sir George Dasent, he decided to set about making a major collection of the popular tales of the West Highlands. He, therefore, appointed fluent Gaelic speakers to go about the country collecting tales from people who could recite them from memory. His principal collectors were Hector Urquhart, game keeper at Ardkinglas, Loch Fyne, and Hector MacLean, schoolmaster at Ballygrant, Islay, and later he acquired the services of John Dewar, a woodman on the Argyll Estates, and Alexander Carmichael, an exciseman. He himself also undertook collecting trips in the Hebrides. He insisted that the transcriptions of the stories be as close as possible to the words of their informants. In 1860–1862 the first four volumes of* Popular Tales of the West Highlands *appeared. Campbell himself was largely responsible for the translations – which again were as literal as possible. Hector MacLean saw the books through the press. Campbell also had the* Dewar Manuscripts *(a million and a quarter words of oral tradition collected by John Dewar from 1862–1871 at the behest of the Duke of Argyll) bound into seven volumes and sent to Inveraray castle where they are preserved. In 1872 he produced* Leabhar na Féinne, *a collection of heroic ballads. He died in 1885.*

From Campbell's papers J. G. MacKay edited two further volumes of oral tradition: More West Highland Tales *Vol. 1 (1940) and Vol. 2 (1960). There is also a great deal of as yet unpublished material relating to oral tradition in the Campbell of Islay papers in the National Library of Scotland.*

The Tale of the Hoodie, was collected by Hector MacLean from Ann MacGilvray, Kilmeny, Islay in April, 1859. It is a supernatural tale about a woman who loses her three sons and her husband, who is a man by day and a hoodie crow by night. She loses her husband because she failed to bring a comb of supernatural significance at a crucial juncture. Eventually all is put to rights. The grouping of events into threes throughout the tale would make it easier for the reciter to remember the story. Campbell's own footnote on possible interpretations of the tale and on the significance of the comb is included at the end of the tale.

Bha tuathanach ann roimhe so; agus bha triùir nighean aige. Bha eud a' postadh aig obhainn. Thàinig feannag mu'n cuairt's thuirt e ris an té bu shine, 'Am pòs thu mise, a nighean an tuathanaich.' 'Cha phòs mis' thu, 'bheathaich ghrànnda: is grannda am beathach an fheannag,' ars'ise. Thàinig e thun na dàrna té an la 'r na mhàireach, 's thuirt e rithe, 'Am pòs thu mise.' 'Cha phòs mi féin,' ars'ise; ' 's grànnda am beathach an fheannag.' An treas la thuirt e ris an te b'òige, 'Am pòs thu mise, a nighean an tuathanaich.' 'Pòsaidh,' ars'ise; 's bòidheach am beathach an fheannag.' An la'r na mhàireach phòs eud. Thuirt an fheannag rithe, 'Cò 'ca is fheàrr leat mise a bhith am fheannag 'san latha 'sam dhuine 'san oidhche, na bhith 'san oidhche am fheannag 's am dhuine 'san latha?' ' 'S fhearr leam thu bhith a'd' dhuine 'san latha 's a'd' fheannag 'san oidhche,' ars'ise. As a dhèigh so bha e na òganach ciatach 'san latha, 's na fheannag 's an oidhche. Am beagan làithean an déigh dhaibh pòsadh thug e leis i 'ga 'thigh féin. Ann an ceann tri ràithean bha mac aca. Anns an oidhche tháinig an aon cheòl timchioll an taighe bu bhòidhche 'chualas riamh. Chaidil a h-uile duine, 's thugadh air folbh am pàisde. Thanig a h-athair thun an doruisd

'sa mhadainn. Dh' fheòraich e dé mur a bha h-uile h-aon an siod; 's bha
duilichinn mhòr air gun tugadh air folbh am pàisde, eagal agus gum biodh
coir' air a dhèanadh air féin air a shon. Ann an ceann tri ràithean a rithisd
bha mac eile aca. Chuireadh faire air an tigh. Thàinig ceòl ra bhòidheach
mar a thàinig roimhid timchioll an taighe; chaidil a h-uile duine 's thugadh
air folbh am pàisde. Thàinig a h-athair thun an doruisd sa mhadainn.
Dh'fheòraich e an robh gach ni ceart; ach bha 'm pàisde air a thoirt air
folbh, 's cha robh fhiòs aige dé a dhèanadh e leis an duilichinn. Ann an
ceann tri ràithean a rithisd bha mac eile aca. Chaidh faire 'chur air an tigh
mar a b' àbhaist. Thàinig ceòl timchioll an taighe mar a thàinig roimhid;
chaidil gach neach, 's thugadh am pàisde air folbh. Nur a dh' éiridh iad an
la 'r na mhàireach chaidh iad gu hàite tàmh eìle a bha aca, e fein 's a' bhean,
's a' phiuthar chéile. Thuirt e riu air an rathad, 'Feuch nach do
dhichuimhnich sibh ni 'sam bith.' Urs' a' bhean, 'DHIOCHUIMHNICH
MI MO CHIR GHARBH.' Thuit an carbad anns an robh eud 'na chual
chrìonaich, 's dh' fhalbh esan 'na fheannag. Thill a dha phiuthair
dhachaidh 's dh' fholbh ise 'na dhéighsan. Nur a bhiodh esan air mullach
cnoic leanadh ise e feuch am beireadh i air, 's nur a ruigeadh ise mullach a
chnoic bhiodh esan san lag an taobh eile. Nur a thàing an oidhche 's i
sgìth, cha robh àite tàmh na fuireachd aice. Chunnaic i tigh beag soluisd
fada uaithe 's ma b' fhada uaithe cha b' fhada a bha ise 'ga ruigheachd. Nur
a ràinig i an tigh sheas i gu dìblidh aig an dorusd. Chunnaic i balachan
beag feadh an taighe, 's theòigh i ris gu h-anabarrach. Thuirt bean an
taighe rithe tighinn a nìos, gu robh fios a seud 's a siubhail aice-se. Chaidh
i laidhe, 's cha bu luaithe thainig an latha na dh' éiridh i. Chaidh i 'mach, 's
nur a bha i 'mach bha i o chnoc gu cnoc feuch am faiceadh i feannag.
Chunnaic i feannag air cnoc, 's nur a rachadh ise air a' chnoc bhiodh an
fheannag 'san lag, nur a rachadh i do'n lag bhiodh an fheannag air cnoc
eile. Nur a thàinig an oidhche cha robh àite taimh na fuireachd aice.
Chunnaic i tigh beag soluisd fada uaithe 's ma b' fhada uaithe cha b' fhada
'bha ise 'g a ruigheachd. Chaidh i gus an dorusd. Chunnaic i balachan air
an urlar ris an do theòigh i gu ra mhòr. Chuir bean an taighe a laidhe i.
Cha bu mhoich' a thàinig an latha na ghabh i 'mach mar a b'àbhaist.
Chuir i seachad an latha so mar na làithean eile. Nur a thainig an oidhche
ràinig i tigh. Thuirt bean an taighe rithe tighinn a nìos; gu 'robh fios a
seud 's a siubhail aice-se; nach d' rinn a fear ach an tigh fhàgail bho cheann
tiota beag; i 'bhith tapaidh, gum b' i siod an oidhche ma dheireadh dhi
fhaicinn, 's gun i 'chadal, ach strì ri gréim a dhèanadh air. Chaidil ise, 's
thàinig esan far an robh i, 's lig e tuiteam do dh' fhàinn, air a làimh dheas.
Nur a dhuisg ise an so thug i làmh air breith air, 's rug i air ite d'a sgéith.
Leig e leatha an ite, 's dh' fhalbh e. Nur a dh' éiridh i 'sa mhadainn cha

robh fios aice dé a dhèanadh i. Thuirt bean an taighe gu'n deach e thairis
air cnoc neamh air nach b'urrainn ise dol thairis gun chrùidhean d'a
làmhan agus d'a casan. Thug i dhi aodach fir 's thuirt i rithe dol a dh'
ionnsachadh na goibhneachd gus am biodh i comasach air crùidhean a
dhèanadh dhì féin. Dh' ionnsaich i 'ghoibhneachd cho math 's gun d' rinn
i crùidhean d'a làmhan agus d'a casan. Dh 'fholbh i thairis air a chnoc
neamh. An latha sin féin an déigh dhi dol thairis air a chnoc neamh bha
pòsadh ri bhith aig a fear ri nighean duine uasail mhòir a bha 'sa bhaile.
Bha rèis anns a' bhaile an latha sin, 's bha h-uile h-aon ri bhith aig an rèis
ach an coigreach a thàinig thairis air a'cnoc neamh. Thainig an còcaire a
h-ionnsuidh, 's thuirt e rithe an rachadh i 'na àite a dhèanadh biadh na
bainnse, 's gu 'faigheadh e dol thun na réise. Thuirt i gu' rachadh. Bha i
furachail daonnan càite am biodh fear na bainnse 'na shuidhe. Lig i
tuiteam do 'n fhàinne agus do 'n ite 'sa bhrot a bha air a bheulaobh. Leis a
chiad spàin thog e'm fàinne, 's leis an ath spàin thog e 'n ite. Nur a thàinig
am ministir a làthair a dheanadh a phòsaidh cha phòsadh esan gus am
faigheadh e fios co a rinn am biadh. Thug iad a' làthair còcaire an duine
uasail, 's thuirt esan nach b'e siod an còcaire a rinn am biadh. Thug iad an
làthair an so an t-aon a rinn am biadh. Thuirt esan gum b'e siod a' bhean
phòsda-san a nis. Dh' fholbh na geasan dheth. Thill iad air an ais thairis air
a' chnoc neamh; ise a tilgeil nan crùidhean as a deigh da 'ionnsuidhsan nur
a thigeadh i treis air a h-aghaidh, 's esan 'ga leantainn. Nur a thàinig eud
air an ais thar a' chnoic, chaidh iad thun nan tri taighean anns an robh ise.
B'e sin tri taighean a pheathraichean-san, thug iad leo an tri mic. Thàinig
iad dhachaidh g'an tigh féin, 's bha iad gu toilichte.

THE TALE OF THE HOODIE

There was ere now a farmer, and he had three daughters. They were
waulking[1] clothes at a river. A hoodie[2] came round and he said to the
eldest one, 'M-POS-U-MI, Wilt thou wed me, farmer's daughter?' 'I won't
wed thee, thou ugly brute. An ugly brute is the hoodie,' said she. He came

---

[1] *Postadh.* A method of washing clothes practised in the Highlands – viz., by dancing on
them barefoot in a tub of water.
[2] Hoodie – the Royston crow – a very common bird in the Highlands; a sly, familiar,
knowing bird, which plays a great part in these stories. He is common in most parts of
Europe.

to the second one on the morrow, and he said to her, 'M-POS-U-MI, Wilt thou wed me?' 'Not I, indeed,' said she; 'an ugly brute is the hoodie.' The third day he said to the youngest, 'M-POS-U-MI, Wilt thou wed me, farmer's daughter?' 'I will wed thee,' said she; 'a pretty creature is the hoodie,' and on the morrow they married.

The hoodie said to her, 'Whether wouldst thou rather that I should be a hoodie by day, and a man at night; or be a hoodie at night, and a man by day?' 'I would rather that thou wert a man by day, and a hoodie at night,' says she. After this he was a splendid fellow by day, and a hoodie at night. A few days after they married he took her with him to his own house.

At the end of three quarters they had a son. In the night there came the very finest music that ever was heard about the house. Every man slept, and the child was taken away. Her father came to the door in the morning, and he asked how were all there. He was very sorrowful that the child should be taken away, for fear that he should be blamed for it himself.

At the end of three quarters again they had another son. A watch was set on the house. The finest of music came, as it came before, about the house; every man slept, and the child was taken away. Her father came to the door in the morning. He asked if every thing was safe; but the child was taken away, and he did not know what to do for sorrow.

Again, at the end of three quarters they had another son. A watch was set on the house as usual. Music came about the the house as it came before; every one slept, and the child was taken away. When they rose on the morrow they went to another place of rest that they had, himself and his wife, and his sister-in-law. He said to them by the way, 'See that you have not forgotten any thing'. The wife said, 'I FORGOT MY COARSE COMB.' The coach in which they were fell a withered faggot, and he went away as a hoodie.

Her two sisters returned home, and she followed after him. When he would be on a hill top, she would follow to try and catch him; and when she would reach the top of a hill, he would be in the hollow on the other side. When night came, and she was tired, she had no place of rest or dwelling; she saw a little house of light far from her, and though far from her she was not long in reaching it.

When she reached the house she stood deserted at the door. She saw a little laddie about the house, and she yearned to him exceedingly. The housewife told her to come up, that she knew her cheer and travel. She laid down, and no sooner did the day come than she rose. She went out, and when she was out, she was going from hill to hill to try if she could see a hoodie. She saw a hoodie on a hill, and when she would get on the hill the hoodie would be in the hollow, when she would go to the hollow, the hoodie would be on another hill. When the night came she had no place of rest or dwelling. She saw a little house of light far from her, and if far from her she was not long reaching it. She went to the door. She saw a laddie on the floor to whom she yearned right much. The housewife laid her to rest. No earlier came the day than she took out as she used. She passed this day as the other days. When the night came she reached a house. The housewife told her to come up, that she knew her cheer and travel, that her man had but left the house a little while, that she should be clever, that this was the last night she would see him, and not to sleep, but to strive to seize him. She slept, he came where she was, and he let fall a ring on her right hand. Now when she awoke she tried to catch hold of him, and she caught a feather of his wing. He left the feather with her, and he went away. When she rose in the morning she did not know what she should do. The housewife said that he had gone over a hill of poison over which she could not go without horseshoes on her hands and feet. She gave her man's clothes, and she told her to go to learn smithying till she should be able to make horseshoes for herself.

She learned smithying so well that she made horseshoes for her hands and feet. She went over the hill of poison. That same day after she had gone over the hill of poison, her man was to be married to the daughter of a great gentleman that was in the town.

There was a race in the town that day, and every one was to be at the race but the stranger that had come over the hill of poison. The cook came to her, and he said to her, Would she go in his place to make the wedding meal, and that he might get to the race.

She said she would go. She was always watching where the bridegroom would be sitting.

She let fall the ring and the feather in the broth that was before him. With the first spoon he took up the ring, with the next he took up the feather. When the minister came to the fore to make the marriage, he would not marry till he should find out who had made ready the meal. They brought up the cook of the gentleman, and he said that *this* was not the cook who made ready the meal.

They brought up now the one who had made ready the meal. He said, 'That now was his married wife.' The spells went off him. They turned back over the hill of poison, she throwing the horse shoes behind her to him, as she went a little bit forward, and he following her. When they came back over the hill, they went to the three houses in which she had been. These were the houses of his sisters, and they took with them the three sons, and they came home to their own house, and they were happy.

I have a great many versions of this tale in Gaelic; for example, one from Cowal, written from memory by a labourer, John Dewar. These are generally wilder and longer than the version here given.

This has some resemblance to an infinity of other stories. For example – Orpheus, Cupid and Psyche, Cinderella's Coach, The Lassie and her Godmother (Norse tales), East o' the Sun and West o' the Moon (ditto), The Master Maid (ditto), Katie Wooden Cloak (ditto), The Iron Stove (Grimm), The Woodcutter's Child (ditto), and a tale by the Countess d'Aulnoy, Prince Cherie.

If this be history, it is the story of a wife taken from an inferior but civilized race. The farmer's daughter married to the Flayer 'FEANNAG', deserted by her husband for another in some distant, mythical land, beyond far away mountains, and bringing him back by steady, fearless, persevering fidelity and industry.

If it be mythology, the hoodie may be the raven again, and a transformed divinity. If it relates to races, the superior race again had horses – for there was to be a race in the town, and every one was to be at it, but the stranger who came over the hill; and when they travelled it was in a coach, which was sufficiently wonderful to be magical, and here again the comb is mixed up with the spells.

There is a stone at Dunrobin Castle, in Sutherland, on which a comb is carved with other curious devices, which have never been explained. Within a few hundred yards in an old grave composed of great slabs of stone, accidentally discovered on a bank of gravel, a man's skeleton was found with teeth worn down, though perfectly sound, exactly like those of an old horse. It is supposed that the man must have ground his teeth on dried peas and beans – perhaps on meal, prepared in sandstone querns. Here, at least, is the COMB near to the grave of the farmer. The comb which is so often found with querns in the old dwellings of some pre-historic race of Britons; the comb which is a civilized instrument, and which in these stories is always a coveted object worth great exertions, and often magical.

The Paps of Jura

from The White Blackbird

ANDREW YOUNG (1885–1971)

Andrew Young was born in Elgin and educated for the ministry of the United Free Church. After War service he took up a charge in the Presbyterian Church in England, later being ordained as a priest of the Church of England. His nature poetry, as in this spare account of the Paps of Jura, was much admired and much of it continued to be inspired by the Scottish landscape.

Before I crossed the sound
  I saw how from the sea
These breasts rise soft and round,
  Not two but three;

Now, climbing, I clasp rocks
  Storm-shattered and sharp-edged,
Grey ptarmigan their flocks,
  With starved moss wedged;

And mist like hair hangs over
  One barren breast and me,
Who climb, a desperate lover,
  With hand and knee.

Legend of the Corrievrechan

GEORGE MACDONALD (1824–1905)

George MacDonald, born in Huntly, Aberdeenshire, claimed descent from one of the survivors of the massacre of Glencoe. Educated at King's College, Aberdeen, he was ordained to the ministry of the Congregational Church in England. Chiefly remembered as the author of fantasy novels for adults and children, a field in which he influenced later writers such as C. S. Lewis. He also wrote novels set in contemporary Scotland.

This poem retells the legend of the great Corrievreckan whirlpool between Jura and Scarba and retells it with a welcome degree of humour and an unexpected final twist. Dull souls who choose not to believe that the whirlpool was named after Prince Breacan of Denmark will continue to claim that this fearsome tidal race is named from the appearance of the streaky colour of the water in its overfalls – Corrie Bhreacain or speckled corrie.

Prince Breacan of Denmark was lord of the strand,
    And lord of the billowy sea;
Lord of the sea and lord of the land,
    He might have let maidens be!

A maiden he met with locks of gold,
    Straying beside the sea:
Maidens listened in days of old,
    And repented grievously.

Wiser he left her in evil wiles,
    Went sailing over the sea;
Came to the lord of the Western Isles:
    Give me thy daughter, said he.

The lord of the Isles he laughed, and said:
  Only a king of the sea
May think the Maid of the Isles to wed,
  And such, men call not thee!

Hold thine own three nights and days
  In yon whirlpool of the sea,
Or turn thy prow and go thy ways
  And let the isle-maiden be.

Prince Breacan he turned his dragon prow
  To Denmark over the sea:
Wise women, he said, now tell me how
  In yon whirlpool to anchor me.

Make a cable of hemp and a cable of wool
  And a cable of maidens' hair,
And hie thee back to the roaring pool
  And anchor in safety there.

The smiths of Greydule, on the eve of Yule,
  Will forge three anchors rare;
The hemp thou shalt pull, thou shalt shear the wool,
  And the maidens will bring their hair.

Of the hair that is brown thou shalt twist one strand,
  Of the hair that is raven another;
Of the golden hair thou shalt twine a band
  To bind the one to the other!

The smiths of Greydule, on the eve of Yule,
  They forged three anchors rare;
The hemp he did pull, and he shore the wool,
  And the maidens brought their hair.

He twisted the brown hair for one strand,
  The raven hair for another;
He twined the golden hair in a band
  To bind the one to the other.

He took the cables of hemp and wool,
    He took the cable of hair,
He hied him back to the roaring pool,
    He cast the three anchors there.

The whirlpool roared, and the day went by,
    And night came down on the sea;
But or ever the morning broke the sky
    The hemp was broken in three.

The night it came down, the whirlpool it ran,
    The wind it fiercely blew;
And or ever the second morning began
    The wool it parted in two.

The storm it roared all day the third,
    The whirlpool wallowed about,
The night came down like a wild black bird,
    But the cable of hair held out.

Round and round with a giddy swing
    Went the sea-king through the dark;
Round went the rope in the swivel-ring,
    Round reeled the straining bark.

Prince Breacan he stood on his dragon prow,
    A lantern in his hand:
Blest be the maidens of Denmark now,
    By them shall Denmark stand!

He watched the rope through the tempest black,
    A lantern in his hold:
Out, out, alack! one strand will crack!
    It is the strand of gold!

The third morn clear and calm came out:
    No anchored ship was there!
The golden strand in the cable stout
    Was not all of maidens' hair.

'S Fhada Thall Tha Mise
(Far Away am I)

from Moch Is Anmoch

DONALD A. MACNEILL (1924–95)

TRANSLATION BY ALASTAIR MACNEILL SCOULLER

Many Gaelic poems and songs are full of longing and nostalgia for the homeland from which the composer has been exiled. In many cases that exile was compulsory. In the wake of the Highland Clearances thousands of Gaels were forced to emigrate to the furthest parts of the globe. The writer of 'S Fhada Thall Tha Mise *was much more fortunate in that his exile was far less traumatic and he was soon to return to his native Isles of Colonsay and Oronsay – but this little poem is none the less telling for that. Donald MacNeill, or Donald Garvard as he was much better known, was born on the Island of Oronsay. He attended primary school on Colonsay (to which Oronsay is joined at low tide) and then proceeded to Keil School in Dumbarton for his secondary education. After some years in the R.A.F. spent in Canada and the South of England he returned to Colonsay where, for thirty years, he was tenant of Garvard Farm which looks across the strand to Oronsay. Donald was a distinguished local bard and he and his wife Joan contributed much to island life with their literary and musical talents.*

'S fhada, 's fhada thall tha mise,
'S fhada thall bho 'n eilean àluinn,
Eilean àiluinn snàmh 'san iar,
Ailleagan gu bràth 'nam chridh'.
'S fhada, 's fhada thall tha mise.

Orasa nan tràighean grinneal,
Tràighean grinneal mìn gan sluaisreadh,
Stuadhantan ùr bho uchd a' chuain
Bualadh fuaimneach mar o chionn.
Orasa nan tràighean grinneal.

'Sann 'nad thàmh a fhuair mi m'àrach,
Fhuair mi m'àrach òg is m'altrum.
Làithean samhraidh, maothach, blàth,
Casruisgt' ruith mi taobh Loch Bàn.
'Sann 'nad thàmh a fhuair mi m'àrach.

'S truagh an-diugh an tìr nan Gall mi,
Tìr nan Gall is mi 'nam aonar;
Daoine coibhneil air gach taobh,
Ach 'se Beurla th'air gach beul.
'S truagh an-diugh an tìr nan Gall mi.

FAR AWAY AM I

Far, far away am I,
far away from the lovely island,
the lovely island, floating in the west,
a little jewel, forever in my heart.
Far, far away am I.

Oronsay of the sandy beaches,
beaches of fine sand, sifted by the waves,
fresh breakers from the bosom of the ocean
crashing loudly as of old.
Oronsay of the sandy beaches.

In your tranquillity I was brought up,
was brought up and was nursed;
warm and gentle days of summer,
running barefoot by Loch Bàn.
In your tranquillity I was brought up.

Sad am I today in the land of strangers,
all alone in the land of strangers,
kindly people all around,
but English is on every tongue.
Sad am I today in the land of strangers.

'Loch Fyneside and Kintyre'

from The Highlands and Western Isles of Scotland

JOHN MACCULLOCH (1773–1835)

John MacCulloch was born in Guernsey but descended from a Galloway family. Educated at Edinburgh University, where he graduated in medicine at the age of twenty in 1793, his chief intellectual passion was geology and mineralogy. He was appointed geologist to the trigonometrical survey of Great Britain, which would eventually produce the first Ordnance Survey maps. From 1811 to 1821 he travelled each year in Scotland assembling a great body of scientific data. In 1824 he published, in the form of letters to his friend Sir Walter Scott, the four volumes of The Highlands and Western Isles of Scotland *from which our extract is taken.*

MacCulloch, like many travellers of his period, had a critical eye for the picturesque and not all of the scenery of Argyll matches up to his high standard. The reader is advised that if the Cowal shore of Loch Fyne were to be neglected 'he would lose very little'. However, a better tourism experience may be had on the Kintyre coast from Skipness to Campbeltown which is 'almost everywhere various and amusing'. MacCulloch does not fail to point out the human attractions of the area – his account of the public washing place at Kilkerran, near Campbeltown, and the 'concourse of the fair sex' assembled there with 'bare legs and arms' – suggests an enquiring mind which was not confned to consideration of the theory of the picturesque or the details of mineralogy.

Like many early writers MacCulloch spells Kintyre as Cantyre – which is, indeed, closer to the Gaelic 'Cean-tire' – headland or promontory (literally lands-end) and Campbeltown has still not had the second 'l' elided from its spelling.

We must pass on to Loch Fyne, the great length and rude boundary of which, excite the very natural expectation of finding much picturesque scenery in the course of its circumnavigation. This, however, is not the case; and though presenting many pleasing, and even picturesque scenes during its far-prolonged extent, there is a great disproportion of blank and uninteresting matter. If the tourist were to commence by neglecting the whole of the eastern shore together, even from Lamont Point to Inveraray, he would lose very little. In general, the shores on this side are smooth and even, without those features so necessary to beauty and variety, which consist in bays and promontories. If there are a few exceptions, they are of so little importance, that it is as little necessary to describe them as it would be for a traveller to waste his time in searching after them. Castle Lauchlan is, perhaps, the point which is almost alone worthy of notice.

It is on the west side that the beauties of Loch Fyne must be sought, and though scattered, they are numerous, even from its entrance to its extremity. But they are, still, little more than fragments of landscape, however pleasing they may often be. There is no one place where this inlet displays any general view, as happens at so many points upon Loch Lomond and elsewhere: as the mountain outline is never characteristic, but, on the contrary, tame or unpleasant, and as the sides do not fold and lock over in that manner which is almost necessary to the production of beauty, in lakes of so extensive a sweep. To call the landscape of Loch Fyne shore scenery, will, perhaps, be to define it in the most correct manner; and, considered as such, this inlet will afford much entertainment all along its west shore, to those who are content to admire, without thinking it necessary that every thing should be a picture or a regular landscape.

It would be as tedious an attempt to indicate those spots which are peculiarly worthy of notice, as it would be difficult to specify them for want of points of reference. But as there is a road all along this side of the loch, the traveller has his choice of proceeding by land or by water. Each will afford some differences; and, in many places, nothing can exceed the beauty of the road, conducted as it is, often among woods and under rocks, or itself impending over the sea, or entangled on the margin of the water among creeks and promontories. From Skipnish Point as far as East Loch Tarbet, the shore is generally fine; the land above being high, the sea margin frequently rising into cliffs, and there being generally a great profusion of wood. The village and bay of Loch Tarbet form a very singular spot, wild alike and unexpected; and, from it, there is a very short communication, by land, with the western sea. A ruined castle, built by the Argyll family, looks down from the hill above; and, by this little town, the road between Campbelltown and Inveraray passes. Upwards, as far as Loch Gilp, the shore continues interesting, as is the road within the land, for a space of many miles. Loch Gilp Head is a neat village; and though the commerce through the Crinan canal is not considerable, it is sufficient, in many seasons, to render this port a lively scene.

It has been the misfortune of the Crinan canal to have generally had a supply of water insufficient to maintain the waste of its leakage; which is considerable, as a great portion of it is built, not sunk in the earth, and, as it is said, that it has been imperfectly puddled. For many years, therefore, it only admitted of small boats; but it has been lately repaired, so as again, nearly at least, to serve the purposes for which it was originally intended. Its advantages to the fishing boats and the smaller vessels that trade between the west coast and the Clyde, are considerable; not only in saving great contingent delay in the navigation round the Mull of Cantyre, but, to the smaller fishing boats, some danger. It is a wild and not unpleasing walk by the side of this canal; but, except at the two extremities, there is not much beauty. The anchorage of Silvercraigs, near Loch Gilp, is one of the most striking and picturesque spots in Loch Fyne; from the intricacy of the several creeks and bays, and the lofty and rocky promontories by which they are separated. Hence, indeed, the coast onwards to Inveraray, deserves to be minutely examined; and it is only by a minute examination that its various beauties will be detected. To enumerate them would be impossible; but the greatest changes of character occur near the high hill and promontory where the iron foundry is situated, and again, beyond this, to Inveraray. He who may make this journey by land, can scarcely miss the different scenes which it presents; but if the voyage by water is adopted, it is necessary to keep the boat close in shore the whole way, and to allow an entire day for this portion alone. Inveraray itself has already passed in review.

Returning now to Skipnish Point, its castle must be pointed out, as a ruin of considerable size and in a state of good preservation. Neither the structure nor the situation, however, are peculiarly picturesque; but there is hence a fine view of the Clyde, in which Arran, as usual, forms a leading object. Hence to Campbelltown, is a succession of sea coast, which is almost everywhere various and amusing, and that, whether we take the high road, which follows the margin of the water, or pursue the line of the shore in a boat. The coast itself is intricate with hill and dale, and with bays and promontories and rocks, sometimes woody, at others populous and cultivated, and, in a few places, bare and open, but still always entertaining. Arran, accompanying it for a long way, forms a fine object in the distance, while the ships, for ever standing up or down the Clyde, add life to the whole. But we must pass it over, and suppose ourselves safe at anchor in Campbelltown harbour.

Fertile as is the west coast in harbours, there is not one that excels this;

which, besides being spacious enough to contain a large fleet, is perfectly land locked, easily entered, and has the best possible holding ground. The high and bold rock, Devar, covers it from the sea completely; being attached to the land on the south side by a spit of shingle, which has probably, in later times, rendered that a peninsula which was once an island. The rock produces some beautiful varieties of green, as well as of brown porphyry, easily wrought, to be obtained of any size, and extremely ornamental when polished, but as yet neglected. Sweden, with far less capital and far less industry (or of reputation for that at least) than ourselves, contrives to fill all Europe with the elegant produce of an article, similar, yet far inferior in beauty and utterly without variety, whereas this rock produces not less than ten or twelve distinct kinds.

To the south, the harbour of Campbelltown is bounded by the high and bold mountain land which forms the Mull of Cantyre; but, northward, the country is merely hilly. This latter boundary is bare and without beauty; but the southern one is, not only bold and various, but is tolerably wooded, in a country where much wood is not expected. The burying ground of Kilkerran, named after Saint Kiaran, is a very pleasing, and not an unpicturesque spot; while it is also rendered a very lively scene by the concourse of the fair sex employed in washing; the public laundry being on the banks of the small stream which runs past it, and displaying all the well-known variety which results from blazing fires, huge black kettles, smoke, linen, tubs, bare legs and arms, and merriment. This would be an admirable scene for Wilkie: the landscape adding charms to the fair, and the fair reflecting them back on the landscape. The castle of Kilkerran, which once stood here, is said to have been built by James the fifth; but it is imagined that there was a castle long before that, which was taken by Haco in his expedition, already mentioned. Some caves along the shore are pointed out, where St Kiaran is reported to have lived the life of a hermit: and Kilhouslan here also preserves the traces of its ancient burying ground and chapel.

Campbelltown, with Stornaway and Inverlochy, is one of the three boroughs erected by James VI, with the professed view of civilizing the Highlands. It is a place of considerable, but variable, commerce; as that commerce consists in the herring fishery, itself unfortunately too variable. It occupies the end of the bay on both sides, and is a town, not only of a very reputable appearance, but of considerable extent and population. Some extensive piers serve for receiving the smaller class of shipping; and as it is always swarming with fishing boats and vessels of different kinds, it forms one of the gayest and liveliest scenes imaginable. Detached villas and single houses, scattered about the shore and the sides of the hills, not only add much to the ornamental appearance of the bay, but give an air of taste and opulence to the whole. A more picturesque and beautiful situation for a maritime town could not well be found; and, from different points, it presents some fine views; uniting all the confusion of town architecture with the wildness of alpine scenery, the brilliancy of a lake, and the life, and bustle, and variety, incidental to a crowded harbour and pier. There is a very beautiful and perfect stone cross at the market place, which, popular report says, was brought from Iona at the Reformation. The sculptures are as fresh as if but just executed, and consist of various foliages and Runic knots, designed and wrought with great taste, together with some emblematical figures of demons and angels, to which the same praise cannot be assigned. If I mistake not, for I have not his book, Pennant also mentions it as having belonged to Iona. This however is an error; as is proved by an inscription in black letter, extremely well cut, which says, 'Hæc est crux Domini Yvari M. H. Eachyrna quondam rectoris de Kyrecan et Domini Andre nati ejus rectoris de Kilcoman qui hanc crucem fieri faciebant'.

It is not difficult to perceive, on examining the land round Campbelltown, that the sea once flowed between the harbour and Machrianish Bay on the west coast, so that the Mull of Cantyre was formerly an island. Much of that tract has lately been drained and cultivated. Through this flat, a canal leads to a coal mine, situated near the bay; the produce of which, though not of a good quality, serves for the consumption of the town. The bay itself is wide, open, sandy, and shallow, producing a great surf in west winds; nor is there any thing picturesque in this quarter, unless it be under the high cliffs. The same may indeed be said of the country in general round Campbelltown; although it is pleasing, and, were it better wooded, would even be beautiful.

The Manse

from Reminiscences of a Highland Parish

NORMAN MACLEOD (1812–72)

Norman Macleod was one of the most famous and popular Scottish churchmen of the mid-nineteenth century who combined a demanding job as Minister of a large city-centre parish, Glasgow Barony, a high profile role as a Chaplain to Queen Victoria and a variety of tasks in the Church of Scotland, travelling to India on Church business, culminating in his becoming Moderator of the General Assembly in 1869. To this he added an active career as a writer and as editor from 1860–1872 of the mass circulation religious magazine Good Words.

The son and grandson of ministers also called Norman Macleod, and with a minister uncle and two minister cousins and a minister brother, Norman Macleod was part of a remarkable clerical dynasty. His uncle John (1801–1872) and his father (1783–1862) were both in their time Moderators of the General Assembly and his father was also a noted Gaelic poet and writer. The author of the haunting Farewell to Fiunary which is included in the North Argyll section of this anthology, he established two Gaelic periodicals and came to be known as 'Caraid nan Gaidheal' – the Friend of the Gaels. The dynasty continued with the grandson of the author of this extract – George Fielden Macleod (1895–1991), who was the founder of the Iona Community, the fifth member of his family to become Moderator of the General Assembly. He was created a life peer in 1967 as Lord Macleod of Fiunary.

The author of Reminiscensces of a Highland Parish was born at Campbeltown when his father was Minister there but spent much of his early life at his grandfather's manse near Fiunary in Morvern, which is the 'Highland Parish' he describes. He also had his earliest education at the parish school of Morvern. The description of life in the manse is colourful and vivid and also serves as a useful corrective to many impressions of Highland Presbyterianism as a joyless and bleak faith. Macleod writes:

A striking characteristic of the manse life was its constant cheerfulness. One cottager could play the bagpipes, another the fiddle. The minister was an excellent performer on the latter, and to have his children dancing in the evening was his delight.

There lived in the Island of Skye, more than a century ago, a small farmer or 'gentleman tacksman.' Some of his admirably-written letters are now before me; but I know little of his history beyond the fact revealed in his correspondence, and preserved in the affectionate traditions of his descendants, that he was 'a good man,' and among the first, if not the very first, in the district where he lived who introduced the worship of God in his family.

One great object of his ambition was to give his sons the best education that could be obtained for them, and in particular to train his first-born for the ministry of the Church of Scotland. His wishes were fully realized, for that noble institution, the parochial school, provided in the remotest districts teaching of a very high order, and produced admirable classical scholars – such as even Dr. Johnson talks of with respect.

And in addition to the school teaching there was an excellent custom then existing among the tenantry in Skye, of associating themselves to obtain a tutor for their sons. The tutor resided alternately at different farms, and the boys from the other farms in the neighbourhood came daily to him. In this way the burden of supporting the teacher, and the difficulties of travelling on the part of the boys, were divided among the several families in the district. In autumn, the tutor, accompanied by his more advanced pupils, journeyed on foot to Aberdeen to attend the University. He superintended their studies during the winter, and returned in spring with them to their Highland homes to pursue the same routine. The then Chief of Macleod was one who took a pride in being surrounded by a tenantry who possessed so much culture. It was his custom to introduce all the sons of his tenants who were studying at Aberdeen to their respective professors, and to entertain both professors and students at his hotel. On one such occasion, when a professor remarked with surprise, 'Why, sir, these are all gentlemen!' Macleod replied, 'Gentlemen I found them, as gentlemen I wish to see them educated, and as gentlemen I hope to leave them behind me.'[1]

The 'gentleman tacksman's' eldest son acted as a tutor for some time, then as parochial teacher, and finally became minister of 'the Highland

---

[1] 'At dinner I expressed to Macleod the joy which I had in seeing him on such cordial feelings with his clan. "Government," said he, "has deprived us of our ancient power; but it cannot deprive us of our domestic satisfactions. I would rather drink punch in one of their houses (meaning the houses of the people), then be enabled by their hardships to have claret in my own." ' – Boswell's *Life of Johnson*, vol. iv. p. 275.

parish.' It was said of him that 'a prettier man never left his native island.' He was upwards of six feet in height, with a noble countenance, which age only made nobler.

He was accompanied from Skye by a servant-lad, whom he had known from his boyhood, called 'Ruari Beg,' or Little Rory. Rory was rather a contrast to his master in outward appearance. One of his eyes was blind, but the other seemed to have stolen the sight from its extinguished neighbour to intensify its own. That grey eye gleamed and scintillated with the peculiar sagacity and reflection which one sees in the eye of a Skye terrier, but with such intervals of feeling as human love of the most genuine kind could alone have expressed. One leg, too, was slightly shorter than the other, and the manner in which he rose on the longer or sunk on the shorter, and the frequency or rapidity with which the alternate ups and downs in his life were practised, became a telegraph of his thoughts, when words, out of respect to his master, were withheld. 'So you don't agree with me, Rory?' 'What's wrong?' 'You think it dangerous to put to sea to-day?' 'Yes; the mountain-pass also would be dangerous?' 'Exactly so. Then we must consider what is to be done.' Such were the remarks which a series of slow or rapid movements of Rory's limbs would draw forth from his master, though no other token were afforded of his inner doubt or opposition. A better boatman, a truer genius at the helm, never took a tiller in his hand; a more enduring traveller never trod the heather; a better singer of a boat-song never cheered the rowers, nor kept them as one man to their stroke; a more devoted, loyal, and affectionate 'minister's man' and friend never lived than Rory – first called 'Little Rory,' but as long as I can remember, 'Old Rory.' More of him anon, however. The minister and his servant arrived in the Highland parish nearly ninety years ago, almost total strangers to its inhabitants, and alone they entered the manse to see what it was like.

I ought to inform my readers in the south, some of whom – can they pardon the suspicion if it be unjust? – are more ignorant of Scotland and its Church than they are of France or Italy and the church of Rome, – I ought to inform them that the Presbyterian Church is established in Scotland, and that the landed proprietors in each parish are bound by law to build and keep in repair a church, suitable school, and parsonage or 'manse,' and also to secure a portion of land or 'glebe' for the minister. Both manses and churches have of late years improved immensely in Scotland, so that in many cases they are now far superior to those in some of the rural parishes of England. But much still remains to be accomplished in this department of architecture and taste. Yet even at the time I speak of, the manse was in its structure rather above than below the houses occupied by the ordinary gentry, with the exception of 'the big house' of the chief. It has been replaced by one more worthy of the times; but it was nevertheless respectable, as the sketch of it on the title-page shows.

The glebe was the glory of the manse! It was among the largest in the county, consisting of about sixty acres, and containing a wonderful combination of Highland beauty. It was bounded on one side by a 'burn,' whose torrent rushed far down between lofty steep banks clothed with natural wood, ash, birch, hazel, oak, and rowan-tree, and which poured its dark moss-water over a series of falls, and through deep pools, 'with beaded bubbles winking at the brim.' It was never tracked along its margin by any human being, except herd-boys and their companions, who swam the pools and clambered up the banks, holding by the roots of trees, starting the kingfisher from his rock, or the wild cat from his den. On the other side of the glebe was the sea, with here a sandy beach, and there steep rocks and deep water, and small grey islets beyond; while many birds, curlews, cranes, divers, and gulls of all sorts, gave life to the rocks and shore. Along the margin of the sea there stretched a flat of green grass which suggested the name it bore, namely, 'the Duke of Argyle's walk.' And pacing along that green margin at evening, what sounds and wild cries were heard of piping sea-birds, chafing waves, the roll of oars, and the song from fishing-boats, telling of their return home. The green terrace-walk which fringed the sea was but the outer border of a flat that was hemmed in by the low precipice of the old upraised beach of Scotland. Higher still was a second storey of green fields and emerald pastures, broken by a lovely rocky knoll, called Fingal's hill, whose grey head, rising out of green grass, bent towards the burn, and looked down into its own image reflected in the deep pools which slept at its feet. On that upper table-land, and beside a clear stream, stood the manse and garden sheltered by trees. Beyond the glebe began the dark moor, which swept higher and higher, until crowned by the mountain-top looking away to the Western Islands and the peaks of Skye.

The minister, like most of his brethren, soon took to himself a wife, the daughter of a neighbouring 'gentleman tacksman,' and the granddaughter of a minister, well born and well bred; and never did man find a help more meet for him. In that manse they lived for nearly fifty years, and there were born to them sixteen children; yet neither father nor mother could ever lay hand on a child and say, 'We wish this one had not been.' They were all a source of unmingled joy.

A small farm was added to the glebe, for it was found that the plant required to work sixty acres of arable and pasture land could work more without additional expense. Besides, John, Duke of Argyle, made it a rule at that time to give farms at less than their value to the ministers on his estates; and why, therefore, should not our minister, with his sensible, active, thrifty wife, and growing sons and daughters, have a small one, and thus secure for his large household abundance of food, including milk and butter, cheese, potatoes, and meal, with the excellent addition of mutton, and sometimes beef too? And the good man did not attend to his parish less that his living was thus bettered; nor was he less cheerful or earnest in duty because in his house 'there was bread enough and to spare.'

The manse and glebe of that Highland parish were a colony which ever preached sermons, on week-days as well as Sundays, of industry and frugality, of courteous hospitality and bountiful charity, and of the domestic peace, contentment, and cheerfulness of a holy Christian home.

Several cottages were built by the minister in sheltered nooks near his dwelling. One or two were inhabited by labourers and shepherds; another by the weaver, who made all the carpets, blankets, plaids, and finer webs of linen and woollen cloths required for the household; and another by old Jenny, the henwife, herself an old hen, waddling about and *chucking* among her numerous family of poultry. Old Rory with his wife and family, was located near the shore, to attend at spare hours to fishing, as well as to be ready with the boat for the use of the minister in his pastoral work. Two or three cottages besides were inhabited by objects of charity, whose claims upon the family it was difficult to trace. An old sailor – Seòras nan Long, 'George of the Ships,' was his sole designation – had settled down in one, but no person could tell anything about him, except that he had been born in Skye, had served in the navy, had fought at the Nile, had no end of stories for winter evenings, and span yarns about the wars and 'foreign parts.' He had come long ago in distress to the manse, from whence he had passed after a time into the cottage, and there lived – very much as a dependent on the family – until he died twenty years afterwards. A poor decayed gentlewoman, connected with one of the old families of the county, and a tenth cousin of the minister's wife, had also cast herself, in her utter loneliness, on the glebe. She had only intended to remain a few days – she did not like to be troublesome – but she knew she could rely on a blood relation, and she found it hard to leave, for whither could she go? And those who had taken her in never thought of bidding this sister 'depart in peace, saying, Be ye clothed;' and so she became a neighbour to the sailor, and was always called 'Mrs.' Stewart, and was treated with the utmost delicacy and respect, being fed, clothed, and warmed in her cottage with the best which the manse could afford. And when she died, she was dressed in a shroud fit for a lady, while tall candles, made for the occasion, according to the old custom, were kept lighted round her body. Her funeral was becoming the gentle blood that flowed in her veins; and no one was glad in their heart when she departed, but all sincerely wept, and thanked God she had lived in plenty and died in peace.

Within the manse the large family of sons and daughters managed, somehow or other, to find accommodation not only for themselves, but also for a tutor and governess. And such a thing as turning any one away for want of room was never dreamt of. When hospitality demanded such a small sacrifice, the boys would all go to the barn, and the girls to the chairs and sofas of parlour and dining-room, with fun and laughter, joke and song, rather than not make the friend or stranger welcome. And seldom was the house without either. The 'kitchen-end,' or lower house, with all its indoor crannies of closets and lofts, and outdoor additions of cottages, barns, and stables, was a little world of its own, to which wandering pipers, parish fools, and beggars, with all sorts of odd-and-end characters, came, and where they ate, drank and rested. As a matter of course, the 'upper house' had its own set of guests to attend to. The traveller by sea, whom adverse winds and tides drove into the harbour for refuge; or the traveller by land; or any minister passing that way; or friends on a visit; or lastly and but rarely, some foreign 'Sassanach' from the Lowlands of Scotland or England, who wanted then to explore the unknown and remote Highlands, as one now does Montenegro or the Ural Mountains, – all these found a hearty exception.

One of the most welcome visitors was the packman. His arrival was eagerly longed for by all, except the minister, who trembled for the small purse in presence of the prolific pack. For this same pack often required a horse for its conveyance. It contained a choice selection of everything which a family was likely to require from the Lowland shops. The haberdasher and linen-draper, the watchmaker and jeweller, the cutler and hairdresser, with sundry other crafts in the useful and fancy line, were all fully represented in the endless repositories of the pack. What a solemn affair was the opening up of that peripatetic warehouse! It took a few days to gratify the inhabitants of manse and glebe, and to enable them to decide how their money should be invested. The boys held sundry councils about knives, and the men about razors, silk handkerchiefs, or, it may be, about the final choice of a silver watch. The female servants were in nervous agitation about some bit of dress. Ribbons, like rainbows, were unrolled; prints held up in graceful folds before the light; cheap shawls were displayed on the back of some handsome lass, who served as a model. There never were seen such new fashions or such cheap bargains! And then how 'dear papa' was coaxed by mamma; and mamma again by her daughters. Each thing was so beautiful, so tempting, and was discovered to be so necessary! All this time the packman was treated as a friend. He almost always carried pipe or violin, with which he set the youngsters a-dancing, and was generally of the stamp of him whom Wordsworth has made illustrious. The news gathered on his travels was as welcome to the minister as his goods were to the minister's family. No one in the upper house was so vulgar as to screw him down, but felt it due to his respectability to give him his own price, which, in justice to those worthy old merchants, I should state was generally reasonable.

The manse was the grand centre to which all the inhabitants of the parish gravitated for help and comfort. Medicines for the sick were weighed out from the chest, yearly replenished in Edinburgh or Glasgow. They were not given in homœopathic doses, for Highlanders, accustomed to things on a large scale, would have had no faith in globules, and faith was half their cure. Common sense and common medicines were found helpful to health. The poor, as a matter of course, visited the manse, not for an order on public charity, but for aid from private charity, and it was never refused in kind, such as meal, wool, or potatoes. There being no lawyers in the parish, lawsuits were adjusted in the manse; and so were marriages not a few. The distressed came there for comfort, and the perplexed for advice; and there was always something material as well as spiritual to share with them all. No one went away empty in body or soul. Yet the barrel of meal failed not, nor did the cruse of oil waste. A 'wise' neighbour once remarked, 'That minister with his large family will ruin himself, and if he dies they will be beggars.' Yet there has never been a beggar among them to the fourth generation. No saying was more common in the mouth of this servant than the saying of his Master, 'It is more blessed to give than to receive.'

A striking characteristic of the manse life was its constant cheerfulness. One cottager could play the bagpipe, another the fiddle. The minister was an excellent performer on the latter, and to have his children dancing in the evening was his delight. If strangers were present, so much the better. He had not an atom of that proud fanaticism which connects religion with suffering, as suffering, apart from its cause.[1]

---

[1] A minister in a remote island parish once informed me that, 'on religious grounds,' he had broken the only fiddle in the island! His notion of religion, I fear, is not rare among his brethren in the far west and north. We are informed by Mr Campbell, in his admirable volumes on the *Tales of the Highlands*, that the old songs and tales are also being put under the clerical ban in some districts, as being too secular and profane for the pious inhabitants. What next? Are the singing-birds to be shot by the kirk-sessions?

Here is an extract from a letter written by the minister in his old age, some fifty years ago, which gives a very beautiful picture of the secluded manse and its ongoings. It is written at the beginning of a new year, in reply to one which he had received from his first-born son, then a minister in a distant parish:-

'What you say about the beginning of another year is quite true. But, after all, may not the same observations apply equally well to every new day? Ought not daily mercies to be acknowledged, and God's favour and protection asked for every new day? and are we not as ignorant of what a new day as of what a new year may bring forth? There is nothing in nature to make this day in itself more worthy of attention than any other. The sun rises and sets on it as on other days, and the sea ebbs and flows. Some come into the world and some leave it, as they did yesterday and will do tomorrow. On what day may not one say, "I am a year older than I was this day last year"? Still I must own that the first of the year speaks to me in a more commanding and serious language than any other common day; and the great clock of time, which announced the first hour of this year, did not strike unnoticed by us.

'The sound was too loud to be unheard, and too solemn to pass away unheeded. "*Non obtusa adeo gestamus pectora Poeni.*" We in the manse did not mark the day by any unreasonable merriment. We were alone, and did eat and drink with our usual innocent and cheerful moderation. I began the year by gathering all in the house and on the glebe to prayer. Our souls were stirred up to bless and to praise the Lord: for what more reasonable, what more delightful duty, than to show forth our gratitude and thankfulness to that great and bountiful God from whom we have our years, and days, and all our comforts and enjoyments? Our lives have been spared till now; our state and conditions in life have been blessed; our temporal concerns have been favoured; the blessing of God has co-operated with our honest industry; our spiritual advantages have been great and numberless; we have had the means of grace and the hope of glory; in a word, we have had all that was requisite for the good of our body and soul; and shall not our souls and all that is within us, all our powers and faculties, be stirred up to bless and praise His name?

'But to return. This pleasant duty being gone through, refreshments were brought in, and had any of your clergy seen the crowd (say thirty, great and small, besides the family of the manse), they would pity the man who, under God, had to support them all! This little congregation being dismissed, they went to enjoy themselves. They entertained each other by turns. In the evening, I gave them one end of the house, where they danced and sang with great glee and good manners till near day. We enjoyed ourselves in a different manner in the other end. Had you popped in unnoticed, you would have seen us all grave, quiet, and studious. You would see your father reading *The Seasons*; your mother, *Porteous' Lectures*; your sister Anne, *The Lady of the Lake*; and Archy, *Tom Thumb*!

'Your wee son was a new and great treat to you in those bonny days of rational mirth and joy, but not a whit more so than you were to me at his time of life, nor can he be more so during the years to come. May the young gentleman long live to bless and comfort you! May he be to you what you have been and are to me! I am the last that can honestly recommend to you not to allow him get too strong a hold of your heart, or rather not to allow yourself *doat too much* upon him. This was a peculiar weakness of my own, and of which I had cause more than once to repent with much grief and sore affliction. But your mother's creed always was (*and truly she has acted up to it*), to enjoy and delight in the blessings of the Almighty, while they were spared to her, with a thankful and grateful heart, and to part with them when it was the will of the gracious Giver to remove them, with humble submission and meek resignation.'

'The Young Gillespie'

from Gillespie

JOHN MACDOUGALL HAY (1880–1919)

*If some Scots clergymen-writers like S.R. Crockett and 'Ian Maclaren'
wrote novels depicting a couthy, kindly, small-town Scotland filled with
sentimental descriptions of the douce lives of the toilers in the kailyard,
another clergyman-novelist, J. MacDougall Hay, reacted against this
school and gave a dark and tortured picture of Scottish small-town life. Set
in 'Brieston' – in fact Hay's native town of Tarbert on Loch Fyneside – the
story is an attack on what Hay saw as the growing materialism of Scotland
and Scottish society. The quotation on the title page from the Book of
Proverbs 'He that is greedy of gain, troubleth his own house' could
certainly be applied to the central figure, Gillespie Strang, for whom the
making of money becomes the chief figure and driving force. Our extract,
the first four brief chapters, establish the troubled background from which
Gillespie springs and his early attempts at winning financial mastery over
his fellow men.*

*Dedicated to that other great novelist of Argyll, Neil Munro, Gillespie
was Hay's first novel and was published in 1914. His much less well-
known second novel* Barnacles *appeared in 1916. Hay, the son of a Tarbert
herring buyer, was educated at Tarbert High School and Glasgow
University. After working as a schoolmaster and freelance journalist, he
became a minister of the Church of Scotland being ordained to Elderslie,
Renfrewshire in 1909. He served there until his death at the age of thirty-
nine. Hay's birth date is frequently, but erroneously, given as October
1881 but was in fact 1880 as he appears in the Census of April 1881.*

Chapter I

Somewhat by east of the bay two of the Crimea cannon, each on a
wooden platform, lifted to seaward dumb mouths which once had
thundered at Sevastopol. A little west of the derelict guns, and almost at
the end of the shore-road, stood a gaunt two-storeyed house. Its walls

were harled, its gables narrow and high, and its plain windows, whitened
in winter with sea-salt, gave it the appearance of an old high-browed lady,
with her white hair tightly drawn back from her forehead. This house, at
the root of the hills, bleached with the gales of centuries, and imminent
upon a beach of gravel, had a sinister appearance. From a distance one
was infected with a sense of austere majesty at first sight of the house. It
came as a discovery, nearer hand, that it was the tall gables which
produced this effect. Attention, however, was attracted, not to the gables,
but to a sign which hung over the door. Dimly traced on this heart-
shaped sign was the half-defaced head of a man, and a hand grasping a
dagger. The hand stabbed down with sleuth-like malignity. The place had
once been an inn and of considerable repute; but horror came to nest
there in the inscrutable way in which it attaches to certain places. Two
men had come up from the sea in the dusk, and put in for the night at the
inn. His wife being sick, Alastair Campbell went up in the morning to
rouse the men. He found one of them lying on his back on the floor as if
sunk in profound meditation. A bone handle rested on his left breast.

'Clare tae Goäd,' said Campbell, 'I thought it was the dagger o' the sign
above the door. A cold grue went doon my back.' The slain man, one-
eyed, with a broad black beard, was a Jew. His pockets had been rifled.
The hue and cry was raised, but the tall, swarthy fellow had vanished
even more completely than the dead man, where he lay nameless in the
south-west corner of the graveyard.

Fear fell upon the inn. It was named the 'Ghost'. The painted dagger
seemed to grate aloft when the wind blew. Campbell took to drink, and
used to wander through the house at night, candle in hand. His wife
became worn, watching him, and, always ailing, died within the year on
child-bed. It came to this at last that her husband sat in the bar all day
drinking with every wastrel, and too sodden at nightfall to make a
reckoning. He roved the rooms, shouting with terrible blasphemy on a
concealed left-handed devil to come out and show himself. Fishermen
sailing past said that they saw lights dancing about the rigging of the
'Ghost' in the grey of dawn. Soon all the bottles in the bar were emptied.
Campbell's comrades from the town dropped off, and the scavengers
who remained held the pewter measure beneath the tap as Campbell
tilted up each barrel in turn. Of all that he had done, of all that had
happened to him in his downfall and degradation, this was the most
pitiable.

'This is the last nicht, my he'rties,' he cried, tilting up the last barrel.
Without the sign creaked ominously in the scuffling wind. 'Hark to it!' he
yelled; 'the bloody dagger's speakin'. Here's to it;' and with an oath he

held the tankard to his mouth. His bloodshot eyes rolled in his inflamed face. 'By Goäd, boys, I'll fire the hoose ower my heid and burn oot the bloody Spaniard.' The scavengers stamped out the fire, and carried him upstairs to the bed of the room where he had discovered the Jew lying on the floor, sunk in eternal meditation. He kicked and screamed in mortal terror, the veins standing out on his brow like whip-cords, and the sweat drenching his face. In the midst of a scream he clapped his hands to his head and heaved upon the bed, and the room became suddenly quiet with the dumbness that follows a thunderclap. Campbell had taken a shock. The coyotes at his bedside held the tankard to his twisted mouth; the liquid trickled impotently down over his chin, and they knew that he was done. At the turn of the night Campbell joined hands with the bearded Jew, and together they went into the Shadow to look for retribution on their maimed and scarred lives.

Through the night the creaking of the sign without was as the rattling of Death's skeleton keys.

Chapter II

Richard Glamis Strang bought the inn. Nobody else would bid for such a nest of bad odour. Mr Strang, untainted with the supernatural of the West Highlands, was young and about to marry. He had established himself in Duntyre. He was not a native of these parts, having sailed from the Heads of Ayr, where his folk had been ling-fishers. For a year he had lived penuriously, like a Viking, in the fo'c'sle of one of the derelict smacks heeled on the beach, and took to the herring fishing. He wore a thin silver chain twisted round his neck in a double loop. Its ends disappeared with a heavy silver watch beneath his oxter. Over his jersey he wore a waistcoat lined with red flannel, which peeped abroad at the armpits. Only in the coldest weather did he wear a jacket. A hardy, tall, weather-beaten man with a stoop, taciturn and slow of speech, whose large hands gripped like steel. His eyes, grey and keen as blades, were seated in those depths which sea-vigil digs in the head of man. He took the sea in his little boat, working his lines during the winter, and in the spring he sold her to a boat-hirer, and offered money down for a share in a fishing-boat. He told the crew he had come from Ayr to found a home in the west. He was accepted; his skill recognised; his seamanship became a matter of wonder. None in the fleet could steer as he by the weather-ear. He went upon his own ground unquestioned, till on a Saturday night at the 'Shipping Box', a Macdougall, a red-haired, vitriolic man, half drunk, called him by an indecent name, saying he was a Lowland interloper. A strain of Irish blood in Mr Strang surged up into his pale face, and his eyes glittered like swords upon the little red man, who mouthed at him.

'Come on,' he spluttered. 'Dae ye ken who I am? I'm the man that boiled a kettle in the lee o' a sea. Come on, ye Ayrshire bastard, I'll show ye the wy tae fush herrin'.'

A plump smack sounded abroad, and the Macdougall went down under the palm of Mr Strang. A laugh from some twenty salt-hardened throats burst boisterously on the fallen hero's ears.

'Dived like a solan, Erchie,' someone cried; and the Macdougall rose, his coward heart fluttering in fear.

'By the jumping Jehosiphat!' he cried, 'but you're a man,' and put forth his hand. Mr Strang took it and nodded.

'We're aye learnin', Erchie, to work to windward,' he said with a quiet smile.

Thus was he enlarged upon the imagination of men. Thus do men found the pillars of their house upon clay, rust, and mire.

He fell in love with one of the girls of the town, a Macmillan, lissom, white as milk, red as the dawn, with an eye for mirth and an abundance of sympathy – a trusty, wise mate. He had been reared in an iron school; bred to the sea with nerves of steel informed against the chances of gales, the darkness of fogs, the welter of snow-showers. He had the sailing lore by rote; and putting no store by anything but his business in the waters, neither legend nor superstition, took the inn at an easy rate, made some alterations, but left the sign above the door, where on surly nights it swung and groaned as if lamenting the weird upon the ill-fated house. On tempestuous winter nights of the first year of their wedded life, when they sat in the stone-flagged kitchen, her tales of the countryside came upon him, not with the stuff of surprise, but of magic. She had fed on oral romance and was its herald, proclaiming to him the deeds of her ancestors of Knapdale, and their mad ploy on the playground of half the county. Outside the seas thundered and clawed the beach; the old sign of the faded head mourned and jabbered; the sea-fowl screamed over the roof; and the house shook to the hammers of the gale. To the man the Lord of Hosts was abroad upon the air, and the wings of His angel troubled the deep.

The whole thing was so different from the sordid life of an Ayrshire fishing-port, which had no leisure and little inspiration for romance in its pale flat lands, that his life became clothed upon with wonder, and he lived in a world with more in it of magic than of reality. He sat under the elusive deft hands of a seer, who wove upon him a garment rich with pearls and shone upon with a haunting light, here and here alluring and splendid; but there also stained with the shadows of what was grim, terrible, and foreboding. He could not feel himself sib to this glancing wife. This strange food of reality for her had always been to him the thinnest stuff of dreams – things he had heard of vaguely, things so improbable and intangible in a world of deep-sea lines and strife with winds, tides, and piratical dog-fish that scarcely the phantom of their ghostly presence had passed upon the face of his seaboard. Now he heard them, plucked from the life of a people, and chanted as their gospel by a girl who crept close to him, shivering at the sadness of her tale. As the sea without droned the antiphon, and the homeless wind upon the hill cried the antistrophe, he thought it was a wilding elfin thing he loved who was one with the witch-wind upon the waste, and with the changeling brumous sea. At the end of the tale, as a dog that is half drowned shakes the water from its pelt, he shook himself free from an undefined sinister influence.

One evening, when dark-bluish shadows lay upon the snow, she had been telling tales of olden bickerings – how one of her race had been hanged by the Duke of Argyle from the tall mast of his galley within the harbour there at the west end of the Island; of one that had been out in the '45 and had fled the country to France, and had married there – there was a strain of French blood in her veins; of another that had come out of the foreign wars limping under the weight of a major's commission, and had found his grave in the lee of Brussels at Waterloo; and then suddenly veered to an ancient tale of a heroine of her race who had slain her son to save her lover. She ceased talking. Her husband looked at her with simple level eyes. In the silence they heard the cry of wild geese high up in the sky – the ghostly birds, instinct-driven, passing as the arrow of God through the heavens to their decreed place.

'We are driven by something deep within us that we have got from our ancestors, to do strange things that were allowed in their age, but are unlawful now,' she said. 'Honk! Honk!' vibrant and clear as a bell it rang out high over the snow in response – the bugling of birds borne along by the 'something deep' within them – and was heard by these frigate-birds, a man and a woman, sitting facing one another in the pitiable belief that they, alone of all God's creatures, can stem the call of destiny.

She told of her who had slain her son to save her lover, and of the terrible doom that rested on the name ever since, and was not yet fulfilled, that fratricide, parricide, or matricide would yet stain their house and open the ancient scar again before the house and name perished for ever.

'Oh, my dear, dear husband, if the doom should fall on you or on our children!' She lifted a scared white face searchingly to his. Alas! that every evangel must have behind it a doom.

'I vowed again and again never to marry to escape it' – a faint smile stole across her serious face – 'but love for you compelled me. Oh, Dick! Dick!' she wound her arms about his neck. 'You love me, don't you? Tell me again that you do. Our love must keep the doom at bay.'

He struggled back again to the place of reality from that twilit land to which she had led him. He was vexed with her imagined woe.

'Doom be blowed,' he cried; 'it's as dead as a red herring.'

'Oh, Dick! Dick!' she visualised the haggard spectre riding the back of her house; 'you must love me to fight it. You do, don't you?'

'As weel as I love my mother, lyin' i' the mools o' Ayr Kirkyaird,' he answered solemnly.

She held up her mouth to him.

'Mary,' he adjured her, 'the time's gane by for ony mair nonsense o' thae olden times. Doom be hanged. Wha's tae kill either you or me? We're mairrit eighteen months lucky, an' hae nae wean yet.'

'I'd like to have a baby, a wee girlie; but I'm afraid, terribly afraid.'

He jumped to his feet, flushed and angry.

'Feart o' an auld wife's story.'

'Hush, Dick, hush; even this house isn't canny. There's a curse on it. Do you hear it? That creaking sign scares the life out of me at nights, when you're at the fishing. I can't sleep for listening to it.'

He clapped his two big hands together.

'Doon it comes noo; where's the hammer?'

He searched, but could not find it.

'Never mind, Dick,' her eyes followed him through the kitchen, 'you can take it down in the morning.'

But in the morning the frost had frozen the wind, and Dick was gone to shoot 'the big lines' ten miles away on the Nesskip banks. The sign was forgotten; and the wild geese had passed on unerringly, unquestioningly, on the path of destiny.

Chapter III

Six months later Richard Strang came to face something that was elemental. His wife was pregnant. As she became heavier with child he deserted his work to comfort her, but could not drive away her fear.

'Pray God it's a girl; a girl can do no harm;' and again she harped on the ancient tale, and summoned up the black rider that rode with such sinister menace on its back.

'Mary,' he cried, fumbling impotently with his hands, desirous to strangle this hideous ghost, 'will ye bring the doom on yoursel'?'

'Oh, no! No!' she moaned, wringing her hands.

'You're like to,' he answered bitterly. 'You'll kill yoursel' an' the wean in your womb wi' fright.'

She cowered, but clung despairingly to the arms of her cross.

'Oh, no! No, Dick! It won't be that way, however it comes.'

He was fairly angry now.

'Let me hear nae mair o' this trash an' nonsense. Your wild ancestors is no goin' to herry my nest. If they had to labour at the oar there wad be nane o' this.' His voice had a ring of pride in it. It was the first time he had referred to his people. 'It may be bonny to tell; but I'm thinkin' it wad hae been better for them to hae earned an honest penny like me an' mine.' He got up and strode through the kitchen, the iron of his sea-boots ringing on the flags. 'They were a bonny crew wi' their ongoins. As for oor folk, they were skilly at the lines an' the oar. They werna trokin' wi' princes that hadna a penny to their name. I don't ken as ony were hangit or got a red face for being ca'ed a thievery set. We didna brag o' being rebels an' shoutherin' a gun; oor name wasna cried aboot the countryside for dirty work wi' the lassies and ploys at the inns.'

She put out her two blue-veined hands to him piteously, her eyes big with fear, her breasts heaving rapidly. He pushed them away. 'We didna ride hell-gallopin' on black stallions, an' leave the weemin' at hame scared o' their life.'

She burst out sobbing, her face like clay. He strode up to her. 'Mary! Mary! My lamb, I'm no angry at ye, lassie; I'm vexed at the wy ye're vexin' yersel' wi' a' this clishmaclaiver.'

'Dick! Dick! Oh! Oh!! Oh!!! don't look at me that way; don't be angry with me; you'll kill me.'

He gathered her in his arms with a groan.

'Downa greet; downa greet mair; it's a lassie that's comin'.'

The sobs trailed away.

'If it's a boy, leave him to me. I'll teach him hoo tae handle the tiller, no' the dirk. Just bide till you see.' And he comforted her.

Five months later he made fast his boat to an iron staple beneath the guns and hurriedly leapt ashore. Last night his wife had taken a fancy for whitings. Since daybreak he had searched three banks. The white fish, strung on by the gills to his fingers, shone in the dusk as angels of mercy come up out of the sea. As Richard Strang stepped within his door and stood in the passage at the foot of the stair, he heard a wailing cry in the room above – thin, fretting, querulous. His heart stopped in its beat. Open-mouthed he listened, with his massive dark head leaning forward. The sign rasped above the door; and mingling with its harsh noise was that feeble whimper. The hand of something alive, which had that moment drawn in from a far-off impenetrable deep, beyond the confines of the world, touched his heart with tender fingers. A new life from inscrutable eternity mingled with his being. Out of a vast silence it had come, away back in the ages. He gasped. Was she right after all? Did ancestry stalk Time and become reincarnate? That wail seemed to drift up from the dim spaces of a far unknown. Lugubriously overhead the sign rasped and ground out its baleful note. Once more the wail rang out, now strong and lusty. Tiny fingers creeping over his heart, set it drumming in his breast. 'Good God!' he whispered, 'The baby's born,' and shaking the fish from his fingers he tooks the stairs in three bounds, and saw the pallid face of his wife turned to the wall. The room was heavy with the dumbness and mystery which pass into the chambers of birth. Lucky Ruagh from the Back Street was bending over a long-shaped, dark-haired head. His wife turned a face of woe to him, as she stretched out a thin white arm and pulled his face down to her.

'Oh, Dick! Dick! It's a boy.'

Stunned, he could answer nothing; and when he was again at the foot of the stair he was listening to a wail which, borne down upon the wind of Time out of an inimical midnight past, and passing beneath the heavens like an arrow of God, struck unerringly into his heart, as he stood listening to the scurry of the wind rasping the rusty dagger overhead. With every swing of the drunken sign the dagger was plunged downwards with a snarl.

Chapter IV

Man is the blindest of God's creatures. We concert measures and cast the most sanguine of plans, and all the time are weaving a mesh for ourselves. We harness life and put a snaffle bit in its mouth and, gathering up the reins, direct our hopeful course. All the time we are trotting down a road that has been prepared for us. Richard Strang was determined to conquer heredity by habit. The vision which he had seen of the spirit of ancestry gleaming out of the past had terrified him, and it was he who was now afraid of the doom. He had established the house of Strang and, forgetting that heredity is stronger than the bands of habit, planned a definite mode of life for his son. Purblind, he was but fashioning the dynamite that was yet to ruin his house. The son took after him. He trained the boy to the sea; gave him no books to read; took him from school at the bare age of fourteen. The tales of his romance were figures; his tradition was record catches of fish. The only doom the boy feared was loss of gear in a gale. The parents pathetically believed that if the lad got no stupid stories into his head he was safe. The son not only inherited his father's temperament; but where his father judged of the chances of the sea, the boy dreamed of them. From training as well as by nature he became close-fisted. Where the father was keen the son was greedy. The parents, dreading the very word 'ancestors', secretly rejoiced; and the father even tempted fate one idle night by asking the lad if he ever read a story-book. The boy curled his lip. 'Story-books 'ill no boil the pot.' The parents smiled. Purblind!

Mrs Strang had no more children. Life became fuller for her. She lay awake at night when husband and son were on the sea, not from any fear of doom but from fear of the perils of the deep. The boy grew supple, tall, broad, commonplace in mind, a worshipper of things. At twenty, when his father had given him his own bank-book, he began to dominate the house. His mother, folk noticed, was failing. She was troubled with a little hacking cough, and seemed to have grown lately. She was out a good deal, by Doctor Maclean's advice. Her favourite walk was up to the town, round its curving shore street to the north road, which brought her to Galbraith's farm. She had often wondered why Mrs Galbraith had become a farmer's wife, for this woman read books of philosophy and poetry, played the piano, and could discourse about Nature, its beauties, its secrets, and its wayward moods, to Mrs Strang by the hour as they sat on the brae, looking down on the fishing-fleet in the harbour and on the town. Once or twice Mrs Strang's son accompanied her on these walks.

'Gillespie,' she asked him once, 'what secrets have you and Mr Galbraith got together?' There was a pleasant ring of maternal pride in her voice. It was difficult to know if Gillespie Strang ever flushed. He had his mother's high colour. It was brick-red on the nape of his bull-dog neck. Gillespie looked fixedly ahead.

'There's nae secrets. He's learnin' me to ferret an' trap rabbits for a pastime.'

Times were never so good. It was a word with the elder fishermen, 'When spring comes in with spring tides and a new moon the fishing is sure to be good.' Each herring meant money. Gillespie was constantly on the sea. At twenty-five he had a strong name in the bank, and Lowrie the banker would cross the street, seen of men, and talk civilly to him. Every man's fortune is in a lockfast box, of which he has the key. Some men use it skilfully; some blunder and break the lock; many tell themselves they are unable, and live by assisting other men to use their key. Gillespie, a master of craft, had the wards well oiled. None was defter with the key. He looked to unlock a fortune, this wiry supple youth.

He had extended the scope of his operations from the sea to the hill. This hybrid life put him in bad odour with everybody. To be a fisherman is always a fisherman; to be a farmer always a farmer. Gillespie was despised as an idiot, who wrought clashing irons in the fire. His eye was as quick on the gun as on the line; as cunning with the snare as with the tiller. He made a bargain with Lonend, whose farm marched with Galbraith's, for the rights of fishing, shooting, and trapping over his lands. He worked like two men; his robust frame was seldom fatigued. He visited his snares at dawn, when he had returned from a night's fishing. Secretly he snared the runs in the graveyard. Superstition made him immune from detection. In the winter when he could not tempt the sea, he shot rabbits and roamed the forest for white hares. He arranged with a Glasgow merchant of the Fish Market for the disposal of his hares, rabbits, wild-duck, and trout. He was seldom in his father's house. If he was not on the sea, draining his nets of their ultimate fin, he was at Lonend. He was now on his way there with his mother; but suddenly left her in the hollow below Galbraith's farm and skirted the edge of the Fir Planting. In this sere time of the year the place looked bleached and grey, and was full of a haunting melancholy. It was empty, save for a solitary man ploughing the Laigh Park. He was a tall spare man, loosely knit, whose hair was turning grey. His face had something of the geniality and frankness of a child's. In the plum-like bloom of the winter dusk he ploughed the lea, urging his ministry of faith in a pentecost of peace. It was strange to watch him at his work of redemption, for he looked wan, haggard, spent. The fruition of autumn seemed an impossible thing to this prematurely aged man, and his worn grey and brown team. As the pallid sunset fell across the lines of resurrection which his plough turned up, the field looked a half-torn, rifled purse. At the end of the field he turned, with the gait of a man who has weariness even in his bones. In the dimness Gillespie could discern but the faint outline of a figure. He heard a dull creaking of harness, and a monotonous voice urging the drooping horses, which moved beneath a faint cloud. Patiently they drew out of the shadow of the firs and plodded down the field. A curlew cried on the moor above; a vagrant gull flitted by like a ghost with silent swoop. The trees on the east and south sides gathered the gloom about them. In the oppressive stillness they stood up like gaunt sentinels of the man's labour, screening him from the pirate eyes of Gillespie. Inexpressible sadness, and the pathos of human frailty, set their profound significance upon this altar of hope; for though the man was at the beginning of things in his labour, yet he was consumed with the modern cancer of unrest. He was up to the ears in debt to Gillespie. The money had been largely squandered in Brodie's back-room. Late and early he wrestled with the sour soil, relying upon the imperishable husbandry of earth to stop the mouth of the wolf, without perceiving that whisky would make the ground sterile.

With a faint shearing sound the plough lifted the scented fallow, but the aridity of Galbraith's heart would admit no savour of the fresh earth. The dying are not revived with eau-de-Cologne. In the upturned soil Galbraith knew no potency; in its young face felt no resurrection. Only in the doggedness of despair he caught a gleam of far-off gold in the black, shining furrows. He ploughed on mechanically, straight and silent to the end of the field. He was assisting in turning Gillespie's key in the lockfast box.

The early stars arose upon the wood. So benign it all was, and he so weary. He came to a halt in the thick shadows of the Planting. A little wind began to rustle among the skeleton boughs, like the feet of timid animals scurrying in the dark. Suddenly a light flared in the window of the farm. It spoke of the security, the tranquillity, the tenderness of the hearth across the perplexing vastness of this outland brooding night. The ploughman turned his eyes upon it in a long hungry stare. Slowly he unyoked and turned his horses home, and upon them fell the deliberate night, as the moon grew by stealth over the tree-tops and across the half-ploughed field.

Our nature is rarely prophetic of happiness: very little causes to brood over it the sable wings of omens. Thus Galbraith, harassed with vexing thoughts, was not startled on hearing Gillespie's voice as he stepped out of the shadows.

'Makin' heidway wi' the plooghin', Calum.'

This was Gillespie's way – no salutation. There was something sinister in the tone. It was the voice of an overseer.

'It's a dreich job,' Galbraith answered wearily. He sought for no explanation of Gillespie's appearance there at such an hour. The movements of vultures are unquestioned.

The business became rapid – so rapid that Galbraith never finished his 'dreich job'. Gillespie's voice was honeyed.

'I thocht it better to see ye here, no to be vexin' the missis.'

Gillespie lied. He did not want his mother, who was at the farm-house, to pry further into his affairs. Galbraith was nervously plaiting the mane of the half-foundered grey. Man and beast were stooping to the earth in exhaustion.

'It's kin' o thochtfu' o' ye,' Galbraith said, with a gleam of irony.

'Weel, Calum, I dinna want to press ye, but I'm needin' the ready money ee' noo. I'm thinkin' o' buyin' a trawl.'

Galbraith was puzzled. 'Trawling' for herring was illegal.

'The Government 'ill no alloo trawlin'.' In censorship Galbraith plucked at hope. Gillespie, on the other hand, had foresight.

'Ay! But it's comin'.' His exultant voice flouted the song, 'There's a good time coming, boys', in Galbraith's face. 'I've ordered a couple o' trawls frae Greenock. I'm needing the ready money to pey them.' As a matter of fact, he had requisitioned no fewer than half-a-dozen 'trawl' nets, and thereby entered upon another step in his career. He had no intention of using them: that was too risky; but he meant to sell them – secretly. They could only be bought 'sub rosa'. It is the ideal way of commerce for a Gillespie, who could make his own selling price.

'I'm fair rookit oot,' answered Galbraith, in a despondent voice. The grey nickered uneasily, and whinnied towards home.

'I'll maybe hae to foreclose then.' The voice was as suave as Satan's. Galbraith's fingers suddenly ceased from teasing the horse's mane. He half raised his clenched hand to the stars.

'By Göad, ye'll put me to the door!'

Gillespie saw the threatening gesture. He was a coward, physically and morally. Lares and penates were meaningless to him. He cut the red strings which bound these to the heart of the man as readily as he cut cheese. To save his skin he temporised.

'I'd bide off till the fall if I could, Calum,' he said plausibly, 'but thae merchants in Greenock 'ill no' be put off.' He made a gesture implying urgent necessity, and said coaxingly, as if advising a friend:

'What's to hinder ye gettin' Lowrie to back a bill for ye?'

Galbraith regarded him moodily.

'It comes agin the grain,' he answered. He pondered, stubbing the fallow with his toe, then raised his head.

'Hoo muckle will I lift?' he asked. We talk of 'lifting money' out of the bank.

It did not suit Gillespie's book to be clear of Galbraith altogether. He wanted a grip on the farm.

'Let me see, let me see' – in the stillness his breath whistled sharply in his nostrils. 'I'll mand, I think, wi' three hunner.' Galbraith slightly staggered against the grey, which moved forward at the touch.

'Whoa, there!' he called out irascibly. 'Three hunner!' As a straw is more than a straw to a drowning man, so Galbraith in the depths was unable to estimate this sum at its proper value.

Gillespie twittered upon one of his rare laughs.

'Hoots, man, gie Lowrie a lien on the hairvest, an' the hunner's yours lik' the shot o' a gun.'

A man will see resource in the wildest scheme when the roof is cracking over his head.

Galbraith acquiesced. He was the first of many whom Gillespie brought to dance to his pipe.

Lowrie was a withered looking man, bald, clean-shaven. The skin below his chin hung slackly, and was of the grey colour of a plucked fowl's. He nipped at it when dealing with grave matters of finance. He nipped at it now as he interrogated Galbraith. This Lowrie was a man who never went abroad, save to church. He had a beat on the pavement in front of the bank over which he lived; and there, as upon a balcony, he spied upon the town. He knew to a farthing the state of every man, and he astutely estimated their occasions.

'A large sum, if I may say so, a very large sum on a sudden notice.' His small, quick, penetrating eyes searched Galbraith's face. Galbraith, a child of the piping winds and blowsy rains, was ill at ease in this musty atmosphere. The large green safe, with a screw arrangement on the top, appeared to him an ambuscade. Malevolence lurked in it, waiting for threadbare men. And this pursy little man probed him. If they had foregathered in Brodie's back-room, with glasses winking jovially at them – but here the sombre angel of want seemed to shake a mildew from its wings. Galbraith was silently reviling the foxiness of Gillespie which had driven him there.

'May I ask what you need such a large sum for at this time of year?'

Galbraith seized the chance to smite Gillespie. He would show him up.
'It's for Gillespa' Strang,' he blurted out.

The banker's eyebrows went up; the tips of his fingers came evenly
together. He crossed a plump leg.

'Ah! Indeed, for Mr Strang; I see, for Mr Strang. And what call has Mr
Strang upon you?'

'I owe him risin' on five hunner, the fox.'

Galbraith was warming to his task. Lowrie held up a fat preaching
palm.

'No personalities, please. That does no good.'

'He's brocht me to the end o' my tether,' said Galbraith bitterly. The
banker sighed the sigh of a man of sorrows, as who should say, 'They all
come to me to deliver them,' but his tones were incisive.

'Will Mr Strang not accept a lien on your crops?'

Galbraith shook his head.

'That is unfortunate. Mr Strang is a keen business man, and in the
interests of my employers I do not feel myself justified in accepting your
bond. You see, Mr Strang has a prior claim.' The banker hesitated a
moment, and looked as if plunged in thought. The next he rose abruptly.

'I'm sorry to say that I cannot consider your proposal, Mr Galbraith.
Extremely sorry.' With his left hand he plucked at the slack beneath his
chin; his right he extended in a dry official way to Galbraith.

'Mr Grant.' He raised his voice.

A tall, fair-haired man appeared, with a pen in the cleft of his ear. He
had peeped over the top of the glazed glass portion of the door before
entering.

'Mr Grant, please show Mr Galbraith out.'

Galbraith, in tow of the banker's clerk, vanished from the malice which
loured from the green steel safe, and its screw apparatus which ground
down the lives of needy men.

The banker sat down and wrote a note to Mr Strang, junr., at the
'Ghost', desiring the favour of an interview with him at his earliest
convenience. He proposed to himself to inform Mr Strang privately of
the visit of Mr Galbraith. In this fashion the banker sought the
confidence of 'solid men'. Gillespie came late to that interview, for in the
meanwhile Galbraith had passed to that Bank, where the deeds done in
the body, whether they be good or whether they be evil, are husbanded
till the Books are opened.

The Smoky Smirr o Rain

from Wind on Loch Fyne

GEORGE CAMPBELL HAY (1915–84)

*George Campbell Hay was the son of the novelist John MacDougall Hay,
the author of* Gillespie. *After his minister father's death in 1919, George
Campbell Hay returned from the Manse of Elderslie, Renfrewshire to the
family home at Tarbert on Loch Fyne where he grew up before going to
study modern languages at Oxford. Tarbert and the life of Loch Fyne was
the inspiration for much of his work, including the collection from which
this poem is taken. Hay wrote in English, Scots, and Gaelic (as Dèorsa
MacIain Dèorsa) and translated poetry from a variety of European
languages.*

A misty mornin' doon the shore wi a hushed an' caller air,
an' ne'er a breath frae East or Wast tie sway the rashes there,
a sweet, sweet scent frae Laggan's birks gaed breathin' on its ane,
their branches hingin' beaded in the smoky smirr o rain.

The hills aroond war silent wi the mist alang the braes.
The woods war derk an' quiet wi dewy, glintin' sprays.
The thrushes didna raise for me, as I gaed by alane,
but a wee, wae cheep at passin' in the smoky smirr o rain.

Rock an' stane lay glisterin' on aa the heichs abune.
Cool an' kind an' whisperin' it drifted gently doon,
till hill an' howe war rowed in it, an' land an' sea war gane.
Aa was still an' saft an' silent in the smoky smirr o rain.

The Country of the Mull of Kintyre

from Highways and Byways in the West Highlands

SETON GORDON (1886–1977)

Seton Gordon was born in Aboyne, Aberdeenshire on the edge of the Grampian Mountains. From the publication of his first book, Birds of the Loch and Mountain, *in 1907 at the age of 21, he rapidly became known as one of Scotland's leading writers on natural history and topography. A specialist in ornithology, his pioneering works on the Golden Eagle and other Scottish mountain birds broke new ground.*

His two charming collections of description and legend, history and topography: Highways and Byways in the Central Highlands *and* Highways and Byways in the West Highlands, *first published in the 1930s, have always found readers and have recently been reprinted.*

This chapter on the Mull of Kintyre and its hinterland is typical of Seton Gordon's writing with its feel for landscape, its intimate knowledge of Highland history, customs and folklore and its passion for natural history. It paints a delightful picture of this fascinating corner of Argyll and sketches Kintyre's close associations with Ireland from the time of the Dalriadic settlement and St Columba through Bruce to the wars of Montrose.

The long peninsula of Kintyre or Cantyre (in Gaelic Ceann Tíre, the Head of the Land) which terminates in the wild headland of the Mull has long associations with its sister country of Ireland over the sea. On Kintyre landed Fergus Mór, first king of Dalriada (whose name is present in the burn of Tirfergus), and Adamnan relates that Columba on a visit to Kintyre, spoke with the captain and crew of a vessel newly arrived from France. On that occasion Columba had come from Iona, but there is a tradition of the country that the saint originally made his way from Ireland to Iona by way of the coast of Kintyre and stayed there awhile, before residing for a time in the cave at Ellary on the shore of Loch Caolisport. At a later date King Haco's fleet rounded the Mull and captured the strong fortress of Dunaverty, compelling the Scottish knight who held it for Alexander III to surrender the castle, and appointing Guthorn Bakkakoff as governor in his place. The oldest name for the Mull of Kintyre is Epidion Akron (Greek–Ptolemy), the Epidian Cape, from the Epidii, the Celtic folk who inhabited the Kintyre. The name became in the Old Irish Ard Echde. In Adamnan it is Caput Regionis, a literal translation of the Gaelic name Ceann Tíre. In the Norse Sagas it is Saltire or Satiri, the Land's Heel.

The traveller making his way to the Mull of Kintyre from the north, passes along a stretch of wind-swept country, level and productive, at the edge of which the long Atlantic swell breaks white even in calm weather. On the grey autumn day when I wandered south along this beautiful coast-line I could see Islay and Jura on the horizon to the west. There was a deep blueness on those island hills, and heavy shade was on them except for one small pool of golden sunshine on the heathery coast of Jura. In the middle distance rose the long island of Gigha with its small neighbour Cara, and on the far horizon lay Rathlin with the hills of Ireland beyond it. I passed the castle of Largie, where the MacDonalds still hold their old lands, and even in the most wind-swept places saw many small gardens bright with flowers. It was delightful to me, coming from the garden-less district of northern Skye, to find that the people of Kintyre had so great a love of flowers. Within a stone's throw of some of those cottage gardens creamy seas broke lazily upon the low sandy shore, where oyster catchers were feeding and bathing, and lapwings were circling in great flocks high overhead. Here was the Spirit of Ocean – of the open unbridled Atlantic – and a Hebridean atmosphere. Yet here were no small crofts, as in the Hebrides, but large farms with well-filled stackyards. The potato crop was being lifted, and so many weeks had passed without rain that clouds of dust rose and were suspended on the quiet air as the work proceeded. To reach the Mull of Kintyre it is necessary (if one is to keep to the road) to pass through the town of Campbeltown. The old name of the place is Ceann Loch Cille Chiaráin, the Head of St Ciaran's Loch, and the old name of the parish is Kilkerran.

In the new *Statistical Account* mention is made of 'St Kiaran, the apostle of Kintyre', whose cave is situated four miles from Campbeltown. 'In the centre of the cave is a small circular basin, which is always full of fine water, supplied by the continual dropping from the roof of the cave. There is also a rudely sculptured cross on a stone, upon which the saint is said to have sat and prayed. This St Kiaran was highly esteemed by his contemporary, St Columba, who wrote a sacred ode upon his death, in which he celebrates his virtues. The ode is still extant; it commences, "Quantum Christe! Apostolum Mundo Misisti Hominem. Lucerna hujus insulae".'

In the same account, written in the year 1843, is the following: 'In the centre of the main street of Campbeltown an ancient cross forms a principal feature of attraction. It is richly ornamented with sculptured foliage. It has on one side this inscription: "This is the cross of Mr Ivar M. K. Eachran, once Rector of Kyregan, and Master Andrew his son, Rector of Kilcoman, who erected this cross".'

Near Campbeltown is Machrihanish, where a celebrated golf course has been laid out on the sandy *machair*: the road to the links branches off about a couple of miles south of Campbeltown from the road which leads to the Mull.

Near the Mull of Kintyre the character of the land changes. Here are wide moors with small glens leading down to the sea, and many hills, some of them rising steeply from the ocean. The narrow road to the lighthouse on the Mull winds through this hilly country and it is now possible to drive a car all the way to the gates of the lighthouse. At the highest point of the road, which must be a full thousand feet above sea level, I left it and turning to my right climbed Beinn na Lice, a hill of 1,400 feet which rises here. Crossing green slopes of crowberry, where blue hares fed, I soon reached the cairn on the hill-top. There was a profound silence on the hill and a soft grey light was over land and sea. Rathlin, blue and mysterious, rose across the calm ocean strait named of old Sruth na Maoile, where the children of Ler were compelled by witchcraft to remain in the shape of swans during 300 long years. Rathlin lies so close to the Irish shore that it is interesting to remember it was for long reckoned as one of the Hebrides, and was a part of the kingdom of the Isles. On Rathlin Robert the Bruce was concealed by his ally Angus Og, Lord of the Isles, and when the kingdom of the Isles was surrendered to the Scottish Crown in 1476 the island became a part of the lands of MacDonald of Islay. Rathlin is mentioned by Adamnan, who writes of it as 'insula quæ vocatur Rechru', and the Isle was known as Rechrin before the variant Rathlin was used. Between Rathlin and Ireland I could see no waves on that great tidal stream known in early times as Coire Bhreacáin (not to be confused with the strait of the same name between Jura and Scarba) and written of by the learned Adamnan as Charybdis Brecani. The tale of Breccán who was drowned in this whirlpool with all his company of fifty ships, is told in the Book of Ballymote. Breccán lived before Columba's day, and it is recorded that Columba was once in peril from the whirlpool, and when the *curach* appeared likely to be overwhelmed Breccán appeared in friendly greeting and the coracle safely crossed the steep waves of the tidal stream.

A haze was now spreading fast northward over the ocean, but I could see the high rocks of Fair Head behind Rathlin and the misty outline of the Antrim mountains to the south. Jura and Islay were now faint on the horizon, while to the east Ailsa Craig was a dim cone rising from an invisible sea. North-east were the hills of Arran, now seen with difficulty in increasing mist and haze. More than a thousand feet below me was the lighthouse, beyond which gannets from Ailsa Craig could be seen travelling out to sea in the direction of Islay, flying very low above the tidal stream that was flowing north. When I had almost reached the lighthouse I saw many grouse flying over the steep heather-covered hillside; it was unexpected to find them so near the open Atlantic. A friendly wheatear, on migration perhaps, flitted from stone to stone. I had a kindly welcome from the head lighthouse-keeper, who told me that he had, a few months before my visit, been transferred from Barra Head to this station. He said that the bird life on the Mull was disappointing after Barra. The lighthouse on the Mull of Kintyre is one of those stations sending out directional finding wireless waves to shipping in time of fog, and two powerful wireless aerials stand close to the lighthouse.

As I reached the top of the hill road once more I looked back over the ocean and saw pools of soft sunlight which relieved the haze that was momently thickening. Soon the coast of Ireland was hidden from view and even the island of Sanda, a few miles off the shore of the Mull and the most southerly point of Argyll, was scarcely seen against gathering clouds. On Sanda are the ruins of a chapel dedicated to St Ninian.

I returned to Campbeltown by way of the village of Southend and passed, perhaps a mile before reaching it, a pleasant sandy bay flanked on the east by a small rocky peninsula. On this peninsula are the remains of the old fortified castle of Dunaverty. As early as the year 710 there is a record of this *dùn* having been besieged, but it will be known to posterity as the site of 'as disgraceful, bloody, and indiscriminate a massacre as the pen of history has ever recorded'. It was in the year 1647. The power of Montrose had been broken and at Dunaverty almost his last adherents were besieged by Leslie's army. The garrison of the castle consisted of MacDonalds and MacDougalls under the leadership of Archibald MacDonald of Sanda. The garrison held out until their water supply was cut off by the besiegers, and when a party from the garrison attempted to supply themselves from a stream near the base of the rock they were all slain. A flag of truce was then sent out, and the garrison surrendered to the mercy of the kingdom. 'General Leslie,' says the new *Statistical Account*, 'afterwards made a nice distinction, that the besieged had yielded themselves to the kingdom's mercy and not to his, and, availing himself of this infamous casuistry . . . the whole garrison were put to the sword except one young man.' That young man's name was MacDougall, and he owed his life to the good offices of Sir James Turner, adjutant in Leslie's army. But before the garrison of Dunaverty surrendered, the infant son of Archibald MacDonald of Sanda was carried secretly by his nurse from the fortress under cover of darkness and the baby was hidden in a cave that to this day is known as MacDonald's Cave. The nurse was Flora MacCambridge and the baby's name was Ronald.

Little remains to-day of the old fortress of Dunaverty on the grassy mound overlooking that broad bay with its red sandy shore. It was October when I visited the place, but the last summer had been unusually fine and warm and the sea rocket still flowered at the edge of the sandy shore while, to complete the illusion of summer, eider drakes called from the waters of the bay. I spoke with a fisherman who told me that he had often come across human bones in the sand here, and that he had also found old bullets. He said that when the foundations of the house which stands immediately beneath the castle were being laid, many human bones were unearthed. But before that, in the year 1822 after an unusually high tide, accompanied by a gale of wind, the sand was drifted from a bank near the ruined castle, and an immense number of human bones and skulls were laid bare.

A few hundred yards from Dunaverty, and near the public road, is to be seen a small enclosure. Here are buried Archibald Mór and Archibald Òg of Sanda, the leaders of the force who were massacred and who shared the fate of their men. It is narrated that MacDonald of Largie was also murdered in cold blood and is buried here. As though ashamed of that disaster which overtook its inmates the castle of Dunaverty has almost entirely vanished. When Robert the Bruce passed some nights here on his way from Saddell to Rathlin the fortress was considered well-nigh impregnable, for the sea almost surrounds the *dùn* and on the landward side was a fosse, covered with a drawbridge. The district shortly after the massacre was visited by the plague, so that the whole countryside was depopulated.

It was evening when I passed again through Campbeltown – now a changed place to what it was in the days when the great MacDonald had a castle here – and the sun was sinking as I arrived at the western seaboard of Kintyre. From a sky overspread by soft cloud a shaft of glowing light shone on sea and land, suffusing the long Atlantic combers that broke upon the shore where perhaps the great Fergus, first king of Dalriada, landed from his *birlinn* or galley. Faintly across the sea was Gigha, mysterious across drowsy waters, and as darkness settled on the coast the tremulous uncompleted autumn songs of wandering curlews mingled with the low murmur of advancing seas.

A Phaidrín do dhúisg mo dhéar
(Thou rosary that hast waked my tear)

AIFFRIC NIC COIRCEADAIL

TRANSLATION BY W. J. WATSON

A Phaidrín do dhúisg mo dhéar (Thou rosary that hast waked my tear) *is
recorded in the Book of the Dean of Lismore. It is the personal, simple and
sincere lament of a wife for her husband, Niall Og, who has died very
young and left her devastated.*

*Niall Og is thought to have been chief of Clan Neill and Constable of
Castle Sween for the Lord of the Isles from 1455 until his death. He also
owned lands in Gigha where he appears to have lived with his family. His
wife extols the virtues of her young husband and points out that he was a
generous patron of poets who would come from as far as the south of
Ireland for his patronage. Gigha will now be desolate without him and
Castle Sween, the scene of so much happiness for them both in the past, she
will not be able to look upon again. The ending of the poem is made more
poignant by the use of metaphor. The family (father, mother and child) is
compared to a cluster of three nuts. God has taken the choicest nut, the
father, and left the family inconsolable.*

*A very interesting feature of the poem is the reference to the rosary
which begins and concludes the poem. In Catholic devotional practice the
rosary is one of the great prayers of the church to Mary the Mother of God,
seeking her intercession with her Son for mankind. Rosary beads are held
in the hand and run through the fingers to enable suppliants to count their
prayers (mostly 'Aves' or 'Hail Marys') as they are being said. The sight of
the rosary in her husband's hand reminds the young wife of his goodness
and sparks off her grief. It is appropriate that the poem ends with a prayer
to Mary since the rosary is so particularly associated with her.*

A Phaidrín do dhúisg mo dhéar,
ionmhain méar do bhitheadh ort;
ionmhain cridhe fáilteach fial
'gá raibhe riamh gus a nocht.

Dá éag is tuirseach atáim,
an lámh má mbítheá gach n-uair,
nach cluinim a beith i gclí
agus nach bhfaicim í uaim.

Mo chridhe-se is tinn atá
ó theacht go crích an lá dhúinn;
ba ghoirid do éist ré ghlóir,
ré h-agallaimh an óig úir.

Béal asa ndob aobhdha glór,
dhéantaidhe a ghó is gach tír:
leómhan Muile na múr ngeal,
seabhag Íle na magh mín.

Fear ba ghéar meabhair ar dhán,
ó nach deachaidh dámh gan díol;
taoiseach deigh-einigh suaire séimh,
agá bhfaightí méin mheic ríogh.

Dámh ag teacht ó Dhún an Óir
is dámh ón Bhóinn go a fholt fiar:
minic thánaig iad fá theist,
ní mionca ná leis a riar.

Seabhag seangglan Sléibhe Gaoil,
fear do chuir a chaoin ré cléir;
dreagan Leódhuis na learg ngeal,
éigne Sanais na sreabh séimh.

A h-éagmhais aon duine a mháin
im aonar atáim dá éis,
gan chluiche, gan chomhrádh caoin,
gan ábhacht, gan aoibh i gcéill.

Gan duine ris dtig mo mhiann
ar sliocht na Niall ó Niall óg;
gan mhuirn gan mheadhair ag mnáibh,
gan aoibhneas an dáin im dhóigh.

Mar thá Giodha an fhuinn mhín,
Dún Suibhne do-chím gan cheól,
faithche longphuirt na bhfear bhfial:
aithmhéala na Niall a n-eól.

Cúis ar lúthgháire má seach,
gusa mbímis ag teacht mall:
's nach fuilngim a nois, mo nuar,
a fhaicinn uam ar gach ard.

Má bhrisis, a Mheic Dhé bhí,
ar bagaide na dtrí gcnó,
fa fíor do ghabhais ar ngiall:
do bhainis an trian ba mhó.

Cnú mhullaigh a mogaill féin
bhaineadh do Chloinn Néill go nua:
is tric roighne na bhfear bhfial
go leabaidh na Niall a nuas.

An rogha fá deireadh díbh
's é thug gan mo bhrígh an sgéal:
do sgar riom mo leathchuing rúin,
a phaidrín do dhúisg mo dhéar.

Is briste mo chridhe im chlí,
agus bídh nó go dtí m'éag,
ar éis an abhradh dhuibh úir,
a phaidrín do dhúisg mo dhéar.

Muire mháthair, muime an Ríogh,
go robh 'gam dhíon ar gach séad,
's a Mac do chruthuigh gach dúil,
a phaidrín do dhúisg mo dhéar.

THOU ROSARY THAT HAST WAKED MY TEAR

Thou rosary that hast waked my tear, dear the finger that was wont to be on thee; dear the heart, hospitable and generous, which owned thee ever until to-night.

Sad am I for his death, he whose hand thou didst each hour encircle; sad that I hear not that that hand is in life, and that I see it not before me.

Sick is my heart since the day's close is come to us; all too short a time it listened to his speech, to the converse of the goodly youth.

A mouth whose winning speech would wile the hearts of all in every land; lion of white-walled Mull, hawk of Islay of smooth plains.

The man whose memory for song was keen, from whom no poet-band went without reward; a chief nobly generous, courteous and calm, with whom was found a prince's mind.

Poets came from Dún an Oir,[1] poets too from the Boyne to seek his curling hair; oft did they come drawn by his fame, not more often than they got from him all their wish.

Slim bright hawk of Sliabh Gaoil,[2] a man who showed kindness to the Church; dragon of Lewis of bright slopes, salmon of Sanas[3] of quiet streams.

For want of one man all lonely am I after him, without sport, without kindly talk, without mirth, without cheer to show.

Without one man to whom my mind draweth of the stock of MacNeill since young Neil is gone; ladies lack mirth and joy; I am without hope of gladness in song.

Sad is the state of smooth-soiled Gigha; Dún Suibhne[4] I see without music, that greensward of a stronghold of generous men; the sorrow of the MacNeills is known to them.

Cause of our joyous mirth in turn, to which we were wont to go in stately wise, while now, alas! I endure not to view it from each height.

If Thou, Son of the living God, hast made a breach upon the cluster of three nuts,[5] true it is that Thou hast taken our choice hostage; Thou hast plucked the greatest of the three.

From Clann Neill hath been newly plucked the topmost nut of their cluster; often do the choicest of the generous men come down to the MacNeills' last bed.

The latest, choicest of them, it is the tale of him that hath sapped my strength; my loved yokefellow hath parted from me, thou rosary that hast waked my tear.

My heart is broken within my body, and will be so until my death, left behind him of the dark fresh eyelash, thou rosary that hast waked my tear.

Mary Mother, who did nurse the King, may she guard me on every path, and her Son who created each creature, thou rosary that hast waked my tear.

[1] Dún an Oir: in Cape Clear Island, off south-west coast of Ireland.
[2] Sliabh Gaoil: hill in south Knapdale.
[3] Sanas: Machrihanish in Kintyre.
[4] Dún Suibhne: Castle Sween.
[5] The cluster of three nuts is a metaphor for father, mother and child.

Remember Me

from Beyond This Limit

NAOMI MITCHISON (1897–1999)

Although born in Edinburgh and descended from a family of Perthshire landowners, the Haldanes, Naomi Mitchison's claims to be considered as a writer of Argyll are strongly founded. She and her husband Richard, a barrister and Labour MP, settled at Carradale in Kintyre in 1937 and she lived at Carradale House until her death there in January 1999 at the age of 101.

Naomi Mitchison's themes for her fiction were enormously varied – her subjects included the Haldane family's history, in a fine historical novel set after the Jacobite Rising of 1745, The Bull Calves; *mythology, ancient history, science fiction, contemporary novels set in Kintyre such as* Lobsters on the Agenda *and books for children. In non-fiction she wrote several volumes of memoirs and a volume based on her Mass Observation diaries during the 1939–45 War.*

Our choice from her extensive output, the product of over seventy years of active creation, reflects her active concern and engagement with political and social issues. It was written when the author was in her eighties and is a dark tale of life in Argyll after a nuclear war.

My name is Jessie MacKinnon. I was on the District Council for ten years and since then on the Community Council; I was Vice-Chairman, and indeed I am acting Chairman now. There was this and that committee and group in our small community a few miles out from Oban. My husband had a small mixed farm, which did well enough and gave him plenty of time in the winter for reading and wood-work. He was a great reader. After he died I carried on working the farm with one old man, for I liked doing it, but Rob and Sandy used to come out with their families and help me in holiday times. Sometimes in summer I used to let to a few boarders, nice folk. They came back mostly, I remember; they were all terribly taken with my garden, all of them, and the view. I had children. I had friends. It is all past.

My little granddaughter Fiona was staying with me, Rob and Mary's youngest. It is because of her that it is at all worth my while to be alive, and sometimes looking at her I wonder. For I ask myself has she truly escaped? She is beginning to grow up, to have the thoughts that come naturally to a young girl. But then? At least she looks better than most of the other children. Better indeed than some of them, poor wee mites.

This is the way it was with me. It was a light west wind and I was out in my garden, looking into the wind, so that I never saw the flash east over Glasgow. I only – somehow knew that something had happened. I turned and I saw the cloud go up. Then another. I thought about Rob and Mary; well, I will not speak of that now, nor of much else. My other son was in the Midlands of England: himself and – all of them. No word has come through. Nor will it now.

Queer things went through my head. The old man who helps on the farm, Colin Mor, came over from the sheds. He said 'They have done it' and then he stared round and began muttering about would the pensions go on. I looked at him and it changed to some kind of prayer. And then it was one of my neighbours, Miss Paterson, who had the rockery with the fancy heaths and the gentians. She watched the cloud with me and I felt her hand on my arm. She said, in a shaky voice 'No more Strathclyde now Jessie.' You see, we had all been speaking together about the new local government set-up and how badly it was turning out for us on the fringes, and then we both looked at one another and I knew she had said that in the hope of taking my mind off what she knew it must be on. And with that I remembered how she had a sister and brother-in-law in Helensburgh. So some way we managed a small laugh, and then I said, 'We'd best get down to Connel.' That was the Civil Defence Centre by the loch, and we had both said we would go over and help if there was ever any need, though some way we thought there never would be. We could not have brought ourselves to think otherwise. They had a stock of medicines and blankets and all that down there. She said hesitating 'Have you tried the phone?' I said no, for I knew, I knew. But yet now she had said it I lifted the receiver and dialled the number I knew so well. But there was nothing, nothing at all.

I gave Fiona a book and some sweeties and a great petting, saying I'd be gone for a while. She had not noticed a thing, indoors. I told her I would lock the door in case bad people were to come, but it was mostly to stop her going out – and touching anything. The flowers were still blooming, but if the wind changed –

We drove down to Connel and even then I began to wonder about petrol. We waited with others. Some of us tried to reason out why it had happened. The laird's wife said they had been small bombs or rockets, if it had been one of the big ones we would all be dead. 'Theatre weapons' she said and somehow naming it made it less terrible. One could hold it in the mind then. But the thing was, we had thought we were out of the world danger, that a small country such as we are today need not be drawn in. We did not know then what was being done over our heads. I am not even clear today, for the news that gets through is not to be trusted. No more than one can trust the grass or the sky. Not any more.

It was on into the evening before the first of the buses got through, and then the rest, and I looking, looking for my own ones. Just in case. It was not until a week or two after when they began to die that I could bring myself to be glad that Rob and Mary and Andy and Jean had not been among them; that it was all over for them, almost before I had seen the cloud. The only train that got through had been standing at Garelochhead; the driver was burned, but he carried on, the decent man; I remember he did not die for quite a while. He lifted a load all up from there to Arrochar; the woods were all on fire round him; it was the ones who had been working their gardens or that who had the burns. No train from further down Loch Long had a chance. The ones who came on the buses were from Alexandria and Balloch, the western edge of Dumbarton even. There were a few from Helensburgh who got across to the Lomond-side road, but they had been badly caught by the Holy Loch bomb. They had the most terrible things to tell us; some of them seemed to be going to live, but they had these burns that did not heal. The blankets were mostly used to bury them in. That is, until we began to see that there would be no more blankets and we could not afford to let the dead have any of them. The laird's wife brought down stuff from the Big House. Their son and his family were in Australia; they had not heard yet when I saw them last, and if the son were ever to get here, what would he find?

Miss Paterson had given up hope for her sister and brother-in-law. She was working hard, wearing herself out. I could see how Dr Bowles was counting on her; he was an elderly man who had come out to the highlands mainly for the fishing and golf and the pleasure of it here, as it was in those days. He had read the leaflets but had barely taken them in. The young doctor from Oban, Dr MacAndrew, knew more. But I could see how even he flinched from the burns. It was later that Miss Paterson told me about how hard it was to forget that her sister had a baby coming, her first. There were wee coats and socks that Elsie Paterson had been knitting, put away in tissue paper. For weeks after she kept dreaming she was putting another one away in the press. And then she woke. Those were the kind of dreams I had too.

That first night the wind blew itself out and there was a calm. But even while it seemed to be blowing there must have been a current away above us that was bringing some of the evil stuff west and over. I have some sense and I kept Fiona in the house, but myself I was working for the refugees. The District Nurse was on leave. She never came back. I started by bringing all my milk over to the centre; I thought it was the best way I could help. Dr Bowles had been pleased at first, but young Dr MacAndrew – he is dead now but he was a fine young man – said to me that it was as good as poisoned. 'Throw it away!' he said, and he told me quick while he was dressing a burn, for we still had dressings in those days, that the milk would be full of radioactive iodine and must on no account be given to anyone, above all not a child. It could damage the child's thyroid gland and give it a cancer or turn it into an idiot.

We all know that now. Too well do we know it. But then it was news and not everyone believed. Dr MacAndrew said to me 'Go round to your neighbours, Mrs MacKinnon, and warn them every one, and above all those with bairns. And mind, not a drop to Fiona.' So I did just that, but half of them laughed at me; it seemed against nature that good milk with nothing at all wrong in the look of it could hurt a child. So it came about that before a year had passed I saw my nearest neighbour's three turning from lively bright children into listless miseries. One of them has just died; we all know that is best.

Yet at the time it seemed just crazy; Fiona had been with me just because she'd had the measles and was needing good food. I did not think to do this extra washing of the vegetables which I do, not until later. Even so it had me puzzled, for we get our water from the high loch and it would be bound to get as much fall-out as the grass. I had not thought it out; when I did I began drawing water out of the old well, that is fed by a spring from far underground. I look and look at Fiona and wonder, did I keep enough of the stuff away from her? Or will she have something secretly eating at her? It is, I suppose, probable that she escaped. But I cannot help thinking sometimes that I did not do enough.

I have even tried to pray for Fiona, but I just cannot get myself to believe that it is any use now. I don't know even how she has taken it all. She clings onto me, but not too badly. She never or hardly ever speaks of what has been. Only at birthday or Christmas time. Mostly she tries to take the burden off me, more perhaps than a child her age should do.

I had of course to tell her, but not until we were totally certain, beyond the reach of hope. I think she knew by then. She asked about her uncle Sandy and the cousins, down south. Betty was her own age. I said we should not hope too much. By that time we had come to the conclusion that a string of these rocket bombs had been targetted across all the industrial parts of Scotland and England. Strategic destruction that is called. Not murder.

The police came over with their geiger counters, walking about the fields and houses. After a time they said it was safe or just about. 'Not like nearer in' I mind they said. One or two had been as far as Inveraray and they say the things ticked away there. Over the Rest they did not go. Nobody did. Arrochar – it is just a name now. But, for all they said, I found it hard to believe that our own land was unhurt.

Gradually we got a drift in of survivors, not like the first lot, though some had small burns or radiation sickness which did not kill at once; some of these have survived. But most were people who came where they thought there would be food. Some had their living knocked away. Some had been staying in hotels, though the full tourist season had not been on when the thing happened. The hotels shut and the guests had no way of going back to wherever they had come from; they were cut off except from the west. They drove as far as their petrol would take them and offered money, but what was the use of that? Still and all, those of us like myself who had rooms, took them in if they seemed decent. I had first an old lady and got mortally tired of her; she did nothing but complain. Then I took in an Edinburgh couple with two small children; I thought Fiona might like them. Mr Drummond did not look strong; he had been in some kind of an office with good pay; he seemed to think that some day he'd be back and find it going on. Indeed he tried to bluster at first and sell me his car for a great price, but his wife had more sense and we got together.

She would help with the housework and cooking, but she turned out to be a poor cook, having only done it in a town. He would dig, help on the farm and so on. I thought, well, he could dig up the back part of my garden behind the dyke which I had not bothered about for long enough, and we would put in more vegetable seeds. He agreed. We went to Oban together and got plenty of seeds. The shops still took money, in hope, one supposes, that some day it would be worth something. He did not know much about gardening but came back with a heavy spade and fork, and he certainly worked and did not complain about his blisters or the nettle stings. But we did not see much of each other.

They were in what had been Rob and Mary's room. I would wake in the night and hear them moving and for seconds, until my mind cleared, I would have the warm feeling that they were mine, not these strangers. I was not the only one to have that feeling about the incomers.

Yet in a way it was worse for them, since they had lost everything, while we still had our homes. I knew that and yet I could not be welcoming. So they were apt to get together and let out to one another how they felt about us. One can get the feel of this kind of thing in a small community and we could not blame them. But more had gone on to Oban and even to the islands and Ardnamurchan. And one or two had skills we needed; there is a brisk wee dressmaker from up Stirling way who never seems short of eggs or potatoes or even flowers.

Looking back on last year I find it hard some way to remember just when things happened. The electricity still goes on sometimes and was good enough for a while, since most of the hydro-electric stations were far enough from the towns. The others, the coal-fired ones, were put out of action at once. They say the great building at Longannet is still standing and the turbines inside it. Some day perhaps it will be possible for people to go back into it, start it all up again. Not in my time, nor yet in Fiona's. But the Falkirk bomb destroyed most of the works and until we can build up some kind of industry in Scotland there's power to spare. But things go wrong at our own sub-station level and there is no way of getting repairs. Some of the men have gone into the outskirts for short times and tried to get what supplies and spares they could carry away in barrows. But it is terribly risky, even with rubber boots and gloves. We would never urge anyone to do it.

It stands to reason that there was no petrol after the first month, even with the hard rationing. There was fighting over the last of it in Oban, and two of the police badly hurt. Perhaps this was to be expected. Here we just accepted it decently. But I'm wondering how long my poor old pony will last; he had to eat the grass and it must have been thick with fall-out. For that matter even if the wind had not changed, the stuff would have got back to us right round the world. As it must have come to everyone everywhere, even those who sent out the planes: but not strongly – I could wish it had been. We all worry about our beasts; I gave the first milk to the calves and they are not looking too grand for yearling queys and stots. The milk should be safe now with the radioactive iodine worn off and I could wish I had more of it, but the cows are just not in calf. We are hoping it will wear off as the ones with the geiger counters say, and it is great news when we hear of a new calf, even if it may be a bitty misshapen. But some of us small farmers depended on the A.I. centre with the stuff driven out to us, and that had to close down at once; it is queer how much we took for granted in the old days, now we are back to something much older. Maybe this summer when the flush of grass is on I shall be able to make a bit butter; it is something one misses, and Mrs Drummond seemed to think there'd be bound to be margarine at least, in the shops. Some of the folk with big deep-freezes and the Oban hotels themselves bought it up, but some of this was lost when the electricity went off, and the rest of us were not sorry for them.

It was the same going back to old ways with the fishing and all the boats depending on diesel, not just the engines but the winches and every new bit of machinery. The nets they had were far and away too heavy to haul by hand. But the fishermen got going, I'll say that for them; the big boats are laid up, but the small ones are out with lines and lobster pots and their trawl nets cut up into something lighter. It's the queerest thing, but already there seem to be more fish coming back; I have dried and salted a few. Yet I am doubtful about some of them. I remember Dr MacAndrew saying to a meeting of housewives 'It is this stuff the herring feed on, the plankton, that gets hold of the radioactive material that has fallen into the water, and it stands to reason the herring will be full of it, and so will the mackerel.' Yes, I remember that day well, for soon after that he got ill himself and knew there was nothing to be done. He had gone as far as Crianlarich to try to help the doctor there and both of them had gone down with the radiation sickness. I used to go over and sit with him once in a while. He would not go into hospital. It was crowded out and he said to me 'We mustn't waste resources. Remember that, Mrs MacKinnon.' His voice had gone thin by then, he was vomiting now and again; I wiped his face for him and he was saying he was sorry and trying to smile.

Yes, I have remembered. We have to make do with our own food. The tins in the shops are all done, even the kinds one never used to buy. I am lucky that my hens are still laying. Nearer Glasgow most of the poultry as well as the cattle died. They say there is hardly a cattle beast left in Dalmally and Tyndrum, as well as Strachur way. South of Tarbert there is nothing alive. One of the things had been targetted on Macrihanish. It was hard somehow the way we in western Scotland had been loaded up with these things which have brought destruction down on us and we were never even consulted. Defence, they said! When the haze came creeping over everything and the eastern sky glared like hellmouth – some way I had expected this – I kept in all the beasts from the inbye land and the hens, just as I kept in Fiona. I mind now I slapped her for running out. My heart bleeds for it but I know I was right. But the way I was placed I could not get the sheep from the high ground – indeed we had nowhere to put them under cover, none of us – and things have gone badly there. We would find a dead sheep here or there and when it came to lambing time, there were dead lambs and sick ewes. It is the same for all of us.

Maybe all this worrying about what we shall have to eat and to wear and how to mend our house is some help against the deep grief which we almost all have and the feeling night and day that we are cut off. The telly went blank, though for a time some people kept trying it; they couldn't believe it was over for ever. My radio never got much beyond Radio Scotland and Clyde. But I kept on trying. Once or twice I have heard foreign voices; I thought I could even make out a bit of French once, but it was faint and I could not get anything from it. Yet there are other people, maybe in the same fix as ourselves. If once we could get to them! But how? Fiona found an old newspaper at the bottom of a press and read the big headings, the football and all that. Finished. Finished. Then she found the strip cartoons and she was at me to know what happened next, so we made up stories. But I was glad to burn that newspaper and all the cheery lies it had in it. I can remember that it used to be said by the Americans and the Russians and the Chinese that they could stand an atomic war because it would only kill one in three or maybe one in four of their populations. I do not care one bit if there are no Americans left or no Russians or no Chinese. I would not lift one finger to help any of them if I saw one in trouble. Yet once I was a good church member with a great belief in human brotherhood. It is as though love has been killed in me.

Some of the folk round here have been going to the church and seem to be all the better for an hour of hymn-singing. But not me. I went once and the Minister kept on about sin and how we were being punished. But it seemed to me that all he had in mind was the wee kind of sins, gambling and fornication and drink. And the sins that brought all this on us were of a different kind altogether and nothing to do with God looking on to see if the boys were playing cards for money at the back of the haystack. We brought it on ourselves. It was not God. Without our intending it surely, but that made no difference.

At first we tried to go on with local government as it was. But it was too difficult. We had too much to do, all of us, and the Strathclyde administration was finished as though it had never been and the District Council could not go on. For a while we telephoned to Lochgilphead, but then the lines went down in a storm that November and could not be repaired. Even in Lochgilphead there were some people burned and a terrible lot of sickness later. The hospital there was to receive casualties from Glasgow; some got through, but most were scared of heading south again; it was too near the Holy Loch. I don't know how they got on later. Nobody has been that far for months, though we might manage it maybe next year. The District Engineer that we used to see at the Oban meetings tried to get through to Dunoon. He was a brave man, but it is just not enough to be brave. He is dead.

But when it comes to the bit, local government, whatever you call it, depends on grants from the central government. And there is no government. There is no centre. Schools only go on because we, the parents and grandparents, pay the teachers in eggs or potatoes, peats or meal. I gave one of them a box my husband had made; it had a lock and key. That matters these days. Public health is gradually breaking down for want of equipment. One of the married District Nurses who had retired came on again when it was clear that our own nurse would never come back from her leave. She had us all out gathering sphagnum moss and drying it for dressings and for use when there were no more sanitary towels to be had. We need to think of everything.

There is no postal service with no petrol for the vans. And I will never get the letters I used to look for. Never. Never. But our old Postie got hold of a pony and is starting running a service on his own, in and out of Oban, with the odd passenger and letter or parcel. He says that it's happening in north and mid-Argyll, and indeed we are beginning to get in touch, though everything is gone beyond Ballachulish. It must have been Inverness and Fort William that they picked out. Postie sends in the bill himself, using up the old forms and saying what he will take instead of pounds. There are still a few people who use the old money. But it is little used compared with things, most of all food, and that is how we pay Postie.

Well then, it seemed to Miss Paterson and me that we should at least get the Community Council started up again, so we called a meeting, just going round. The Chairman himself had been away at the time and, well, he never came back. So it was myself that needed to take the decision. So far we have had three meetings. It is not much more than six or seven miles for anyone to come in and up to now we have managed to give the executive committee a cup of tea, but they must bring their own sugar. There had been some thefts already, so we asked the policeman to come. Things were awkward for him because he had carried out the emergency orders, but then they had stopped. Oban Headquarters was not much better off, and there had already been some crimes there, the real thing I mean, not just young people showing off. Our own policeman came in and told me they were going out armed now in Oban, but for himself he could not see himself doing anything of the kind, for after all we were all decent folk.

I was taking the meeting and maybe I saw a bitty further ahead. Anyway I proposed from the Chair that our Police Force representative should be asked in the name of the community to go out armed. It has turned out to be just as well, though there was only the one time he has had to shoot – so far. He was upset about it himself, although he missed; but the gang were scared and ran, and it has kept certain ones away. The laird's wife brought in the gun, with her husband's compliments, and he would have come in himself if he had felt able. Postie went over later and asked if he could have the pair to it. I believe he has had to use it, though he will not say.

Old Dr Bowles came to the meeting, and I kept thinking if only it could have been Dr MacAndrew, for the old man was flustered and seemed some way unable to think ahead. He kept saying we ought to get in supplies, vaccines and antibiotics and that, though he knew as well as the rest of us that this was nothing but speaking into the wind. I had bought bottles of aspirin and cough mixture and disinfectant before the Oban chemist I mostly went to was out of them. The shop is shut now, and so are most of the others in Oban. I wish I had got more sugar, but I did not wish to appear grasping; most of it has gone already, though it is nice to see the jam and jelly I have. The laird has diabetes and there is no more insulin; it is weeks now since I have seen either of them. I had not wanted to ask the Minister to the meeting, but he came and started in about sin. I told him he was out of order, and a fair few laughed.

The incomers came to the meeting and mostly sat by themselves in the two back rows, except for the dressmaker body who sat with friends near the front. They wanted a piece of land ploughed up for themselves and one of the farmers who has a pair of good horses, offered to plough and harrow around an acre for them, free. But they must get their own seeds. It seemed fair enough to the rest of us, though clearly some of them thought they could do with more. They are managing with seeds this year and so are we all, but next year? Oats and barley will go on, and potatoes, but our turnips and field carrots will scarcely ripen seed so far north and I cannot see most of the greens doing it, still less beans and peas.

The talk at the meeting, which used in the old days to be about the footpath to the school and danger from cars, or else about the bus time tables, was now about food and security from raiders and what was happening elsewhere. Postie was good and offered to find out where the rest of the Community Councils were getting together. Indeed he has done just that and maybe it will be possible to build something up. It could be the only way. We have even had a representative coming from from Argyll across the loch and we hope to send someone over to mid-Argyll. We hear from the fishermen that there have been troubles in Mull and the folk in the big hotel waving money about and trying to get hold of a plane, but we will face that when it comes. Meanwhile we will strengthen ourselves. Several of our young folk have got out their old saddles and are keen enough to ride to a meeting. They have been making bows and arrows, even. But most of the time we needed to talk about getting together for this and that which had to be done urgently. I suppose it will be like this all over wherever people have escaped and maybe we are luckier than some.

The old Oban Town Council, that was there before Strathclyde, had got together, such as were left of them, and they sent over, trying to rope us in, with talk of rating the district and that. But they had little to offer us, except for office space and acres of paper and clips and rubber bands, and it was clear that what they wanted from us would be oatmeal and mutton. So we decided to write back a polite and formal letter, but to let it be known we would not be playing their game.

It was clear to all of us that we'd need to gò back to the old ways for the harvesting. A few of us had a bit of diesel oil laid by for the tractors, and some used it for harvesting, making out that something would happen one day, some help was bound to come. But it seemed to me that I would keep the little I had for the winter ploughing. My pony is not up to it. I slept with the key of the padlock under my pillow and I let it get about that I had a gun; who would know that I only have five cartridges? Though there was a time not so long ago when one could leave one's house door unlocked and no thought of harm.

Colin Mor has been terrible at first, asking for this or that, even if he knew I had none of it, but now he has settled in and is working hard. The queer thing was he wanted to keep getting his wages in cash. I told him that money was not worth having, but if that was what he wanted it suited me. I drew out all I had in my account, and borrowed quickly against my shares, though nobody, least of all the bank manager, knows if they will ever be worth anything again. But Colin Mor was happy, putting it away wherever it is he does put it, under his mattress maybe, and he was with us for harvest. He snares an odd rabbit and I make a stew with my onions and give him his share. The Drummonds did not like it at first, but they soon got over that. All of us got together when it came to a fine spell in September, and cut the oats with scythes and bound by hand; I tried to wear gloves at first, but they hinder one and we had to be quick; now I am worried about the skin on my right forefinger.

What we could not harvest at the back-end was fed to the beasts, though we were careful to keep plenty of seed. There may be enough fertiliser in the stores for next year's grain and grass, but it will need to be shared and not let the big farmers, least of all the ones in Mull, get too much of a share of it. By now we had almost forgotten which field was whose; we were needing to think all together. Again we needed to thresh by hand, since there was no fuel for the big thresher. But it is easy enough to make a flail, though hard and slow work using one. We had to grind the grain as best we could. I had a hand coffee mill and Fiona does half an hour at it after school. We were speaking at the last Community Council meeting about the possibility of getting one of the old water mills somewhere in Argyll working again. We were well aware by now that there would be no flour coming in and we must depend on our own oatmeal and barley meal. It is queer to think how little one used to value a loaf of bread.

We dug the potatoes with graips as we could not use the tractor spinners, all getting together as in the old days. Not one wee potato did we miss! We had a good feeling that they at least would be safe, though how can we be sure, for the evil stuff works down into the soil. We would find dead worms here and there. But we notice that there are far too many grubs and caterpillars and such and not the birds that used to clear them off for us. For the poor birds that were flying about in the air while it was at its worst dropped and died; it was sad to see that. One is glad of a sparrow now even. I wonder will the swallows ever come back.

I do not know how long we can go on. For the first year we still had some stores; I even made a Christmas cake for Fiona and a few other of the young ones. I used the last bit of margarine that I had been saving up and Mrs. Drummond managed to find some sugar; there was a brooch she used to wear and I think that is how it went. But it started Fiona onto speaking about her last Christmas and all the fun and happiness they'd had together. And I had to leave the room quickly; it was more than I could bear. We have kept hoping that a ship might come in from somewhere. But it never does. And our health is going down. I have sore places on my insteps and my face, and my hair has fallen out in patches. There was a time I would have minded about that. Now I only mind anything because of Fiona. Yes, and the Community Council. But it is too soon to know what will happen either to the Community Council or to the children. Perhaps when we do know it will seem that we were still happy when we did not know.

5
LORN
Introduction

The Irish-born Lorn, brother of Fergus MacErc, gave his name to the territory to the north of what is now called Mid-Argyll and in the sixth century was Dalriada. As the *Duan Albanach* records:

> Three sons of Erc, the son of pleasant Eachaid, three men who got the blessing of Patrick, took Scotland – great were their deeds – Loarn, Fergus and Angus. Ten years Loarn, with distinguished renown, was in the Kingdom of Argyle . . .

By Lorn we have taken to mean all of the lands within a rough parallelogram reaching from Loch Awe in the south to Loch Leven in the north. From the Firth of Lorn east to the Moor of Rannoch – a land of great contrasts, crammed with names and places of story and myth as well as other associations. From Celtic myth comes the story of Deirdre, forever associated with beautiful Loch Etive, which divides Lorn into two parts Upper and Nether Lorn. Marion Campbell's version runs:

> Glen Etive. Etive triple-guarded, by the Herdsman of the black-rock plaid above it in the mist, watching the road dive under his elbow from Glencoe; loch edged with faintest track each side, ten miles to the narrows and a glacial sill; six miles more of wide waters and the tidal Falls of Lora to lock the outer door; a fiord within a fiord . . . You could have been safe anywhere along the locked fiord, safe from king's lust and king's revenge in your hut on the hillside remote from the guarded courts, you white-handed girl of the doomed beauty, you Deirdre of the Sorrows . . .

The long coast of the Firth of Lorn and Loch Linnhe has many spectacular views across to inshore islands like Seil and the Garvellachs, and farther out to Mull with Ben More above all. In the part of the Upper Lorn known as Appin, the views are crowned by the great hills of North Argyll across Loch Linnhe. In the middle ground, it is the island of Lismore which 'provides a grandstand view of some of the finest scenery, landscape and seascape, in all Scotland' (Rev. Ian Carmichael).

Lismore, which means 'The Great Garden' or 'The Great Enclosure', is another of Argyll's seemingly inexhaustible stock of places of interest and of historical or in this case ecclesiastical and literary significance. A Pictish saint, Moluag, is believed to have brought Christianity here at or around the same time that Columba was in Iona and later a cathedral was built in the thirteenth century for the diocese of Argyll. Here too, as described elsewhere in this anthology, was the site associated with *The Book of the Dean of Lismore* and its confirmation of an ancient Gaelic oral tradition.

Appin was of course the scene of the dramatic events surrounding the 1752 murder of Colin Campbell of Glenure and described in Robert Louis Stevenson's Jacobite tales *Kidnapped* and *Catriona*:

> This is a Campbell that's been killed. Well, it'll be tried in Inverara, the Campbell's head place; with fifteen Campbells in the jury-box, and the biggest Campbell of all (and that's the Duke) sitting cocking on the bench.

Stevenson's interest in what became known as the Appin Murder owed much to legends he had heard while on childhood holiday visits to the Highlands. Like Scott before him and Neil Munro later, he shows a distinctively Scottish talent for capturing the essence of a landscape, as the 'Earraid' extract in the Mull and North Argyll chapter illustrates.

Oban has been variously described as the Charing Cross of the Highlands and the Gateway to the Hebrides. Although the great days of the excursion steamers are long gone the bustling little port still provides vital communication links for the Inner and Outer Hebrides and is still a railhead for the West Highland Line, or that part of it which might be termed 'Argyll's own railway'. Although Oban was founded only two hundred years ago as a fishing village there are many places of historical interest nearby. The Macdougalls of Lorn held both Dunollie and Dunstaffnage castles, until the latter was granted to the Campbells by Robert Bruce, after the Macdougalls backed the wrong side during the Bruce's guerrilla campaign which raged through Lorn in 1308.

Lorn has a long coastline lit by sunsets over Hebridean seas but it also has a wild and vast interior, with dark associations for the Macdougalls, the Campbells and of course the MacDonalds. Glencoe, the Moor of Rannoch and the Black Mount are some of the evocative places in what we might call Upper Lorn, with seven or eight peaks of over 3,000 feet. Stevenson, Munro, Duncan Ban Macintyre and T. S. Eliot are all writers who have found inspiration in this broken ground.

To complete the description of the district known as Lorn: Cruachan Ben, as it is often called, crouches over Loch Awe in Lorn's bottom corner on the landward side. The massive Cruachan long attracted visitors, poets like William Wordsworth, but also day trippers to the massive hydro-electric scheme. David Graham Campbell writing in 1978 in the 'Portrait' series observed:

> Lorn is no longer a district of large landowners; power has passed back to the elements. The most significant thing about Lorn today (at any rate for the outside world) is Cruachan Beinn. Not only do its peaks dominate the landscape, but an astonishing feat of engineering has hollowed out inside it a space as large as St Paul's Cathedral, in which there is the most powerful generating station in Scotland.

Historically, Loch Awe served as a kind of twenty-two mile long natural moat, which formed a barrier against invasion of the Campbells' Inveraray power base. These were days when the name Argyll stood for an individual as much as a territory. When it was for many indeed 'A Far Cry to Loch Awe'.

'The Sound of Mull'

from The Lord of the Isles

WALTER SCOTT (1771–1832)

This terrific account of the seascape of the coast of the Lorn district of Argyll comes from the Notes to the first Canto of Scott's 1815 epic poem. The Lord of the Isles deals with the exploits of the Bruce in and around Lorn in 1307 on his return to Scotland following the murder of the Red Comyn. The poem tells of the love of Edith of Lorn for Ronald, Lord of the Isles. Edith waits in Lorn:

> *. . . where a turret's airy head,*
> *slender and steep, and battled round,*
> *O'erlook'd dark Mull! Thy mighty Sound,*
> *Where thwarting tides, with mingled roar,*
> *Part thy swarth hills from Morven's shore.*

The Lord of the Isles *never attained the popularity of* Marmion *nor* The Lay of the Last Minstrel *and we have chosen to give an extract from Scott's notes to the poem. Rather like some of Bernard Shaw's prefaces to his plays the notes make for probably more entertaining and certainly more informative reading today. Also of interest are the circumstances in which Scott gathered the information about the landscapes and seacapes in which he sets the poem. As usual, he preferred to add to his verses the kind of colouring which comes from first-hand experience and knowledge of places. On this occasion he took the opportunity to acquire some of this background colour, while sailing around Scotland in the late summer of 1815 as a guest of the Commissioners of the Northern Lights. On board the Lighthouse yacht Pharos he collected much that was of use for this poem (and, incidentally, for a novel* The Pirate*). An extract from Scott's journals of the trip, published as* The Voyage of the Pharos *can be found in the chapter Mull and North Argyll.*

– Dark Mull! thy mighty Sound. – St VII p. 13

The Sound of Mull, which divides that island from the continent of Scotland, is one of the most striking scenes which the Hebrides afford to the traveller. Sailing from Oban to Aros, or Tobermory, through a narrow channel, yet deep enough to bear vessels of the largest burthen, he has on his left the bold and mountainous shores of Mull; on the right those of that district of Argyleshire, called Morven, or Morvern, successively indented by deep salt-water lochs, running up many miles inland. To the south-eastward arise a prodigious range of mountains, among which Cruachan Ben is pre-eminent. And to the north-east is the no less huge and picturesque range of the Ardnamurchan hills.

Many ruinous castles, situated generally upon cliffs overhanging the ocean, add interest to the scene. Those of Dunolly and Dunstaffnage are first passed, then that of Duart, formerly belonging to the chief of the warlike and powerful sept of Macleans, and the scene of Miss Ballie's beautiful tragedy, entitled the *Family Legen*d. Still passing on to the northward, Artornish and Aros become visible upon the opposite shores; and, lastly, Mingarry, and other ruins of less distinguished note.

In fine weather, a grander and more impressive scene, both from its natural beauties, and associations with ancient history and tradition, can hardly be imagined. When the weather is rough, the passage is both difficult and dangerous, from the narrowness of the channel, and in part from the number of inland lakes, out of which sally forth a number of conflicting and thwarting tides, making the navigation perilous to open boats. The sudden flaws and gusts of wind which issue without a moment's warning from the mountain glens, are equally formidable. So that in unsettled weather, a stranger, if not much accustomed to the sea, may sometimes add to the other sublime sensations excited by the scene, that feeling of dignity which arises from a sense of danger.

'The Battle of the Pass of Brander'

from The Bruce

JOHN BARBOUR (c. 1320–95)

John Barbour is often called the 'Father of Scottish Literature', because of his authorship of The Bruce, *the earliest known poem in Scots of any length. The poem was probably written in the 1370s and celebrates King Robert and his part in the Wars of Independence. Barbour himself called it a 'romance' and in style it resembles these stories with a chivalric theme. The tale is in broad terms faithful to historical fact, more so than Blind Harry's* Wallace. *Famous passages include that beginning:*

> A! fredome is a noble thing!
> Fredome mays man to haif liking

The extract from the poem is followed by another of Walter Scott's notes to The Lord of the Isles. *In this Scott also describes the battle.*

> The king and his men held thar way,
> And quhen intill the pas war thai
> Entryt the folk of Lorne in hy
> Apon the king raysyt the cry
> And schot and tumblit on him stanys
> Rycht gret and hevy for the nanys,
> Bot thai scaith nocht gretly the king
> For he had thar in his leding
> Men that lycht and deliver war
> And lycht armouris had on thaim thar
> Sua that thai stoutly clamb the hill
> And lettyt thar fayis to fulfill
> The maist part of thar felny.
> And als apon the tother party
> Come James of Douglas and his rout
> And schot apon thaim with a schout
> And woundyt thaim with arowis fast,

And with thar swerdis at the last
Thai ruschyt amang thaim hardely,
For thai of Lorn full manlely
Gret and apert defens gan ma.
Bot quhen thai saw that thai war sua
Assaylit apon twa partys
And saw weill that thar ennemys
Had all the fayrer off the fycht
In full gret hy thai tuk the flycht,
And thai a felloun chas gan ma
And slew all that thai mycht ourta,
And thai that mycht eschap but delay
Rycht till ane water held thar way
That ran doun be the hillis syd.
It was sa styth and depe and wid
That men in na place mycht it pas
Bot at ane bryg that beneuth thaim was.
To that brig held thai straucht the way
And to brek it fast gan assay,
Bot thai that chassyt quhen thai thaim saw
Mak arest, but dred or aw
Thai ruschyt apon thaim hardely
And discumfyt thaim uterly,
And held the brig haile quhill the king
With all the folk off his leding
Passyt the brig all at thar ese.
To Jhone off Lorne it suld displese
I trow, quhen he his men mycht se
Oute off his schippis fra the se
Be slayne and Chassyt in the hill,
That he mycht set na help thartill,
For it angrys als gretumly
To gud hartis that ar worthi
To se thar fayis fulfill thar will
As to thaim selff to thole the ill.

NOTES ON THE HOUSE OF LORN

The House of Lorn, as we observed in a former note, was, like the Lord of the Isles, descended from a son of Somerled, slain at Renfrew, in 1164. This son obtained the succession of his mainland territories, comprehending the greater part of the three districts of Lorn, in Argyleshire, and of course might rather be considered as petty princes than feudal barons. They assumed the patronymic appellation of MacDougal, by which they are distinguished in the history of the middle ages.

The Lord of Lorn, who flourished during the wars of Bruce, was Allaster (or Alexander) MacDougall, called Allaster of Argyll. He had married the third daughter of John, called the Red Comyn, who was slain by Bruce in the Dominican church at Dumfries, and hence he was a mortal enemy of that prince, and more than once reduced him to great straits during the early and distressed period of his reign, as we shall have repeated occasion to notice. Bruce, when he began to obtain an ascendancy in Scotland, took the first opportunity in his power to requite these injuries. He marched into Argyleshire to lay waste the country. John of Lorn, son of the chieftain, was posted with his followers in the formidable pass between Dalmally and Bunawe.

It is a narrow path along the verge of the huge and precipitous mountain, called Cruachan Ben, and guarded on the other side by a precipice overhanging Loch Awe. The pass seems to the eye of a soldier as strong, as it is wild and romantic to that of an ordinary traveller. But the skill of Bruce had anticipated this difficulty. While his main body, engaged in a skirmish with the men of Lorn, detained their attention to the front of their position, James of Douglas, with Sir Alexander Fraser, Sir William Wiseman, and Sir Andrew Grey, ascended the mountain with a select body of archery, and obtained possession of the heights which commanded the pass. A volley of arrows descending upon them directly warned the Arygleshire men of their perilous situation, and their resistance, which had hitherto been bold and manly, was changed into a precipitate flight. The deep and rapid river of Awe was then (we learn the fact from Barbour with some surprise) crossed by a bridge. This bridge the mountaineers attempted to demolish, but Bruce's followers were too close upon their rear; they were, therefore, without refuge and defence, and were dispersed with great slaughter.

'A Model Seaport'

from In Scotland Again

H. V. MORTON (1892–1979)

Morton was one of the most successful travel writers in the period before and immediately after the Second World War. His popular and easy style made his books extremely successful commercially: In Search of Scotland, *for example, passed through six impressions in six months.*

This extract comes from In Scotland Again, *published in 1933, and it shows some of the best features of Morton's style – this manages to combine a quantity of information with a relaxed approach to story telling. Anecdotes of people he meets on his journeys also feature in Morton's writing and here he makes some nice points about Scotland and England through the encounter on the boat with a fellow-Londoner. The following passage from the introduction to the book sums up his humorous but affectionate approach to writing about Scotland. The traveller is crossing the Border:*

> *So, as he dipped down over the arched backs of the fells, his mind, seeking relief from the gnawing of his stomach, began to dwell with passionate intentness upon the kind of food that he would so soon be eating. He would arrive in Scotland at that beautiful moment known as 'high tea'. He would sit down in the coffee-room of a country hotel that seemed to be waiting for the arrival of Charles Dickens and his friends. There would be a huge silver urn on a vast mahogany sideboard. A foxed engraving on the wall would show Cromwell in the act of removing the bauble, or perhaps it would be Charles I defending himself in Westminster Hall, for all Scottish hotels are fascinated by the more embarrassing moments in English history. And a little Highland exile with a few freckles round her nose would come to him and ask, in a voice like a wind blowing gently through the glens of Lochaber, what he would like to eat. There would be Findon haddock, fried plaice, eggs, eggs and bacon, and probably steak; for such is the tremendous foreground of 'high tea'. In the background would be baps and bannocks and scones, white bread and brown bread, gingerbread and currant bread, and apple jelly and jam.*

And no doubt there were many such hotels in Oban.

The shop windows of Oban are, in the season, as hysterical as Walter Scott's welcome to George IV. They blaze with clan tartan, they shine with cairngorms, they glitter with skean dhus, and there are in Oban probably more comic postcards about Scotsmen (printed in England) than in any other town of this size in the world.

Oban, like Stratford-on-Avon, has a dual personality. One Oban turns with agreeable eagerness to the tourist; the other is a possibly less tartan Oban reserved for winter, the fireside and friends. I have never seen this Oban, but I have no doubt that it is a good-looking, friendly one.

I think that Oban is one of the most beautiful coast towns in Scotland. On a bright day there is something Mediterranean about it. The gentle western hills slope gracefully to the water; the buildings fringe the waterside, and on the hills are villas. I have heard men criticize the Roman arena which broods over Oban. This miniature Colosseum, which a local banker in a classical moment erected as a family memorial, gives a distinct and alien character to the place. It is quite pointless and out-of-place, but then so are the majority of memorials!

There cannot be anywhere in the world a more model seaport. All the untidy aspects of shipping are absent from Oban. It is the kind of seaport that a millionaire might create if he wanted one of his own. Even the south pier, where the purely commercial ships tie up, looks on a busy day as if it had been arranged by a committee of the Royal Academy. The herring girls knit stockings and jumpers as they sit on boxes waiting for their 'shift' to move on into the packing yards.

In these yards barrels of herrings are swiftly packed for America and, I believe, Russia. The girls stand at long troughs, the sleeves rolled over their sturdy arms, and slit-slit-slit-splash, in three automatic movements they gut the silver shoals.

Tied up to the jetty are the little, tough-looking trawlers, dirty from days at sea; a picturesque huddle of masts and funnels and high fo'c'sles, and through open hatchways you can see the herrings lying, silver and red-eyed, in crushed ice.

And Oban, more so than any town on the west coast of Scotland, is a place of happy memories.

It is from Oban that thousands of people set out to visit the enchanted Western Isles which lie out in the Atlantic and do not seem to belong to this world. It is to Oban that the little steamers bring back travellers from the west. After weeks spent out of the world in lovely places, Oban, with its hectic shop windows, seems a kind of metropolis.

There is in Oban, too, a promise of the west, just as the unearthly winds of Connemara blow through the grey streets of Galway, in Ireland. There is a touch of the Gaelic in the air. And in the evening as a western sunset burns in the sky and you look towards the mountains of Mull, you feel that you stand on the frontier of a new land.

I took the road north-east from Oban and came to the ruins of a great castle which stands on a promontory where Loch Linnhe enters Loch Etive. This was the famous strong-hold of Dunstaffnage. It is from this old ruin that the Captain of Dunstaffnage takes his ancient title. A guide book that should know better states that the Duke of Argyll, as chief of the Clan Campbell, is the hereditary keeper of Dunstaffnage. This is not so. In 1910 the Duke claimed the title, but Angus John Campbell, the present holder and the twentieth Captain of Dunstaffnage, made good his claim in the Court of Session that his ancestors had held the title since 1436.

It has been a magnificent castle: now it is merely a shell with nine-foot-thick walls from which is one of the finest views on the west coast.

Stand, as I did, in the afternoon of one of those summer days that swing in from the Atlantic in October, and you will never forget the crumbling ramparts of Dunstaffnage. You look eastward up Loch Etive towards the twin peaks of Ben Cruachan; westward over the narrow sea are the blue mountains of Mull and Morven; to the north is Loch Nell with its fringe of saffron weed.

Round you are woods stained with autumn colours; the rowans turning crimson, the chestnuts bright gold above the deep russet of dead bracken, and at the back of the hills wear the last heather of the year.

Lying neglected beside a wall in this castle is a magnificent cannon, which should be rescued and placed in a museum.

'It came from the Spanish Armada,' said the young man who opened the gates of Dunstaffnage to me. 'It was taken out of Tobermory Bay, but no one thinks anything of it.'

It is possible with difficulty to read the name of its maker: Asuerus Koster, of Amsterdam.

The greatest memory of Dunstaffnage is that of the Coronation Stone, which is to-day in Westminster Abbey beneath that famous chair on which so many schoolboys have carved their names. This stone was the ancient Coronation Stone of the Irish kings. It was said to have been Jacob's pillow on the plains of Luz.

When the Scots came over from Ireland to settle in Caledonia they brought this stone with them, first to Iona and then to Dunstaffnage, which became the capital of the Dalriadic kingdom. Afterwards, when Scone became the capital, the Stone of Destiny went there, and remained from 850 until the year 1297, when Edward I removed it to Westminster Abbey.

There is another memory in this castle. In 1746 a boat came over from the Western Isles bringing Flora Macdonald as a state prisoner to Dunstaffnage. She was on her way to London to be tried for helping Prince Charles Edward to escape after Culloden. She was kept there for ten days . . .

Among the trees at the back is one of those ruined kirkyards so frequent in Scotland, where the shrubs and the weeds push apart the gravestones. The gravestones nod together, the green mould grows on the walls, the spiders spin shrouds from tomb to tomb, and there is no sound but the whisper of autumn leaves and the high little song of a robin rising and falling on the still air.

These graveyards are melancholy things. If I had nothing else to do I would like to go round Scotland, as Old Mortality did in the Covenanting Country, tidying them up and weeding a bit here and there.

* * *

I met him in the boat that slips out in the evening from Oban into the Sound of Mull. Our fellow passengers were farmers and drovers returning to their islands from a cattle sale. There was a varied cargo, including a calf in a sack. It looked like the conjurer's pretty assistant who permits herself to be tied up in view of the audience.

The little man interested me, because he was not the sort of man whom you would expect to meet on the road to the Hebrides.

He looked as though some mighty wind had taken him up from Queen Victoria Street or Cheapside and dropped him neatly in this boat. He was the perfect little Londoner. When he walked the deck I seemed to hear the clicking of a garden gate, and when he stood against the rail the great hills behind him seemed to lose their gaunt outlines and form into something like St Paul's Cathedral.

I was rather frightened by him because he looked talkative and the kind of man who knows all about dahlias or postage stamps . . .

We steamed out past Kerrera towards Mull. A few gulls followed us and the setting sun was in our eyes. All round us were the grape-blue hills hushed in peace, and above the hum of the engines I could hear the crew making jokes in Gaelic.

Se we set our course for that world beyond the world – the Western Isles.

'That's nice,' said the little man, knocking his pipe out on the rail.

I found that he was looking at the sunset which burned in the third movement of its symphony behind Duart Castle. The sea was a blinding sheet of silver that moved and shivered as if with millions of small fish.

Beyond was the hypnotic peace of lonely places, a peace that was calling me on to wild hills and desolate valleys so that I wanted to stand in silence.

'I said that's rather nice,' repeated the little man.

I was about to employ a curt snub, when I looked down at the little man and liked him.

'D'you live here, in Scotland?' he asked.

'No.'

'I don't, either,' he said simply.

'You're from London?'

'How d'you know that?' he asked.

'Oh, instinct, a guess, that's all.'

'D'you know Brixton? You do? Well; that's interesting. Glad to meet you. Funny to think of the Number Three 'buses going up past the town hall, up to Tulse Hill – d'you know Tulse Hill? – and Herne Hill and the Croxted Road. D'you know that part? Thurloe Park Road and Dulwich. Nice part. I always say it's the nicest part of London; but it's funny to think of it all the same, isn't it?'

'I suppose it is.'

And the sunset burnt itself out in gold and red above Ben More.

I wondered, and I wondered again, why this dear little fellow was losing himself on the road to the isles; but I was too lazy to tackle him and find out.

The peace of the isles, which is like no other peace on earth, was falling over me like a mist and drenching me. I was content to babble about London and to look out at the hills, thinking that no solitude and no simplicity like this exist east of the Balkan States.

A bell rang. The engines stopped. The ship drifted. Down below we saw a long boat and three islanders in it, jet black against the silver of the sea. Five farmers got into it and a few herdsmen. One was drunk and fell down. Everybody laughed. They held bulky brown paper parcels. A new bicycle was carefully lowered. A mail bag was flung in, a little one hardly bigger than a woman's handbag. There was a slim parcel containing the morning newspapers. The bell rang.

The ship moved off; and we saw the long boat rowing to the near-by shore, where a few scattered lights shone on the mountain-side.

The little community had experienced its daily contact with the outside world. It had received its letters, its newspapers, a new bicycle for Jeanie and its mysterious brown paper packages from Oban.

The moon was rising and the *Lochinvar* went on through the silent Sound with a light at her masthead.

In twenty minutes or so the engine-room bell rang again, the boat sidled up to a little jetty and made fast. Here we landed the calf.

There was a tin shed and a life-belt hanging on it, and behind dark hills shouldered the sky. The entire population was on the jetty; old men leaning on sticks, hatless young maids, great clumsy youths, all gazing eagerly at the boat which was the one sensation of the day. They looked at the little man and myself and took in every detail about us, whispering and wondering.

There were shouted conversations between the islanders in the boat and those on the jetty. They all knew one another. Then the engines threshed the water and we moved off to 'Good-byes' and Gaelic farewells and waving hands, leaving them in the silence and the shadow of their hills.

'You wouldn't think this could go on twenty-four hours from London, would you?' said the little man. 'Think of Piccadilly Circus now, not that I go up west much these days, but – think of it!'

I was getting rather tired of this sort of thing, but still I liked the little man. He was full of wonder. He had something to say which he could not express, and I was too lazy to help him to say it. At the same time, I wished that he would get it off his chest.

'It's cold. Come down in the cabin and have a drink.'

'I don't drink,' said the little man.

'Well, have some tea.'

'That would be very nice.'

We sat on plush seats in the little cabin. The artificial flowers trembled in their vases as the ship went over the still waters. On a panel let into the wall *Lochinvar* was escaping on horseback with a fair maiden.

'Are you on holiday?'

'Yes; it's a funny place to come for a holiday all alone. My family think I'm potty. They like Eastbourne. But, you know, I find that London gets on my nerves a bit. I think every one ought to get away from London. It isn't natural is it? If I had money I'd go right round the world.'

'Why do you come to a place like this?'

'I like being alone. I like to stand in these boats – I came here last year, only earlier – and think that London's going on just the same and I'm right out of it. Of course, I'm always glad to get back. But would anyone believe London is only a day's journey away from – this?'

He waved his hand towards the portholes and we saw a mountain slide past.

'Then you find that getting right away gives you – what? Balance?'

'That's it. I go down to an office every day, and I suppose if all goes well I shall do so until I drop or get too old. But I never get worried or fed up when I miss a train or have to stand all the way from Brixton in a tram, because I think of – all this. You know. Quiet! Mind, I don't like too much of it. If I were here alone too long I'd get restless and fed up, but three or four days just put me right.'

He said a lot more on these lines. I thought he was very sound. He was in search of detachment. He had found the antidote that most Londoners need so badly.

We came slowly into Tobermory Bay.

A half moon was bright in the sky. We could see a fringe of houses, white in the moonlight, curving round the harbour, and nothing but sleeping hills and silence as deep as the ocean.

The farmers and the herdsmen were stamping about the deck and looking towards the lights of home. They were adventurers. They had been to Scotland for the day. They had sold their cattle. They had bought all the things their wives had ordered them to buy. They had had a few drinks and felt full of virtue.

We landed on the jetty. There was a crowd of perhaps fifty people present, standing in the light of oil flares watching every face as it came down the gang plank. Then we walked through the deserted street beside the harbour. There was no sound but that of a river tumbling over rocks somewhere near. We were right out of the world, 'over the hills and far away'.

The little man looked at me:

'By Jove!' he said, 'it's difficult to . . .'

'Its incredible,' I said quickly.

'An TV'
('The TV')

from Eadar Fealla-dhà Is Glaschu

IAIN CRICHTON SMITH (1927–98)

TRANSLATION BY IAIN CRICHTON SMITH

Iain Crichton Smith (Iain Mac a'Ghobhainn) was born in Glasgow in 1928. Soon after his family moved to the Island of Lewis. A native speaker of Gaelic, he had his schooling at the Nicolson Institute and then proceeded to Aberdeen University. In 1955 he moved to Argyll to take up a teaching post in Oban High School which he retained until 1977 when he retired to become a full time writer. He then moved to Taynuilt where he lived and worked until his death in 1998.

He was a prolific and accomplished writer in English and Gaelic. As a novelist with no fewer than ten titles to his credit he will be best remembered for Consider the Lilies, *a novel set during the Highland Clearances which has become a minor classic. In Gaelic his novel* An t-Aonaran (The Hermit) *was his most accomplished work in this genre and is undoubtedly one of the best Gaelic novels so far written. He also published many collections of short stories in both English and Gaelic and his innovative contribution to Gaelic short story writing has done much to make that aspect of Gaelic literature the vibrant art form that it is today.*

Crichton Smith was also a capable dramatist, again in both languages, but it is for his poetry above all that his reputation will endure. His principal collections are, in English: Thistles and Roses *(1961),* Deer on the High Hills *(1962),* The Law and the Grace *(1965),* Hamlet in Autumn *(1972),* The Village and Other Poems *(1989) and* The Leaf and the Marble *(1998); and in Gaelic* Bìobuill is Sanasan-Reice *(1965),* Eadar Fealla-Dha is Glaschu *(1974) and* Na h-Eilthirich *(1983).*

With other major Gaelic poets like Sorley MacLean, George Campbell Hay and Derick Thomson, Crichton Smith sought to extend the range of Gaelic poetry to make it more responsive to the wider world whilst at the same time keeping it true to its own roots and traditions. 'An TV' is a good example of this. The poem appears to be a random collection of quips about television, but it is much more carefully controlled than that. It is a complex satirical poem which seeks to show us how our life has become

conditioned and to some extent dehumanised by television. By referring to
Plato and Berkeley, philosophers of international stature and significance,
he emphasises how true reality is kept from us by television. In the climax
in the last two stanzas, however, Crichton Smith's points are made more
telling by allusions to two Gaelic songs which he particularly admired.

> You my love are more dear to me
> than 'Softly Softly'
> than 'Sportsnight with Coleman'

echoes 'Mo Ribhinn Og, Bheil Cuimhn'Agad?' ('Young Girl Do You
Remember?') where the speaker declares,

> You my love are dearer to me
> than my mother who reared me when I was young.

To replace the love of a mother, as is implied by the allusion, with a TV
crime series and a sports programme shows a terrible loss of values. In the
last stanza Crichton Smith delivers his most powerful blow. It refers to the
very beautiful love song, 'Fi-l-óro', often associated with the great 18th-
century poet William Ross. In it the rejected suitor wishes he could be
alone for many years with his love

> In locked rooms with iron gates
> And the key thrown away and a blind man looking for them.

To ask if there is a TV in the room in such circumstances simply
undermines any real understanding of the depth of human emotion.

(1)
Tha a' ghrian ag éirigh gach latha
á faileasan falbhach –
air an TV.

(2)
Cha do chreid sinn gu robh Eirinn ann
gus am faca sinn i iomadh oidhche –
air an TV.

(3)
Tha e nas fhaisge air Humphrey Bogart
na tha e air Tormod Mór –
on fhuair e an TV.

(4)
Arsa Plato –
'Tha sinn ceangailte ann an uaimh' –
'se sin an TV.

(5)
Thàinig nighean a-steach do rùm
gun bholtrach gun fhiamh –
ás an TV.

(6)
Mu dheireadh chaill e an saoghal
mar a thubhairt Berkeley –
cha robh ann ach an TV.

(7)
Cheannaich e 'War and Peace',
Tolstoy, tha mi ciallachadh,
an déidh fhaicinn air an TV.

(8)
Nuair a chuir e ás an TV.
chaidh an saoghal ás –
chaidh e fhéin ás.

(9)
Cha dàinig a làmhan air ais thuige
no a shùilean
gus an do chuir e air an TV.

(10)
Ròs ann am bóla air an TV,
na nithean a th'anns an t-saoghal,
's na nithean nach eil.

(11)
Fhuair e e fhéin ann an sgialachd
's chan fhaigheadh e aisde
air an TV.

(12)
Bha e anns an sgialachd:
Bha e anns an rùm.
Cha robh fhios càit an robh e.

(13)
'S tu a ghràidh is fheàrr leam
na *Softly Softly*
na *Sportsnight with Coleman*.

(14)
An seòmraichean glaiste le geatachan iarainn
ach, a ghràidh,
a bheil TV annta?

THE TV

(1)
The sun rises every day
from moving shadows –
on the TV.

(2)
We did not believe in the existence of Ireland
till we saw it many nights –
on the TV.

(3)
He knows more about Humphrey Bogart
than he knows about Big Norman –
since he got the TV.

(4)
Said Plato –
'We are tied in a cave' –
that is, the TV.

(5)
A girl came into the room
without perfume without expression –
on the TV.

(6)
At last he lost the world
As Berkeley said –
there was nothing but the TV.

(7)
He bought 'War and Peace',
I mean Tolstoy,
after seeing it on the TV.

(8)
When he switched off the TV
the world went out –
he himself went out.

(9)
His hands did not come back to him
or his eyes
till he put on the TV.

(10)
A rose in a bowl on the TV set,
the things that are in the world,
the things that are not.

(11)
He found himself in a story
and he could not get out of it
on the TV.

(12)
He was in the story:
He was in the room
He did not know where he was.

(13)
You, my love, are dearer to me
than Softly Softly
than Sportsnight with Coleman.

(14)
'In locked rooms with iron gates' –
but, my love,
do they have TV?

'Deirdre's Lament for Scotland'

from Irische Texte Vol. 2, Ed. Stokes and Windisch

ANONYMOUS

There are many versions of the tragic story of Deirdre and the Sons of Uisnech. The earliest variant was recorded as long ago as the twelfth century in the early Irish Manuscript known as the Book of Leinster. *A very fine variant was recorded as recently as 1867 on the island of Barra by Alexander Carmichael, the great folklorist whose own home was the island of Lismore in the Firth of Lorn. The extract given here comes from the Scottish fifteenth-century Glen Masain manuscript recorded in* Irische Texte Vol. 2, *Leipzig, 1880, edited by Whitley Stokes and Ernst Windisch.*

The tale begins at a feast at the court of King Conchobar in Emain Macha in Ulster. During the celebrations the birth of Deirdre to the wife of Feidhlim, the King's story-teller, is announced. The King's Druid, Cathbad, prophesied that she would grow up to be a great beauty and the cause of great woe in the province. The nobles instantly wish that she be put to death to prevent future strife but Conchobar intervenes saying that he will keep her and rear her to be his own wife. When she grows up, however, she meets Naisi, an extremely handsome young man and a kinsman of Conchobar, and falls deeply in love with him. Although at first he is extremely reluctant, Naisi eventually allows himself to be persuaded to elope with her and so with his two brothers Ardan and Ainnle and their trains they flee to Loch Etive in Scotland. There they pass the time in idyllic bliss until Conchobar sends his emissary Fergus MacRoich to entreat their return. He finds them in their hunting booth playing chess. They are persuaded that Conchobar's invitation is genuine and reluctantly return to Ulster. It was, however, a cruel trick and, although Fergus had acted in good faith, Naisi and his brothers and their followers were attacked and defeated by the hosts of Conchobar soon after their arrival. Deirdre was grief-stricken at the death of her lover and refused to raise her head or smile for a year. So angered was Conchobar with this behaviour that he sent her away with Eogan, the man who had slain Naisi. As they drove away in Eogan's chariot Conchobar hurled a dreadful insult at her at which she leapt from the vehicle and dashed her head against a pillar stone.

The extract which follows is the lament of Deirdre as she leaves Glen Etive and Scotland for the last time.

Inmain tír an tír út thoir
Alba conahingantaib:
nocha ticfuinn eisdi ille
mana tísainn le Noise.

Inmain Dun-fidhgha is Dún Finn,
inmain in dun osa cinn
inmain Inis Draigen de
is inmain Dun Suibnei.

Caill Cuan!
gair tiged Ainnle, mo núar!
fa gair lim dobí intan
is Naíse an-oirear Alban.

Glenn Láid!
docollainn fan, mboirinn caoimh:
iasg is sieng is saill bruic
fa hí mo chuid an Glend Laigh.

Glenn Masain!
ard a crimh, geal a gasáin;
donímais collud corrach
ós inbir mungaich Masáin.

Glenn Eitci!
ann dotogbhus mo céttig,
alaind a fidh, iar néirghe
buaile gréne Glenn Eitchi.

Glenn Urchán!
bahi inglenn diriug dromcháin
nochor uallcha fer a aoisi
ná Nóise an Glenn Urcháin.

Glenn Da Rúadh
mochen gach fer dána dúal
is binn guth cúach ar cráib cruim
ar in mbinn ós Glinn Da Rúadh.

Inmain Draigen is trén traigh,
inmain a uisce ingainimh glain:
nocha ticfuinn seide anoir
mana tísuinn lem inmain.

DEIRDRE'S LAMENT FOR SCOTLAND

A loveable land is yon land in the east,
Alba with its marvels.
I would not have come hither out of it
Had I not come with Naisi.

Loveable are Dun-fidga and Dun-Finn,
Loveable the fortress over them,
Loveable Inis Draigende   [*Inistrynich, Loch Awe*]
And loveable Dun Suibni.

Caill Cuan!
Unto which Ainnle would wend, alas!
It was short I thought the time
And Naisi in the region of Alba.

Glenn Laid!
I used to sleep under a fair rock.
Fish and venison and badger's fat
This was my portion in Glen Laid.

Glenn Masain!   [*in Cowal*]
Tall its garlic, white its branchlets:
We used to have an unsteady sleep
Over the grassy estuary of Masain.

Glenn Etive!
There I raised my first house.
Delightful its wood, after rising
A cattlefold of the sun is Glenn Etive.

Glenn Urchain   [*Glen Orchy*]
It was the straight fair-ridged glen.
Not prouder was any man of his age
Than Naisi in Glen Urchain.

Glenn Da-Ruad!   [*Glendaruel*]
My love to every man who hath it as a heritage!
Sweet is cuckoos' voice on bending branch
On the peak over Glenn Da-Ruad.

Beloved is Draigen over a strong beach:
Dear its water in pure sand;
I would not have come from it, from the east,
Had I not come with my beloved.

Osnadh carad i gCluain Fraoich
(The sigh of a dear one is in the Meadow of Fraoch)

THE BLIND ONE FROM CLUAIN (fl. 14th century)

TRANSLATION BY NEIL ROSS

Osnadh carad i gCluain Fraoich *(The sigh of the dear one is in the meadow of Fraoch) is one of the great heroic ballads from the Book of the Dean of Lismore.*

Fraoch, the hero of the ballad, is in love with Fionnabhair, daughter of Meadhbh (Maeve) Queen of Connacht in Ireland. The Queen is jealous and, since she cannot have Fraoch, she plots his death. Feigning illness she sends Fraoch to fetch magic rowan berries from a tree which grows on an island in a nearby loch. It is, however, guarded by a monster. Finally the monster attacks Fraoch and both die in a gruesome fight. Fionnabhair stricken with grief at the death of her lover also dies.

This powerful ballad is ascribed by the Dean of Lismore to An Caoch ó Chluain, the Blind One from Cluain, an Irish poet of the fourteenth century. Although the poem is clearly set in Ireland and was almost certainly composed in County Roscommon, it became very popular in Scotland. So well established did it become in Scotland that it became localised, among other places, in Argyll at the head of Loch Awe: a strong local tradition grew up that the island of Fraoch Eilean, near Kilchurn Castle, was the scene of the action of the tale. The prior existence of the local names Cruachan and Fraoch which correspond to names mentioned in the ballad would have facilitated the legend taking root in this area. Fraoch, however, is simply the Gaelic for 'heather'. Fraoch Eilean, therefore, simply means 'heather island'. The hero's name Fraoch is a proper name, a quite different word but one which looks the same as the Gaelic word for 'heather'.

1. Osnadh carad i gCluain Fraoich,
   osnadh laoich i gcaiseal chró;
   osnadh do-ní tuirseach fear,
   agus dá nguileann bean óg.

2. Ag so thair an carn fá bhfuil
Fraoch mac Fiodhaigh an fhuilt mhaoith,
fear do-rinn buidheachas badhbh;
is uaidhe shloinntear Carn Fraoich.

3. Gul aonmhná i gCruachain soir,
truagh an sgéal fá bhfoil an bhean;
's é do-bheir a h-osnadh trom
Fraoch mac Fiodhaigh na gcolg sean.

4. Is í an aoinbhean do-ní an gul,
ag dul dá fhois go Cluain Fraoich,
Fionnabhair an fhuilt chais fhiail,
inghean Mheidhbhe agá mbiaid laoich.

5. Inghean Oilealla as úr folt
is Fraoch anocht taobh ar thaobh;
gé mór fear dár tairgeadh í,
níor ghrádhuigh sí fear acht Fraoch.

6. Fuaighis Meadhbh Moighe hAoi
cairdeas Fraoich fá fearr i ngliaidh,
an chúis fár chréachtach a chorp,
tré gan locht do dhéanamh ria.

7. Do cuireadh é gus an bhás;
taobh ré mná ní tug ón olc;
mar fuair a oidheadh lé Meidhbh,
inneósad gan cheilg anos.

8. Caorthann do bhí ar Loch Máigh,
do-chímís an tráigh fá dheas;
gacha ráithe gacha mí,
toradh abaigh do bhí air.

9. Sásamh bídh na caora sin,
fá milse ná mil a bhláth;
do chongbhadh an caorthann dearg
fear gan bhiadh go ceann naoi dtráth.

10. Bliadhain ar shaoghal gach fhir
do chuireadh sin, fá sgéal dearbh;
go mbudh fhóirthin do lucht cneadh
fromhadh a mheas is é dearg.

11. Do bhí amasach 'na dhiaidh,
gérbh é liaigh chabhartha an t-sluaigh,
péisd nimhe do bhí 'na bhun,
do bhac do chách dul dá bhuain.

12. Do líon easláinte throm throm
inghean Eachach na gcorn saor;
d'fhiosrughadh créad táinig ria,
do cuireadh lé fios ar Fraoch.

13. Adubhairt Meadhbh nach biadh slán
go bhfuighbheadh lán a bos maoth
do chaoraibh an locha fhuair,
gan duine dá mbuain acht Fraoch.

14. 'Cnuasach riamh ní dhearna mé,'
ar mac Fiodhaigh go ngné dheirg;
'gion go ndearnas é,' ar Fraoch,
'rachad do bhuain chaor do Mheidhbh.'

15. Gluaisis Fraoch fá fearr i n-ágh
uainne do shnámh ar an loch;
fuair an phéisd is í 'na suain
is a ceann suas ris an ndos.

16. Fraoch mac Fiodhaigh an airm ghéir
táinig ón phéisd gan fhios di;
tug sé a sheanultach chaor ndearg
mar a raibhe Meadhbh dá tigh.

17. 'Acht gé maith a dtugais leat,'
adubhairt Meadhbh as geal cruth,
'ní fhóir mise, a laoich luain,
acht slat do bhuain as a bun.'

18. Tograis Fraoch, 's níor ghiolla tim,
snámh arís ar an linn bhuig;
's níor fhéad, acht gé mór a ágh,
teacht ón bhás i raibhe a chuid.

19. Gabhais an caorthann ar bharr,
tairrngidh an crann as fhréimh,
ag tabhairt dó a chos i dtír,
mothuighis dó arís an phéisd.

20. Beiris air agus é ar snámh
is gabhais a lámh 'na craos;
do ghabh seisean ise ar ghiall;
is truagh gan a sgian ag Fraoch.

21. Fionnabhair an fhuilt chais fhiail
do-rad chuige sgian go n-ór;
leadraidh an phéisd a chneas bán,
is teasgaidh a lámh ar leódh.

22. Do thuiteadar bonn ar bonn
ar tráigh na gclach gcorr so theas,
Fraoch mac Fiodhaigh is an phéisd;
truagh, a Dhé, mar tug an treas.

23. Gé comhrag, ní comhrag cearr:
rug leis a ceann iona láimh;
ó ad-chonnaic an inghean é,
do-chuaidh 'na néal ar an tráigh.

24. Éirghis an inghean ón támh,
gabhais an lámh, budh lámh bhog;
gé tá so 'na cuid na n-éan,
mór an t-éacht do-rinn i bhfos.

25. Is ón bhás sin fuair an fear
Loch Máigh do lean don loch;
atá an t-ainm se de go luan
'gá ghairm anuas gus anos.

26. Beirear ann sin go Cluain Fraoich
crop an laoich go caiseal chró;
ar an gcluain tugadh a ainm;
is mairg mhaireas dá ló.

27. Carn Láimhe an carn sa rém thaoibh,
ó láimh Fhraoich do baisteadh soin:
fear nachar iompuigh i dtreas,
fear ba dhásach neart i dtroid.

28. Ionmhain an béal nár ob dhámh,
dá mbídís mná ag toirbheirt phóg;
ionmhain tighearna na sluagh,
ionmhain gruadh ná dheirge an rós.

29. Duibhe ná fiach barr a fhuilt,
deirge a ghruadh ioná fuil laoig;
fá míne ioná cubhar sreabh,
gile ioná an sneachta cneas Fraoich.

30. Caise ioná an casnaidhe a fholt,
guirme a rosg ná oighreadh leac;
deirge ioná partaing a bhéal,
gile a dhéad ioná bláth feath.

31. Airde a shleagh ioná crann siúil,
binne ioná téad ciúil a ghuth;
snámhaidhe do fhearr ná Fraoch
nochar shín a thaobh ré sruth.

32. Fá leithne ioná comhla a sgiath,
ionmhain triath do bhí ré druim;
comhfhada a lann is a lámh;
leithne a cholg ná clár do luing.

33. Truagh nach i gcomhrag ré laoch
do thuit Fraoch do bhronnadh ór;
dursan a thuitim lé péisd:
truagh, a Dhé, nach maireann fós.

THE SIGH OF A DEAR ONE IS IN THE MEADOW OF FRAOCH

1. The sigh of a dear one is in the Meadow of Fraoch, the sigh of a hero on a bloody bier; a sigh that saddens a man and makes a maid to weep.

2. Here in the east is the cairn beneath which lies smooth-haired Fraoch, son of Fiodhagh, a man who gladdened carrion birds; 'tis from him the Cairn of Fraoch is named.

3. The weeping of a single woman is in Cruachan to the east; sad the tale that grieves her; the cause of her heavy sigh is Fraoch son of Fiodhagh of ancient blades.

4. The one woman who thus weeps, as she goes to the Meadow of Fraoch to see him, is Fionnabhair of noble curling locks, daughter of Meadhbh of the warrior hosts.

5. Oilill's daughter of resplendent hair and Fraoch this night lie side by side; though to many a man she has been offered, yet has she loved no man save Fraoch.

6. Meadhbh of Magh nAoi secured the friendship of Fraoch, peerless in combat; yet he would not be her lover; this is the cause that his body was full of wounds.

7. He was driven to death; his grace towards ladies could not save him from harm; how he met destruction through Meadhbh I will now relate without guile.

8. A rowan tree there was upon Loch Máigh; we could see the strand in the south; every quarter, every month, ripe fruit was there upon it.

9. Choice food were these berries, sweeter than honey was the rowan's bloom; the red rowan sustained a man without other food for the space of nine days.

10. A year could this tree add to the life of every man, a true tale; a remedy for such as were hurt was to taste its fruit when it was red.

11. Though it was a healing physician to the people, yet ever near it, ready to attack, was a poisonous monster, to check all men from plucking its fruit.

12. A heavy, heavy sickness fell upon Meadhbh, daughter of Eochaidh of noble goblets; to inquire the cause of her complaint, she sent for Fraoch.

13. Meadhbh declared she should never be well until she should get the fill of her soft palms of the rowan berries of the cold lake, no man to pluck them but Fraoch.

14. 'Never have I gathered berries,' quoth Fiodhagh's son of ruddy face; 'nevertheless,' said he, 'I will go to pluck berries for Meadhbh.'

15. Fraoch who excelled in fight set out from us to swim the lake; he found the monster asleep, its head aloft against the tree.

16. Fraoch, the keen-weaponed son of Fiodhagh, came back unseen by the monster; he brought a great armful of red berries to Meadhbh in her house.

17. 'Though what thou hast brought is good,' said Meadhbh fair of form; 'naught avails me, thou haloed hero, save to cut a sapling from the root.'

18. Fraoch was willing, no faint youth, to swim once more the watery pool; nor might he, though great his valour, flee the death that was his lot.

19. He seized the rowan by the top, and pulled the stem from its root; the monster this time perceived him as he drew to shore.

20. It seized him as he swam, and grasped his hand in its mouth; he laid hold of the beast by the jaw; alas, that Fraoch should lack his knife.

21. Fionnabhair of noble curling locks threw to him a knife set with gold; the monster mauled his fair skin, it mangled and bit off his hand.

22. Together they fell upon this southern strand of jagged stones, Fraoch son of Fiodhagh and the monster; sad, alas, the story of the fray.

23. As for the fight, 'twas no clumsy one: he bore off the monster's head in his (one) hand; when the maiden saw him she fainted on the shore.

24. The maiden arose from her swoon and took his hand, his soft hand; though it be now but food for the birds, yet great the deed it did in life.

25. From that death that the hero met, Loch Máigh remains the lake's name; by that name the loch is ever known since then and for ever.

26. Then is brought to the Meadow of Fraoch the hero's body to a bloody bier; to the meadow his name was given; alas for such as survive him.

27. The Cairn of the Hand is this cairn beside me, from Fraoch's hand it is called, a warrior who turned not back in fray, a man of bold strength in fight.

28. Beloved the mouth that denied not poets, the mouth to which maidens would grant kisses; beloved the captain of hosts, the cheek than which the rose was not redder.

29. Blacker than raven his locks, redder his cheeks than calf's blood; softer than foam of streams, whiter than snow the skin of Fraoch.

30. More curled than ringlets from the plane his hair, bluer his eye than a sheet of ice; his mouth redder than scarlet, his teeth whiter than woodbine bloom.

31. Loftier his spear than a ship's mast, sweeter than harp-string his voice; a swimmer better than Fraoch never stretched his side to stream.

32. Broader was his shield than a door's leaf, beloved the chief who was behind it; of equal length were his blade and his arm, and broader his sword than a ship's plank.

33. Sad that not in combat with a hero did Fraoch fall who lavished gold; pitiable that he should fall by a monster; sad, alas, that he lives not still.

'Loch Awe to Loch Etive'

from Recollections of a Tour Made in Scotland, 1803

DOROTHY WORDSWORTH (1771–1855)

Dorothy Wordsworth's journal of the tour she made in Scotland with her brother William in 1803 has long been regarded as the perfect complement to his verses written on Scottish subjects and in Scottish locales. Part of the attraction of Scotland which lured the pair and their friend Coleridge north from their Lakeland home was literary. They had fallen first of all for the astonishing appeal of Macpherson's Ossian (although Wordsworth later recanted) nearly forty years after that phenomenon burst upon the literary world. A more recent interest was the rural appeal which Burns's poems and lyrics held for a poet who sought for simplicity and the authentic voice of the people.

The grandeur of the hills and lochs of the northern country was also an objective for the Wordsworths who by this time had developed an affection for and a knowledge of nature, amounting to a whole philosophy. The different responses which they made to their tour were to greatly influence the opening up of the Highlands to literary and cultural tourism in the coming years. Their meeting with Scott later on the journey is a reminder that this was before the appearance of The Lady of the Lake *became Scott's first contribution to Highland tourism. Dorothy's constant comparisons with her beloved Lakes do pall a little, but the quiet simplicity of the narrative and her marvellous powers of observation of the scene and the Highland people, such as the children she encounters by Loch Awe, are clearly shown in this extract.*

The extract shows Dorothy meandering in the Loch Awe area of Argyll and we learn of her general preference for harmonious scenery rather than the very extremes of, for example, the Moor of Rannoch ('The road to Rannoch as dreary as possible'). Unlike Hogg – travelling in the Western Highlands in the same year – the Wordsworths seek out the gentler approach to Glencoe by way of Loch Etive, catch their first sight of the beautiful western ocean and leave us with this beautiful description:

> Our eyes settled upon the island of Mull, a high mountain, green in the sunshine and overcast with clouds – an object as inviting to the fancy as the evening sky in the west and though of a terrestrial green, almost as visionary. We saw that it was an island of the sea, but were unacquainted

with its name; it was of a gem-like colour and soft as the sky.

The romantic picture of Kilchurn Castle is enhanced by William's poem on the same subject.

Went over the hill, and saw nothing remarkable till we came in view of Loch Awe, a large lake far below us, among high mountains – one very large mountain right opposite, which we afterwards found was called Cruachan. The day was pleasant – sunny gleams and a fresh breeze; the lake – we looked across it – as bright as silver, which made the islands, three or four in number, appear very green. We descended gladly, invited by the prospect before us, travelling downwards, along the side of the hill, above a deep glen, woody towards the lower part near the brook; the hills on all sides were high and bare, and not very stony: it made us think of the descent from Newlands into Buttermere, though on a wider scale, and much inferior in simple majesty.

After walking down the hill a long way we came to a bridge, under which the water dashed through a dark channel of rocks among trees, the lake being at a considerable distance below, with cultivated lands between. Close upon the bridge was a small hamlet, a few houses near together, and huddled up in trees – a very sweet spot, the only retired village we had yet seen which was characterized by 'beautiful' wildness with sheltering warmth. We had been told at Inverary that we should come to a place where we might give our horse a feed of corn, and found on inquiry that there was a little public-house here, or rather a hut 'where they kept a dram'. It was a cottage, like all the rest, without a sign-board. The woman of the house helped to take the horse out of the harness, and, being hungry, we asked her if she could make us some porridge, to which she replied that 'we should get that', and I followed her into the house, and sate over her hearth while she was making it. As to fire, there was little sign of it, save the smoke, for a long time, she having no fuel but green wood, and no bellows but her breath. My eyes smarted exceedingly, but the woman seemed so kind and cheerful that I was willing to endure it for the sake of warming my feet in the ashes and talking to her. The fire was in the middle of the room, a crook being suspended from a cross-beam, and a hole left at the top for the smoke to find its way out by: it was a rude Highland hut, unadulterated by Lowland fashions, but it had not the elegant shape of the ferry-house at

Loch Ketterine, and the fire, being in the middle of the room, could not be such a snug place to draw to on a winter's night.

We had a long afternoon before us, with only eight miles to travel to Dalmally, and, having been told that a ferry-boat was kept at one of the islands, we resolved to call for it, and row to the island, so we went to the top of an eminence, and the man who was with us set some children to work to gather sticks and withered leaves to make a smoky fire – a signal for the boatman, whose hut is on a flat green island, like a sheep pasture, without trees, and of a considerable size: the man told us it was a rabbit-warren. There were other small islands, on one of which was a ruined house, fortification, or small castle: we could not learn anything of its history, only a girl told us that formerly gentlemen lived in such places. Immediately from the water's edge rose the mountain Cruachan on the opposite side of the lake; it is woody near the water and craggy above, with deep hollows on the surface. We thought it the grandest mountain we had seen, and saying to the man who was with us that it was a fine mountain, 'Yes,' he replied, 'it is an excellent mountain,' adding that it was higher than Ben Lomond, and then told us some wild stories of the enormous profits it brought to Lord Breadalbane, its lawful owner. The shape of Loch Awe is very remarkable, its outlet being at one side, and only about eight miles from the head, and the whole lake twenty-four miles in length. We looked with longing after that branch of it opposite to us out of which the water issues: it seemed almost like a river gliding under steep precipices. What we saw of the larger branch, or what might be called the body of the lake, was less promising, the banks being merely gentle slopes, with not very high mountains behind, and the ground moorish and cold.

The children, after having collected fuel for our fire, began to play on the green hill where we stood, as heedless as if we had been trees or stones, and amused us exceedingly with their activity: they wrestled, rolled down the hill, pushing one another over and over again, laughing, screaming, and chattering Erse: they were all without shoes and stockings, which, making them fearless of hurting or being hurt, gave a freedom to the action of their limbs which I never saw in English children: they stood upon one another, body, breast, or face, or any another part; sometimes one was uppermost, sometimes another, and sometimes they rolled all together, so that we could not know to which body this leg or that arm belonged. We waited, watching them, till we were assured that the boatman had noticed our signal. – By the bye, if we had received proper directions at Loch Lomond, on our journey to Loch Ketterine, we should have made our way down the lake till we had come opposite to the ferryman's house, where there is a hut, and the people who live there are accustomed to call him by the same signal as here. Luckily for us we were not so well instructed, for we should have missed the pleasure of receiving the kindness of Mr and Mrs Macfarlane and their family.

A young woman who wanted to go to the island accompanied us to the water-side. The walk was pleasant, through fields with hedgerows, the greenest fields we had seen in Scotland; but we were obliged to return without going to the island. The poor man had taken his boat to another place, and the waters were swollen so that we could not go close to the shore, and show ourselves to him, nor could we make him hear by shouting. On our return to the public-house we asked the woman what we should pay her, and were not a little surprised when she answered, 'Three shillings.' Our horse had had a sixpenny feed of miserable corn, not worth threepence; the rest of the charge was for skimmed milk, oat-bread, porridge, and blue milk cheese: we told her it was far too much; and, giving her half-a-crown, departed. I was sorry she had made this unreasonable demand, because we had liked the woman, and we had before been so well treated in the Highland cottages; but, on thinking more about it, I satisfied myself that it was no scheme to impose upon us, for she was contented with the half-crown, and would, I daresay, have been so with two shillings, if we had offered it her at first. Not being accustomed to fix a price upon porridge and milk, to such as we, at least, when we asked her she did not know what to say; but, seeing that we were travelling for pleasure, no doubt she concluded we were rich, and that what was a small gain to her could be no great loss to us.

When we had gone a little way we saw before us a young man with a bundle over his shoulder, hung on a stick, bearing a great boy on his back; seeing that they were travellers, we offered to take the boy on the car, to which the man replied that he should be more than thankful, and set him up beside me. They had walked from Glasgow, and that morning from Inverary; the boy was only six years old, 'But,' said his father, 'he is a stout walker,' and a fine fellow he was, smartly dressed in tight clean clothes and a nice round hat: he was going to stay with his grandmother at Dalmally. I found him good company; though I could not draw a single word out of him, it was a pleasure to see his happiness gleaming through the shy glances of his healthy countenance. Passed a pretty chapel by the lake-side, and an island with a farm-house upon it, and corn and pasture fields; but, as we went along, we had frequent reason to regret the want of English hedgerows and English culture; for the ground was often swampy or moorish near the lake where comfortable dwellings among green fields might have been. When we came near to the end of the lake we had a steep hill to climb, so William and I walked; and we had such confidence in our horse that we were not afraid to leave the car to his guidance with the child in it; we were soon, however, alarmed at seeing him trot up the hill a long way before us; the child, having raised himself up upon the seat, was beating him as hard as he could with a little stick which he carried in his hand; and when he saw our eyes were on him he sate down, I believe very sorry to resign his office: the horse slackened his pace, and no accident happened.

When we had ascended half-way up the hill, directed by the man, I took a nearer footpath, and at the top came in view of a most impressive scene, a ruined castle on an island almost in the middle of the last compartment of the lake, backed by a mountain cove, down which came a roaring stream. The castle occupied every foot of the island that was visible to us, appearing to rise out of the water; mists rested upon the mountain side, with spots of sunshine between; there was a mild desolation in the low grounds, a solemn grandeur in the mountains, and the castle was wild, yet stately, not dismantled of its turrets, nor the walls broken down, though completely in ruin. After having stood some minutes I joined William on the high road, and both wishing to stay longer near this place, we requested the man to drive his little boy on to Dalmally, about two miles further, and leave the car at the inn. He told us that the ruin was called Kilchurn Castle, that it belonged to Lord Breadalbane, and had been built by one of the ladies of that family for her defence during her Lord's absence at the Crusades, for which purpose she levied a tax of seven years' rent upon her tenants; he said that from that side of the lake it did not appear, in very dry weather, to stand upon an island; but that it was possible to go over to it without being wet-shod. We were very lucky in seeing it after a great flood; for its enchanting effect was chiefly owing to its situation in the lake, a decayed palace rising out of the plain of waters! I have called it a palace, for such feeling it gave to me, though having been built as a place of defence, a castle or fortress. We turned again and reascended the hill, and sate a long time in the middle of it looking on the castle and the huge mountain cove opposite, and William, addressing himself to the ruin, poured out these verses: –

> Child of loud-throated War! the mountain stream
> Roars in thy hearing; but thy hour of rest
> Is come, and thou art silent in thy age.

We walked up the hill again, and, looking down the vale, had a fine view of the lake and islands, resembling the views down Windermere, though much less rich. Our walk to Dalmally was pleasant: the vale makes a turn to the right, beyond the head of the lake, and the village of Dalmally, which is, in fact, only a few huts, the manse or minister's house, the chapel, and the inn, stands near the river, which flows into the head of the lake. The whole vale is very pleasing, the lower part of the hill-sides being sprinkled with thatched cottages, cultivated ground in small patches near them, which evidently belonged to the cottages.

We were overtaken by a gentleman who rode on a beautiful white pony, like Lilly, and was followed by his servant, a Highland boy, on another pony, a little creature, not much bigger than a large mastiff, on which were slung a pair of crutches and a tartan plaid. The gentleman entered into conversation with us, and on our telling him that we were going to Glen Coe, he advised us, instead of proceeding directly to Tyndrum, the next stage, to go round by the outlet of Loch Awe to Loch Etive, and thence to Glen Coe. We were glad to change our plan, for we wanted much to see more of Loch Awe, and he told us that the whole of the way by Loch Etive was pleasant, and the road to Tyndrum as dreary as possible; indeed, we could see it at that time several miles before us upon the side of a bleak mountain; and he said that there was nothing but moors and mountains all the way. We reached the inn a little before sunset, ordered supper, and I walked out. Crossed a bridge to look more nearly at the parsonage-house and the chapel, which stands upon a bank close to the river, a pretty stream overhung in some parts by trees. The vale is very pleasing; but, like all other Scotch vales we had yet seen, it told of its kinship with the mountains and of poverty or some neglect on the part of man.

Ora Dìona
(Prayer of Protection)
COLLECTED AND TRANSLATED BY
ALEXANDER CARMICHAEL (1832–1912)

Carmina Gadelica *is the Latin title (meaning* Gaelic Hymns*) given to the vast collection of Gaelic oral tradition, mainly in verse, assembled by Alexander Carmichael. It is one of the great treasures of the Scottish Gaelic heritage.*

Alexander Carmichael was born on the Island of Lismore and later worked as an exciseman on the west coast and in the Hebrides. Throughout his life he was concerned with the preservation of oral tradition; he was one of John Francis Campbell's collectors for Popular Tales of the West Highlands *(1860–62) and he was a contributor to Dr Alexander Nicolson's* Gaelic Proverbs *(1881). His greatest work, however, was the collection of the* Carmina Gadelica *which he gathered throughout the West Highlands and islands between 1855 and 1899 and which were subsequently published in five volumes between 1900 and 1954. The* Carmina *consist of a wide variety of prayers, invocations, incantations, hymns, blessings and waulking songs which suggest a deep spirituality in the communities in which they were recited. Many of the items appear to be of pre-Reformation and some of pagan origin.*

This 'Prayer of Protection' was collected by Carmichael in 1882 from Mrs Ann Livingstone in Taynuilt. She had been born and brought up in Glen Kinglass on Loch Etive where she learned much traditional lore. In this prayer Michael is Saint Michael, the Archangel, and Brigid is Saint Bride or Brigid of Kildare in Ireland. Both of these saints received particular veneration in the West Highlands. Neil Munro's novel Children of Tempest, *which draws heavily on Carmichael's notes, depicts devotional practices connected with these saints being carried out in South Uist.*

Mhìcheil na mìl,
A Mhìcheil nan lot,
Dìon mi bho mhìghean
Luchd mìoruin a nochd,
Luchd mìoruin a nochd.

A Bhrighde nan nì,
A Bhrighde nam brot,
Dìon mi bho dhìmeas
Sìodhach nan cnoc,
Sìodhach nan cnoc.

A Mhoire na mìn
A Mhoire na moit,
Cobhair mi 's dìon
Le do lìon-anart broit,
Le do lìon-anart broit.

A Chrìosda na crìbh,
A Chrìosda na crois,
Spìon mi bho lìona
Luchd spìde nan olc,
Luchd spìde nan olc.

Athair nan anrach,
Athair nan nochd,
Tarr mi gu sgàth-thaigh
Slànaighear nam bochd,
Slànaighear nam bochd.

PRAYER OF PROTECTION

Thou Michael of militance,
Thou Michael of wounding,
Shield me from the grudge
Of ill-wishers this night,
Ill-wishers this night.

Thou Brigit of the kine,
Thou Brigit of the mantles,
Shield me from the ban
Of the fairies of the knolls,
The fairies of the knolls.

Thou Mary of mildness,
Thou Mary of honour,
Succour me and shield me
With thy linen mantle,
With thy linen mantle.

Thou Christ of the tree,
Thou Christ of the cross,
Snatch me from the snares
Of the spiteful ones of evil,
The spiteful ones of evil.

Thou Father of the waifs,
Thou Father of the naked,
Draw me to the shelter-house
Of the Saviour of the poor,
The Saviour of the poor.

Address to Kilchurn Castle

WILLIAM WORDSWORTH (1770–1850)

The ruins of the Campbell stronghold of Kilchurn were much admired by the Wordsworths on their 1803 tour of Scotland (see previous extract). The little promontory on which it stood is now an islet and, as the English writers observed, it makes a magnificent picture with the great bulk of Cruachan in the background. To confirm the information given by Dorothy in her Recollections of a Tour in Scotland *the following facts may be added. The oldest part, a tower, was built in the fifteenth century by Sir Colin Campbell of Glenorchy; to this additions were made by the First Earl of Breadalbane and the castle was abandoned soon after serving as a garrison for government forces in the '45.*

Child of loud-throated War! the mountain Stream
Roars in thy hearing; but thy hour of rest
Is come, and thou art silent in thy age;
Save when the wind sweeps by and sounds are caught
Ambiguous, neither wholly thine nor theirs.
Oh! there is life that breathes not; Powers there are
That touch each other to the quick in modes
Which the gross world no sense hath to perceive,
No soul to dream of. What art Thou, from care
Cast off – abandoned by thy rugged Sire,
Nor by soft Peace adopted; though, in place
And in dimension, such that thou might'st seem
But a mere footstool to yon sovereign Lord,
Huge Cruachan, (a thing that meaner hills
Might crush, nor know that it had suffered harm;)
Yet, he, not loth, in favour of thy claims
To reverence, suspends his own; submitting
All that the God of Nature hath conferred.
All that he holds in common with the stars,
To the memorial majesty of Time

Impersonated in thy calm decay!
Take, them, thy seat, Vicegerent unreproved!
Now, while a farewell gleam of evening light
Is fondly lingering on thy shattered front,
Do thou, in turn, be paramount; and rule
Over the pomp and beauty of a scene
Whose mountains, torrents, lake, and woods, unite
To pay thee homage; and with these are joined,
In willing admiration and respect,
Two Hearts, which in thy presence might be called
Youthful as Spring. – Shade of departed Power,
Skeleton of unfleshed humanity,
The chronicle were welcome that should call
Into the compass of distinct regard
The toils and struggle of thy infant years!
Yon foaming flood seems motionless as ice;
Its dizzy turbulence eludes the eye,
Frozen by distance; so, majestic Pile,
To the perception of this Age, appear
Thy fierce beginnings, softened and subdued
And quieted in character – the strife,
The pride, the fury uncontrollable,
Lost on the aerial heights of the Crusades![1]

---

[1] The tradition is, that the castle was built by a Lady during the absence of her Lord in Palestine.

Cead Deireannach nam Beann
(Final Farewell to the Bens)

DUNCAN BAN MACINTYRE (1724–1812)

TRANSLATION BY ANGUS MACLEOD

Duncan Macintyre is frequently known in Gaelic as Donnachadh Bàn nan Oran (Fair Duncan of the Songs). He was born at Drum Liaghart near the shore of Loch Tulla and was later to marry Mary MacNicol, daughter of the local innkeeper at Inveroran – his Màiri Bhàn Og (Fair Young Mary). He served as soldier in the Argyll Regiment of Militia and fought – somewhat reluctantly it would seem – against the Jacobites. He was then employed as a keeper in Glen Lochay, on Ben Dorain and in Glen Etive. In 1766 he left the Highlands for Edinburgh and a post in the City Guard and this was followed by a period in the Breadalbane Fencibles. Cead Deireannach nam Beann *was composed in September, 1802 when as an old man he paid a final visit to the land of his childhood and earlier life.*

Above all Donnachadh Bàn's forte was as a poet of nature and the deer and this is well illustrated in his very fine long poems Oran Coire a'Cheathaich, (Song to the Misty Corrie) *and* Moladh Ben Dóbhrain (Praise of Ben Dorain). (The latter is available in a brilliant translation by the modern poet Iain Crichton Smith.) Cead Deireannach nam Bean *is a series of poignant and nostalgic recollections of nature, of the deer and of happy times with the people he knew from his days as a keeper. He also registers his anguished disapproval of the destruction of the deer forests to make way for sheep.*

Donnachadh Bàn composed about 6000 lines of poetry, but he could neither read nor write and these had to be noted down by others at his dictation. Dr John Stuart, minister of Luss, compiled the first complete edition of his poems. This translation of 'Cead Deireannach nam Beann' is taken from The Songs of Duncan Bàn Macintyre, *edited by the late Angus MacLeod, a highly respected Gaelic scholar and Rector of Oban High School.*

Bha mi 'n dé 'm Beinn Dóbhrain
'S 'na còir cha robh mi aineolach;
Chunna' mi na gleanntan
'S na beanntaichean a b' aithne dhomh:
B' e sin an sealladh éibhinn
Bhith 'g imeachd air na sléibhtean,
'N uair bhiodh a' ghrian ag éirigh,
'S a bhiodh na féidh a' langanaich.

'S aobhach a' ghreigh uallach,
'N uair ghluaiseadh iad gu faramach;
'S na h-éildean air an fhuaran,
Bu chuannar na laoigh bhallach ann;
Na maoislichean 's na ruadhbhuic,
Na coilich dhubha 's ruadha –
'S e 'n ceòl bu bhinne chualas
'N uair chluinnt' am fuaim 'sa' chamhanaich.

'S togarrach a dh' fhalbhainn
Gu sealgaireachd nam bealaichean,
Dol mach a dhìreadh garbhlaich
'S gum b' anmoch tighinn gu baile mi;
An t-uisge glan 's am fàile
Th' air mullach nam beann àrda,
Chuidich e gu fàs mi,
'S e rinn domh slàint' is fallaineachd.

Fhuair mi greis am àrach
Air àirighnean a b' aithne dhomh,
Ri cluiche 's mire 's mànran
'S bhith 'n coibhneas blàth nan caileagan;
Bu chùis an aghaidh nàduir
Gum maireadh sin an dràsd ann,
'S e b' éigin bhith 'gam fàgail
'N uair thàinig tràth dhuinn dealachadh.

Nis on bhuail an aois mi
Fhuair mi gaoid a mhaireas domh,
Rinn milleadh air mo dheudach,
'S mo léirsinn air a dalladh orm;
Chan urrainn mi bhith treubhach

Ged a chuirinn feum air,
'S ged bhiodh an ruaig am dhéidh-sa
Cha dèan mi ceum ro-chabhagach.

Ged tha mo cheann air liathadh
'S mo chiabhagan air tanachadh,
'S tric a leig mi mialchù
Ri fear fiadhaich ceannardach;
Ged bu toigh leam riamh iad,
'S ged fhaicinn air an t-sliabh iad,
Cha téid mi nis g' an iarraidh
On chaill mi trian na h-analach.

Ri am dol anns a' bhùireadh
Bu dùrachdach a leanainn iad,
'S bhiodh uair aig sluagh na dùthcha,
Toirt òrain ùra 's rannachd dhaibh;
Greis eile mar ri cairdean
'N uair bha sinn anns na campan,
Bu chridheil anns an am sinn,
'S cha bhiodh an dram oirnn annasach.

'N uair bha mi 'n toiseach m' òige
'S i ghòraich a chum falamh mi;
'S e Fortan tha cur òirnne
Gach aon nì còir a ghealladh dhuinn;
Ged tha mi gann a stòras,
Tha m'inntinn làn de shòlas,
On tha mi ann an dòchas
Gun d' rinn nighean Deòrs' an t-aran
domh.

Bha mi 'n dé 'san aonach
'S bha smaointean mór air m' aire-sa,
Nach robh 'n luchd-gaoil a b' àbhaist
Bhith siubhal fàsaich mar rium ann;
'S a' bheinn as beag a shaoil mi
Gun dèanadh ise caochladh,
On tha i nis fo chaoraibh
'S ann thug an saoghal car asam.

'N uair sheall mi air gach taobh dhìom
Chan fhaodainn gun bhith smalanach,
On theirig coill is fraoch ann,
'S na daoine bh' ann, cha mhaireann iad;
Chan 'eil fiadh r' a shealg ann,
Chan 'eil eun no earb ann,
Am beagan nach 'eil marbh dhiubh,
'S e rinn iad falbh gu baileach as.

Mo shoraidh leis na frìthean,
O 's mìorbhailteach na beannan iad,
Le biolair uaine 's fìoruisg,
Deoch uasal rìomhach cheanalta;
Na blàran a tha prìseil,
'S na fàsaichean tha lìonmhor,
O 's àit a leig mi dhìom iad,
Gu bràth mo mhìle beannachd leò.

FINAL FAREWELL TO THE BENS

I was on Ben Dobhrain yesterday,
no stranger in her bounds was I;
I looked upon the glens
and the bens that I had known so well;
this was a happy picture –
to be tramping on the hillsides,
at the hour the sun was rising,
and the deer would be a-bellowing.

The gallant herd is joyous,
as they moved off with noisy stir;
the hinds are by the spring,
and the speckled calves looked bonny there;
then the does and roe-bucks,
the black-cocks and the grouse cocks –
the sweetest music ever heard
was their sound when heard at dawn of day.

Blithely would I set out
for stalking on the hill passes,
away to climb rough country,
and late would I be coming home;
and clean rain and the air
on the peaks of the high mountains,
helped me to grow, and gave me
robustness and vitality.

I earned my living for a time,
at shielings that I knew full well,
with frolic, fun, flirtation,
enjoying maidens' tender fellowship;
'twere contrary to nature
that this should still obtain there;
we had perforce to leave them,
when the time arrived to separate.

Now since old age has stricken me,
I have an ailment that will cleave to me,
that has wrought havoc on my teeth,
while my vision is beclouded;
I am not fit for exploit
though I might find it needful,
and though pursuit were on my trail,
I could not step out very fast.

Although my head is hoary
and my locks have become scanty,
oft have I loosed a deer-hound
against a wild, high-headed one:
though I, who loved them always,
were to see them on the hillside,
now, being sadly short of breath,
I cannot go a-chasing them.

In their rutting season,
devotedly I followed them;
then an interlude with country folk,
while giving them new songs and verse;
another spell with comrades,

while we were campaigning:
cheery were we then,
nor was the dram to us a novelty.

When I was in my early youth,
'twas folly kept me destitute;
'tis Providence bestows on us
each fair thing that was promised us;
though I am scant of riches,
my mind is full of solace,
for I trust that George's daughter
will have provided bread for me.

Yesterday I was on the moor,
and grave reflections haunted me:
that absent were the well-loved friends
who used to roam the waste with me;
since the mountain, which I little thought
would suffer transformation,
has now become a sheep-run,
the world, indeed, has cheated me.

As I gazed on every side of me
I could not but be sorrowful,
for wood and heather have run out,
nor live the men who flourished there;
there's not a deer to hunt there,
there's not a bird or roe there,
and the few that have not died out
have departed from it utterly.

Farewell to the deer forests –
O! they are wondrous hill-country,
with green cress and spring water,
a noble, royal, pleasant drink;
to the moor plains which are well beloved,
and the pastures which are plentiful,
as these are parts of which I've taken leave,
my thousand blessings aye be theirs.

'Glencoe'

from The History of England

THOMAS BABINGTON MACAULAY (1800–59)

Macaulay is the quintessential Whig historian – immensely popular in his day and well into the twentieth century, and synonymous with the documenting of the Revolution Settlement and the presenter of the case for his great hero William III. This extract comes from The History of England *which he only took up to 1697 and here Macaulay gives an epic account of what others have described as a mere footnote in history. Macaulay develops a powerful political theme to his story and sets the context with fine portraits of all the main protagonists. He allocates the blame for the Glencoe massacre to various of the dramatis personae but fails to acknowledge the important involvement of William in the story. Subsequent evaluations have tended to reinforce the king's culpability in the events, but even Macaulay's account remains astonishingly vivid and readable, and is a key element of the Whig version of British and Scottish history.*

Macaulay's preferred method was to prepare for writing a narrative such as this by exploring on the ground the scenes and set-pieces in which he sets his narrative. The superb account of the 'glen of weeping' itself shows the power of this scene-setting technique which he derived from one of his literary models, Sir Walter Scott. Macaulay has a sympathy for Scots and Scotland derived from his grandfather who was minister of Cardross church on the fringes of Argyll.

John Earl of Breadalbane, the head of a younger branch of the great house of Campbell, ranked high among the petty princes of the mountains. He could bring seventeen hundred claymores into the field; and, ten years before the Revolution, he had actually marched into the Lowlands with this great force for the purpose of supporting the prelatical tyranny. In those days he had affected zeal for monarchy and episcopacy: but in truth he cared for no government and no religion. He seems to have united two different sets of vices, the growth of two different regions, and of two different stages in the progress of society. In his castle among the hills he had learned the barbarian pride and ferocity of a Highland chief. In the

Council Chamber at Edinburgh he had contracted the deep taint of treachery and corruption. After the Revolution he had, like too many of his fellow nobles, joined and betrayed every party in turn, had sworn fealty to William and Mary, and had plotted against them. To trace all the turns and doublings of his course, during the year 1689 and the earlier part of 1690, would be wearisome. That course became somewhat less tortuous when the battle of the Boyne had cowed the spirit of the Jacobites. It now seemed probable that the Earl would be a loyal subject of their Majesties, till some great disaster should befall them. Nobody who knew him could trust him: but few Scottish statesmen could then be trusted; and yet Scottish statesmen must be employed. His position and connections marked him out as a man who might, if he would, do much towards the work of quieting the Highlands; and his interest seemed to be a guarantee for his zeal. He had, as he declared with every appearance of truth, strong personal reasons for wishing to see tranquillity restored. His domains were so situated that, while the civil war lasted, his vassals could not tend their herds or sow their oats in peace. His lands were daily ravaged: his cattle were daily driven away: one of his houses had been burnt down. It was probable, therefore, that he would do his best to put an end to hostilities.

He was accordingly commissioned to treat with the Jacobite chiefs, and was entrusted with the money which was to be distributed among them. He invited them to a conference at his residence in Glenorchy. They came: but the treaty went on very slowly. Every head of a tribe asked for a larger share of the English gold than was to be obtained. Breadalbane was suspected of intending to cheat both the King and the clans. The dispute between the rebels and the government was complicated with another dispute still more embarrassing. The Camerons and Macdonalds were really at war, not with William, but with Mac Callum More; and no arrangement to which Mac Callum More was not a party could really produce tranquillity. A grave question therefore arose, whether the money entrusted to Breadalbane should be paid directly to the discontented chiefs, or should be employed to satisfy the claims which Argyle had upon them. The shrewdness of Lochiel and the arrogant pretensions of Glengarry contributed to protract the discussions. But no Celtic potentate was so impracticable as Macdonald of Glencoe, known among the mountains by the hereditary appellation of Mac Ian.

Mac Ian dwelt in the mouth of a ravine situated not far from the southern shore of Lochleven, an arm of the sea which deeply indents the western coast of Scotland, and separates Argyleshire from Invernesshire. Near his house were two or three small hamlets inhabited by his tribe.

The whole population which he governed was not supposed to exceed two hundred souls. In the neighbourhood of the little cluster of villages was some copsewood and some pasture land: but a little further up the defile no sign of population or of fruitfulness was to be seen. In the Gaelic tongue, Glencoe signifies the Glen of Weeping: and in truth that pass is the most dreary and melancholy of all the Scottish passes, the very Valley of the Shadow of Death. Mists and storms brood over it through the greater part of the finest summer; and even on those rare days when the sun is bright, and when there is no cloud in the sky, the impression made by the landscape is sad and awful. The path lies along a stream which issues from the most sullen and gloomy of mountain pools. Huge precipices of naked stone frown on both sides. Even in July the streaks of snow may often be discerned in the rifts near the summits. All down the sides of the crags heaps of ruin mark the headlong paths of the torrents. Mile after mile the traveller looks in vain for the smoke of one hut, or for one human form wrapped in a plaid, and listens in vain for the bark of a shepherd's dog, or the bleat of a lamb. Mile after mile the only sound that indicates life is the faint cry of a bird of prey from some storm beaten pinnacle of rock. The progress of civilisation, which has turned so many wastes into fields yellow with harvests or gay with apple blossoms, has only made Glencoe more desolate. All the science and industry of a peaceful age can extract nothing valuable from that wilderness: but, in an age of violence and rapine, the wilderness itself was valued on account of the shelter which it afforded to the plunderer and his plunder. Nothing could be more natural than that the clan to which this rugged desert belonged should have been noted for predatory habits. For, among the Highlanders generally, to rob was thought at least as honourable an employment as to cultivate the soil; and, of all the Highlanders, the Macdonalds of Glencoe had the least productive soil, and the most convenient and secure den of robbers. Successive governments had tried to punish this wild race: but no large force had ever been employed for that purpose; and a small force was easily resisted or eluded by men familiar with every recess and every outlet of the natural fortress in which they had been born and bred. The people of Glencoe would probably have been less troublesome neighbours if they had lived among their own kindred. But they were an outpost of the Clan Donald, separated from every other branch of their own family, and almost surrounded by the domains of the hostile race of Diarmid. They were impelled by hereditary enmity, as well as by want, to live at the expense of the tribe of Campbell. Breadalbane's property had suffered greatly from their depredations; and he was not of a temper to forgive such injuries. When, therefore, the

Chief of Glencoe made his appearance at the congress in Glenorchy, he was ungraciously received. The Earl, who ordinarily bore himself with the solemn dignity of a Castilian grandee, forgot, in his resentment, his wonted gravity, forgot his public character, forgot the laws of hospitality, and, with angry reproaches and menaces, demanded reparation for the herds which had been driven from his lands by Mac Ian's followers. Mac Ian was seriously apprehensive of some personal outrage, and was glad to get safe back to his own glen. His pride had been wounded; and the promptings of interest concurred with those of pride. As the head of a people who lived by pillage, he had strong reasons for wishing that the country might continue to be in a perturbed state. He had little chance of receiving one guinea of the money which was to be distributed among the malecontents. For his share of that money would scarcely meet Breadalbane's demands for compensation; and there could be little doubt that, whoever might be unpaid, Breadalbane would take care to pay himself. Mac Ian therefore did his best to dissuade his allies from accepting terms from which he could himself expect no benefit; and his influence was not small. His own vassals, indeed, were few in number: but he came of the best blood of the Highlands: he kept up a close connection with his more powerful kinsmen; nor did they like him the less because he was a robber; for he never robbed them; and that robbery, merely as robbery, was a wicked and disgraceful act, had never entered into the mind of any Celtic chief. Mac Ian was therefore held in high esteem by the confederates. His age was venerable; his aspect was majestic; and he possessed in large measure those intellectual qualities which, in rude societies, give men an ascendancy over their fellows. Breadalbane found himself, at every step of the negotiation, thwarted by the arts of his old enemy, and abhorred the name of Glencoe more and more every day.

But the government did not trust solely to Breadalbane's diplomatic skill. The authorities at Edinburgh put forth a proclamation exhorting the clans to submit to King William and Queen Mary, and offering pardon to every rebel who, on or before the thirty-first of December 1691, should swear to live peaceably under the government of their Majesties. It was announced that those who should hold out after that day would be treated as enemies and traitors. Warlike preparations were made, which showed that the threat was meant in earnest. The Highlanders were alarmed, and, though the pecuniary terms had not been satisfactorily settled, thought it prudent to give the pledge which was demanded of them. No chief, indeed, was willing to set the example of submission. Glengarry blustered and pretended to fortify his house. 'I will not,' said Lochiel, 'break the ice. That is a point of honour with me. But my tacksmen and people may use their freedom.' His tacksmen and people understood him, and repaired by hundreds to the Sheriff to take the oaths. The Macdonalds of Sleat, Clanronald, Keppoch, and even Glengarry, imitated the Camerons; and the chiefs, after trying to outstay each other as long as they durst, imitated their vassals.

The thirty-first of December arrived; and still the Macdonalds of Glencoe had not come in. The punctilious pride of Mac Ian was doubtless gratified by the thought that he had continued to defy the government after the boastful Glengarry, the ferocious Keppoch, the magnanimous Lochiel had yielded: but he bought his gratification dear.

At length, on the thirty-first of December, he repaired to Fort William, accompanied by his principal vassals, and offered to take the oaths. To his dismay, he found that there was in the fort no person competent to administer them. Colonel Hill, the Governor, was not a magistrate; nor was there any magistrate nearer than Inverary. Mac Ian, now fully sensible of the folly of which he had been guilty in postponing to the very last moment an act on which his life and his estate depended, set off for Inverary in great distress. He carried with him a letter from Hill to the Sheriff of Argyleshire, Sir Colin Campbell of Ardkinglass, a respectable gentleman, who, in the late reign, had suffered severely for his Whig principles. In this letter the Colonel expressed a good natured hope that, even out of season, a lost sheep, and so fine a lost sheep, would be gladly received. Mac Ian made all the haste in his power, and did not stop even at his own house, though it lay nigh to the road. But in that age a journey through Argyleshire in the depth of winter was necessarily slow. The old man's progress up steep mountains and along boggy valleys was obstructed by snow storms; and it was not till the sixth of January that he presented himself before the Sheriff at Inverary. The Sheriff hesitated. His power, he said, was limited by the terms of the proclamation; and he did not see how he could swear a rebel who had not submitted within the prescribed time. Mac Ian begged earnestly and with tears that he might be sworn. His people, he said, would follow his example. If any of them proved refractory, he would himself send the recusant to prison, or ship him off for Flanders. His entreaties and Hill's letter overcame Sir Colin's scruples. The oath was administered; and a certificate was transmitted to the Council at Edinburgh, setting forth the special circumstances which had induced the Sheriff to do what he knew not to be strictly regular.

The news that Mac Ian had not submitted within the prescribed time was received with cruel joy by three powerful Scotchmen who were then at the English Court. Breadalbane had gone up to London at Christmas in order to give an account of his stewardship. There he met his kinsman

Argyle. Argyle was, in personal qualities, one of the most insignificant of the long line of nobles who have borne that great name. He was the descendant of eminent men, and the parent of eminent men. He was the grandson of one of the ablest of Scottish politicians; the son of one of the bravest and truehearted of Scottish patriots; the father of one Mac Callum More renowned as a warrior and as an orator, as the model of every courtly grace, and as the judicious patron of arts and letters, and of another Mac Callum More distinguished by talents for business and command, and by skill in the exact sciences. Both of such an ancestry and of such a progeny Argyle was unworthy. He had even been guilty of the crime, common enough among Scottish politicians, but in him singularly disgraceful, of tampering with the agents of James while professing loyalty to William. Still Argyle had the importance inseparable from high rank, vast domains, extensive feudal rights, and almost boundless patriarchal authority. To him, as to his cousin Breadalbane, the intelligence that the tribe of Glencoe was out of the protection of the law was most gratifying; and the Master of Stair more than sympathised with them both.

The feeling of Argyle and Breadalbane is perfectly intelligible. They were the heads of a great clan; and they had an opportunity of destroying a neighbouring clan with which they were at deadly feud. Breadalbane had received peculiar provocation. His estate had been repeatedly devastated; and he had just been thwarted in a negotiation of high moment. Unhappily there was scarcely any excess of ferocity for which a precedent could not be found in Celtic tradition. Among all warlike barbarians revenge is esteemed the most sacred of duties and the most exquisite of pleasures; and so it had long been esteemed among the Highlanders. The history of the clans abounds with frightful tales, some perhaps fabulous or exaggerated, some certainly true, of vindictive massacres and assassinations. The Macdonalds of Glengarry, for example, having been affronted by the people of a parish near Inverness, surrounded the parish church on a Sunday, shut the doors, and burned the whole congregation alive. While the flames were raging, the hereditary musician of the murderers mocked the shrieks of the perishing crowd with the notes of his bagpipe. A band of Macgregors, having cut off the head of an enemy, laid it, the mouth filled with bread and cheese, on his sister's table, and had the satisfaction of seeing her go mad with horror at the sight. They then carried the ghastly trophy in triumph to their chief. The whole clan met under the roof of an ancient church. Every one in turn laid his hand on the dead man's scalp and vowed to defend the slayers. The inhabitants of Eigg seized some Macleods, bound them hand

and foot, and turned them adrift in a boat to be swallowed up by the waves, or to perish of hunger. The Macleods retaliated by driving the population of Eigg into a cavern, lighting a fire at the entrance and suffocating the whole race, men, women, and children. It is much less strange that the two great Earls of the house of Campbell, animated by the passions of Highland chieftains, should have planned a Highland revenge, than that they should have found an accomplice, and something more than an accomplice, in the Master of Stair.

The Master of Stair was one of the first men of his time, a jurist, a statesman, a fine scholar, an eloquent orator. His polished manners and lively conversation were the delight of aristocratical societies; and none who met him in such societies would have thought it possible that he could bear the chief part in any atrocious crime. His political principles were lax, yet not more lax than those of most Scotch politicians of that age. Cruelty had never been imputed to him. Those who most disliked him did him the justice to own that, where his schemes of policy were not concerned, he was a very good natured man. There is not the slightest reason to believe that he gained a single pound Scots by the act which has covered his name with infamy. He had no personal reason to wish the Glencoe men any ill. There had been no feud between them and his family. His property lay in a district where their tartan was never seen. Yet he hated them with a hatred as fierce and implacable as if they had laid waste his fields, burned his mansion, murdered his child in the cradle.

To what cause are we to ascribe so strange an antipathy? This question perplexed the Master's contemporaries; and any answer which may now be offered ought to be offered with diffidence. The most probable conjecture is that he was actuated by an inordinate, an unscrupulous, a remorseless zeal for what seemed to him to be the interest of the state. This explanation may startle those who have not considered how large a proportion of the blackest crimes recorded in history is to be ascribed to ill regulated public spirit. We daily see men do for their party, for their sect, for their country, for their favourite schemes of political and social reform, what they would not do to enrich or to avenge themselves. At a temptation directly addressed to our private cupidity or to our private animosity, whatever virtue we have takes the alarm. But virtue itself may contribute to the fall of him who imagines that it is in his power, by violating some general rule of morality, to confer an important benefit on a church, on a commonwealth, on mankind. He silences the remonstrances of conscience, and hardens his heart against the most touching spectacles of misery, by repeating to himself that his intentions are pure, that his objects are noble, that he is doing a little evil for the sake of a great good. By degrees he comes altogether to forget the turpitude of the means in the excellence of the end, and at length perpetrates without one internal twinge acts which would shock a buccaneer. There is no reason to believe that Dominic would, for the best archbishopric in Christendom, have incited ferocious marauders to plunder and slaughter a peaceful and industrious population, that Everard Digby would, for a dukedom, have blown a large assembly of people into the air, or that Robespierre would have murdered for hire one of the thousands whom he murdered from philanthropy.

The Master of Stair seems to have proposed to himself a truly great and good end, the pacification and civilisation of the Highlands. He was, by the acknowledgment of those who most hated him, a man of large views. He justly thought it monstrous that a third part of Scotland should be in a state scarcely less savage than New Guinea, that letters of fire and sword should, through a third part of Scotland, be, century after century, a species of legal process, and that no attempt should be made to apply a radical remedy to such evils. The independence affected by a crowd of petty sovereigns, the contumacious resistance which they were in the habit of offering to the authority of the Crown and of the Court of Session, their wars, their robberies, their fireraisings, their practice of exacting black mail from people more peaceable and more useful than themselves, naturally excited the disgust and indignation of an enlightened and politic gownsman, who was, both by the constitution of his mind and by the habits of his profession, a lover of law and order. His object was no less than a complete dissolution and reconstruction of society in the Highlands, such a dissolution and reconstruction as, two generations later, followed the battle of Culloden. In his view the clans, as they existed, were the plagues of the kingdom; and of all the clans the worst was that which inhabited Glencoe. He had, it is said, been particularly struck by a frightful instance of the lawlessness and ferocity of those marauders. One of them, who had been concerned in some act of violence or rapine, had given information against his companions. He had been bound to a tree and murdered. The old chief had given the first stab; and scores of dirks had then been plunged into the wretch's body. By the mountaineers such an act was probably regarded as a legitimate exercise of patriarchal jurisdiction. To the Master of Stair it seemed that people among whom such things were done and were approved ought to be treated like a pack of wolves, snared by any device, and slaughtered without mercy. He was well read in history, and doubtless knew how great rulers had, in his own and other countries, dealt with such banditti. He doubtless knew with what energy and what severity James the Fifth had put down the mosstroopers of the border, how the chief of Henderland had been hung over the gate of the castle in which he had prepared a banquet for the King; how John Armstrong and his thirty six horsemen, when they came forth to welcome their sovereign, had scarcely been allowed time to say a single prayer before they were all tied up and turned off. Nor probably was the Secretary ignorant of the means by which Sixtus the Fifth had cleared the ecclesiastical state of outlaws. The eulogists of that great pontiff tell us that there was one formidable gang which could not be dislodged from a stronghold among the Apennines. Beasts of burden were therefore loaded with poisoned food and wine, and sent by road which ran close to the fastness. The robbers sallied forth, seized the prey, feasted, and died; and the pious old Pope exulted greatly when he heard that the corpses of thirty ruffians, who had been the terror of many peaceful villages, had been found lying among the mules and packages. The plans of the Master of Stair were conceived in the spirit of James and of Sixtus; and the rebellion of the mountaineers furnished what seemed to be an excellent opportunity for carrying those plans into effect. Mere rebellion, indeed, he could have easily pardoned. On Jacobites, as Jacobites, he never showed any inclination to bear hard. He hated the Highlanders, not as enemies of this or that dynasty, but as enemies of law, of industry, and of trade. In his private correspondence he applied to them the short and terrible form of words in which the implacable Roman pronounced the doom of Carthage. His project was no less than this, that the whole hill country from sea to sea, and the neighbouring islands, should be wasted with fire and sword, that the Camerons, the Macleans, and all the branches of the race of Macdonald, should be rooted out. He therefore looked with no friendly eye on schemes of reconciliation, and, while others were hoping that a little money would set everything right, hinted very intelligibly his opinion that whatever money was to be laid out on the clans would be best laid out in the form of bullets and bayonets. To the last moment he continued to flatter himself that the rebels would be obstinate, and would thus furnish him with a plea for accomplishing that great social revolution on which his heart was set. The letter is still extant in which he directed the commander of the forces in Scotland how to act if the Jacobite chiefs should not come in before the end of December. There is something strangely terrible in the calmness and conciseness with which the instructions are given. 'Your troops will destroy entirely the country of Lochaber, Lochiel's lands, Keppoch's, Glengarry's and Glencoe's. Your power shall be large enough. I hope the soldiers will not trouble the government with prisoners.'

This despatch had scarcely been sent off when the news arrived in London that the rebel chiefs, after holding out long, had at last appeared before the Sheriffs and taken the oaths. Lochiel, the most eminent man among them, had not only declared that he would live and die a true subject to King William, but had announced his intention of visiting England, in the hope of being permitted to kiss His Majesty's hand. In London it was announced exultingly that all the clans had submitted; and the announcement was generally thought most satisfactory. But the Master of Stair was bitterly disappointed. The Highlands were then to continue to be what they had been, the shame and curse of Scotland. A golden opportunity of subjecting them to the law had been suffered to escape, and might never return. If only the Macdonalds would have stood out, nay, if an example could but have been made of the two worst Macdonalds, Keppoch and Glencoe, it would have been something. But it seemed that even Keppoch and Glencoe, marauders who in any well governed country would have been hanged thirty years before, were safe. While the Master was brooding over thoughts like these, Argyle brought him some comfort. The report that Mac Ian had taken the oaths within the prescribed time was erroneous. The Secretary was consoled. One clan, then, was at the mercy of the government, and that clan the most lawless of all. One great act of justice, nay of charity, might be performed. One terrible and memorable example might be made.

Yet there was a difficulty. Mac Ian had taken the oaths. He had taken them, indeed, too late to be entitled to plead the letter of the royal promise; but the fact that he had taken them was one which evidently ought to have been brought under consideration before his fate was decided. By a dark intrigue, of which the history is but imperfectly known, but which was, in all probability, directed by the Master of Stair, the evidence of Mac Ian's tardy submission was suppressed. The certificate which the Sheriff of Argyleshire had transmitted to the Council at Edinburgh was never laid before the Board, but was privately submitted to some persons high in office, and particularly to Lord President Stair, the father of the Secretary. These persons pronounced the certificate irregular, and, indeed, absolutely null; and it was cancelled.

Meanwhile the Master of Stair was forming, in concert with Breadalbane and Argyle, a plan for the destruction of the people of Glencoe. It was necessary to take the King's pleasure, not, indeed, as to the details of what was to be done, but as to the question whether Mac Ian and his people should or should not be treated as rebels out of the pale of the ordinary law. The Master of Stair found no difficulty in the royal closet. William had, in all probability, never heard the Glencoe men mentioned except as banditti. He knew that they had not come in by the prescribed day. That they had come in after that day he did not know. If he paid any attention to the matter, he must have thought that so fair an opportunity of putting an end to the devastations and depredations from which quiet and industrious population had suffered so much ought not to be lost.

An order was laid before him for signature. He signed it, but, if Burnet may be trusted, did not read it. Whoever has seen anything of public business knows that princes and ministers daily sign, and indeed must sign, documents which they have not read; and of all documents a document relating to a small tribe of mountaineers, living in a wilderness not set down in any map, was least likely to interest a Sovereign whose mind was full of schemes on which the fate of Europe might depend. But, even on the supposition that he read the order to which he affixed his name, there seems to be no reason for blaming him. That order, directed to the Commander of the Forces in Scotland, runs thus: 'As for Mac Ian of Glencoe and that tribe, if they can be well distinguished from the other Highlanders, it will be proper, for the vindication of public justice, to extirpate that set of thieves.' These words naturally bear a sense perfectly innocent, and would, but for the horrible event which followed, have been universally understood in that sense. It is undoubtedly one of the first duties of every government to extirpate gangs of thieves. This does not mean that every thief ought to be treacherously assassinated in his sleep, or even that every thief ought to be put to death after a fair trial, but that every gang, as a gang, ought to be completely broken up, and that whatever severity is indispensably necessary for that end ought to be used. It is in this sense that we praise the Marquess of Hastings for extirpating the Pindarees, and Lord William Bentinck for extirpating the Thugs. If the King had read and weighed the words which were submitted to him by his Secretary, he would probably have understood them to mean that Glencoe was to be occupied by troops, that resistance, if resistance were attempted, was to be put down with a strong hand, that severe punishment was to be inflicted on those leading members of the clan who could be proved to have been guilty of great crimes, that some active young freebooters, who were more used to handle the broad sword than the plough, and who did not seem likely to settle down into quiet labourers, were to be sent to the army in the Low Countries, that others were to be transported to the American plantations, and that those Macdonalds who were suffered to remain in their native valley were to be disarmed and required to give hostages for good behaviour. A plan very nearly resembling this had, we know, actually been the subject of much discussion in the political circles of Edinburgh. There can be little doubt that William would have deserved well of his people if he had, in this manner, extirpated, not only the tribe of Mac Ian, but every Highland tribe whose calling was to steal cattle and burn houses.

The extirpation planned by the Master of Stair was a different kind. His design was to butcher the whole race of thieves, the whole damnable race. Such was the language in which his hatred vented itself. He studied the geography of the wild country which surrounded Glencoe, and made his arrangements with infernal skill. If possible the blow must be quick, and crushing, and altogether unexpected. But if Mac Ian should apprehend danger, and should attempt to take refuge in the territories of his neighbours, he must find every road barred. The pass of Rannoch must be secured. The Laird of Weem, who was powerful in Strath Tay, must be told that, if he harbours the outlaws, he does so at his peril. Breadalbane promised to cut off the retreat of the fugitives on one side, Mac Callum More on another. It was fortunate, the Secretary wrote, that it was winter. This was the time to maul the wretches. The nights were so long, the mountain tops so cold and stormy, that even the hardiest men could not long bear exposure to the open air without a roof or a spark of fire. That the women and children could find shelter in the desert was quite impossible. While he wrote thus, no thought that he was committing a great wickedness crossed his mind. He was happy in the approbation of his own conscience. Duty, justice, nay charity and mercy, were the names under which he disguised his cruelty; nor is it by any means improbable that the disguise imposed upon himself.

Hill, who commanded the forces assembled at Fort William, was not entrusted with the execution of the design. He seems to have been a humane man; he was much distressed when he learned that the government was determined on severity; and it was probably thought that his heart might fail him in the most critical moment. He was directed to put a strong detachment under the orders of his second in command, Lieutenant Colonel Hamilton. To Hamilton a significant hint was conveyed that he had now an excellent opportunity of establishing his character in the estimation of those who were at the head of affairs. Of the troops entrusted to him a large proportion were Campbells, and belonged to a regiment lately raised by Argyle, and called by Argyle's name. It was probably thought that, on such an occasion, humanity might prove too strong for the mere habit of military obedience, and that little reliance could be placed on hearts which had not been ulcerated by a feud such as had long raged between the people of Mac Ian and the people of Mac Callum More.

Had Hamilton marched openly against the Glencoe men and put them
to the edge of the sword, the act would probably not have wanted
apologists, and most certainly would not have wanted precedents. But
the Master of Stair had strongly recommended a different mode of
proceeding. If the least alarm were given, the nest of robbers would be
found empty; and to hunt them down in so wild a region would, even
with all the help that Breadalbane and Argyle could give, be a long and
difficult business. 'Better,' he wrote, 'not meddle with them than meddle
to no purpose. When the thing is resolved, let it be secret and sudden.' He
was obeyed; and it was determined that the Glencoe men should perish,
not by military execution, but by the most dastardly and perfidious form
of assassination.

On the first of February a hundred and twenty soldiers of Argyle's
regiment, commanded by a captain named Campbell and a lieutenant
named Lindsay, marched to Glencoe. Captain Campbell was commonly
called in Scotland Glenlyon, from the pass in which his property lay. He
had every qualification for the service on which he was employed, an
unblushing forehead, a smooth lying tongue and a heart of adamant. He
was also one of the few Campbells who were likely to be trusted and
welcomed by the Macdonalds: for his niece was married to Alexander, the
second son of Mac Ian.

The sight of the red coats approaching caused some anxiety among the
population of the valley. John, the eldest son of the Chief, came,
accompanied by twenty clansmen, to meet the strangers, and asked what
this visit meant. Lieutenant Lindsay answered that the soldiers came as
friends, and wanted nothing but quarters. They were kindly received, and
were lodged under the thatched roofs of the little community. Glenlyon
and several of his men were taken into the house of a tacksman who was
named, from the cluster of cabins over which he exercised authority,
Inverriggen. Lindsay was accommodated nearer to the abode of the old
chief. Auchintriater, one of the principal men of the clan, who governed
the small hamlet of Auchnaion, found room there for a party commanded
by a serjeant named Barbour. Provisions were liberally supplied. There
was no want of beef, which had probably fattened in distant pastures; nor
was any payment demanded: for in hospitality, as in thievery, the Gaelic
marauders rivalled the Bedouins. During twelve days the soldiers lived
familiarly with the people of the glen. Old Mac Ian, who had before felt
many misgivings as to the relation in which he stood to the government,
seems to have been pleased with the visit. The officers passed much of
their time with him and his family. The long evenings were cheerfully
spent by the peat fire with the help of some packs of cards which had

found their way to that remote corner of the world, and of some French brandy which was probably part of James's farewell gift to his Highland supporters. Glenlyon appeared to be warmly attached to his niece and her husband Alexander. Every day he came to their house to take his morning draught. Meanwhile he observed with minute attention all the avenues by which, when the signal for the slaughter should be given, the Macdonalds might attempt to escape to the hills; and he reported the result of his observations to Hamilton.

Hamilton fixed five o'clock in the morning of the thirteenth of February for the deed. He hoped that, before that time, he should reach Glencoe with four hundred men, and should have stopped all the earths in which the old fox and his two cubs – so Mac Ian and his sons were nicknamed by the murderers – could take refuge. But, at five precisely, whether Hamilton had arrived or not, Glenlyon was to fall on, and to slay every Macdonald under seventy.

The night was rough. Hamilton and his troops made slow progress and were long after their time. While they were contending with the wind and snow, Glenlyon was supping and playing at cards with those whom he meant to butcher before daybreak. He and Lieutenant Lindsay had engaged themselves to dine with the old Chief on the morrow.

Late in the evening a vague suspicion that some evil was intended crossed the mind of the Chief's eldest son. The soldiers were evidently in a restless state; and some of them muttered strange exclamations. Two men, it is said, were overheard whispering. 'I do not like this job,' one of them muttered: 'I should be glad to fight the Macdonalds. But to kill men in their beds' – 'We must do as we are bid,' answered another voice. 'If there is any thing wrong, our officers must answer for it.' John Macdonald was so uneasy that, soon after midnight, he went to Glenlyon's quarters. Glenlyon and his men were all up, and seemed to be getting their arms ready for action. John, much alarmed, asked what these preparations meant. Glenlyon was profuse of friendly assurances. 'Some of Glengarry's people have been harrying the country. We are getting ready to march against them. You are quite safe. Do you think that, if you were in any danger, I should not have given a hint to your brother Sandy and his wife?' John's suspicions were quieted. He returned to his house, and lay down to rest.

It was five in the morning. Hamilton and his men were still some miles off; and the avenues which they were to have secured were open. But the orders which Glenlyon had received were precise; and he began to execute them at the little village where he was himself quartered. His host Inverriggen and nine other Macdonalds were dragged out of their beds, bound hand and foot, and murdered. A boy twelve years old clung round the Captain's legs, and begged hard for life. He would do anything; he would go any where: he would follow Glenlyon round the world. Even Glenlyon, it is said, showed signs of relenting: but a ruffian named Drummond shot the child dead.

At Auchnaion the tacksman Auchintriater was up early that morning, and was sitting with eight of his family round the fire, when a volley of musketry laid him and seven of his companions dead or dying on the floor. His brother, who alone had escaped unhurt, called to Serjeant Barbour, who commanded the slayers, and asked as a favour to be allowed to die in the open air. 'Well,' said the Serjeant, 'I will do you that favour for the sake of your meat which I have eaten.' The mountaineer, bold, athletic, and favoured by the darkness, came forth, rushed on the soldiers who were about to level their pieces at him, flung his plaid over their faces, and was gone in a moment.

Meanwhile Lindsay had knocked at the door of the old Chief and had asked for admission in friendly language. The door was opened. Mac Ian, while putting on his clothes and calling to his servants to bring some refreshment for his visitors, was shot through the head. Two of his attendants were slain with him. His wife was already up and dressed in such finery as the princesses of the rude Highland glens were accustomed to wear. The assassins pulled off her clothes and trinkets. The rings were not easily taken from her fingers: but a soldier tore them away with his teeth. She died on the following day.

The statesman, to whom chiefly this great crime is to be ascribed, had planned it with consummate ability: but the execution was complete in nothing but guilt and infamy. A succession of blunders saved three fourths of the Glencoe men from the fate of their chief. All the moral qualities which fit men to bear a part in a massacre Hamilton and Glenlyon possessed in perfection. But neither seems to have had much professional skill. Hamilton had arranged his plan without making allowance for bad weather, and this at a season when, in the Highlands, the weather was very likely to be bad. The consequence was that the fox earths, as he called them, were not stopped in time. Glenlyon and his men committed the error of despatching their hosts with firearms instead of using the cold steel. The peal and flash of gun after gun gave notice, from three different parts of the valley at once, that murder was doing. From fifty cottages the half naked peasantry fled under cover of the night to the recesses of their pathless glen. Even the sons of Mac Ian, who had been especially marked out for destruction, contrived to escape. They were roused from sleep by faithful servants. John, who, by the death of his father, had become the patriarch of the tribe, quitted his dwelling just as twenty soldiers with fixed bayonets marched up to it. It was broad day long before Hamilton arrived. He found the work not even half performed. About thirty corpses lay wallowing in blood on the dunghills before the doors. One or two women were seen among the number, and a yet more fearful and piteous sight, a little hand, which had been lopped in the tumult of the butchery from some infant. One aged Macdonald was found alive. He was probably too infirm to fly, and as he was above seventy, was not included in the orders under which Glenlyon had acted. Hamilton murdered the old man in cold blood. The deserted hamlets were then set on fire; and the troops departed, driving away with them many sheep and goats, nine hundred kine, and two hundred of the small shaggy ponies of the Highlands.

It is said, and may but too easily be believed, that the sufferings of the fugitives were terrible. How many old men, how many women with babes in their arms, sank down and slept their last sleep in the snow; how many, having crawled, spent with toil and hunger, into nooks among the precipices, died in those dark holes, and were picked to the bone by the mountain ravens, can never be known. But it is probable that those who perished by cold, weariness, and want were not less numerous than those who were slain by the assassins. When the troops had retired, the Macdonalds crept out of the caverns of Glencoe, ventured back to the spot where the huts had formerly stood, collected the scorched corpses from among the smoking ruins, and performed some rude rites of sepulture. The tradition runs that the hereditary bard of the tribe took his seat on a rock which overhung the place of slaughter, and poured forth a long lament over his murdered brethren and his desolate home. Eighty years later that sad dirge was still repeated by the population of the valley.

The survivors might well apprehend that they had escaped the shot and the sword only to perish by famine. The whole domain was a waste. Houses, barns, furniture, implements of husbandry, herds, flocks, horses, were gone. Many months must elapse before the clan would be able to raise on its own ground the means of supporting even the most miserable existence.

Chì Mi na Mòr-Bheanna
(The Mist-covered mountains of Home)

JOHN CAMERON (fl. 1860)

TRANSLATION BY MALCOLM MACFARLANE

Chì Mi na Mòr-Bheanna *which is now sung to a beautiful slow and haunting air was originally intended to be sung to the catchy tune 'Johnny stays long at the Fair'. Its composer John Cameron hailed from Ballachulish at the entrance to Glencoe. The song was published in Archibald Sinclair's* An t-Oranaiche (The Gaelic Songster) *in 1879 where its full title is given as* Duil ri Baile-Chaolais Fhaicinn air a Cheud Là do 'n Fhogharadh, 1856 *('Anticipation of Seeing Ballachulish on the First Day of Autumn, 1856'). Cameron also published a religious work* Dan Spioradail, *in 1862 and was bard to the Ossianic Society. The English version* The Mist Covered Mountains of Home *is by the distinguished writer, translator and editor, Malcolm MacFarlane (Calum MacPhàrlain) (1853–1931) – another Argyllshire man – from Dalavich on Loch Awe and later Paisley.*

Séist
O chì, chì mi na mòr-bheanna,
O chì, chì mi na còrr-bheanna,
O chì, chì mi na coireachan,
Chì mi na sgòran fo cheò.

Chì mi gun dàil an t-àite 'san d' rugadh mi;
Cuirear orm fàilte 'sa chànain a thuigeas mi;
Gheibh mi ann aoidh agus gràdh 'nuair ruigeam,
Nach reicinn air thunnachan òir.

Chì mi ann coilltean, chì mi ann doireachan;
Chì mi ann màghan bàna is toraiche;
Chì mi féidh air làr nan coireachan,
Fàlaicht' an trusgan de cheò.

Beanntaichean àrda is àillidh leacainnean;
Sluagh ann an còmhnuidh is còire cleachdainnean;
'S aotrom mo cheum a'leum g'am faicinn
Is fanaidh mi tacan le deòin.

Fàilt' air na gorm-mheallaibh tholmach, thulachnach;
Fàilt' air na còrr-bheannaibh mòra, mulanach;
Fàilt' air na coilltean, is fàilt' air na h-uile –
O! 's sona bhi 'fuireach 'nan còir.

THE MIST-COVERED MOUNTAINS OF HOME

Chorus
Hoo, O! Soon shall I see them O;
Hee O! see them, O see them O;
Ho-ro! Soon shall I see them,
The mist-covered mountains of home.

There shall I visit the place of my birth;
And they'll give me a welcome, the warmest on earth;
All so loving and kind, full of music and mirth,
In the sweet-sounding language of home.

There I shall gaze on the mountains again;
On the fields and the woods and the burns in the glen;
And away 'mong the corries, beyond human ken,
In the haunts of the deer I shall roam.

There I'll converse with the hard-headed father,
And there I shall jest with the kind-hearted mother;
O, light is my heart as I turn my steps thither,
The ever-dear precincts of home.

Hail! to the mountains with summits of blue;
To the glens with their meadows of sunshine and dew;
To the women and men ever constant and true,
Ever ready to welcome one home.

'The King's House'

from A Tour of the Highlands in 1803

JAMES HOGG (1770–1835)

This account of a visit paid by Hogg to the Western Highlands and Islands (in the same year as the Wordsworths and Coleridge were trekking over much of the same ground) was given by the 'Ettrick Shepherd' in a series of letters to Sir Walter Scott. It was the second excursion Hogg had made north of the Highland line – he had given a similar 'whimsical account' of the Northern Highlands in the previous year.

Scott, who was then Sheriff of Selkirkshire, befriended Hogg and brought him into the public eye, through publishing a number of Hogg's ballads in the second volume of the Minstrelsy of the Scottish Border. *Hogg had got these ballads from his mother and Scott, like others of Hogg's patrons, saw him as something of a primitive with only a perfunctory education but one with direct access to folklore and tradition.*

Hogg had come to the Moor of Rannoch by way of Inveraray and there had received some hospitality from the Duke of Argyll – perhaps this accounts for his failure to make any allusion, as travellers usually did, to the Massacre of Glencoe, even though he was in the vicinity. Leaving Argyll, Hogg went on to make an extensive tour of the West Coast and reached as far as Lewis. In contrast to his earlier omission he does go on to make several references to the '45 and confesses: 'While traversing the scenes where the patient sufferings of one party and the cruelties of the other were so affectingly displayed, I could not help being a bit of a Jacobite in my heart and blessing myself that in those days I did not exist, or I should certainly have been hanged.'

The King's house was supposedly built for General Wade and is now a hotel and remains popular with walkers and climbers, many of whom take the high route over to Ballachulish as Hogg did in 1803.

But if I go backward and forward this way I shall never get from Inveraray; therefore suppose me all at once on the road early in the morning on which I proceeded up Glen Aray, viewed two considerable cataracts romantically shrouded in woods, and at length arrived on the borders of Loch Awe, or Loch Howe. My plan was to take breakfast at Port Sonachan, and proceed to Oban that night, having letters to some gentlemen of that country, and having a pocket travelling map, I never asked the road of anybody, at which indeed I have a particular aversion, as I am almost certain of being obliged to answer several impertinent questions as an equivalent for the favour conferred.

The road that turns to the left towards Port Sonachan is certainly in danger of being missed by a stranger, for although I was continually on the look-out for a public road to that hand, I never observed it in the least, till at last, seeing no ferry across the lake, nor road from the other side, I began to suspect that I had erred, and condescended to ask of a man if this was the road to Port Sonachan. He told me that I was above a mile past the place where the roads parted. 'And where does this lead?' said I. 'To Tyndrum, or the braes of Glenorchy,' said he; and attacked me with other questions in return, which I was in no humour to answer, being somewhat nettled at missing my intended route, and more at missing my breakfast, but knowing that whatever road I took, all was new to me, I, without standing a moment to consider of returning, held on as if nothing had happened.

About eleven a.m. I came to Dalmally in Glenorchy, where I took a hearty breakfast, but the inn had a poor appearance compared with what I had left. Some of the windows were built up with turf, and, on pretence of scarcity of fuel, they refused to kindle a fire in my apartment, although I was very wet, and pleaded movingly for one. There was nothing in this tract that I had passed deserving of particular attention. The land on the south-east side of the lake is low-lying, interspersed with gentle rising hills, and strong grassy hollows, where good crops of oats and beans were growing. On the other side the hills are high and steep, and well stocked with sheep. One gentleman is introducing a stock of the Cheviot breed on a farm there this season. They had formerly been tried on a farm in the neighbourhood of the church, but the scheme was abandoned in its infancy.

I am, yours, etc.,

J. H.

Dear Sir, – Leaving Dalmally, and shortly after, the high road to Tyndrum, I followed a country road which kept near the bank of the river, and led me up through the whole of that district called *the braes of Glenorchy*. At the bridge of Orchy, (or as it is spelled by some Urguhay), I rejoined the great military road leading to Fort William, and three miles farther on reached Inverournan, the mid-way stage between Tyndrum and the King's house beyond the Black Mount, where I took up my lodgings for the night.

The braes of Glenorchy have no very promising appearance, being much over-run with heath, and the north-west side rocky. But it is probable that I saw the worst part of them, their excellency as a sheep range having for a long time been established; for who, even in the south of Scotland, hath not heard of the farms of Soch and Auch!

The Orchy is a large river and there are some striking cascades in it. The glen spreads out to a fine valley on the lower parts, which are fertile, the soil on the river banks being deep, yet neither heavy nor cold. As you ascend the river the banks grow more and more narrow, till at last they terminate in heather and rocks. Beside one of the cascades which I sat down to contemplate, I fell into a long and profound sleep. The Earl of Breadalbane is the principal proprietor. I was now, at Inverournan, and got into a very Highland and rather a dreary scene. It is situated at the head of Loch Tullich, on the banks of which there yet remains a number of natural firs, a poor remembrance of the extensive woods with which its environs have once been overrun.

Amongst the fellow lodgers, I was very glad at meeting here with a Mr McCallum, who had taken an extensive farm on the estate of Strathconnon, which I viewed last year; who informed me, that all that extensive estate was let to sheep farmers, saving a small division on the lower end, which the General had reserved for the accommodation of such of the natives as could not dispose of themselves to better advantage.

Next morning I traversed the Black Mount in company with a sailor, who entertained me with many wonderful adventures; of his being pressed, and afterwards suffering a tedious captivity in France. This is indeed a most dreary region, with not one cheering prospect whereto to turn the eye. But on the right hand lies a prodigious extent of flat, barren muirs, interspersed with marshes and stagnant pools; and on the left, black rugged mountains tower to a great height, all interlined with huge wreaths of snow. The scenery is nothing improved on approaching to the King's house. There is not a green spot to be seen, and the hill behind it to the westward is still more terrific than any to the south of it, and is little inferior to any in the famous Glencoe behind it. It is one huge cone of mishapen and ragged rocks, entirely peeled bare of all soil whatever, and all scarred with horrible furrows, torn out by the winter torrents. It is indeed a singular enough spot to have been pitched upon for a military stage and inn, where they cannot so much as find forage for a cow, but have their scanty supply of milk from a few goats, which brouse on the wide waste. There were, however, some very good black-faced wedder hoggs feeding in the middle of the Black Mount, but their colour and condition both, bespoke them to have been wintered on a richer and lower pasture, and only to have been lately turned out to that range.

After leaving the King's house I kept the high way leading to Balachulish for about two miles, and then struck off, following the old military road over the devil's stairs, which winds up the hill on one side and down on the other, and at length entered Lochaber by an old stone bridge over a water at the head of Loch Leven; and without meeting with anything remarkable, arrived at Fort William about seven o'clock p.m.

It is upwards of twenty miles from the King's house to Fort William, across the hills, and the road being extremely rough, my feet were very much bruised. The tract is wild and mountainous, the hills on the Lochaber side are amazingly high and steep, and, from the middle upward, are totally covered with small white stones. They form a part of that savage range called *the rough bounds*. Before reaching the town I passed some excellent pasture hills which were thick covered with ewes and lambs.

'Lost on Rannoch'

from John Splendid

NEIL MUNRO (1863–1930)

This is our second extract from Neil Munro's fine historical novel, John Splendid, *which deals, from an Argyll perspective, with the same period and events as Walter Scott's* A Legend of the Wars of Montrose. John Splendid *was Munro's first novel, published in 1898 to considerable critical acclaim. It tells of the return in 1644 from study and the foreign wars of Colin, 'Young Elrigmore', the heir to a small estate in Glen Shira, an ally but not a vassal of MacCailein Mòr, the chief of Clan Campbell. Colin becomes caught up in the Civil War and the campaigns of the Marquis of Montrose and the Covenant Army and the ancient rivalry of Clan Campbell (Diarmaid) and MacDonald. Colin has joined a force which has left the familiar surroundings of Inveraray behind and is following Montrose north towards Lochaber.*

This excerpt gives a graphic description of perhaps Scotland's greatest wilderness, the Moor of Rannoch in the north east corner of Argyll. We have chosen this passage, although we might well have selected other descriptions of the same territory in Munro's greatest novel The New Road *or in Robert Louis Stevenson's* Kidnapped.

I stood on the hillock clothed with its stunted saugh-trees and waited for the day that was mustering somewhere to the east, far by the frozen sea of moss and heather tuft. A sea more lonely than any ocean the most wide and distant, where no ship heaves, and no isle lifts beckoning trees above the level of the waves; a sea soundless, with no life below its lamentable surface, no little fish or proud leviathan plunging and romping and flashing from the silver roof of fretted wave dishevelled to the deep profound. The moorfowl does not cry there, the coney has no habitation. It rolled, that sea so sour, so curdled, from my feet away to mounts I knew by day stupendous and not so far, but now in the dark so hid that they were but troubled clouds upon the distant marge. There was a day surely when, lashing up on those hills around, were waters blue and stinging, and some plague-breath blew on them and they shivered and dried and cracked into this parched semblance of what they were in the old days when the galleys sailed over. No galleys now. No white birds calling eagerly in the storm. No silver bead of spray. Only in its season the cannoch tuft, and that itself but sparsely; the very bluebell shuns a track so desolate, the sturdy gall itself finds no nourishment here.

The grey day crept above the land; I watched it from my hillock, and I shrunk in my clothing that seemed so poor a shielding in a land so chill. A cold clammy dawn, that never cleared even as it aged, but held a hint of mist to come that should have warned me of the danger I faced in venturing on the untravelled surface of the moor, even upon its safer verge. But it seemed so simple a thing to keep low to the left and down on Glenurchy that I thought little of the risk, if I reflected upon it at all.

Some of the stupidity of my venturing out on the surface of Rannoch that day must have been due to my bodily state. I was not all there, as the saying goes. I was suffering mind and body from the strain of my adventures, and most of all from the stormy thrashings of the few days before – the long journey, the want of reasonable sleep and food. There had come over all my spirit a kind of dwam, so that at times my head seemed as if it were stuffed with wool; what mattered was of no account, even if it were a tinker's death in the sheuch. No words will describe the feeling except to such as themselves have known it; it is the condition of the man dead with care and weariness so far as the body is concerned, and his spirit, sorry to part company, goes lugging his flesh about the highways.

I was well out on Rannoch before the day was full awake on the country, walking at great trouble upon the coarse barren soil, among rotten bog-grass, lichened stones, and fir-roots that thrust from the black peatlike skeletons of antiquity. And then I came on a cluster of lochs – grey, cold, vagrant lochs – still to some degree in the thrall of frost. Here's one who has ever a fancy for such lochans, that are lost and sobbing, sobbing, even-on among the hills, where the reeds and the rushes hiss in the wind, and the fowls with sheeny feather make night and day cheery with their call. But not those lochs of Rannoch, those black basins crumbling at the edge of a rotten soil. I skirted them as far off as I could, as though they were the lochans of a nightmare that drag the traveller to their kelpie tenants' arms. There were no birds among those rushes; I think the very deer that roamed in the streets of Inneraora in the November's blast would have run far clear of so stricken a territory. It must be horrible in snow, it must be lamentable in the hottest days of summer, when the sun rides over the land, for what does the most kindly season bring to this forsaken place except a scorching for the fugitive wild-flower, if such there be?

These were not my thoughts as I walked on my way; they are what lie in my mind of the feelings the Moor of Rannoch will rouse in every stranger. What was in my mind most when I was not altogether in the swound of wearied flesh was the spae-wife's story of the girl in Inneraora, and a jealousy so strong that I wondered where, in all my exhausted frame, the passion for it came from. I forgot my friends left in Dalness, I forgot that my compact and prudence itself called for my hurrying the quickest way I could to the Brig of Urchy; I walked in an indifference until I saw a wan haze spread fast over the country in the direction of the lower hills that edged the desert. I looked with a careless eye on it at first, not reflecting what it might mean or how much it might lead to. It spread with exceeding quickness, a grey silver smoke rolling out on every hand, as if puffed continually from some glen in the hills. I looked behind me, and saw that the same was happening all around. Unless I made speed out of this sorrowful place I was caught in the mist. Then I came to the full understanding that trouble was to face. I tightened the thongs of my shoes, pinched up a hole in my waist-belt, scrugged my bonnet, and set out at a deer-stalker's run across the moor. I splashed in hags and stumbled among roots; I made wild leaps across poisonous-looking holes stewing to the brim with coloured water; I made long detours to find the most fordable part of a stream that twisted back and forth, a very devil's cantrip, upon my way. Then a smirr of rain came at my back and chilled me to the marrow, though the sweat of travail a moment before had been on every part of me, and even dripping in beads from my chin. At length I lifted my eyes from the ground that I had to scan most carefully in my running, and behold! I was swathed in a dense mist that cut off every view of the world within ten yards of where I stood. This cruel experience dashed me more than any other misadventure in all my wanderings, for it cut me off, without any hope of speedy betterment, from the others of our broken band. They might be all at Urchy Bridge now, on the very selvedge of freedom, but I was couped by the heels more disastrously than ever. Down I sat on a tuft of moss, and I felt cast upon the dust by a most cruel providence.

How long I sat there I cannot tell; it may have been a full hour or more, it may have been but a pause of some minutes, for I was in a stupor of bitter disappointment. And when I rose again I was the sport of chance, for whether my way lay before me or lay behind me, or to left or right, was altogether beyond my decision. It was well on in the day: high above this stagnant plain among tall bens there must be shining a friendly and constant sun; but Elrigmore, gentleman and sometime cavalier of Mackay's Scots, was in the very gullet of night for all he could see around him. It was folly, I knew; but on somewhere I must be going, so I took to where my nose led, picking my way with new caution among the bogs and boulders. The neighbourhood of the lochs was a sort of guidance in some degree, for their immediate presence gave to a nostril sharpened by life in the wild a moist and peaty odour fresh from the corroding banks. I sought them and I found them, and finding them I found a danger even greater than my loss in that desolate plain. For in the grey smoke of mist those treacherous pools crept noiselessly to my feet, and once I had almost walked blindly into an ice-clear turgid little lake. My foot sank in the mire of it almost up to the knees ere I jumped to the nature of my neighbourhood, and with an effort little short of miraculous in the state of my body, threw myself back on the safe bank, clear of the death-trap. And again I sat on a hillock and surrendered to the most doleful meditations. Noon came and went, the rain passed and came again, and passed once more, and still I was guessing my way about the lochs, making no headway from their neighbourhood, and, to tell the truth, a little glad of the same, for they were all I knew of the landscape in Moor Rannoch, and something of friendship was in their treacherous presence, and to know they were still beside me, though it said little for my progress to Glenurchy, was an assurance that I was not making my position worse by going in the wrong airt.

All about me, when the rain was gone for the last time, there was a cry of waters, the voices of the burns running into the lochans, tinkling, tinkling, tinkling merrily, and all out of key with a poor wretch in draggled tartans, fleeing he knew not whither, but going about in shortened circles like a hedgehog in the sea.

The mist made no sign of lifting all this time, but shrouded the country as if it were come to stay for ever, and I was doomed to remain till the end, guessing my way to death in a silver-grey reek. I strained my ears, and far off to the right I heard the sound of cattle bellowing, the snorting low of a stirk upon the hillside when he wonders at the lost pastures of his calfhood in the merry summer before. So out I set in that direction, and more bellowing arose, and by-and-by, out of the mist but still far off, came a long low wail that baffled me. It was like no sound nature ever conferred on the Highlands, to my mind, unless the rare call of the Benderloch wolf in rigorous weather. I stopped and listened, with my inner head cracking to the strain, and as I was thus standing in wonder, a great form leaped out at me from the mist, and almost ran over me ere it lessened to the semblance of a man, and I had John McIver of Barbreck, a heated and hurried gentleman of arms, in my presence.

He drew up with a shock, put his hand to his vest, and I could see him cross himself under the jacket.

'Not a bit of it,' I cried: 'no wraith nor warlock this time, friend, but flesh and blood. Yet I'm bound to say I have never been nearer ghostdom than now; a day of this moor would mean death to me.'

He shook me hurriedly and warmly by the hand, and stared in my face, and stammered, and put an arm about my waist as if I were a girl, and turned me about and led me to a little tree that lifted its barren branches above the moor. He was in such a confusion and hurry that I knew something troubled him, so I left him to choose his own time for explanation. When we got to the tree, he showed me his black knife – a very long and deadly weapon – laid along his wrist, and 'Out dirk,' said he; 'there's a dog or two of Italy on my track here.' His mind, by the stress of his words, was like a hurricane.

Now I knew something of the Black Dogs of Italy, as they were called, the abominable hounds that were kept by the Camerons and others mainly for the hunting down of the Gregarich.

'Were they close on you?' I asked, as we prepared to meet them.

'Do you not hear them bay?' said he. 'There were three on my track: I struck one through the throat with my knife and ran, for two Italian hounds to one knife is a poor bargain. Between us we should get rid of them before the owners they lag for come up on their tails.'

'You should thank God who got you out of a trouble so deep,' I said, astounded at the miracle of his escape so far.

'Oh ay,' said he; 'and indeed I was pretty clever myself, or it was all bye with me when one of the black fellows set his fangs in my hose. Here are his partners; short work with it, on the neck or low at the belly with an up cut, and ward your throat.'

The two dogs ran with ferocious growls at us as we stood by the little tree, their faces gaping and their quarters streaked with foam. Strong cruel brutes, they did not swither a moment, but both leaped at McIver's throat. With one swift slash of the knife my companion almost cut the head off the body of the first, and I reckoned with the second. They rolled at our feet, and a silence fell on the country. Up McIver put his shoulders, dighted his blade on a tuft of bog-grass, and whistled a stave of the tune they call 'The Desperate Battle'.

'If I had not my lucky penny with me I would wonder at this meeting,' said he at last, eyeing me with a look of real content that he should so soon have fallen into my company at a time when a meeting was so unlikely. 'It has failed me once or twice on occasions far less important;

but that was perhaps because of my own fumbling, and I forgive it all because it brought two brave lads together like barks of one port on the ocean. "Up or down?" I tossed when it came to putting fast heels below me, and "up" won it, and here's the one man in all broad Albainn I would be seeking for, drops out of the mist at the very feet of me. Oh, I'm the most wonderful fellow ever stepped heather, and I could be making a song on myself there and then if occasion allowed. Some people have genius, and that, I'm telling you, is well enough so far as it goes; but I have luck too, and I'm not so sure but luck is a hantle sight better than genius. I'm guessing you have lost your way in the mist now?'

He looked quizzingly at me, and I was almost ashamed to admit that I had been in a maze for the greater part of the morning.

'And no skill for getting out of it?' he asked.

'No more than you had in getting into it,' I confessed.

'My good scholar,' said he, 'I could walk you out into a drove-road in the time you would be picking the bog from your feet. I'm not making any brag of an art that's so common among old hunters as the snaring of conies; but give me a bush or a tree here and there in a flat land like this, and an herb here and there at my feet, and while winds from the north blow snell, I'll pick my way by them. It's my notion that they learn one many things at colleges that are no great value in the real trials of life. You, I make no doubt, would be kenning the name of an herb in the Latin, and I have but the Gaelic for it, and that's good enough for me; but I ken the use of it as a traveller's friend whenever rains are smirring and mists are blowing.'

'I daresay there's much in what you state,' I confessed, honestly enough; 'I wish I could change some of my schooling for the art of winning off Moor Rannoch.'

He changed his humour in a flash. 'Man,' said he, 'I'm maybe giving myself overmuch credit at the craft; it's so seldom I put it to the trial that if we get clear of the Moor before night it'll be as much to your credit as to mine.'

As it happened, his vanity about his gift got but a brief gratification, for he had not led me by his signs more than a mile on the way to the south when we came again to a cluster of lochans, and among them a large fellow called Loch Ba, where the mist was lifting quickly. Through the cleared air we travelled at a good speed, off the Moor, among Bredalbane braes, and fast though we went it was a weary march, but at last we reached Loch Tulla, and from there to the Bridge of Urchy was no more than a meridian daunder.

The very air seemed to change to a kinder feeling in this, the frontier of the home-land. A scent of wet birk was in the wind. The river, hurrying through grassy levels, glucked and clattered and plopped most gaily, and bubble chased bubble as if all were in a haste to reach Lochow of the bosky isles and holy. Oh! but it was heartsome, and as we rested ourselves a little on the banks we were full of content to know we were now in a friendly country, and it was a fair pleasure to think that the dead leaves and broken branches we threw in the stream would be dancing in all likelihood round the isle of Innishael by nightfall.

We ate our chack with exceeding content, and waited for a time on the chance that some of our severed company from Dalness would appear, though McIver's instruction as to the rendezvous had been given on the prospect that they would reach the Brig earlier in the day. But after an hour or two of waiting there was no sign of them, and there was nothing for us but to assume that they had reached the Brig by noon as agreed on and passed on their way down the glen. A signal held together by two stones on the glen-side of the Brig indeed confirmed this notion almost as soon as we formed it, and we were annoyed that we had not observed it sooner. Three sprigs of gall, a leaf of ivy from the bridge arch where it grew in dark green sprays of glossy sheen, and a bare twig of oak standing up at a slant, were held down on the parapet by a peeled willow withy, one end of which pointed in the direction of the glen.

It was McIver who came on the symbols first, and 'We're a day behind the fair,' said he. 'Our friends are all safe and on their way before us; look at that.'

I confessed I was no hand at puzzles.

'Man,' he said, 'there's a whole history in it! Three sprigs of gall mean three Campbells, do they not? and that's the baron-bailie and Sonachan, and this one with the leaves off the half-side is the fellow with the want. And oak is Stewart – a very cunning clan to be fighting or foraying or travelling with, for this signal is Stewart's work or I'm a fool; the others had not the gumption for it. And what's the ivy but Clan Gordon, and the peeled withy but hurry, and – surely that will be doing for the reading of a very simple tale. Let us be taking our ways, I have a great admiration for Stewart that he managed to do so well with this thing, but I could have bettered that sign, if it were mine, by a chapter or two more.'

'It contains a wonder deal of matter for the look of it,' I confessed.

'And yet,' said he, 'it leaves out two points I consider of the greatest importance. Where's the Dark Dame, and when did our friends pass this way? A few chucky-stones would have left the hour plain to our view, and there's no word of the old lady.'

I thought for a second, then, 'I can read a bit further myself,' said I; 'for there's no hint here of the Dark Dame because she was not here. They left the *suaicheantas* just of as many as escaped from –'

'And so they did! Where are my wits to miss a tale so plain?' said he. 'She'll be in Dalness yet, perhaps better off than scouring the wilds, for after all even the MacDonalds are human, and a half-wit widow woman would be sure of their clemency. It was very clever of you to think of that now.'

I looked again at the oak-stem, still sticking up at the slant. 'It might as well have lain flat under the peeled wand like the others,' I thought, and then the reason for its position flashed on me. It was with just a touch of vanity I said to my friend, 'A little colleging may be of some use at woodcraft too, if it sharpens Elrigmore's wits enough to read the signs that Barbreck's eagle eye can find nothing in. I could tell the very hour our friends left here.'

'Not on their own marks,' he replied sharply, casting his eyes very quickly again on twig and leaf.

'On nothing else,' said I.

He looked again, flushed with vexation, and cried himself beat to make more of it than he had done.

'What's the oak branch put so for, with its point to the sky if –?'

'I have you now!' he cried; 'it's to show the situation of the sun when they left the rendezvous. Three o'clock, and no mist with them; good lad, good lad! Well, we must be going. And now that we're on the safe side of Argile there's only one thing vexing me, that we might have been here and all together half a day ago if yon whelp of a whey-faced MacDonald in the bed had been less of the fox.'

'Indeed and he might have been,' said I, as we pursued our way. 'A common feeling of gratitude for the silver –'

'Gratitude!' cried John, 'say no more; you have fathomed the cause of his bitterness at the first trial. If I had been a boy in a bed myself, and some reckless soldiery of a foreign clan, out of a Sassenach notion of decency, insulted my mother and my home with a covert gift of coin to pay for a night's lodging, I would throw it in their faces and follow it up with stones.'

Refreshed by our rest and heartened by our meal, we took to the drove-road almost with lightness, and walked through the evening till the moon, the same that gleamed on Loch Linnhe and Lochiel, and lighted Argile to the doom of his reputation for the time being, swept a path of gold upon Lochow, still hampered with broken ice. The air was still, there was no snow, and at Corryghoil, the first house of any dignity we came to, we went up and stayed with the tenant till the morning. And there we learned that the minister and the three Campbells and Stewart, the last with a bullet in his shoulder, had passed through early in the afternoon on their way to Cladich.

The Great Exodus

from Children of the Dead End

PATRICK MACGILL (1890–1963)

Patrick MacGill's sensational first novel, Children of the Dead End, *broke new ground in Scottish working-class literature by giving an insider's view of life as a tramp, navvy and agricultural labourer. MacGill's hero, Dermod Flynn, an acknowledged self-portrait, comes to Scotland from Donegal as a young man to work on the potato harvest, falls into bad ways and sinks to becoming a tramp. Later he works on the railway and then finds employment labouring at the great Kinlochleven hydro-electric works in Argyll. This huge undertaking, built to power the new aluminium smelting plant there, employed vast numbers of navvies who lived, worked and, all too often, died in conditions of danger and squalor between 1905 and 1909.*

Our extract describes the end of the building contract and the dismissal of Dermod, his friend Moleskin Joe and all the other 'ragged, unkempt scarecrows of civilisation' who had laboured on the scheme.

Children of the Dead End *was published in 1914 with considerable critical and commercial success and another sensational novel,* The Rat-Pit, *dealing with Dermod Flynn's lost love, Norah Ryan, followed in 1915. A series of war-time novels, based on MacGill's front-line experiences won considerable praise as did a later return to the setting of* Children of the Dead End *in* Moleskin Joe.

We'll lift our time and go, lads,
The long road lies before,
The places that we know, lads,
Will know our like no more.
Foot forth! the last bob's paid out,
Some see their last shift through,
But the men who are not played out
Have other jobs to do.

From 'Tramp Navvies'

'Twas towards the close of a fine day on the following summer that we were at work in the dead end of a cutting, Moleskin and I, when I, who had been musing on the quickly passing years, turned to Moleskin and quoted a line from the Bible.

'Our years pass like a tale that is told,' I said.

'Like a tale that is told damned bad,' answered my mate, picking stray crumbs of tobacco from his waistcoat pocket and stuffing them into the heel of his pipe. 'It's a strange world, Flynn. Here today, gone tomorrow; always waitin' for a good time comin' and knowin' that it will never come. We work with one mate this evenin', we beg for crumbs with another on the mornin' after. It's a bad life ours, and a poor one, when I come to think of it, Flynn.'

'It is all that,' I assented heartily.

'Look at me!' said Joe, clenching his fists and squaring his shoulders. 'I must be close on forty years, maybe on the graveyard side of it, for all I know. I've horsed it since ever I can mind; I've worked like a mule for years, and what have I to show for it all today, matey? Not the price of an ounce of tobacco! A midsummer scarecrow wouldn't wear the duds that I've to wrap around my hide! A cockle-picker that has no property only when the tide is out is as rich as I am. Not the price of an ounce of tobacco! There is something wrong with men like us, surely, when we're treated like swine in a sty for all the years of our life. It's not so bad here, but it's in the big towns that a man can feel it most. No person cares for the likes of us, Flynn. I've worked nearly ev'rywhere; I've helped to build bridges, dams, houses, ay, and towns! When they were finished, what happened? Was it for us – the men who did the buildin' – to live in the homes that we built, or walk through the streets that we laid down? No earthly chance of that! It was always, "Slide! we don't need you any more," and then a man like me, as helped to build thousand houses big as castles, was hellish glad to get the shelter of a ten-acre field and a shut gate between me and the winds of night. I've spent all my money, have I? It's bloomin' easy to spend all that fellows like us can earn. When I was in London I saw a lady spent as much on fur to decorate her carcase with as would keep me in beer and tobacco for all the rest of my life. And that same lady would decorate a dog in ribbons and fol-the-dols, and she wouldn't give me the smell of a crust when I asked her for a mouthful of bread. What could you expect from a woman who wears the furry hide of some animal round her neck, anyhow? We are not thought as much of as dogs, Flynn. By God! Them rich buckos do eat an awful lot. Many a time I crept up to a window just to see them gorgin' themselves.'

'I have often done the same kind of thing,' I said.

'Most men do,' answered Joe. 'You've heard of old Moses goin' up the hill to have a bit peep at the Promist Land. He was just like me and you, Flynn, wantin' to have a peep at the things which he'd never lay his claws on.'

'Those women who sit half-naked at the table have big appetites,' I said.

'They're all gab and guts, like young crows,' said Moleskin. 'And they think more of their dogs than they do of men like me and you. I'm an Antichrist!'

'A what?'

'One of them sort of fellows as throws bombs at kings.'

'You mean an Anarchist.'

'Well, whatever they are, I'm one. What is the good of kings, of fine-feathered ladies, of churches, of anything in the country, to men like me and you? One time, 'twas when I started trampin' about, I met an old man on the road and we mucked about, the two of us as mates, for months afterwards. One night in the winter time, as we were sleepin' under a hedge, the old fellow got sick, and he began to turn over and over on his beddin' of frost and his blankets of snow, which was not the best place to put a sick man, as you know yourself. As the night wore on, he got worse and worse. I tried to do the best I could for the old fellow, gave him my muffler and my coat, but the pains in his guts was so much that I couldn't hardly prevent him from rollin' along the ground on his stomach. He would do anythin' just to take his mind away from the pain that he was sufferin'. At last I got him to rise and walk, and we trudged along till we came to a house by the roadside. 'Twas nearly midnight and there was a light in one of the windows, so I thought that I would call at the door and ask for a bit of help. My mate, who bucked up somewhat when we were walkin', got suddenly worse again, and fell against the gatepost near beside the road, and stuck there as if glued on to the thing. I left him by himself and went up to the door and knocked. A man drew the bolts and looked out at me. He had his collar on back to front, so I knew that he was a clergyman.

"What do you want?" he asked.

"My mate's dyin' on your gatepost," I said.

"Then you'd better take him away from here," said the parson.

"But he wants help," I said. "He can't go a step further, and if you could give me a drop of brandy –"

'I didn't get any further with my story. The fellow whistled for his dog, and a big black animal came boundin' through the passage and started snarlin' when it saw me standin' there in the doorway.

"Now, you get away from here," said the clergyman to me.

"My mate's dyin'", I said.

"Seize him," said the man to the dog.'

'What a scoundrel that man must have been,' I said, interrupting Moleskin in the midst of his story.

'He was only a human being, and that's about as bad as a man can be,' said Joe. 'Anyway, he put the dog on me and the animal bounded at the thick of my leg, but that animal didn't know that it was up against Moleskin Joe. I caught hold of the dog by the throat and twisted its throttle until it snapped like a dry stick. Then I lifted the dead thing up in my arms and threw it right into the face of the man who was standin' in the hallway.

"Take that an' be thankful that the worst dog of the two of you is not dead," I shouted. "And when it comes to a time that sees you hangin' on the lower cross-bars of the gates of heaven, waitin' till you get in, may be kept there till I give the word for you to pass through."

'My mate was still hangin' on the gatepost when I came back, and he was as dead as a maggot. I could do nothin' for a dead man, so I went on my own, leavin' him hangin' there like a dead crow in a turnip field. Next mornin' a cop lifted me and I was charged with assaultin' a minister and killin' his dog. I got three months hard, and it was hard to tell whether for hittin' the man or killin' the dog. Anyway, the fellow got free, although he allowed a man to die at his own doorstep. I never liked clergy before, and I hate them ever since; but I know, as you know, that it's not for the likes of you and me that they work for.'

'Time to stop looking at your work, boys!' interrupted Red Billy, as he approached us, carrying his watch and eternal clasp-knife in his hands. 'Be damned to you, you could look at your work all day, you love it so much. But when you go to the pay-office tonight, you'll hear a word or two that will do you good, you will!'

On arriving at the pay-office, every man in turn was handed his lying time and told that his services were no longer required. Red Billy passed the money out through the windows of the shack which served as money-box. Moleskin came after me, and he carefully counted the money handed to him.

'Half-a-crown wrong in your tally, old cock,' he said to Red Billy. 'Fork out the extra two-and-a-tanner, you unsanctified, chicken-chested cheat. I didn't think that it was in your carcase to cheat a man of his lyin' time.'

'No cheatin',' said Billy.

'Well, what the hell –!'

'I'm, two-and-a-tanner short –'

'No cheatin',' piped Billy maliciously.

'I'll burst your nut, you parrot-faced, gawky son of a Pontius Pilate, if you don't fork out my full lyin' time!' roared Moleskin.

'I always charge two-and-six for a pair of boots and the same for a clasp-knife,' said the ganger.

Billy had a long memory, and Joe was cornered and crestfallen. I, myself, had almost forgotten about the knife which Joe had lifted from Red Billy on the morning of our arrival in Kinlochleven, and Joe had almost lost memory of it as well.

'I had the best of that bargain,' Red Billy went on sweetly. 'The knife was on its last legs and I just intended to buy a new one. A half-crown was a good penny for a man like me to spend, so I thought that if Moleskin paid for it, kind of quiet like, it would be a very nice thing for me–a–very–nice–thing–for–me.'

'I grant that you have the best of me this time,' said Moleskin, and a smile passed over his face. 'But my turn will come next, you know. I wouldn't like to do you any serious harm, Billy, but I must get my own back. I have only to look for that old woman of yours and send her after you. I can get her address easy enough, and I have plenty of time to look for it. You don't care much for your old wife, Billy, do you?'

Billy made no answer. It was rumoured that his wife was a woman with a tongue and a temper, and that Billy feared her and spent part of his time in endeavouring to get out of her way. Joe was working upon this rumour now, and the ganger began to look uncomfortable.

'Of course, if I get my half-crown and another to boot, I'll not trouble to look for the woman,' said Joe. 'It won't be hard to find her. She'll have gone back to her own people, and it is well known that they belong to Paisley. Her brothers are all fightin' men, and ready to maul the man that didn't play fairly with their own blood relations. By God! they'll give you a maulin', Billy, when I send them after you. They'll come up here, and further, until they find you out. You'll have to shank it when they come, run like hell, in fact, and lose your job and your lyin' time. If you give me seven-and-six I'll not give you away!'

'I'll give you the half-crown,' said Billy.

'I'm losin' my time talkin' to you,' said Joe pleasantly, and he pulled out his watch. 'Every minute I stop here I'm goin' to put my charge up a shillin'.'

'I'll give you the five shillin's if you go away and keep clear of Paisley,' growled the ganger. 'Five shillin's! You dammed cheat! Are you not content with that?'

'One minute,' said Joe solemnly. 'Eight-and-six.'

'My God!' Billy cried. 'You're goin' to rob me. I'll give you the seven-and-six.'

We were heartily enjoying it. There were over one hundred men looking on, and Joe, now master of the strained situation, kept looking steadfastly at his watch, as if nothing else in the world mattered.

'Two minutes; nine-and-six,' he said at the end of the stated time.

'Here's your nine-and-six!' roared Billy, passing some silver coins through the grating. 'Here, take it and be damned to you!'

Joe put the money in his pocket, cast a benevolent glance at Billy, and my mate and I went out from Kinlochleven. We did not go into the shack which we had occupied for over a year. There was nothing there belonging to us, all our property was on our backs or in our pockets, so we turned away straight from the pay-office and took to the road again.

The great procession filed down the hillside. Hundreds of men had been paid off on the same evening. The job was nearly completed, and only a few hands were required to finish the remainder of the labour. Some men decided to stay, but a great longing took possession of them at the last moment, and they followed those who were already on the road.

Civilisation again! Away behind the hunchbacked mountains the sunset flamed in all its colours. Islands of jasper were enshrined in lakes of turquoise, rivers of blood flowed through far-spreading plains of dark cumulus that were enshrouded in the spell of eternal silence. Overhead the blue was of the deepest, save where one stray cloud blushed to find itself alone in the vastness of the high heavens.

We were an army of scarecrows, ragged, unkempt scarecrows of civilisation. We came down from Kinlochleven in the evening with the glow of the setting sun full in our faces, and never have I looked on an array of men such as we were. Some were old, lame men who might not live until they obtained their next job, and who would surely drop at their post when they obtained it. These were the veterans of labour, crawling along limply in the rear, staggering over boulders and hillocks, men who were wasted in the long struggle and who were now bound for a new place – a place where a man might die. They had built their last town and were no longer wanted there or anywhere else. Strong lusty fellows like myself took the lead. We possessed hale and supple limbs, and a mile or two of a journey meant very little to any of us.

Now and again I looked behind at the followers. The great army spread out in the centre and tailed away towards the end. A man at the rear sat down and took a stone out of his boot. His comrades helped him to his feet when he had finished his task. He was a very old, decrepit, and weary man; the look of death was in his eyes, but he wanted to walk on. Maybe he would sit down again at the foot of the mountain. Maybe he would sleep there, for further down the night breezes were warmer, much warmer, than the cold winds on the hillside. Probably the old fellow thought of these things as he tumbled down the face of the mountain; and perhaps he knew that death was waiting for him at the bottom.

Some sang as they journeyed along. They sang about love, about drink, about women and gambling. Most of us joined in the singing. Maybe the man at the rear sang none, but we could not hear him if he did, he was so far behind.

The sun paled out and hid behind a hump of the mountain. Overhead a few stars twinkled mockingly. In the distance the streams could be heard falling over the cliffs. Still the mountain vomited out the human throng, and over all the darkness of the night settled slowly.

What did the men think of as they walked down from Kinlochleven? It is hard to say for the inmost thoughts of a most intimate friend are hidden from us, for they lack expression and cannot be put into words. As to myself, I found that my thoughts were running back to Norah Ryan and the evenings we spent on the shores of the Clyde. I was looking backward; I had no thoughts, no plans, for the future.

I was now almost careless of life, indifferent towards fortune, and the dreams of youth had given place to a placid acceptance of stern realities. On the way up to the hills I had longed for things beyond my reach – wealth, comfort, and the love of fair women. But these thoughts had now given place to an almost unchanging calm, an indifference towards women, and an almost stoical outlook on the things that are. Nothing was to me pleasurable, nothing made me sad. During the last months in Kinlochleven I had very little desire for drink or cards, but true to custom I gave up neither. With no man except Moleskin did I exchange confidences, and even these were of the very slightest. To the rest of my mates I was always the same, except perhaps in the whisky saloon or in a fight. They thought me very strong in person and in character, but when I pried deeply into my own nature I found that I was full of vanity and weaknesses. The heat of a good fire after a hard day's work caused me to feel happier; hunger made me sour, a good meal made me cheerful. One day I was fit for any work; the next day I was lazy and heedless, and at times I so little resembled myself that I might be taken for a man of an entirely opposite character. Still, the river cannot be expected to take on the same form in shine as in shadow, in level as in steep, and in fall as in freshet. I am a creature of environment, an environment that is eternally changing. Not being a stone or clod, I change with it. I was a man of many humours, of many inconsistencies. The pain of a corn changed my outlook on life. Moleskin himself was sometimes disgusting in my sight; at other times I was only happy in his company. But all the time I was the same in the eyes of my mates, stolid, unsympathetic, and cold. In the end most of my moods went, and although I had mapped out no course of conduct, I settled into a temperate contentment, which, though far removed from gladness, had no connection with melancholy.

Since I came to Kinlochleven I had not looked on a woman, and the thoughts of womankind had almost entirely gone from my mind. With the rest of the men it was the same. The sexual instinct was almost dead in them. Women were merely dreams of long ago; they were so long out of sight that the desire for their company had almost expired in every man of us. Still, it was strange that I should think of Norah Ryan as I trudged down the hillside from Kinlochleven.

The men were still singing out their songs, and Joe hummed the chorus through the teeth that held his empty pipe as he walked along.

Suddenly the sound of singing died and Moleskin ceased his bellowing chorus. A great silence fell on the party. The nailed shoes rasping on the hard earth, and the half-whispered curse of some falling man as he tripped over a hidden boulder, were the only sounds that could be heard in the darkness.

And down the face of the mountain the ragged army tramped slowly on.

'Saskatchewan'

LORN MACINTYRE (1942–)

Born in Taynuilt and deeply rooted in Argyllshire history and culture, Macintyre, poet, short story writer and novelist is working on a large-scale series of Argyllshire novels, The Chronicles of Invernevis. *This short story, which appeared in* The Flamingo Book of New Scottish Writing 1998, *is a reminder, with its Canadian Highland dancer, of the overseas Argyll, the Argyll of the Diaspora and the Clearances.*

It's Games Day. The sun has risen over the bay and is coming through my cotton curtains, laying a golden quilt on my bed. I hear Father crossing the landing, then the rasp of his razor as he shaves, singing a Gaelic song. He is secretary of the Games and he knows that everything is ready on the field above the town. The marquees that came on the cargo boat have been erected; the latrines dug. He rinses his razor under the tap and I hear the Old Spice I gave him for his Christmas being slapped on. Mother is now up, going down to the kitchen.

I go to the corner of my bedroom and lift up the two swords. They have authentic looking hilts, but the blades are made of silver-painted wood. I cross them on the carpet and lace up my pumps. Today I am dancing at the Games, and this year I hope to win the sword dance. I have been practising all winter, making the floor of my bedroom vibrate, with Mother claiming that the ceiling in the sitting-room will come down on top of her as she watches a soap on our temperamental set which sometimes has to be slapped to restore the signal. But Father came up to watch me dancing, sitting on the bed as I danced by the window over my dud swords.

'I'll be amazed if you don't win it this year, Marsali.'

It's Games morning and I'm practising, landing on my toes as softly as possible to save them for the competition. Soon Mother will call up that breakfast is ready, but I will eat nothing more than a brown egg because I have seen competitors in previous years throwing up behind the marquee.

I know where Father is. He is at the sitting-room window, watching for the dark blue bow of the steamer to slide up to the pier. It left one of the islands in the dawn and is packed with spectators for the Games. Many of them are Father's customers in the bank, but that isn't why I hear the door closing as he goes down to the pier to wait by the gangway. It's for the pleasure of hearing the Gaelic of another island spoken. I have put my swords away and can see the first of the spectators coming along the street from my high window. The men have raincoats folded over their shoulders and caps pushed to the backs of their heads as they look into the window of Black the ironmonger's. Their stout wives are at the other window where knitting needles are crossed in balls of wool.

The procession up to the field musters at the memorial clock and is led by the laird with a plaid over his shoulder and a long stick. The pipe band behind him is followed by the spectators, going past the aromatic wild roses on the back brae. But I am already on the field, my number pinned to my frilled blouse. I have on my pumps and am practising in the subdued coolness of the tent, using my swords. Mothers are fussing round other competitors, straightening the pleats of kilts and exhorting them to dance as well as they can.

A girl comes in. She is pretty, with a blue velvet bonnet angled on her blonde hair, and a plaid, held at her shoulder by a cairngorm brooch, trailing at her heels. She is carrying a holdall that says Canadian Pacific, and in her other hand she has two large swords.

'Hi,' she says to us all, and comes across to the corner of the tent where I am exercising to make my toes supple. 'I'm Jeannie Maclean.'

I go into my bag and check the programme. There is no such name down for the sword dance. She sees me looking at her quizzically and she says: 'I'm a late entry. Mom posted the form a month ago but it never reached here. I went to see the secretary and he says I can compete since I've come such a long way.'

'Where are you from?' I ask.

'Saskatchewan.'

Immediately that name takes on a romantic resonance and I want her to say it again.

'It's in Canada,' she informs me, lacing up her pumps. 'We have wheat fields that go on for miles.'

I am trying to imagine the ripe golden crop waving in the breeze when she adds more information. 'Our people came from this island.'

'From here?' I say, surprised.

'U-huh. They were cleared last century and they found their way to Saskatchewan. They did pretty well. We have four combine harvesters on our farm and my father has a herd of Aberdeen Angus he shipped across.'

It's not a boast but a factual statement.

'Are these real swords?' I enquire, reaching across to touch them.

'Claymores. My folks brought them across from this island. My grandfather said we fought with them at Culloden.'

'If they came from here they must have spoken Gaelic,' I say.

'Sure, but we lost it when we intermarried. My great-grandmother was a squaw. I'd love to learn Gaelic.' (She pronounces it Gale-ick.) 'Do you speak it?'

I nod, but I'm getting too involved in this conversation instead of preparing for the competition. She, after all, is a rival, and as she lays the swords on the turf and begins a practice dance, I see how good she is. She's dancing as she converses with me, her shadow turning on the canvas wall of the tent. 'I've been doing this since I was three, first with two wooden spoons on the floor of the kitchen. I need to win today. Mom's outside.'

I don't want to stay in the tent to watch her practise because it's undermining my confidence, so I go over the hill, past the latrines, already busy with early drinkers, to a quiet hollow where I lay down my swords in the hum of insects and make my own music with my mouth to dance to. But I feel there is something lacking. My feet are heavy and I am aware of the clumsiness of my hands above my head. As I turn my foot touches a blade, and I stop, upset.

I hear Father's voice through the megaphone calling the competitors for the sword dance. As I go back over the hill I feel he has betrayed me by letting the girl from Saskatchewan – I am beginning to hate the name – enter for the competition when the rule says entries in advance. The dancing judges from the mainland are sitting in the shade of a lean-to beside the platform, with paper to mark the competitors on the card tables about their knees. I sit on the hill to watch, but I am not impressed by the standard.

'Number 79, Jeannie Maclean.'

She comes up on to the platform with her swords under her arm and there is a confab among the judges. Yes, she can use her own swords, as long as the steward lays them down. He makes them into a cross for her on the boards. She puts her hands on her hips and bows to the judges as the pipes tune up. I see from the first steps what a beautiful dancer she is. I am watching her toes and they hardly seem to touch the boards, springing in the air above the blades, now touching a diced stocking. The people around me on the hillside are enthralled. To my left there is a woman also wearing a Maclean kilt, with a cape. She is standing, holding up her thumbs to her dancing daughter.

Jeannie Maclean is turning in the air, her kilt swirling. She is twenty
seconds off the trophy which is waiting in a table in the secretary's tent.
Four nights ago I watched father polishing it, and he told me: 'Your name
will be on this, Marsali.'

Jeannie Maclean is performing her last movement when she comes
down, heavily. I see the side of the pump touch the blade which slices
through the leather. She is lying on the boards, holding her bleeding foot,
and her mother is shouting behind me instead of going down to her
injured daughter. 'You damn fool!'

Father calls for Dr MacDiarmid through the megaphone and he comes
in his Bermuda shorts with his medical bag. Jeannie Maclean is helped off
the platform and hops to the first-aid tent, her hand on the doctor's
shoulder, to have her foot stitched.

It's my turn to dance and I turn to bow to the judges in the lean-to.
How dearly now do I wish that the trophy for the sword dance was going
across the ocean to Canada, to sit in a glass case in a prairie house where
Gaelic was once spoken. But Jeannie Maclean is out of the competition.
As my toes touch the boards I am dancing to the refrain: Sas-katch-ew-
an, Sas-katch-ew-an. I see Father crossing the field, his secretary's rosette
on his lapel. He has come to watch me and he stands, smiling in
encouragement. I know I have never danced better because this is a
performance for him. Sas-katch-ew-an, Sas-katch-ew-an. I am reaching
for the sky. Mother is on the hillside waving but she has never really been
interested in Highland Dancing or Gaelic because she's from the
mainland.

I can feel my toes so sure, as they come down between the blades. I
turn to face my father, my knuckles on my hips. This is for you, Father,
for all the patience and love, for the Gaelic words you give me. I turn to
face the marquee. I can see a slumped shadow on the canvas, another
shadow hanging over it, an arm raised. This is for you Jeannie Maclean,
with your wounded foot, your treacherous swords and your angry mom.
I have nothing but pity and love, and as I bow to the judges and the
applause rises I know that one day I will go to Saskatchewan.

Rannoch, by Glencoe

T. S. ELIOT (1888–1965)

Thomas Stearns Eliot, although an American, lived in England from a comparatively early age. He achieved fame here and became closely identified with English poetry and the higher criticism. His sympathies were with high culture and Anglicanism but in this short poem he sketches images of a landscape very different from those he knew best. Like many writers before him he senses the sad memories and associations of Glencoe ('The road winds in listlessness of ancient war'). They are alien to him even though he actually bears a Scots name.

This little arresting poem makes a suitable coda to a chapter which has included much about the high places of Argyll and their 'thin air'.

Here the crow starves, here the patient stag
Breeds for the rifle. Between the soft moor
And the soft sky, scarcely room
To leap or soar. Substance crumbles, in the thin air
Moon cold or moon hot. The road winds in
Listlessness of ancient war,
Languor of broken steel,
Clamour of confused wrong, apt
In silence. Memory is strong
Beyond the bone. Pride snapped,
Shadow of pride is long, in the long pass
No concurrence of bone.

Acknowledgements

'Dunadd', chapter 5 of *Argyll the Enduring Heartland* by Marion Campbell © Marion Campbell 1995

'Is mairg dá ngalar an grádh' by Isabel of Argyll, translated by W.J. Watson, from *The Book of the Dean of Lismore*, reprinted by permission of Scottish Gaelic Texts Society and Scottish Academic Press

'Gillespeg Gruamach' from *John Splendid* by Neil Munro, reprinted by permission of The Neil Munro Society

The Provost and the Queen from *Lunderston Tales* by Robin Jenkins, reprinted by permission of Polygon

'Adiutor laborantium' by St Columba, translated by T.O. Clancy and G. Markus, from *Iona, the Earliest Poetry of a Celtic Monastery*, reprinted by permission of EUP

'Treasure Trove', from *Complete Para Handy* by Neil Munro, Birlinn Limited, reprinted by permission of The Neil Munro Society

'Oran na priosonach' by John Maclean, translated by Donald Meek, from *Tuath is Tighearna*, Scottish Texts Society and Scottish Academic Press, 1995

'Ardnamurchan Story', Introduction from *Night Falls on Ardnamurchan* by Alasdair Maclean, reproduced by permission of Victor Gollancz

'Ni h-éibhneas gan Chlainn Domhnaill' by Giolla Coluim Mac an Ollàimh, translated by W.J. Watson, from *The Book of the Dean of Lismore*, reprinted by permission of Scottish Gaelic Texts Society and Scottish Academic Press

'Fios chun a'Bhàird' by William Livingstone, translated by Donald Meek, from *Tuath is Tighearna*, Scottish Texts Society and Scottish Academic Press, 1995

'The Paps of Jura' from *The White Blackbird*, by Andrew Young, reprinted by permission of Carcanet

''S Fhada Thall Tha Mise', by Donald A. MacNeill, translated by Alastair Macneill, from *Moch is Anmoch*, reprinted by permission of House of Lochar

'The smoky smirr o rain', from *Wind on Loch Fyne* by George Campbell Hay. The publisher acknowledges the W.L. Lorimer Memorial Trust

'The Country of the Mull of Kintyre', from *Highways and Byways in the West Highlands* by Seton Gordon, reprinted by permission of Birlinn Ltd

'A Phadrín do dhúisg mo dhéar' by Aiffric Nic Coirceadail, translated by W.J. Watson, from *The Book of the Dean of Lismore*, reprinted by permission of Scottish Gaelic Texts Society and Scottish Academic Press

'Remember Me', from *Beyond This Limit* by Naomi Mitchison, reprinted by permission of Scottish Academic Press © Naomi Mitchison

'A Model Seaport', from chapters 11 and 12 of *In Scotland Again* by H.V. Morton, reprinted by permission of Methuen

'An TV', from *The Permanent Island* by Ian Crichton Smith, reprinted by permission of Carcanet

'Cead Deireannach nam beann' by Duncan Macintyre, translated by Angus Macleod in *The Songs of Duncan ban Macintyre*, reprinted by permission of The Scottish Gaelic Texts Society

'Lost on Rannoch', from *John Splendid*, by Neil Munro, reprinted by permission of The Neil Munro Society

'The Great Exodus', from *Children of the Dead End* by Patrick MacGill © The Estate of Patrick MacGill

'Saskatchewan' by Lorn Macintyre, reprinted by permission of the author

'Rannoch, by Glencoe' by T.S. Eliot, reprinted by permission of Faber & Faber